THE SWEETEST BURN

A Broken Destiny Novel

JEANIENE FROST

A Broken Destiny Novel

THE SWEETEST BURN

ISBN-13: 978-0-373-80395-8

The Sweetest Burn

www.HQNBooks.com

Printed in U.S.A.

To my husband, Matthew, for a thousand reasons I can think of,
and ten thousand more that I've probably forgotten.

CHAPTER ONE

"Et tu, Brute?" I muttered as I walked along the beach, pulling my cardigan a little tighter against the salt-scented breeze. It would be hot soon, as per usual in Miami, but at this predawn hour, the spring air was a little cool for the knee-length dress I'd thrown on to look for my missing pet.

"Brutus!" I called out, loudly this time. "Where are you?"

I'd been calling him for over fifteen minutes with no response, and I was getting worried. He had never been away from home this close to dawn before. I might not have wanted Brutus when he'd been dumped on me, and he definitely wasn't anyone's idea of a normal pet, but over the past couple months, I'd really come to care for him.

Every night for the past two months, he left the house at dusk and was back by 5:00 a.m. at the latest. Before me, Brutus had spent his entire life in darkness, so he didn't just hate sun; he was afraid of it. That's why, when he hadn't shown up by five thirty this morning, I'd gone looking for him. North Shore Open Space Park in Miami was one of his favorite places, and at this hour, the stretch of beach I walked along was deserted.

I scowled at the slowly lightening horizon, my worry increasing. "Brutus!" I yelled again. He'd better not be avoiding me because he'd broken the rules and had eaten someone.

Even if he'd done nothing wrong, if I didn't find him soon, he'd probably break into someone's house to avoid the sunlight. If that happened, God help the homeowner if they noticed him and tried to shoo him outside. Talk about an incident that would make the evening news.

"Did you lose something?" an unfamiliar male voice asked from right behind me.

I stiffened. No one else had been on the beach moments ago. Even with the sounds of the surf, my recently upgraded senses should have picked up on someone running straight at me, and he would've had to run to cover that much distance in mere seconds.

There was another explanation for how the man behind me had so suddenly and soundlessly appeared, but if that was the case, then one of us wouldn't be leaving this beach alive.

I couldn't let on that I knew something might be wrong. I turned around and fixed a false smile on my face.

"You startled me!" I said, hoping I sounded more surprised than scared.

A lock of black hair fell over the stranger's face as he smiled back at me. "Sorry. I heard you yelling, so I came over to see if you needed any help."

He looked a few years older than me, putting him in his early to midtwenties. Though he was on the skinny side, he was also cute in a boyish sort of way. If I'd have met him when I was back at college last semester, I would've thought the shadows that appeared and disappeared beneath his skin were figments of my imagination. After all, I'd been diagnosed with hallucinations by more than a few doctors. Problem was, now I knew I wasn't crazy, although some days, I wished I were.

Then, I saw his eyes shine like an animal's that had caught the light, evidence of the supernatural equivalent of *tapetum lu-*

cidum. My suspicions had been correct. The guy in front of me might look human to anyone who didn't have my abilities—which was over 99 percent of the world—but he wasn't. He was a demon minion.

"I do need a little help," I said, still smiling although my heart had started to race. "I'm looking for my, ah, dog."

"Sure," he said, casually taking my arm. "I think I saw a dog over this way."

Both of us were lying. Brutus was no dog, and there hadn't been one anywhere around here. Still, I let him lead me toward the brush that grew along the sea wall. As I walked, I hitched my dress up on the side that he couldn't see. I'd learned a few things in the past several months since I discovered that minions and demons existed. The most important lesson? Never leave your house unarmed.

Even as I reached for the knife strapped to my thigh, I glanced at the sky. Brutus was over nine feet tall, as wide as two gorillas and had leathery wings that could double as swords, so now would be a *really* good time for him to show up.

He didn't, though, and I drew in a deep breath for courage. Okay, so I was alone on a dark, deserted beach with a minion who'd been endowed with superhuman strength from whatever demon he served. Not good, but hysterics wouldn't help. I knew that from experience.

"You seem nervous," the minion remarked.

He sounded amused by the prospect, and that was like a shot of adrenaline to my body. Minions and demons had ruined countless lives, not to mention killed my parents, kidnapped my sister and almost killed me more times than I could count. This jerk thought that I was just another human slave to bring back to his demon master's realm. Well, I had a surprise for him.

I whirled, balancing my weight on my right leg while kicking out with my left. At the same time, I pulled the knife out, smashing it into his face with more force than any human should be able to muster. That, combined with the minion's downward momentum from suddenly getting his feet kicked out from under him, caused him to drop like a stone. My roommate, Costa, had been training me in hand-to-hand combat, and it had paid off. For the barest second, the minion's shocked gaze met mine, and I felt a savage thrill at the disbelief in his gaze.

Who's afraid now? I thought fiercely.

I shouldn't have taken that brief moment to celebrate. Even with a knife sticking out of his face, he was still deadly. His hands closed over my ankles, yanking hard. I lost my balance and fell backward, twisting away at once to avoid his immediate tackle. He landed on sand instead of me, but then his fists smashed into my lower body. I doubled over, feeling like I'd been hit by a truck. He held on and started to crawl up my body, his grin visible even through the streams of blood coming from where the knife stuck out of his face.

I couldn't break his grip, so I didn't try. When he made it up to my thigh, my knee smashed into his face with all the extra-human strength I had in me. Pain reverberated up my leg, but this time, I didn't spare a single second before attacking again. I grabbed his head and yanked it to the side as hard as I could. A *crack* sounded and the minion's whole body went limp.

I managed to roll away, my knees and ribs throbbing so much that vomiting felt like a good way to celebrate. Still, I was exultant. Looks like those fighting lessons had really paid off! In fact, Costa had trained me so well, my actions had felt more like muscle memory instead of a conscious decision to kill some-one. I *had* killed the minion, though, and he wasn't the first one, although he was the first one that I'd taken on by myself with only a normal weapon.

Being a killer hadn't been anywhere on my list of life goals six months ago, when I'd been a junior at WMU. Since then, I'd had to learn how to do that as well as do a lot of other strange, unpleasant things. *Thank you, unexpected supernatural lineage. You are the gift that keeps on giving.*

With a suddenness that still startled me, the minion's body dissolved until nothing but ashes remained. They began to blow away in the same ocean breeze that whipped my hair around like dozens of dark brown scarves. The way minions and demons turned to ash after death was the only considerate thing they did.

Even though everything hurt, I heaved myself up from the sand. Bruised and battered or no, I still had to find Brutus.

I was in the process of brushing the sand off me when my surroundings changed in an instant. The sand turned to sheets of ice, the light became pitch darkness and the sounds from the surf ceased with such abruptness that the new silence was ominous. The worst part was the cold. My teeth began to chatter, and the frigid air felt like it scattered razors across my skin.

Just as quickly, the dark, frozen world disappeared, leaving me back on the beach with a warm, salt-scented breeze and mauve-colored shades of dawn starting to paint the horizon. Still, I felt stiff from more than the cold that seemed to linger on the air. That hazy, alternate version of this area wasn't a full-on sensory hallucination, although all of my former doctors would've sworn otherwise. Instead, it was a glimpse of a realm that hovered right over this one.

Physicists call it M theory—the idea that different dimensional layers existed next to each other. I called it a shitload of trouble, because that sunless, icy world was a demon realm. My lineage gave me the ability to catch glimpses of these deadly realms, but for some reason, I hadn't spotted this one before. If I'd known that a demon realm existed right on top of this place, I would've never walked this beach at all, let alone by myself before the sun was fully up.

Before I could turn around to leave, a large slash suddenly appeared in the air and three people stepped out of it. At once, the supernatural tattoo on my right arm began to burn. I gripped it without looking away, and the part of my brain that wasn't freaking out figured out what was going on.

The minion I'd killed hadn't snuck up on me using his supernatural stealth and speed. He'd simply crossed from a demon realm into this one through a gateway that I hadn't known was there.

I didn't have time to wonder if the realm was new, or if it had always been there and was now accessible to this world through an ominous crack. The three new minions seemed startled to see me, but then their gazes roved from the blood on my dress and cardigan to the very incriminating pile of minion ashes near my feet. When the palest one stretched out hands that turned into living, writhing snakes, it was all I could do not to scream.

Not three minions. Two minions and an unkillable, shape-shifting *demon*.

Standing and fighting would be suicide, so I snatched my knife from the pile of minion ashes and began to run. The demon barked out an order in a language I recognized all too well, then the minions gave chase, and they were *fast*. If I had been a normal human, they would have had me in five seconds flat, but I wasn't normal, and right now, I was glad about that.

I was also glad I had a mental map of the closest hallowed ground near the North Shore park. In fact, I'd memorized every plot of hallowed ground near my house just in case something like this happened. St Joseph's Catholic Church was about seven streets away. If I made it, the demon couldn't touch me because demons couldn't cross hallowed ground. Minions could, but I'd already killed one today. Why not go for more?

Since sand was harder to run on, I headed toward the sidewalk along the park, needing the flat ground to increase my speed. Behind me, I could hear the minions cursing. They hadn't expected me to make them work for this. That gave me grim satisfaction as I darted around benches and tables in the deserted picnic area. My knees and ribs still throbbed from my earlier fight, but nothing was as great a painkiller as survival instinct. As I ran, I counted down the wooden street markers in the park for encouragement. Eighty-Third Street. Eighty-Fourth. The church was just after Eighty-Seventh Street. I was going to make it.

Then, even though he was much farther away, I heard the demon yell, "She's the Davidian!" in a rage-filled roar, and I knew all bets were off. My speed might have been preventing the minions from capturing me, but it also outed me as number one on the demon's most-wanted list.

The demon was no longer content to send his minions ahead of him like a bunch of hunting dogs. Several quick glances over my shoulder showed him now tearing after me himself, and he made the minions look as if they'd been moving in slow motion. Benches, tables and other large objects were hurtled my way as he didn't just chase me, but actively tried to kill me.

I ducked and weaved around as many as I could, but some still found their mark. I cursed when something heavy smacked me in the back, and while it made me stumble, I forced myself not to fall. Instead, I put all of my energy into running, staying within the limits of the park despite its greater dangers of projectiles. Taking the main road, A1A, would give me a straight shot to the church, but even at this hour, cars were on it. I couldn't risk someone else getting hurt, and demons loved nothing more than collateral damage.

I'd just rounded a corner that brought me briefly back onto the beach when something slammed into my legs, knocking me over. I rolled at once, making sure not to stab myself in the process, and was back up when a loud, trumpeting snarl sounded overhead.

Brutus, my pet gargoyle, flew toward me, the dawn's rays highlighting his large, beastly form in different shades of pink. I would've been relieved to see him, but I was too shocked by the man riding on Brutus's back.

The minions and demon saw them, too, and at their confused

expressions, I remembered that they didn't see a large man on the back of a hulking, grayish-blue gargoyle. Due to Archon glamour, all they saw was an angrily squawking seagull somehow carrying his muscular male passenger, and from the way they cocked their heads, they didn't know what to make of the sight.

"Ivy, duck!" the man yelled.

I hit the sand even as I reeled with shock. Only one person in the world could treat the deadly gargoyle like a winged pony, and that was the same person who'd broken my heart months ago, and then disappeared.

Adrian.

CHAPTER TWO

Brutus soared over me, and Adrian almost grazed my back from how close he came. Seconds later, I heard multiple thumps and a scream. I rolled over in time to see the minions fall to the ground. Only bloody holes remained where their heads had been, and when Brutus whirled back around, his leathery wings were spattered with red.

Then Adrian jumped off Brutus and torpedoed himself onto the snake-armed demon. Two-hundred-plus pounds of pissed-off male slamming into the demon caused him to plow back into the sand. Adrian's bulk pinned him down, but those coiling serpents surged toward him, gleaming fangs extended to strike.

"Watch out!" I screamed.

Before the first syllable left my lips, Adrian had already grabbed the serpents below their snapping jaws. With a brutal jerk, he ripped their heads off. The demon let out an ear-splitting howl and black blood spurted from where the snakes' headless bodies still protruded from his wrists.

"Adrian," the demon spat. "Don't do this! Your father—"

"Is dead," Adrian cut him off, then ripped the demon's throat out. I caught a glimpse of something pulpy before I turned away, my stomach clenching with disgusted relief. Demon physiology was different, so what Adrian had just torn out was the equivalent of the demon's heart.

Unfortunately, it wouldn't kill him. Only three weapons in the world could kill demons, and one of them had melded into a tattoo on my arm that now hurt as though it had caught fire.

Adrian climbed off the demon. I stared at the snake heads, which, like the demon, weren't turning to ash because the demon wasn't really dead. He was just unconscious, so he wouldn't disintegrate and neither would his severed serpentine arms, apparently.

"Were they poisonous?" I asked, still trying to recover from everything that had just happened.

Adrian glanced at the heads. "Oh yeah," he said, sounding oddly amused. "Demon poison is the deadliest there is."

"Then why did you grab the snakes with your *bare hands*?"

Fear for him sharpened my voice. It took all the self-control I had not to run over and check to make sure that he hadn't been nicked by one of those lethal fangs. I wasn't about to do that, of course. I might be thrilled that he hadn't been killed, but I was still furious with him over other things.

Adrian let out a contemptuous snort. "I know that demon. Vritra is used to everyone running from his snakes, so he never expected me to go right for them. Sometimes, a person's most powerful weapon is also their greatest weakness."

My mind flashed to how close those snakes had come to biting Adrian. "How's that?" I muttered, trying to ignore the roughly lyrical cadence of his accent that was as unusual as he was.

Adrian's gaze raked over me as he came closer. "People count on their most powerful weapon too much, so when it's gone, they don't know what to do. The moments before they figure that out is your best chance to kill them."

A cold-blooded assessment, but his ruthlessness didn't surprise me. It was to be expected since Adrian had been raised by demons, hence the snake-armed demon's comment about Adrian's "father." Foster father would be a more accurate way to describe Demetrius, the demon who'd snatched Adrian up when he was only a child. Demetrius wouldn't be snatching up any more children. I'd seen to that when I killed him.

"What's that?" he asked, suddenly lunging toward me. I jumped back, but Adrian had already grabbed me. His large hands slid along the cardigan covering my arms, and I yanked back, refusing to let him touch me. "There's blood on your clothes," he said, sounding concerned. "Did one of them hurt you?"

"Nope," I lied. Yes, I was still hurt, and that counted for more than my physical injuries. "It's from the other guy, who's probably blown away by now."

His dark blue gaze narrowed. "Another minion attacked you?"

Brutus didn't like that idea, either. He stalked over to the ashes of the other two minions, snarling as he clawed them, as if that would make them any more dead. I went over and patted his wing, grateful for the excuse to turn my attention away from Adrian.

"Don't worry, boy," I crooned. "You got them."

His gorilla-like head dipped as he slimed the side of my face with a lick. I hid my wince. If Brutus saw it, his feelings would be hurt. The fearsome two-ton gargoyle could be as sensitive as a golden retriever at times.

"Where were you, anyway?" I asked, not expecting an answer. Brutus could grunt, chuff, snarl and roar, and while I was getting better at picking up his mood from those, he couldn't speak a single intelligible word.

"With me," Adrian replied. "Sorry, we ran late today."

Today? I stared at him, piecing together the subtext. Adrian couldn't be bothered to even send me a text message these past couple months, but he'd been hanging out with my *gargoyle* on a regular basis? I glared at Brutus. *Just you wait until we get home,*

I silently promised the gargoyle. *Somebody* wasn't getting any raw chuck roast for breakfast after this!

The snake-armed demon's skin was starting to blacken and burn under the dawn's brightening rays. After everything demons had taken from me, I'll admit that the sight pleased me. If I was just a tad more vindictive, I would've videoed it so that my sister, Jasmine, could enjoy it, too.

"What are we going to do with him?" I said, nodding at the demon. "The beach is empty now, but it won't be for long."

Adrian's reply was to say something to Brutus in what I referred to as Demonish. The harsh yet disturbingly beautiful language was where Adrian's unusual accent came from. I only recognized the word for "go," but Brutus understood all of it. As soon as Adrian finished speaking, the gargoyle grabbed the demon and flew off toward the ocean.

"What's he doing?"

"Dropping him far enough away that the demon won't be a threat to any beachgoers," Adrian replied. "If we're lucky, his prolonged exposure to daylight will turn him into a withered husk. Demons can't stand our realm in the sun. I told you that."

He had, which begged the question, why had the demon risked such exposure by entering this world right before dawn?

"Ivy." The low, resonant way Adrian said my name made shivers roll over me, although I'd rather die than let him know that. "It's good to see you."

I didn't want to be, but I was glad to see him, too, and for more reasons than him knowing exactly how to take out Snake Arms. I'd tried to talk myself out of feeling anything for Adrian during the two months since he'd admitted that he had betrayed me and then disappeared. Told myself that what I'd *thought* I felt for him had been due to the extreme circumstances we'd found ourselves in mixed with the temptation of forbidden fruit. Some days, when I only dwelled on the cold logic of the situation, I even believed it. The fact that Adrian had made no attempt to contact me seemed to support that theory. And now, after all this time, he thought that showing up, smiling and flashing me a smoldering look would make everything okay?

"Yeah?" I said, turning my back on him. "Well, now you've seen me." And I walked away from him. "I wouldn't stay here, if I were you," I threw over my shoulder at Adrian. "There's a gateway on the beach. I glimpsed the demon realm only seconds before Snake Arms and his friends came out of it."

"Where?" he asked, catching up to me all too quickly.

"About four blocks this way," I said, cursing myself because now, he had a good reason to keep walking with me.

He reached over, touching my arm. "Ivy, wait—"

"Now, that's funny," I interrupted, jerking away. "Is that what you thought? That I'd just *wait* for you until you felt like showing up again?"

"You asked me to go," Adrian said, his voice roughening with frustration. "In fact, you insisted, remember?"

I began to walk faster. "Who wouldn't need a little time after finding out that you'd lied to me about my real destiny? Then, you didn't even try to make up for what you'd done. No, you disappeared for months without a single word. You knew when I started this that I thought everything would be fine if I used David's hallowed, Goliath-slaying slingshot to save my sister. But after I almost died doing that, you dropped the bomb that it was only step one in a destiny I couldn't avoid, *remember*?"

Don't even get me started on step two and three of my supposedly unavoidable destiny, where fate said that Adrian would literally be the death of me.

He sighed, running his hand through his hair. The front was still longer than the back, and the ocean breeze tousled those thick, dark gold waves. His silver-ringed eyes were deep blue, and even when he scowled, it highlighted lips both full and completely masculine. Adrian was as gorgeous as he was dangerous; another sign of fate's cruel sense of humor when it came to our opposing destinies.

I looked away, blaming my staring at him on post-battle temporary insanity. Once, I'd laughed after almost getting ripped apart by a demon who could turn shadows into weapons. Adrenaline was more sense-depriving than heroin at times.

"Yeah, I remember," Adrian said shortly. "Saying I'm sorry is worthless, so I won't. All I can do is promise that it will never happen again."

I wished it wouldn't, for a lot of reasons. But how could I believe this promise when he still wouldn't even apologize for the last time he'd lied to me? And worse, fate predicted that he would betray me again. Twice, and the final one would end in my death, making me just another dead Davidian in a long line of ones killed by Judians.

Except that I was the *last* descendant of the Biblical King David's line, and thus the only human capable of wielding the hallowed weapons that could bring down demons. Adrian was the last descendant of Judas, and in addition to his incredible, otherworldly powers, he had also inherited the fate to betray and kill Davidians. When we first met, I had believed that he could beat his fate, if he tried. In fact, I'd believed it so much that I'd fallen in love with him. Now, I wasn't so sure, but I had other things to worry about. Like the demons who would surely be after me, my sister and Costa now that we'd killed more of their people.

Adrian grabbed my arm. "Would you stop for a second so we can talk?"

"No," I replied, yanking away. "And if you touch me again, you'll regret it."

"What's your hurry?" he challenged, switching tactics.

I gave him an irritated glance. "I'm worried about my sister and your best friend. Costa's house is on hallowed ground, so it's safe for now, but three minions and a demon going missing from that realm won't go unnoticed, as you of all people should know. The rest of the demons will figure out what happened since no human could've taken them down. Soon, they'll be tearing this place apart looking for us, so Jasmine, Costa and I need to be gone before they do."

He arched a brow. "Well, then, I guess it's a good idea that I stay close to make sure you're safe."

"I can take care of myself, as one very dead minion would tell you if he could," I shot back.

The smile he flashed me was maddening in its cockiness. "Seems like you needed a little help with the rest of them."

He was right, but admitting that would be tantamount to telling him that I wanted him to stay, and I didn't. "Don't flatter yourself. I had a plan. Two more blocks, and I'd have been on hallowed ground. The demon couldn't cross that, and he couldn't wait me out with the sun coming up. And as you once told me, minions are easy to kill."

"Not two at a time when you're still a novice," he replied.

I spun around, and then clenched my teeth when I saw the triumphant look in his eyes. He'd wanted me to keep talking and I'd let him bait me into it.

I began to hike up my dress as I resumed walking. Adrian watched with interest until I reached the straps around my upper thighs. I gave him a censuring look as I pulled out my cell phone. No, I wasn't flashing him. I had to give Costa and Jasmine a heads-up that they needed to start packing. Poor Costa. He'd taken me and my sister in because we couldn't return to our old house—or our old lives—after I'd decimated a demon realm rescuing Jasmine. Now, Costa would be forced to leave his own home, and I had no idea where any of us would go.

But when I looked at my phone, I let out a groan. The front of it was smashed so badly, I could see the plastic casing behind it. Memories of the minion's fists explained how that had happened. My ribs hadn't been the only thing he'd bashed as he'd tried to kill me.

"Do you have a phone?" I asked, breaking my new silence. His mouth tightened. "No."

"Who goes anywhere without a cell phone?" I muttered.

Adrian's features closed off, as if this was somehow a sore subject. "I've been having issues with mine."

We walked in silence for several moments. The sun was almost fully up, and I felt bad for Brutus flying in those rays while taking the demon far out over the ocean, even though I was ticked at Brutus for sneaking behind my back to see Adrian.

"Do you know the worst part of staying away from you these past months?" Adrian asked. "I thought it would be remembering everything that had happened between us, but instead, it was thinking of everything we *didn't* do."

I still said nothing. If he'd missed me so much, ignoring me for months was a real unique way of showing it.

He moved closer, until his big body blocked the wind. I still didn't look up at him, but kept staring straight ahead as if I could will myself back at Costa's with sheer mind power.

"I showed you terrible places when I should have shown you beautiful ones," he went on, his voice deepening. "Told you horrible details about my past instead of letting you get to know the person I'd become, and I taught you how to wield that slingshot instead of teaching you a thousand different things that we would've enjoyed much, much more."

The way his voice caressed that last part made his meaning explicitly clear. Surprise combined with a rush of heat as a treacherous part of myself started imagining what those things might have been. My lack of experience meant I didn't have a lot to go on, but my mind seemed up to improvising. Then, with a mental slap, I forced those thoughts back.

"Too late now," I said in a crisp tone.

Adrian caught me to him, his hands closing like warm steel bands around my arms.

"Ivy, listen. When we met, I didn't think I could beat my fate.

That's why I kept pushing you away, why I didn't tell you who I was at first and why I didn't tell you what I felt until, yes, it was almost too late. But it's not too late." He stared at me until his gaze felt almost palpable with his intensity. "I know what I feel for you, and it's stronger than any destiny. I told you the last time I saw you that I'd make you believe in us again. I meant that, and regardless of how mad you are at me, if you had a hard time resisting me when I was fighting my feelings for you…you won't stand a chance now that I'm not."

My jaw dropped as pride chased away the dangerous warmth that had caused me to sway the tiniest bit closer to him. I'd practically thrown myself at him the last time circumstances had forced us to spend time together, and what had that gotten me? Betrayed and dumped. Damned if I'd let history repeat itself.

"Don't be so cocky," I said, pulling away and starting to walk again. "I'm not the same person, either, so save your efforts. My panties aren't going to fall off just because you've finally decided that you want them to."

His laughter chased after me, sensual and challenging. "Oh, Ivy, they don't need to fall off. I'm happy to tear them."

I let out a frustrated sigh. Adrian wasn't leaving and he wasn't listening to me; I may as well be reliving the first time we met. Back then, he'd saved me from a minion kidnapping while opening my eyes to my "hallucinations" being real. Whether I liked it or not, if history was repeating itself, then his presence meant my life was about to irrevocably change.

Again.

CHAPTER THREE

Since Adrian wasn't going away, I decided to make him pull his weight. When we reached the spot on the beach where I'd grappled with the minion, I gestured in the general vicinity of where I'd spotted the demon realm. I didn't see anything now, but that wasn't a huge surprise. My lineage meant that I was most attuned to hallowed objects, so at best, I only caught random glimpses of dark ones even when I was right on top of them. Adrian's lineage meant that he was most attuned to dark objects, and a demon realm gateway was about as dark as something could get.

"The realm gateway was over there. Do you see it?"

He walked to the spot I'd indicated. Then he held out his hands as if feeling for a doorway, which, in essence, he was.

"It's strange," he said after a pause. "I see the realm and I do feel something, but it's not as strong as a normal gateway would be. Instead of a door, it feels more like…a crack."

"That's what I'm worried about," I said with a fresh sense of dismay. "With the walls between demon realms and our world weakening, cracks are probably turning up all over the place. If it gets worse, those cracks will turn into gaping holes and realms will spill out into this world. And then…"

I stopped speaking because I didn't want to say what would happen next. The only thing worse than knowing was being the only person who could do something to stop it. That's why I'd spent the past two months splitting my time between training and trying to get my sister, Jasmine, through the post-traumatic stress of being a former demon captive. You'd think with all that, I wouldn't have had the energy to focus on Adrian, yet I had. A broken heart was the slowest wound to heal, it appeared.

"I think we're safe for the moment," Adrian said, not addressing my unfinished sentence. "The crack doesn't feel strong enough to let anyone else through. Maybe the sunlight is weakening it."

For now. I rubbed my right hand where the outline of a braided rope ran from my finger all the way up to my elbow. The remains of the ancient, hallowed slingshot no longer burned in that odd way, but touching it was a tangible reminder that Adrian and I had destinies to fulfill: me to possibly save those trapped in the demon realms, and him to probably betray me.

"All right, well, minions are dead, the demon's gone, Brutus should be back any second and I'm almost home, so you can leave. Now," I added.

A scoff preceded his response and the silver rings around his dark blue eyes seemed to gleam.

"I'm not going anywhere, Ivy. Ready or not, I'm back in your life and I'm here to stay."

"But I don't *want you to*," I said, fighting the urge to thump him over the head so the words would sink in.

He only smiled, dazzling and so arrogant that I spun around so I didn't have to look at him anymore. "Yes, I heard you, but while you might not want me—yet—you do need me."

Then, with his lightning quickness, he appeared in front of

me, shoving a small box into my hands. "Speaking of things I didn't get to do before, happy birthday, although one day late."

Shock made me stand still and stare at the box. Twenty-one was a milestone, but no one else had remembered. Not my sister, who was also my best friend, or Costa, my roommate who'd become as close as a brother to me, or Zach, the Archon who sorta mentored me and had supernatural knowledge of just about *everything*. Only Adrian, and I'd never told him when it was.

I couldn't stop myself from opening the unexpected gift. Then I let out a little gasp when I saw the round stone suspended at the end of a long gold chain. The jewel reflected the first rays of sunlight back at me in a rainbow of colors that were so bright, I had to squint while looking at it. Unless it was the most sparkly piece of glass *ever*, Adrian had just given me a diamond the size of a large marble.

"There's no way I can accept this," I almost stuttered, adding, "Did you steal it?" because how else could he have gotten something that cost as much as several high-end cars?

Hints of darkness colored his laughter. "Former demon prince, remember? I might have left all that behind me, but I didn't leave empty-handed."

"You're not a demon, you were just raised by them," I muttered.

He shrugged. "Honorary demon prince, then. Either way, I can afford it. Besides, you lost your other necklace because of me, so don't say you can't accept this one to replace it."

The necklace was so beautiful, a shallow part of me wanted nothing more than to put it on and run to the nearest mirror. I couldn't, of course. For starters, I hadn't looked into a mirror since the night I found out the hard way that some demons use mirrors as portals into our world. Plus...

"This feels like a bribe," I said, holding the necklace out to him. "And you can't make up for everything that's happened with a shiny, expensive gift. Things aren't good between us,

Adrian. Not even close, and if I accepted this, I'd be implying that they were."

He crossed his arms, his posture taking on a very familiar stubbornness. "I'm not trying to bribe you, I'm giving you a birthday gift. Throw it into the surf if you want, but it's yours, so I am not taking it back."

My jaw clenched. He might have been raised in an environment where money was no object, but I could no more toss this diamond into the ocean than I could burn a stack of hundred-dollar bills for warmth, and from the challenging curl to his mouth, he knew that. Still, that didn't mean he was getting his way.

I folded the necklace into my hand and resumed walking. It didn't take my enhanced peripheral vision to see Adrian's smirk as he followed. He thought he'd won this round. *Think again*, I silently told him.

"So, if you're rich, why did we only stay in crappy motels when we first met?" I asked as I kept walking toward Costa's house.

He let out a laugh that managed to combine the lure of ecstasy along with the dangers of addiction.

"Because I was doing everything I could to kill the mood, not that it worked. Even in the ugliest surroundings, I wanted you so much that it almost killed me not to take you in every dingy room those crappy motels had to offer."

"Stop it," I muttered. Thankfully, Brutus picked that moment to fly past us and land in the tallest section of beach shrubs. I ran after the gargoyle, trying to soothe him as he attempted to cover himself with beach brush to avoid the sun.

"It's okay," I was saying when Adrian said, *"Carparata!"* loud enough to snap Brutus's head up.

The Demonish word turned Brutus from a cringing creature into his usual, formidable self. The gargoyle might be my pet now, but to the bone, he still belonged to Adrian. After all,

Adrian was the one who'd given Brutus to me as my protector.
The fact that he'd done so when Adrian had thought he was
sacrificing his life to save mine was yet another reason why he
was so hard to evict from my heart.

Still, I wasn't about to give up trying. "Here you go, my
good Brutus," I said, pulling out the necklace and latching it
around his leathery wrist. Because of his size, it fit like a brace-
let. "Something shiny for you."

The gargoyle held up his arm, looking at the diamond next
to his grayish-blue skin. Then he chuffed as if in approval.

"See?" I said, with a wide grin at Adrian. "He loves it."

The glare Adrian gave me was priceless. Then, with a smile
that was far too confident for my liking, he waved in the direction of Costa's house.

"You can give my gift to Brutus and you can keep stomp-
ing off to Costa's, but no matter what, I'm coming with you.
Realm cracks are appearing and demons and minions are on the
move again. You might have killed Demetrius, giving me the
vengeance I'd wanted for years, but that didn't take me out of
the fight. I still live to kick demon ass, so I wouldn't sit this out
for the world, and if you know anything about me, you should
know that. Besides, Zach's probably aware of all this and waiting back at Costa's for us. As you might recall, Archons may be
nearly immortal, but they're not very patient."

CHAPTER FOUR

Costa's house was a former church, hence the hallowed ground it rested on that demons were unable to cross. The sight of its tall, slanted roof with the cross that Costa hadn't bothered to take down filled me with a mixture of relief and sadness. I couldn't say that I'd been happy here, but I'd felt safe, and that counted for a lot in this world. Now, it was time to leave, and I didn't know if I'd ever see this place again.

Adrian was right; more people were at the house than when I'd left it an hour ago. My sister, Jasmine, seemed startled to see Adrian, but it didn't escape my notice that Costa didn't look surprised. I stifled my snort as we came into the kitchen. Had Adrian been in contact with Costa this whole time, too? Was I literally the *only* person he'd avoided these past couple months?

As I approached the table, Adrian pulled a chair out for me, but I ignored that. "I'll stand."

"Are you two fighting again?" Costa cast a knowing glance between us. "Situation normal, then."

The other person I hadn't seen in the past two months was Zach, but as Adrian had predicated, the Archon now sat at the kitchen table as casually as if he'd dropped by for breakfast. As with minions and demons, at first glance, you wouldn't know there was anything unusual about Zach. His jeans and faded-blue hoodie matched his college-age appearance, and his dark brows, closely cropped hair and mocha-colored skin were a great frame for his deep, walnut-brown eyes.

One look into those eyes, however, and I couldn't imagine anyone not realizing that there was something otherworldly about Zach. His gaze seemed to reach right into your soul, and if he chose to reveal his true nature, the room would be filled with exploding light and deafeningly beautiful voices. The one time Zach had dropped his human disguise to show me that, I'd unwittingly fallen to my knees with tears streaming down my face. You never realized how insignificant you were until confronted with a creature filled with the power and glories of eternity.

Archons—*angels*—were such creatures, so you'd think I'd be glad to see Zach. Instead, I felt a mildly growing sense of dread. Unlike their Hallmark Channel representations, Archons weren't cuddly beings who spent their time sprinkling happy dust onto humanity. Instead, they were fearsome warriors who'd been relegated to the sidelines during the most important battle of the ages, so they were ready to fight no matter how that turned out for mankind. They were also our only allies against demons, so that made them indispensable to us regardless of their seeming indifference toward the fate of my race.

"I'm out of time, aren't I?" I said in lieu of a hello.

Zach didn't take offense. He'd probably invented the custom of not saying hello. "Yes. As the realm walls continue to weaken, new fissures are formed, allowing greater access between the dark worlds and this one. It is only a matter of time until those fissures rupture and parts of the demon world spills out into your realm."

"I found that out the hard way," I said with a sigh. "Three minions and a demon tried to nab me on the beach."

Jasmine's face paled and she ran over to me. "Are you okay? How did you get away? Did they know who you were?"

I gave my younger sister a reassuring squeeze, a pang hitting me as I looked at her. She'd always had my adoptive mother's blond hair, but sometime during her hellish captivity, she'd grown a long white streak down the center of her head. Her pale blue eyes were the same color as my adoptive father's, and seeing them reminded me of him so much, I had to blink back a sudden surge of tears.

Oh, how I missed my parents! They hadn't deserved to die at the hands of minions and demons just because they'd been investigating Jasmine's disappearance. Then again, no one deserved to die at the hands of demons and minions for any reason.

"I'm fine," I reassured Jaz. "I got the first one, Adrian and Brutus took care of the rest. And they didn't know who I was, at first. They were just looking for new slaves."

Zach inclined his head in agreement. "The demons grow bolder as they gain more access to this world."

Maybe it was the fresh wave of grief I'd felt over my parents' death, maybe it was my fear over what I knew I had to do. Either way, I couldn't hold back my brusque reply.

"Remind me again why Archons would allow terrible things to happen to innocent people when they have the power to stop it?"

The gaze Zach turned on me was hard. "A better reason than why your race would rather assign blame to others than work on looking for solutions yourselves."

Yes, humanity had its flaws, but that didn't mean we weren't worth saving, dammit! And I still couldn't figure out if Zach even wanted us to be saved. Some days, he acted as if he did, yet other days, the Archon seemed just as happy to let humanity burn if it meant finally ending the war between Archons and demons.

"If you truly believe your race is worth saving, then you'll be eager to get started," Zach replied, using his mind-reading abilities. How could I forget about those?

I glowered at him. It sucked being reminded that in this case, "somebody" doing something really meant "me."

"I'm ready," I said, which was the biggest lie in the world, but what else could I say? *We're all gonna die!* seemed too defeatist, even if it was probably true.

Zach rose with his usual grace, then cast a sideways glance at Brutus, who was in the darkest corner of the kitchen. He'd be in his room, if he wasn't waiting for his breakfast of raw meat.

"Would someone explain why that gargoyle is wearing the stone of Solomon around his wrist?" Zach asked.

"The what of who?" Jasmine said.

I wondered the same thing, but Adrian replied to Jasmine before I could ask. "Ivy didn't like her birthday present, so she gave it to Brutus," he told my sister.

"Birthday? Oh crap, Ivy, I forgot your birthday!" Jasmine said with a gasp. Costa seemed shocked for a different reason.

"You gave a three-thousand-year-old diamond with famed mystic qualities to *Brutus*?" he asked me.

Zach also gave me a look that seemed to question my sanity. I shifted defensively even as this news rocked me. "I just thought it was a normal diamond," I mumbled.

"It isn't," Adrian said, his arched brow implying that I should have given him a chance to say this earlier. "King Solomon stole this diamond from Asmodeus, a demon king, because it was said to shield its wearer from harm. After Solomon's death, Asmodeus stole it back, and when I was a child, it was given to me because demons wanted to protect the last Judian."

I was openmouthed discovering the diamond's history, not to mention its protective qualities. Adrian hadn't just been trying to buy my forgiveness with an expensive trinket. He'd given me the same talisman he'd had since he was a child. *Damn him for making it harder to stay angry with him*, I thought, my emotions wrestling anew at this.

"Very well," Zach replied, although he would have overheard my inner battle. "Ivy, you will leave at once. Adrian and Costa will accompany you on your search for the staff of Moses."

"Not Adrian," I burst out.

"Yes, Adrian," Zach said in his best don't-argue-with-an-angelic-being tone. "Without him, you won't discover the map."

"There's a map that leads to the staff?" That was a surprise. "One of those would've been helpful when we were trying to find the first hallowed weapon."

Zach shrugged. "It's a map of sorts, and perhaps if you would have looked closer, you would have discovered it when you were searching for the slingshot, too."

Archons and their cryptic-speak, not to mention their lack of initiative that bordered on apathy. Figures there had been a map back then and Zach hadn't told me. For all I knew, he had another map in his pocket now, yet couldn't be bothered to mention that, either. "Or, why don't you just tell me where the staff is, if you know?" I said to cut through all the crap.

"Because this is *your* task to succeed or fail at, Davidian," was Zach's inexorable reply.

Don't hit the Archon, I reminded myself while clenching my fists. We still needed him.

Zach's mouth twitched, as if he found my impotent rage amusing. "Adrian is coming with you, Ivy. Don't bother to list all the reasons why you don't want him to. The fact remains that he must or you will not only fail, you won't survive. That's why I rescinded his ban from seeing you earlier today."

My gaze swung to Adrian. "What do you mean, he rescinded your ban from seeing me?"

A low, almost growling sound left Adrian. "Zach put a supernatural restraining order on me. I couldn't get within a mile of you without suddenly becoming paralyzed, Costa supernaturally forgot every message I tried to send you through him, and if I attempted to call, text or email you, my phone would blow up."

"Really?" Costa looked bewildered. "You and I have talked several times since then, and I don't remember that."

Adrian grunted. "Exactly."

"Cock-blocked by an angel," Costa muttered. "That's new."

I ignored Costa's comment in favor of giving Zach a disbelieving look. "First you supernaturally prevent Adrian from so much as texting me, then you insist that he come along on the search for the staff. What kind of game are you playing?"

Zach's dark brown eyes gave nothing away. "No game. Only fate."

Fate. My teeth ground. I really hated that word.

"Why didn't you tell me about this on the beach?" I asked Adrian, giving up on getting a more definitive answer out of Zach.

Adrian's coloring was darker than normal, and when I caught the look he flashed Zach's way, I realized why. Pride. He'd rather let me think that he was a total jerk than admit that Zach had shut him down so effectively, he'd been helpless. Yes, for longer than I cared to remember, Adrian had had both minions and demons scurrying to do his bidding. Plus, with his incredible strength, speed and fighting skills, almost no one had been able to stop Adrian from doing something he'd set his mind to. In that light, his bruised-ego silence about the way Zach had shut him down was almost understandable.

Almost. Adrian should have told me why he'd abandoned me when I needed him the most. The fact that he hadn't only highlighted that he was thinking more about himself than me. Plus, if he couldn't admit something so small to me, how could I trust him with the *really* big things, like our fates?

And Zach. He got the other end of my stink eye. He could have said something before now, too. Men. They were the same whether they were Archons, humans or Judians.

Something else occurred to me. "Zach lifted his restraining order on you the same day I came across the first minions and demon I've seen in months?" It couldn't be a coincidence…

"It isn't," Zach said, using his intrusive skills again.

My irritation died away. His inconsideration paled next to making sure that I was still alive.

"Thank you," I said, hoping for the hundredth time that Archons were more invested in the fate of humanity than they let on. Aside from my bloodline, I wasn't anyone special, yet Zach had saved me more than a few times. I just wished I understood why so many other people had to suffer and die.

Zach inclined his head, which was his version of "you're welcome." "Preparations have been made. You are to start your search for the staff at once."

"You're forgetting one thing," I pointed out. "We have no idea where Moses's staff might be. This is a big world, and that's not even counting all the demon realms in it, too."

Zach glanced at Adrian, and when they exchanged a meaningful look, my hackles rose. "If either of you even *think* of hiding something from me again—" I began furiously.

"We're not," Adrian interrupted, his gaze piercing as it landed on me. "I told you, Ivy, no secrets and no holding back this time. Moses's staff controls nature, which is why we need it to repair the realm walls and the demons also want it so they can use it to send those same walls crashing down. So, our best bet is to start with places that have natural anomalies. Even while dormant, the staff will affect what's around it."

That made sense, but, "I doubt it'll be as simple as googling places that are known for large congregations of locusts, frogs, lightning bolts or partings of seas," I said tartly. "If so, demons would've found it centuries ago."

Adrian raised a brow. "They've spent a lot of time scouring places with unusual natural phenomena, but they can't sense hallowed objects. Only you can. That's why we're going to find the staff and they're not."

He sounded completely confident. Then again, he was over-looking the most dangerous part of this mission. It wasn't whether or not we could find the staff. It's what could very likely happen if I tried to use it.

"I'm going with you, too," Jasmine said, her words distract-ing me from a topic I didn't want to dwell on.

I turned to my sister. "You've been through enough. We'll find you another place to stay at on hallowed ground, so you'll be safe—"

"You think I'll ever feel safe again?" Her voice filled with more pain than any eighteen-year-old should ever have. "I'm barely holding it together with you and Costa around me 24/7. If you leave me by myself, I'll lose it for sure. And I spent months trapped in a demon realm, so I know what we're up against."

"Jasmine," I tried again.

"I'm *going*." She cut me off with a flash of her old stubborn-ness. "Either help me pack or get out of my way, Ives."

She hadn't called me her pet name from our childhood since we'd rescued her. That, plus the glimpse of her former spunk, melted my resistance away. Who was I to lecture her? She was right. In some ways, she'd been through a lot more than me.

"Fine, then *you* can help *me* pack," I said, trying not to think about how I was going to find the staff while not getting myself killed, my sister hurt or my heart broken again.

"I'll pull our ride around," Adrian stated.

I gave him a doubtful look. "You think we can fit four adults and a winged gargoyle into your vintage metal baby?"

His smile was threatening and promising, like a lion licking its prey while deciding whether to eat it now or later. "We're bringing my Challenger, but we're not riding in it."

Huh? "What's that supposed to mean?"

His smile widened into a grin. "Get packed and you'll find out."

CHAPTER FIVE

I dropped my suitcases when I saw the bus. It was so long that it extended well past the driveway, and it had to be at least three feet taller than Brutus at his full height. Now I knew what Adrian meant about bringing his Challenger but not riding in it. The muscle car was hitched to the back of the bus, and though it wasn't small, it was dwarfed by the black-and-gray behemoth that had the words *Soul Smashers* emblazoned across both sides of it.

Adrian jumped down from the side door, ignoring the steps that led to the bus. "Like it?" he asked, grinning at my expression. "It's not much for speed, but when it comes to space and comfort, this thing has it all."

"You don't say," I managed. "Where did you get this?"

He glanced at it. "This was the tour bus for a band that was trying to be the next Smashing Pumpkins. The Soul Smashers never made it past being a one-hit wonder, which is why they went broke and sold their tour bus to me a few months ago."

I didn't comment on the irony of the last Judian and the last Davidian traveling around in a bus labeled Soul Smashers while trying to prevent a demon apocalypse. Instead, I climbed the steps and peeked inside. Then I blinked, convinced that I'd been glamoured because this couldn't be real.

Plush, black leather couches and a matching leather recliner chair made up what looked like an upscale living room. Mounted wall speakers surrounded a state-of-the-art entertainment area with a large flat-screen TV, and unless I was crazy, across from that was a minibar.

Beyond that, there was a kitchen with the works: granite countertops, a double-door refrigerator, stove, microwave, sink and dishwasher. A dinette area was across from that, with a half bathroom tucked into the corner. And on the opposite wall, right before a door that I assumed led to a bedroom, was a full bar complete with a lower cooler filled with wine bottles.

No wonder these rockers went broke, I thought. They'd been too busy drinking and riding around in style to perform.

When I slid open the pocket door in the back, it revealed a large, king-size bed, and I spied another bathroom in the corner, this one with a shower. The exterior of the tour bus might look at little beat up, but on the inside, everything was brand-new and top-of-the-line. Hell, it was nicer than the house we'd just left, not that I'd ever say such a thing to Costa.

"Better than my Challenger?" Adrian teased.

I turned around to find him standing behind me. He had both my suitcases, but really what caught my attention was his smile. It was almost impish, and the silver rings encircling his irises seemed to gleam brighter from mischief. I couldn't remember seeing Adrian look so…carefree. Under the power of that infectious smile, I smiled back.

"You could fit several of my former dorms in this thing."

He shrugged. "As you said, Brutus is too big to fit in any regular vehicle, plus in addition to the four of us, we also have lots of luggage and weapons." Then Adrian cast an almost casual glance at the bedroom. When his gaze met mine, his smile had a decidedly wicked slant. "This will suit all our needs."

Wow, he wasn't even *trying* to be subtle! Did he really think he'd just walk back into my life and I'd greet him with open legs? Okay, so I'd come close to giving it up before, but I knew better now. We had destinies to fulfill—or in his case, to over-come—so any attraction I *might* still feel for him was irrelevant. Saving people was my top priority. Not getting sweaty with the one person in the world who was fated to betray me.

"We could also have just taken different cars," I said, my chilly look telling him, *It's not happening.*

The single arch of his brow said, *We'll see.*

Jasmine and Costa climbed into the trailer, interrupting our wordless conversation. "Nice, bro," Costa commented, look-ing around with appreciation, but no surprise. Maybe Costa was used to Adrian living large, even if that was a side of him I was just beginning to see.

"Is all this necessary?" was what Jasmine said. I frowned. I agreed, but she sounded snippy, which wasn't like her.

"Our first stop is California," Adrian replied, his new, neu-tral tone not fooling me a bit. He hadn't done this just because we had a long way to go. "Since it will take days to get there, we all may as well be comfortable."

Comfortable, my ass. His glance at the bedroom certainly hadn't been *accidental.*

Jasmine shot a look between us, then she tugged on my arm. "Come on, Ivy. If the bedroom's ours, let's get settled in."

I grabbed my bags and led the way. "The closet's yours, and there are more drawers under the bed," Adrian called out.

"Thanks—"

Jasmine shut the pocket door before I could finish speaking. When she turned around, her arms were crossed in a way that reminded me of our mother when she'd been upset.

"Is something wrong?" I asked.

"Yes," she replied shortly. "You and Adrian are what's wrong."

I was so shocked, it took me a second to find my tongue. "Lower your voice, he can *hear* us," I hissed.

Her blue eyes seemed to turn to ice. "I don't care. He's destiny-bound to betray you and everyone knows it. If it were up to me, he wouldn't be anywhere near you, but Zach insisted."

I didn't know what surprised me more, the harshness in her voice, or this latest revelation. "Zach? When did you talk to him about Adrian coming with us? When I was packing?"

She gave an impatient swipe. "After you left to look for Brutus. Zach showed up and said that you'd be back with Adrian. I begged him not to lift his restriction on Adrian, but you can't tell an Archon to do anything he doesn't want to—"

"You knew about Zach supernaturally preventing Adrian from contacting me?" I cut her off. "And you didn't tell me?"

Jasmine's expression hardened. "Who do you think asked Zach to do it in the first place? Zach agreed that you needed time by yourself. I was hoping you'd get over Adrian if he was forced to leave you alone, but ever since he showed up, it's obvious that you haven't."

I stared at her in disbelief. The blond-haired girl across from me *looked* like my sister, but the Jasmine I knew was sunny, playful and impulsive. Not manipulative, hateful and hard.

"Jaz," I said softly. "What's going on?"

She let out a sound that was half scoff, half sob. "You mean, why do I hate him? Maybe it was seeing my boyfriend tortured to death in front of me in *Adrian's former realm,* or seeing how demons treat people worse than cattle, or being their caged trophy for weeks. Maybe it was finding out that minions murdered our parents while I was away, or maybe it's the fact that both demons and Archons believe that Adrian *absolutely* will fulfill his destiny by betraying you! You're all I have left, Ivy." Her voice broke. "I can't stand to lose you, too."

I felt so ashamed. Here I'd thought that Jasmine had been doing better over the past several weeks. She'd seemed like she'd been coping after her ordeal, but she hadn't, and I'd been blind to it. Seeing Adrian again must've felt like salt in her wounds, and she had already suffered so much.

"You don't have to worry," I told her, my voice rough from holding back tears. "If Zach hadn't made him come, Adrian wouldn't be here. Anything I felt for him before…it was just our supernatural tie because we're the last of our lines. Adrian even warned me about that when we first met. It might have felt like real emotions, but it wasn't, and I'm over that now."

I managed not to choke on the lie. Oh, if only what I still felt for Adrian was the same emotions that had drawn Davidians and Judians together for over two thousand years! Those had been compassion, empathy and the need to save. What I felt was different—stronger and deeper—and as much as I might want to, I couldn't blame any of it on my lineage.

"You don't have to be afraid of Adrian betraying me again," I went on. *I won't let him*, I silently added, but Jasmine needed more reassurance than that. "The day I wiped out the Bennington demon realm, Zach told me that Adrian had a chance to beat his fate. So, the demons might believe that Adrian is *their* weapon, but when you take someone's best weapon away from them, it just makes them easier to kill."

I was paraphrasing Adrian's words from this morning, not that Jasmine needed to know that. She just needed to believe it, and despite all my issues with Adrian, I still *did* believe that he could overcome his fate. I just wasn't willing to bet my life on it anymore, let alone my heart.

I went over to Jasmine and took her hands. She couldn't know that I still had doubts. She was too fragile. "I'm going to get Moses's staff, use it to repair the realm walls and then laugh as the demons choke on their unmet expectations of Adrian," I told her in a strong voice that belied my inner fears. "If you don't trust that he has truly changed, at least trust that Adrian hates demons even more than you do."

Tears welled in her eyes until one of them rolled down her cheek. "Then why do all the demons still believe in him?"

I kept my hands on hers, but my grip loosened. "They need to," I said at last. "Aside from getting lucky and managing to kill me first, Adrian's betrayal is their only hope."

She smiled with more pain than anyone eighteen years old should ever have. "And your only hope is that they're wrong. Someone's going to lose this bet, and whoever does will die."

The truth of that was like razors across my heart. I couldn't show that, so I turned away, starting to unload the contents of our suitcases into the room's drawers and cabinets.

"I know this is winner-take-all," I said at last. "But only people who bet everything stand a chance to win it all. We're going to win, Jasmine. I promise you that."

We have to, I didn't add. If not, and the realm walls eroded enough to fall, or Adrian did betray me to demons as his destiny predicted, then all the horrible things Jasmine had experienced would become everyday life for the rest of humanity.

I couldn't let that happen. I wouldn't.

CHAPTER SIX

Adrian took the first shift driving. He'd been tight-lipped ever since I came out of the bedroom, and it didn't take my new, improved senses to figure out why. He'd overheard my conversation with Jasmine. Whether he was more upset at her low opinion of him or my assurance that I'd never felt anything real for him, I didn't know and I wasn't about to ask.

Costa seemed unusually subdued, too. Of course, that could be because of Brutus's close proximity. Even though we'd shared a house, I'd kept the gargoyle away from Costa as much as I could these past two months. Costa might only see a seagull when he looked at Brutus because of the Archon glamour Zach used to disguise him, but Costa never forgot what Brutus was. Neither did Jasmine, although she seemed to have gotten past her initial trepidation over him. Maybe Costa had seen too much of what Brutus had done when the gargoyle had been the demons' flying version of a guard dog to ever feel comfortable around him.

Because of Brutus's fear of sunlight, we had him in the back bedroom with the windows and door shut. I only hoped he didn't break the bed under his weight or get slime on the pillows; man, that gargoyle could *drool* when he slept! Costa, Jasmine and I were on the couch watching TV, although I don't think any of us were paying attention to what was on the screen. We all appeared to be lost in our own thoughts.

"So, California, here we come," I said, trying to break the new, pensive atmosphere. "Which part are we going to? The beaches, the mountains, Hollywood?"

The look Costa gave me said he knew what I was doing, and it wouldn't work. "Death Valley. Shine *that* turd, Ivy."

Okay, so I had my work cut out for me. Was it riding with Brutus that had Costa so grumpy, or was it knowing that our brief, demon-free interlude was over? "Sun and sand, what's not to love?" I said, accepting his challenge. "Beats the hell out of a freezing, pitch-black demon realm."

A smile ghosted across Costa's lips. "You're right—I *would* take scorpions, dehydration and heat stroke over the realms, but that doesn't mean I like where we're going."

I remembered that Costa hadn't volunteered to come with us. Zach had just stated that Costa was going without bothering to ask his opinion on the matter.

"Do you not want to be here? If so, we can drop you off somewhere, or...do something else?"

Costa's pointed look stopped my awkward attempt at letting him off the hook. "I've come this far, Ivy. I'm seeing it through to the end or I'll die trying."

I flinched. Costa had been through enough to know that death was a real possibility. As he continued to stare at me, his real age seemed to creep into his dark brown gaze. Costa was a good-looking Greek guy who appeared to be in his late twenties, but time moved differently in the realms. In the one Costa had been trapped in, it had slowed to a near standstill. He'd be seventy-five on his next birthday, and every moment of those years filled his stare as he spoke again.

"I'm okay with that, Ivy." His voice was very soft. "The question is, are *you* ready to see this through, no matter what?"

I hoped so. I attempted a confident version of a smile. "Of course. It's my destiny, right?"

He leaned back, flicking away wavy black hair that, along with his olive-toned skin and deep brown eyes, highlighted his Mediterranean heritage. "Destiny is only foreknowledge of choices you have yet to make."

"You've been spending too much time with Zach," I muttered, wishing I'd kept watching the movie instead of trying to lighten the mood. Boy, had that backfired.

"No," Costa said, a harsh smile twisting his mouth. "I just know you want to get through this without hurting anyone except demons or minions, and that's impossible. You've busted your ass training to fight them, but you haven't accepted the fact that you might have to sacrifice everyone on this bus to win this war, and until you're ready to do that, you're *not* ready."

I looked away, my jaw clenching. "I'm doing this *for* everyone on this bus. I already lost my parents, my friends and any hope at a normal life, so if I lost all of you, too…it'd probably be easy for the demons to kill me, because I would have lost everything I'd been fighting for."

Costa's smile was wiped away. "Then you need to find something else to fight for, because there's a good chance that some or all of us will die before this is over. So find that something else, Ivy, because one day, you're going to need it."

As if I needed any more pressure. If this was Costa's version of a pep talk, he sucked at it. I looked at him, Jasmine, and then snuck a glance at Adrian, who drove without the aid of any mirrors because he'd smashed all the ones the bus came with. Breaking the mirrors negated a demon's power to use them as mini-gateways or as spying tools, but they must make driving the bus a little more challenging. If so, Adrian didn't show it. He stared fixedly at the road, but I knew he'd been listening.

Did he agree? Did Jasmine? She looked grimly resigned to what Costa had said, but she had admitted herself that she wasn't a fount of objectivity at the moment. Didn't matter, I decided, renewed determination filling me. I didn't need to find something else to do what had to be done to win this war.

I had all the motivation I needed right here.

I rolled over and stuffed the pillow in a new position under my head. Useless. The bed was comfy, the trailer was quiet, and yet I'd lain here, wide-awake, for hours. I blamed Costa, of course. His little chat had been as encouraging as listening to demons debate my chances, and needless to say, they were pretty sure I wouldn't succeed, either.

Costa meant well, but like Jasmine, I figured he'd been through too much to be optimistic. I couldn't blame him. I'd only been dealing with minions and demons for the better part of five months, and I still felt like I'd aged decades inside. If I'd been imprisoned by them for as long as Costa had, or lost my best friend to them the way Costa had lost Tomas? Yeah, I'd be a bowlful of doom, too, with a side order of bitterness.

"Ivy."

My gaze flew to the door, but it was still closed. A quick glance revealed that Jasmine was the only person in the room with me. I hadn't imagined hearing Adrian say my name from just a few inches away, though, so I strained my ears and waited.

"Ivy, come outside." Adrian's voice was low but clear, and I realized that he was speaking to me through the exterior wall of the trailer. "I need to show you something."

I got up, mostly because I couldn't stand to toss and turn anymore. I doubted something was wrong or Adrian wouldn't be whispering. Plus, we'd parked at the edge of an old cemetery. Hallowed ground meant no demons, even if they could roam around our world at night. It wasn't a deterrent to minions, but there'd need to be a lot of them to pose a threat with Adrian, Brutus and Costa here, not to mention me.

The thought cheered me as I moved quietly through the room. I *wasn't* the same helpless girl I'd been when this whole thing started. What doesn't kill you makes you stronger, right? Well, I'd had lots of things try to kill me, so by extension, I had to be stronger by leaps and bounds.

Once out of the bedroom, I tiptoed past a snoring Costa, who was on the sofa bed. The lone pillow on the floor must have been where Adrian had slept. He rarely used blankets, having long ago become well acclimated to the cold. Like Costa and Jasmine, I piled on the blankets to offset my memories of the dark, icy realms, but Adrian's time there had consisted of him being treated better than a king, so maybe he didn't mind.

Adrian had left the door open a crack, so it made no noise when I opened it to go outside. He'd moved away from my side of the trailer and stood near one of the old tombstones. It took a second for me to realize that Brutus was perched on top of a crypt next to him. If I hadn't spotted his red, iridescent eyes, I might've mistaken the gargoyle for an elaborate statue.

"What's up?" I said, keeping my voice down although we were the only ones who seemed to have difficulty sleeping.

Adrian wore a jacket and jeans, and until he turned to face me, I didn't realize that was all he had on. The jacket was open, and moonlight reflected off the muscles in his chest while shadows gave his abs more definition than they already had. As he walked toward me, every ripple of muscles reminded me of the power contained inside his stunningly sculpted body.

"Is this what you wanted to show me?" I asked, a tiny crack in my voice belying the quip. "If so, that's playing dirty."

A slow smile curled his mouth. "If I were playing dirty, I wouldn't be wearing anything."

Yeah, I thought, dragging my gaze away from his physique,

that might do it. Since I'd never admit that out loud, I said, "Why did you want me to come out? Is it what I said to Jasmine?"

His smile faded. "No, but now that you mention it, that did piss me off. I don't care what your sister thinks of me, but you shouldn't lie about what you feel, and we both know our lineage has nothing to do with what's between us."

Feel, not felt. His deliberate use of the present tense told me that he wasn't buying my being over him. The problem was, I was starting to doubt whether or not I was myself.

"Tell that to every Archon and demon alive," I muttered, mentally kicking myself for bringing the subject up. I should just keep a piece of tape handy so I could slap it over my mouth every time I had the urge to say something reckless.

"I don't care what they think, either," Adrian said silkily, closing the distance between us.

I backed away, holding out my hands to ward him off. "Don't. If this is why you called me out here, I'm leaving."

Hard assessment filled his features, as if judging whether I meant that, but he stopped. "It's not why, but it's been so long since I've been near you that I can't help it. Don't say you haven't missed me, too, or I'll know that you're lying."

"Really? How will you know that?" I said, deciding that I'd much rather challenge him than admit to it.

He came close enough to brush my hair away from my neck, and I told myself it was the night air hitting my skin that made me shiver. His fingers trailed over my neck, lingering on the spot where it felt like my heart was trying to escape through my jugular.

"Because when you lie, your pulse pounds even harder."

I moved away. Damn the memories that had come flooding back at his touch, taunting me with how his hands had felt when they'd explored *other* parts of my body.

"You're wearing the necklace." The masculine satisfaction in his voice scattered more shivers over me. I closed my hand over the pendant, as if concealing it made that any less true.

"With its history, I couldn't risk Brutus losing it," I said defensively.

Adrian laughed, but the knowing sound was nothing compared to the intensity in his gaze. "This time, I don't even have to look at your pulse to know you're lying."

What was I going to say? That some crazed part of me had been so touched by Adrian giving me a priceless stone from his childhood that I'd put the necklace on right before I went to bed? I hadn't thought that anyone would see my momentary act of weakness, yet since I'd forgotten to take it off before I went outside, now it was being used against me.

Brutus interrupted the moment by hopping off the crypt and stretching out his wings to their full extension. Then he chuffed at Adrian as if to say, *Hey, pal, remember me?*

Adrian threw a rueful look at the gargoyle. "You're anxious to get started, I know, but your timing sucks."

I actually loved the gargoyle's timing. In fact, the next hunk of raw pot-roast meat I came across had Brutus's name written all over it. Then I looked more closely at the gargoyle, noticing that he had something around his neck, too.

"What's that?" I asked, pointing.

Adrian cast one more look at the diamond in my cleavage. Then he walked over to Brutus and fingered the straps.

"It's why I called you out here. You're about to have your first flying lesson."

CHAPTER SEVEN

I knew my ears weren't malfunctioning, yet I still repeated his statement as if I'd misheard him. "Flying lesson?" *Are you serious?* my mind added in a screech.

He patted Brutus, murmuring to him in Demonish before he answered me. "I've had Brutus since right after he was born. He was so small, I could carry him around like a baby, and he broke every fragile object in my house when he was learning to fly."

The mental image of baby Brutus learning how to fly was adorable, but it didn't quell my apprehension. "But I don't *want* to learn how to ride Brutus when he flies."

The half smile that had curled Adrian's mouth while he reminisced about Brutus vanished. "You remember why I had to leave you when we rescued Jasmine from the Bennington realm?"

"Yes," I said hoarsely, fighting the memories from that day, but the most painful one came, anyway.

Adrian grasped my head, his silver-sapphire gaze almost burning into mine. "He can't fly with all of us, and I'm the heaviest. Brutus'll take you to the B and B, then you need to cross through the gateway."

I was appalled. "Adrian, you can't—"

He pulled my head down, his mouth searing mine in a kiss that matched the blazing intensity in his eyes. Desperation, desire and despair seemed to pour from him into me, but when he lifted his head, he was smiling.

"I love you, Ivy. I love you, and I didn't betray you. For the first time in my life, I feel like I can do anything."

Then he stuffed the slingshot into my pocket, slapped the gargoyle on his side and yelled, "Tarate!" Those mighty wings began to beat at once, flying Jasmine and me away while leaving Adrian to face a horde of minions alone…

His stare crashed through the memory and compelled me not to look away. "I don't regret staying behind to make sure that you and Jasmine made it out, but if a similar situation happens again, I want us *all* to be able to escape. That's why I've spent the past couple months learning how to ride Brutus when he's flying, and why I trained him to strengthen his wings so that he can fly while carrying very heavy loads."

I had to look away and blink several times to clear the sudden blurriness in my vision. "That's…that's smart."

And brave, ballsy, thoughtful and so many other things I didn't dare say out loud. I'd spent the past two months trying to convince myself that I felt nothing for Adrian. He'd spent that time thinking up new ways to protect me and Jasmine, and while it didn't make up for everything that had happened, it did leave a dent in my heart.

He shrugged, although the intensity didn't leave his gaze. "The bus has its perks, but speed isn't one of them. That makes it terrible for getaways if we come under attack. Brutus has speed, maneuverability, and his hide is so thick, minions would need a rocket launcher to bring him down."

Brutus chuffed, lifting his head a notch higher. If I didn't know better, I'd swear he understood every word because then he fluffed out his wings as though he were preening.

"You're all that and a bag of badass," I told him, smiling when he chuffed again as if in agreement. Then I returned my attention to Adrian. "I get why you wanted to learn how to ride him, but why do you want *me* to?"

Adrian fingered the straps around Brutus's neck, which I now realized was a harness. "It takes strength and concentration. If I were injured, I wouldn't be able to do it, and Brutus maxes out at carrying three people in his arms."

I swallowed hard. I didn't like heights and I hadn't even been good at horseback riding the few times I'd tried it. The thought of trying to ride on a flying *gargoyle's* back made my stomach roil, but the thought of Adrian being left behind again was a thousand times worse. I'd rather puke my guts out than risk that. Hell, I'd rather die, but I'd keep that to myself.

"Okay," I said, forcing a smile as I approached Brutus. "Let's get the flying lesson started."

"Again!" Adrian said, followed by a command of *"Tarate!"* to Brutus. The gargoyle vaulted us upward like he was a reptilian version of a roller coaster.

I slammed back against Adrian, forgetting to hold on to the reins again. Only Adrian's hold on them, plus his thighs gripping Brutus, kept us from falling as Brutus's torque made my stomach feel like it bashed into my spine. The rush of wind turned my hair into tiny whips, and when Brutus propelled us higher with another powerful flap of his wings, my guts left my spine to plummet downward like a free-falling elevator.

The fact that I hadn't thrown up yet was a *miracle*.

"Hold the reins," Adrian ordered, pushing them into my hands. I grasped them and held on because refusing and begging for this to stop wouldn't help. I'd learned that the first time.

Brutus tilted his massive head to glance back at me, as if he could feel that the reins had changed hands. Then he dipped slightly, angling his body downward and to the right. The shift tore a scream from me and it was all I could do not to drop them while grabbing wildly for the sturdier base of his wings.

How had Adrian ever mastered this alone? If he hadn't insisted on staying behind me, I would've fallen off a dozen times over.

"You're doing better," Adrian said, putting his mouth closer to my ear so he didn't have to yell.

"Liar!" was my instant response. He chuckled.

"I told you, no more lies. Now, try looking straight ahead, it'll help with the nausea. Then, try to steer Brutus."

I opened my eyes into mere slits, wishing I'd worn the goggles Adrian had offered me. He'd insisted on giving me his jacket, which I'd thought was his excuse to show more skin, but now, I was grateful that he hadn't taken no for an answer on that. March in the Florida panhandle was cooler than expected, or maybe I'd gotten too used to Miami's perpetual heat. Either way, my fingers felt stiff from the cold, and it might take weeks for the feeling to return to my toes. Between Adrian covering my back and legs and Brutus's large form blocking the wind from my front, the rest of me was warm enough, at least.

The few times I'd previously opened my eyes, I'd looked down out of a masochistic need to see how high we were. Answer: *high*. Now, I took Adrian's advice and looked straight ahead.

At first, I couldn't see much. There were lights, but they were faint, like indistinct stars. After a few hard blinks to clear wind-induced tears, I was able to see more clearly, and another few minutes of concentration later, I realized that Adrian was right. With Brutus flying relatively parallel to the ground and me staring straight ahead, the urge to puke faded.

"Steer him," Adrian urged, touching my arm for emphasis.

I pulled the reins a little to the right. Brutus didn't alter course. I pulled harder and the gargoyle turned, dipping down at the same time. Immediately, I yanked up, and Brutus responded by increasing velocity and torpedoing straight upward.

"Level him out, Ivy!" Adrian yelled, molding his body tighter around mine.

Through my instinctive panic, I remembered the simple lessons Adrian had given me. Pulling up on the reins meant *fly
higher* to Brutus. Pulling down meant *dive*. I needed to pull
straight out for the gargoyle to go back to cruising position, so
I did, although harder than I probably should have.

Brutus leveled out, allowing my organs to realign back to
their proper positions. Adrian's grip on me turned less bruising, and when I pulled on the reins again, I made sure to keep
them absolutely straight. This time, Brutus turned smoothly in
the direction I indicated. Emboldened, I steered him toward the
cluster of lights ahead. Within minutes, we were soaring over
a city, the tops of tall buildings well below us and little dots in
the nearby bay all that marked what might have been large,
luxurious yachts.

I surprised myself by laughing as exhilaration replaced my fear.
It was scary, yes, but I could, in fact, do this. Adrian's laughter
joined mine, and when he gripped me tighter, this time, it had
nothing to do with keeping us from falling off. The gargoyle
was the one soaring over the city, but in that instant, I felt like
I was able to fly, and sharing that indescribable feeling with
Adrian only made the moment more unforgettable.

I was almost sorry several minutes later when Adrian took the
reins and turned Brutus back around. All too soon, it seemed,
the lights from our house on wheels were back in view. One
frightening dive later, we were back on solid ground, and Adrian
issued a command that had Brutus lying down so I could slide
off instead of jumping like Adrian did.

Once I was on my own feet, Adrian took the reins off Brutus, then said something in Demonish that I loosely translated
as "Who's a good boy?" The gargoyle took his praise as his due,
even tilting his head in invitation. Adrian scratched him for a
minute, then left Brutus to come toward me.

If I'd thought he looked luscious with his jacket open, that
was nothing compared to how he looked with it off. His shoul-

ders were so broad, my arms wouldn't fit around them. Muscles flexed under skin tanned a deep gold, and his taut abdomen was set off by jeans that now hung so low, one tug would probably bare everything beneath.

I had a sudden urge to test that theory, and I clasped my hands together to stop myself before I did something crazy.

"So, some ride," I said, more than a little breathless.

He came closer, and the raw hunger that flashed across his features almost leveled me. "The ride isn't why your heart's pounding, Ivy."

He almost growled that last part, and his roughly sensual voice felt like it rubbed me while he spoke. I couldn't admit that he was right, so I took a step backward—and almost tripped over a headstone. Adrian's hand shot out, steadying me, and I shook it off while mentally berating myself.

Smooth, Ivy. Real smooth!

I pushed him away, feeling my heart hammer at the brief sensation of him beneath my hand. Touching him was more than enticing; it was addictive, which was why I had to get away from him before I let him do everything his darkly erotic stare promised me that I'd love.

I took his jacket off and held it out to him. His fingers closed over mine, but instead of taking the jacket, he used it to tug me into his arms. His hair brushed my face as he leaned down, and willpower alone caused me to turn my head at the last second, so that his mouth landed on my cheek instead of my lips.

He didn't fight the movement, but slid his mouth lower until he reached my neck. A moan left me at the feel of his tongue, and I shuddered when he pressed his lips more firmly against my throat. Flicks, circles and light suction had me reeling from sensations, until I needed the arms he wrapped around me. Without them, I might have fallen.

"Ivy." His voice was rough, and the hands that slid over me were achingly possessive. "I want you."

I could feel that in the hard flesh that pulsed against my belly. Deep inside me, an answering throb responded. I'd been overwhelmed, angry, lost, betrayed, burdened and brokenhearted over the past several months, but right now, all I felt was passion that threatened to boil over until it scalded me, and I knew that I would love being burned.

But I couldn't. Doing so wouldn't just be epically stupid—it would be greedy, and greed was something to be avoided at all costs when it came to Adrian and me.

Judas had been guilty of three betrayals: trust, when he stole from the communal funds; greed, when he accepted those thirty pieces of silver; and death, when he identified Jesus to the Temple guards with that final, infamous kiss. Adrian had already betrayed my trust by lying to me about my real destiny. I wasn't about to help him succumb to greed by saying yes now.

"No," I said, pushing him away. Adrian let me back him up. He didn't go far, and his hands flexed into fists as if he were fighting a fierce inner battle.

"Okay, so I still want you," I went on, because that was obvious. "Whether that's destiny, lust or something else, I don't know, but if you care about me like you claim to, you'll stay away from me unless you can *prove* that you're not going to betray me again."

And the only way he could prove that was if we succeeded in finding Moses's staff and used it to repair the realm walls, then found the final, hallowed weapon, and did all of this without getting killed in the process. I may as well have told him that I'd give him a chance only if we were the last two people left on earth.

Even still, I couldn't stop the emotions that rolled over me, breaking through barriers that hadn't been strong enough to hold them. Adrian was right—I did still care for him. And that weakened me in ways my enemies would be too quick to take advantage of.

"I need to stay focused if I have any chance at winning this fight," I continued, my tone hardening. "So, once again, if you really want to show me that you've changed, walk away from me. Now."

He said nothing for so long that I wondered if he was going to walk away without a word. If he did, it would be for the best, which was why I refused to say anything else.

"What if I can prove that I won't betray you again?" he finally asked, surprising me.

I let out a short laugh. "If any of us are still alive after this whole thing is over, sure, I might be up for a date."

"There's a way I can prove I won't betray you without waiting until then, but I'll need Zach." Then his voice dropped, becoming rougher and softer at the same time. "If I can prove to you that you can trust me, that there's no way I'd even be *able* to betray you again, will you give me a chance? A real one?"

I should say no. It might sound like a simple question, but it still possibly had destiny-affecting consequences. Then again, it was as realistic as my saying what I'd do if I won the Powerball, although I had better odds of doing that than Adrian had of proving he'd beat his destiny without actually having to beat it first.

Still, even as the word *no* formed on my lips, something rose up in me. *What was wrong with saying what I'd do if an impossible dream came true?* the part of me that couldn't stop caring for Adrian whispered. After all, millions of people talked about what they'd do if they won the Powerball, and 99.9 percent of them would never find out.

In the end, I gave Adrian the same answer I'd forced myself not to say earlier. "Yes. Prove that…and I'll give you a chance."

CHAPTER EIGHT

Despite being awake for half the night, I woke up before Jasmine. After I brushed my teeth and threw a cardigan over my tank top, I went out into the main room. From the swaying motion of the tour bus, we were already back on the road, but I was surprised to see Adrian driving. Brutus sat behind Adrian's chair, and someone had thrown a large blanket over the gargoyle so that he was completely covered. Costa was awake, yawning as he opened a carton of eggs in the kitchen.

"Oh, let me make breakfast," I said, smiling as I gently moved him aside. It's not that I thought cooking was my duty as a girl. Costa loved to cook, but he also wasn't very good at it, as the past several weeks had proved.

He gave me a hopeful look as he went to the wet bar, where a coffeemaker was now set up. "French toast?"

"Sure. Adrian?" I asked, a little unsure about how I should act. Things between us hadn't changed, and yet I'd agreed that they might, if he could prove that he'd conquered his destiny.

"Nothing for me, I already ate," he replied.

That neutral response told me nothing about his frame of mind. Come to think of it, Adrian had been blunt to the point of aggressiveness about wanting me, yet he hadn't said that he wanted more than sex. Months ago, he'd told me that he loved me, but in fairness, he said it right before he thought he was going to be killed by minions.

Did he still love me? Or—in truth—had he ever loved me? Maybe his saying that back then had been impulse instead of sincerity? He *had* thought he was about to die, after all.

I began breaking eggs and mixing them in a bowl. Noises in the bedroom had to be Jasmine waking up, so I called out, "Jaz? Want French toast?" while still mentally stewing.

"Did you mention breakfast?" Jasmine said with a yawn, appearing in the doorway.

I turned toward her, smiling to cover the confusion that had started to swirl inside me. "Yep. Hungry?"

"Starving," she began, then stopped, staring hard. "I don't believe it," she hissed before going back into the bedroom and slamming the door.

I exchanged a bewildered glance with Costa. "Beats me," he said to my unspoken question.

"I'll be right back," I muttered, wiping egg residue from my hands. Then I slid the door open. "Jaz? What's wrong?"

She was as far away from me as the room allowed, and when she swung around and glared at me, I came in and shut the door. Whatever it was, she obviously thought it was my fault.

"You snuck out to see Adrian last night," she accused.

How had she known? She'd been asleep when I came back in! Then, I pushed my guilt back and straightened. I was a grown woman and I didn't need my little sister's permission to meet with anyone. Plus, I *hadn't* done anything with Adrian.

"Not for what you think," I said, trying to find a balance between *you can't tell me what to do* and *I love you, sis*. "He taught me how to ride Brutus while he's flying. Adrian used that trick to fight the demon from the other day, so it's important that I know it, too, with what we're up against."

An angry kind of hurt filled her gaze. "Oh, so I'm supposed to believe that *Brutus* gave you that hickey?"

For the hundredth time, I cursed my inability to look into a mirror. I'd gotten pretty good at putting on makeup using other reflective surfaces, but they weren't clear enough to show everything, like an incriminating hickey that needed covering.

"I expect you to trust me," I settled on, meeting her gaze squarely. "Nothing is going to happen between me and Adrian. The only, highly unlikely exception to that is if he can prove that he can beat his fate, and that's a very big 'if.'"

Jasmine didn't reply. She just stormed past me and headed toward the front of the former tour bus.

"Jaz, don't!" I shouted, chasing after her.

"Let's get something clear," she snapped when she reached Adrian. "If you betray my sister again, I'll kill you."

I wanted to drag her away, but Adrian held out his hand to me in the universal gesture for *Wait, I've got this.*

"If I betray Ivy again, I'll *let* you kill me," he told Jasmine, a hard little smile playing on his lips. "Deal?"

"You'd better believe it," she muttered, spinning around. "Forget the French toast, I lost my appetite."

"After this, so did I," I snapped.

"Don't worry, Ivy," Adrian said, his tone deceptively mild. "Now that your sister and I have an understanding, all that's left is coming through on what you and I agreed to."

Costa raised a brow, but after Jasmine's little scene, I wasn't about to explain my ultimatum to Adrian last night.

"Tell you later," I said with a sigh.

Then, taking a deep breath, I went back to the kitchen and began mixing the eggs again. All the while, I repeated *she's been though a lot* until it cooled my anger. Jasmine just needed more time to see that Adrian wasn't the same person she'd heard so much about while trapped in his former realm. Right now, the only thing she knew was that fate predicted him to betray me two more times, the final one being permanent. No wonder she wasn't his biggest fan. She didn't have to be so bitchy about everything, but then again...

"She's been through a lot," I said to the room in general.

Adrian's glance at me only lasted a second, yet its effect lingered. "So have you, Ivy."

True, and the fight wasn't even half over yet. The thought made me whisk the eggs far harder than necessary. Costa came over and gave me a supportive pat on the back.

"Don't mind Jasmine's attitude," he said lightly. "I hated Adrian at first, too."

I stopped whisking to whirl around in surprise. "But he pulled you out of a demon realm and saved your life!"

Something dark flashed over Costa's face, marring his tanned, attractive features. "He did, yet I still hated him for a long time because of what happened to me in the realms. Some things, you get over. Some things—" his voice lowered until I doubted that anyone except me could hear him "—you don't."

A chill skittered up my spine. Yes, Costa had suffered horribly in the same realm that Adrian had ruled for almost a century, but I'd been sure that he'd forgiven Adrian since Adrian had walked away from that life to devote himself to destroying demons. Furthermore, Costa had fought side by side with us when we'd searched for the slingshot, and through it all, I'd never had reason to doubt his loyalty.

Yet that unfamiliar hardness in his dark brown gaze now made me wonder...what if I'd been wrong?

CHAPTER NINE

We made it through the next two days without incident. When it was daylight, the four of us took turns driving, once Jasmine and I learned the trick to operating a forty-six-foot-long vehicle that was also towing a car. Once night fell, we parked on hallowed ground, avoiding the chance of running into any demons who ventured out in the dark to play. Brutus was our version of a security system then. While we slept, he was awake, either perching himself on the roof of the bus or flying overhead to scope out danger from the skies.

Despite being in near constant contact with Adrian for the past few days, there seemed to be an invisible wall between us. That could be because Jasmine had practically welded herself to my hip, but I wondered if something else was up.

I should just ask Adrian how he intended to prove that he wouldn't betray me again. Or ask him how he felt about me—the other question I couldn't stop wondering about. Yet I didn't have the courage to do it, and the irony of that wasn't lost on me. How could I hope to win a fight against demons if I didn't even have the guts to wage an emotional battle?

Racetrack Playa in Death Valley, California, was hot, with

sunshine so strong, the rays almost felt tangible. I'd expected mile upon mile of gently rolling sand hills, but the terrain was flat, hard earth that reminded me more of an endless parking lot than a desert. In many ways, it was the exact opposite of a demon realm, yet this area had the same air of desolateness, and if I squinted, the mountains in the distance could have been gargantuan pyramids that demons so loved to show off with.

Jasmine looked around with more bemusement than trepidation, reminding me that the only realm she'd seen had been Adrian's. That had been a paradise compared to some of the others, with petrified trees mimicking a forest and frozen rivers reflecting lights from the magnificent, blue-hued city.

"See all the rocks, Ivy?" Adrian said, breaking through my memories. "Those trails behind them are why we're here."

Countless rocks did litter the cracked ground, ranging in size from baseballs to boulders. Most had trails behind them, indicating that they'd been dragged to their positions. Some of those trails were short, as if a child had pushed the smaller ones a few inches before growing bored, yet some of them stretched out farther than I could see, and it would take several people to move the bigger boulders even an inch.

Why would anyone want to come out to Death Valley just to push around rocks? I wondered. Talk about being in desperate need of a social life. Then I looked more closely at the trails behind the rocks. Something was missing...

"There are no footprints," I said in surprise. "How did those stones move, if no one was out here to move them?"

Adrian gave me an arch look. "Exactly. Scientists recently came up with a reason why the sailing stones moved on their own, but I don't buy it. That's why this place is our first stop. Do you sense anything hallowed at play here?"

The million-dollar question. I took a deep breath, focusing

on the supernatural sensor inside me. After a few moments, I frowned. Nothing. Was this thing inside me even on?

I tried again, closing my eyes as I concentrated harder. Minutes ticked by, and still, nothing. Okay, maybe there wasn't anything sacred within a hundred miles of this place, but then I should have *felt* the lack of it. Instead, all I felt was sweat trickling down my body and a headache coming on.

"Ivy." Adrian's voice was low. "Are you okay?"

I opened my eyes, a sigh hissing through my teeth as I figured out the problem. "No. I'm *completely* out of shape!"

"Says who?" Costa said, giving me a once-over.

I almost kicked a nearby rock out of frustration. "Not like that. I spent the past couple months learning how to fight, but I haven't worked on my hallowed radar since I found the slingshot. That means now, my hallowed radar is as sluggish as if it spent this whole time couch-surfing while bingeing on chips and beer."

Jasmine gave me an incredulous look. "Are you serious?"

"As if I'd joke about this," I muttered.

There had to be a way to jump-start my process. After all, I'd managed to use my hallowed finder back when I didn't even know that I *had* the ability. Of course, back then my life was usually in danger, so that had probably factored into things—

Inspiration hit and I spun around, grabbing Adrian by the arm. "Choke me," I announced. "Survival instinct kicks my abilities into gear, as you proved so memorably before."

A muscle ticked in his jaw. "No."

"But you have to," I said, which should have been obvious. Otherwise, we'd wasted three days driving all the way out here.

His featured tightened. "I only did that before because a child's life was on the line. Unless it's life-or-death, I'm never hurting you again. Besides—" his voice lost its harshness

"—survival instinct isn't the only thing that can trigger your abilities. Adrenaline should work, too."

I let out a short laugh. "So I should find a scorpion and pet it for the sheer terror of the experience?"

His mouth quirked. "You could, but I had something else in mind."

My seat belt was on as tight as I could stand. I also had one hand pressed against the side window while the other gripped the seat divider. In addition to that, my leg was braced against the dashboard so I could wedge my body farther into the seat. Still, it felt like I'd be vaulted out of the car at any moment.

And I couldn't stop smiling. That was the craziest thing. At first, I'd been nervous when Adrian gunned the Challenger to incredible speeds across the desert, leaving Jasmine, Costa and the bus containing Brutus far behind. Then I'd been shocked by how he could spin the muscle car around in circles and cause it to "drift" while still maintaining complete control.

I'd never done something reckless just for the fun of it before. Jasmine had always been the impulsive one. I'd been careful, polishing my mask of normalcy as I went through the motions that were otherwise referred to as life. For the longest time, I blamed my ennui on the medication I took for my hallucinations, but then I found out the pills were placebos. My parents had supplied them, knowing there was no cure for my condition, but not wanting to admit that until they thought I could handle it. What they hadn't known was that the cause of my visions was supernatural instead of medical.

No, I'd numbed myself to the world all on my own, resigning myself to never feeling the things that "normal" people felt. Then I met Adrian. He didn't just wake something up inside me; in many ways, he'd transformed me. No wonder I had such difficulty controlling myself around him. Maybe, for the moment,

I shouldn't even try to. Maybe, like I was doing with this wild car ride, I should just enjoy being reckless instead.

I unclipped my seat belt and slid across the seat. Adrian gave me a startled look, slowing the car at once. I didn't wait for it to stop before I leaned over and pressed my lips to his.

His response was immediate, and electric. He yanked me closer, the momentum from him hitting the brakes slamming me harder against him. I didn't care, because his mouth slanted over mine and his arms crushed me to him. I moaned as his tongue slashed past my lips, tangling with mine until I felt drunk with his taste. I breathed in his scent, reveled in the scrape of his lightly stubbled jaw, then arched in wordless bliss when he pulled me all the way onto his lap.

He kissed me deeper, each stroke of his tongue igniting my senses, until my whole body felt like it vibrated from desire. I was lightheaded, as if everything around me was still spinning, but the car had come to a complete stop. His hands moved down my back with sensual possessiveness before sliding over my hips and staying there. I wasn't aware that I'd been gripping his shirt until it ripped open at the collar. The sound he made as his kiss became bruising caused things low in me to tighten so suddenly, I cried out.

That rush of passion did more than cause me to writhe with need in his arms. With an internal flash that was as intense as a solar flare, my abilities activated and I *felt* that the staff wasn't anywhere nearby. Oh, a few hallowed things were, but nothing as significant as an object that had channeled enough power from on high to control nature. That wouldn't register as a faint "blip" on my radar. It would blast it, just like David's ancient slingshot had when I found it months ago.

Adrian pulled away, his hands now framing my face instead of gripping my hips. "I felt that. What is it?"

"You can feel that?" I asked with a gasp.

He brushed my hair away while his gaze raked over me. "You'd be amazed by some of my abilities, Ivy."

The raw sensuality in his voice promised pleasure and threatened obsession. At the same time, there was something distinctly *not* sexy about my abilities rearing their head right now. To say that I hadn't been focusing on anything hallowed for the past several minutes was putting it mildly.

Yet my abilities had had their priorities in order, even if I hadn't. I uncurled myself from Adrian's embrace and began to scoot back into my seat. His eyes stayed locked onto mine, but he didn't stop me.

"You were right, adrenaline did the trick, but the staff isn't here," I said, voice raspy as I tried to regain control.

"Ah." The word did nothing to tell me what he was thinking about my putting the brakes on—or starting things to begin with. Was he frustrated? Upset? I couldn't stand not knowing.

"You—you could say something *else* about what just happened," I stammered.

The faintest smile tugged his lips, which were fuller from how hard he'd kissed me. "So could you, but if you want me to go first, fine. I love how you taste, how you feel, the little noises you make when you're turned on, and when you ripped my shirt open, I wanted to throw you in the back and fuck you so hard, all the windows would shatter."

Adrian's tone was light and he never lost that half smile, but his stare said that he meant every word.

"You promised." My response was 90 percent a reminder of his vow, and 10 percent a plea for him to forget it.

He reached out, catching my hand in his. Then he brought it to his lips, kissing my knuckles while never breaking his stare.

"That's why we're still in the front seat, but you wanted to know what I was thinking, so I told you."

Then he let go of my hand and moved his seat forward. I looked away, flushing. I hadn't even noticed him moving it back, but I wouldn't have fit on his lap otherwise. Despite my tinge of embarrassment, I also felt a sense of relief. By repositioning his seat, Adrian was further confirming that nothing else was going to happen. I'm the one who'd started this, but I'd only meant it to be a kiss. Not for it to end with sex.

Then again, if my hallowed radar hadn't acted up, who knows how this would have ended? With lots of broken windows?

"Your turn," he said, interrupting that dangerous line of thought. "You're the one who kissed me. Why?"

I squirmed at his bluntness. "Isn't it kinda obvious?"

Another ghost of a smile. "I didn't make you guess what I was thinking when I answered you."

No, he sure hadn't. I looked away, unable to reply while on the receiving end of that deep blue stare. His gaze was too probing, too knowing, and yes, still too enticing.

"I shouldn't have," I said at last. "That makes me a tease, I suppose, but I felt so...free, right before I kissed you." I let out a choppy laugh. "Guess it made me forget all the reasons why I'm not."

"Ivy." The way he said my name forced me to look at him. When I did, he pulled me into his arms before I even realized that he'd moved.

"Adrian—"

"Shh," he murmured. "I don't think I've ever just held you before. I was always pushing you away, and the one time I didn't, we were also in this car." His lips brushed my hair. "Did you know that old Challengers were your aphrodisiac?"

I laughed, relaxing at his loose embrace and his light, bantering tone. "What can I say? I'm into vintage things."

His chuckle rumbled against my back. "I've missed you, Ivy. All of you, so don't think you're not free around me because you are. That means kissing me isn't teasing. I want to do truly filthy things to you, but I can wait. If Zach hurries his Archon ass up, I won't even have to wait long."

I had to say it. "You do know it's extremely twisted that you need an angel's help to hook up, right?"

This time, his laughter had an edge. "I never have before, but with Zach, I can give you the guarantee that you demanded."

I didn't remind him that I'd only promised him a *chance*, not a sure thing. "How does Zach factor into you proving that you can beat your fate?" I asked instead.

He tensed, but then relaxed almost as fast. "It's complicated, so I'd rather show you than tell you."

"That's what my prom date said right before I cracked a beer bottle over his head," I replied, my tone dry. "You told me no more secrets, remember?"

He angled his head so he could look at me, and his expression was serious. "I don't want to tell you right now. That's a choice, not a secret, and yes, there's a difference."

Not in my mind, but I'd given him an ultimatum—a huge one—and he'd sworn to meet it. I still didn't think that it was possible, but I had to admit—the idea was starting to appeal. And if it *was* possible for Adrian to prove that he could beat his fate without having to wait until the end of this war, how could I refuse to honor the only stipulation he'd given me?

"Fine," I said. "You'll tell me, or show me, when Zach does what you want him to." *If he does*, I silently added. Then I changed the subject. "So, the staff's not here. What's next on our list of places filled with unexplainable natural weirdness?"

"It's…" His voice trailed off, then he almost shoved me away. He was out of the car before I could ask what was wrong, but one look around answered that.

When I'd glanced out the window moments ago, the sky had been bright blue. Now, it was deepest indigo that was fast turning to black. With all the crazy lightning, I would've thought a storm was rolling in, except there were no clouds.

Adrian jumped back into the car, slamming it into gear and

hitting the gas. The instant velocity knocked me against the seats hard enough to risk whiplash.

"Call Costa." His tone was urgent. "Tell him to aim for the lightning and get out of here, now."

I began to tear through my purse looking for my cell phone. "What's going on?"

Lightning continued to flash on every horizon, until the perimeter of the landscape was bathed in strobes of dazzling white. At the same time, the sky turned pitch black, and more terrifying, somehow looked like it was starting to fall.

Adrian floored the gas. "This area is being swallowed by a demon realm."

CHAPTER TEN

I'm the first to criticize when people ask dumb questions during a crisis. Seriously, I can't count the times I've thought, *Just shut up and run!* while watching a horror movie. In reality, stupid-babble was a side effect of shock, and despite all that I'd been through, I still wasn't immune to it.

Take me saying, "What? How?" while dialing Costa's cell phone with shaking fingers.

Adrian didn't take his eyes off the nearest lightning storm, which he was driving us straight toward.

"Told you, demon realms are created when they cause parts of their world to slam into ours. I've seen it done before, and this is what it looked like."

Yes, he'd explained realm creation to me months ago. Not that understanding it helped when a nightmare-black sky was bearing down on us like a giant foot about to squash an ant. Costa answered on the second ring, and I didn't wait for him to say hello before blurting out Adrian's instructions.

"Drive for the lightning. A realm's coming down on us!"

"What?" Costa demanded. See? Stupid-babble.

"A realm is about to swallow us," I yelled. "The only way out is through the lightning, so drive, drive, drive!"

I heard Costa shout something to Jasmine, then the line went dead. I checked the phone. No bars. With two worlds about to collide in the same space, that wasn't a surprise. Darkness had now completely enveloped the area around us, making it difficult to see the bands of lightning we were headed toward. Without our headlights, we'd be driving blind, and we needed to see or we'd crash into one of the area's many boulders. When we'd gone on our joy ride, we'd driven well away from the bus, not knowing that there would be any consequences. Now, I only hoped that Costa and Jasmine were closer to the lightning belts than we were, because despite Adrian pushing the muscle car to its limit, the horizon around us was turning completely black.

Then several loud booms shook us. Adrian skidded to a stop, narrowly avoiding a large fissure that opened up in the ground in front of us. The air became heavy, compressing us as if each square inch had been filled with invisible weight. Something far louder than thunder echoed across the sky, making me clutch my ears in a futile attempt to lessen the painful noise.

Adrian put the car in Park and shut off the engine. When his gaze met mine, the grim expectancy in those sapphire depths made what he said almost redundant.

"We can't outrun it. It's here."

I looked out the window—and a scream trembled in my throat. I barely noticed Adrian unclipping his seat belt and pulling me into his arms. With those awful compressing sensations growing worse, only his grip kept me from running out of the car in an instinctive, useless attempt to get away.

"Brace yourself!" he shouted above the deafening noise.

I did, unable to stop staring out the window. The wall of black rushing down upon us lost its impenetrable, inky darkness. Instead, for a few terrifying seconds, it looked like a smoky mirror. I could *see* the top of our car amid the rock-littered landscape, see the cracked ground shuddering and fissuring as if caught in the grip of an earthquake, and then I saw my own pale, stricken face staring up from the windshield when that mirrored reflection crashed down on top of us.

Glass pelted my face before Adrian shoved my head into his chest. I tried to concentrate on how tightly he held me, not on the sudden heaviness in my gut that made me feel like I was being eviscerated in my seat. The noise was the worst; a roaring, blasting sound that seemed to reverberate through my entire body. The urge to run was overwhelming, but at the same time, fear kept me frozen in place.

After what might have been minutes, but felt like hours, Adrian pulled away. He lifted my head, and the faint light from the electronics on the dashboard showed blood running from his ears and from the countless tiny cuts on his face. He leaned over and took some napkins out of his glove box, wiping at my face instead of his. I only realized I was bleeding, too, when I saw that they were stained red after he drew them away.

"Is—is it over?" I asked, surprised that I was barely able to hear my own voice.

He nodded, and I lip-read more than heard him say, "Yes."

I drew a shaking hand through my hair, feeling the bite of countless shards that were stuck inside the brown mass. A glance down revealed that Adrian and I were covered with glass. All of the windows and most of the windshield were gone, and my mind flashed to his prior erotic statement. How I wished these had broken from uncontrollable passion instead of a realm slamming into this section of desert.

Even if Adrian hadn't told me what was happening, I'd have figured it out from the new frigid temperatures and the utter darkness. No moonlight interrupted the unbreakable blackness, either. If the moon existed in demon realms, it was never seen because not even the sun's reflection made it into these frozen facsimiles of hell.

I shivered, shock wearing off enough to remind me that I was dressed in shorts and a tank top. Perfect for an afternoon in Death Valley; highly dangerous for our new surroundings. Adrian caught the shiver and drew his shirt off, causing a small shower of glass to hit the seats. Then he balled it up and began using it to brush the glass off me. He said something, but I only caught a word or two. Then he shouted, which made my ears hurt even more, but at least I understood him.

"Get up slowly, there's glass everywhere."

No shit. I managed to get to the door, wincing at all the new cuts that caused despite my being careful. When I was finally outside, I began brushing the shards off me while my shivers turned into shudders. Where had that wind come from? It felt like it skipped my skin and went straight into my bones.

Adrian got out and walked over to the trunk. When he returned, I was relieved at the thermal pants, boots and ski jacket that he held out to me. Thank God his car was stocked for emergencies, and a demon realm landing on us definitely qualified as an emergency.

I stripped off my torn, bloody shirt and shorts without hesitation. Clad only in a bra and panties, I started to pull on the new clothes when Adrian stopped me.

"Wait," he said, holding up a plastic bag. His headlights, which miraculously hadn't shattered, showed a cake-like substance in the bag that I recognized as manna. Right, better heal my injuries before bleeding all over my new clothes.

I scooped out a handful, wincing as I spread it over the parts of me that were the most red-splattered. You'd think that I could feel where the cuts were, but with being nearly naked in the cold, everything hurt. I sure felt it when the manna began to heal my cuts, though. They stung like I'd jabbed myself with a fork before the pain faded into a slight itchiness. The fabled bread of heaven that had fed the Israelites while they wandered in the desert had more than one use. Manna's healing properties were amazing, but it also had its limits, such as how it couldn't heal a mortal wound. Thankfully, I didn't have one.

Adrian positioned himself behind me and lifted my hair. His hands were gentle as they moved over me, but any enjoyment I would have normally felt faded at the numerous stabs of pain as he spread manna over the cuts on my back. Once he was finished, I hurriedly put on my new clothes and boots, then grabbed a handful of manna and gestured to him.

"Your turn."

Either his ears weren't as damaged as mine or he could lip-read, because he understood although I'd forgotten to shout. He turned around, moving until he was directly in front of the headlights. When I saw his back, I sucked in an appalled breath.

Long, deep gashes rent his skin. Glass was still embedded in multiple slashes, reflecting the light through sheens of red. I couldn't believe he'd treated my insignificant wounds first. He looked like he could bleed to death from some of these!

And he'd gotten them while shielding me from the worst of the fallout when the windows exploded. I blinked back my tears. These wounds should have been mine, but he'd taken them for me. How did I begin to say thank-you for that?

First things first, by healing him. I started to lay my manna-smeared hand on his back, but he stopped me.

"You need to get the glass out first, or it'll be stuck beneath the newly healed skin."

I used my other hand to start picking out the glass, wincing at each inadvertent flinch he made. When I had the largest slash cleared, I laid my manna-coated hand on top of it. His muscles bunched and he clenched his fists, but he didn't make a sound as the wound began to close as if pulled by invisible strings. The rivulets of blood slowed and tan skin replaced the red, puckered line. Then even the new scar vanished. I took in a deep breath. One down, dozens to go.

It took over twenty minutes to clear his back of all the serious wounds. He worked on his front at the same time, so when I was done and he turned around, nothing but smooth, red-stained skin met my gaze. I let out a relieved noise and impulsively hugged him, running my hands over his back as if to reassure myself that all those awful gashes were truly gone.

"Don't do that ever again!" My words were muffled against his chest, which then shook with suppressed laughter.

"Sure, Ivy. The next demon realm that crashes onto us, I'll let you take the brunt of."

Liar. I pulled away, my heart fluttering at the total blackness beyond our headlights. Now that we'd survived the immediate danger, we still had to get out of here. But first, we needed to find out if Costa, Jasmine and Brutus had made it through the lightning in time, or if they'd been swallowed by the new realm. If they were here, we couldn't leave without them.

"Do you have warm clothes, too?" I asked, a practical sort of mentality kicking in. "If you run around in shorts and sandals, the demons will know it's you, Archon disguise or no Archon disguise."

"Zach didn't glamour me, so I'm not in disguise," Adrian said, stunning me. I always saw through Archon glamour as if it wasn't there, so I'd had no idea that everyone else could see the real Adrian now, too.

"Why not? Is Zach *trying* to get you caught by demons?"

He shrugged, but hardness filled his gaze, making me think I wasn't the only one who'd wondered that. "Zach said it wouldn't matter this time, so he refused to do it."

My jaw clenched. Wait until I saw Zach again. I'd shake the truth of his motivations out of him, because it was well past time that the Archon revealed whether he was trying to help Adrian overcome his fate, or trying to doom him to fulfill it.

"Well, even if you run into a nest of demons you've never met before, no one else could stand to be mostly naked in these temperatures without catching hypothermia, so they'd still know it was you," I said, trying to use a quip to conceal how angry I was by this latest revelation.

"If we're lucky, we'll be long gone before more demons arrive," he replied, sounding far calmer than I felt. "There should be only one here now, judging from the times I watched Demetrius absorb new realms."

This was the first time I'd heard him mention Demetrius since the day I'd killed him when I'd used the slingshot to wipe out Adrian's former realm. I liked to believe that I'd walked through Demetrius's ashes at some point. The last thing I wanted to do was ask Adrian to elaborate on a memory that involved his evil former foster father, but I had to. "Why only one?"

Adrian shot me a jaded look. "Because demons are territorial, and none of them want someone else jumping in to claim their new territory after they absorb a realm. Remember, on their end, this place was only a reflection before now, and that made it up for grabs. So, only the demon who did this will be here because he's the only one who would've hitchhiked through on the gravitational field when he caused these two dimensions to collide. The others will come, but for a little while, this place should be demon- and minion-free, except for its creator."

That's right, demon realms started out as nothing more than duplicate reflections of our world. Those reflections were detailed enough to include buildings, cars and other structures, but they weren't tangible. Not until a demon used enough power to smash the reflective world into the real one, "swallowing" it. If we were mostly demon-free now, we had to make the most of it.

"Does this thing still run?" I asked, giving the Challenger a critical look. We didn't need windows to look for Costa and Jasmine, but we could sure use a functional engine.

"I'll check after I've changed into my new clothes," Adrian said, and took off his shorts.

I was so startled to suddenly see him naked that for a few uninhibited moments, I drank in the sight of him. The headlights hid nothing from my view, throwing every chiseled hollow and sinew into stunning relief. If the round, hard globes of his ass and his long, muscled lines weren't impressive enough, the object framed by the tight gold curls between his legs did the trick. *I found the staff,* I caught myself thinking. *And it is* mighty.

"Ivy."

The amusement in Adrian's tone broke through my near-blasphemous thought. I turned away, feeling a blush burn my cheeks. I was going to die from embarrassment and then go straight to hell. That was my real destiny.

"Yes, I have warmer clothes," he went on, his tone turning husky. "I didn't occur to me to change into them until you weren't looking, and now, I'm glad I didn't."

Me, too! the shameless part of me replied, but the rest of me was still cringing over being caught gawking at him as if I'd never seen a naked man before. Okay, so I hadn't in real life, but the movies and the internet had to count for *something.*

"Are you dressed yet?" I said, keeping my back turned.

A rustling sound, then he said, "Enough."

I turned around, marveling that my hearing was back to normal. The manna must have healed more than my cuts. Adrian was now by the trunk of the car, and the taillights revealed that he had on pants and calf-high boots. As I watched, he pulled a sweater over his head, then grabbed a large knife and what looked like a bag of dirt from the trunk.

"What's with the dirt?" I asked.

He tucked the knife into his pants. "It's hallowed."

I hadn't felt anything from it, but with my hallowed sensor being out of shape, that wasn't surprising. Plus, it was only a bag. Not an entire plot of ground. "Grave dirt?" I guessed.

He shot me a quick grin. "Not just any. It's dirt that's tossed onto caskets as relatives say their final goodbyes. All that emotion plus being blessed soil turns it into a weapon, so to demons, it's like little grains of dynamite."

I gave the bag an admiring look. "Do we have any more?"

He tossed it at me. "Nope, so if you need to use it, make it count. Now, let's find our way out of here so we don't have to use any of it."

CHAPTER ELEVEN

The Challenger had a flat tire, but Adrian didn't use manna to fix it. Yes, manna worked on *everything*. Since we were low on our supply and didn't know if we'd need more for future injuries, we just drove at a slow pace, the flat wheel causing us to thump-thump-thump our way across the desert playa.

Adrian kept one hand on the wheel and the other outside the window, feeling the air as if it could provide us with directions. For him, it could. I wanted to look for Jasmine and Costa first, but Adrian said that finding the exit took precedence because without it, we were *all* stuck here.

He was right, but I was still worried over whether they'd made it out or not. If they had, we only had ourselves to hustle out of here, and we'd made it out of demon realms under worse circumstances. If Adrian was right and this place was currently empty, we weren't even in any real danger yet. Well, if you overlooked the fact that we were in a now frozen desert with no water, food or shelter aside from a windowless car, anyway.

Because I had nothing else to do at the moment, I kept texting Costa to see if he'd respond. It was possible he'd get them since Jasmine's cell had briefly worked after she'd been pulled into a realm. It was how I learned that she was in trouble all those months ago, when her frantic texts of help and trapped had put me on a collision course with my fate.

After well over an hour of driving, Adrian turned, and a paved road was revealed in our headlights. We must now be clear of Racetrack Playa. We'd left the bus parked near the Grandstands off this road because no one was supposed to drive onto the Playa. Adrian had ignored that when he took me on our ride, but Costa had followed the rules. Minutes later, I held my breath as we drove by the Grandstand area. So far, no familiar tour bus, but headlights from other vehicles lit up the parking lot, and when I saw large shapes moving around, I was horrified.

"There are *people* here!"

Adrian kept driving after casting a single, grim look at the Grandstand area. "Tourists. They would've gotten dragged along like we did when this area was sucked into the realm."

Horns began to sound behind us, and I thought I heard shouts. "We have to turn around," I stated. "Those people have no idea what just happened. They must be terrified!"

"And you think telling them they've been pulled into a demon realm will help?" he asked sardonically. "Even if they did believe you, that would only make them more hysterical. Only finding the exit will help them, Ivy. If the gateway's gravitational fields haven't settled yet, it might even be weak enough that they'll be able to cross through on their own without me needing to pull them through."

What he said made total sense, yet I was still bothered by the way he said it. I looked behind us, not able to see the cars' headlights anymore even though we hadn't driven that far. That was how complete the darkness was. It swallowed everything—and everyone—within it permanently.

And Adrian sounded as if he didn't care about the people we drove away from. Was that by practicality since there was nothing we could do? Or was it another indicator of the coldness that resided in him from spending the first hundred-plus years of his life as a demon prince? He cared about me, sure. And he cared about Costa, I believed. But when push came to shove, did anyone else matter to him? At all?

"You're right," I said at last, depressed by the thought. "It still feels wrong, though. They don't know where they are, what's going on, or what's coming for them."

That was the worst part, because I *did* know what was coming for them, if we couldn't get them out. Then again, if we didn't find the gateway, we'd be worse off than any of them. We'd been number one on the demon's most-wanted list for months, and how ironic if they ended up nabbing us after something as random as a new land grab...

"Wait, why would demons want to absorb a *desert*?" I asked abruptly. "They use their realm absorbing for showing off, but there's nothing out here except sand, more sand and rocks."

Adrian gave me a thoughtful sideways glance. "They might not want the repercussions of swallowing a populated area. They've gotten away with that for millennia, but it's the information age now. Thousands of people suddenly disappearing would make worldwide headlines and cause mass panic. Still..."

"Demons don't much care about freaking people out?" I supplied. "In fact, it'd probably amuse them to see governments scrambling to come up with an explanation as to why entire cities became ghost towns in a blink. Plus, if demons get their way and the realm walls crumble, then everyone will be able to see those dark, icy realms spill out into our world, and then they'd know for sure that demons exist."

Adrian began to slow the car. "Then, the only other reason they'd use their power to absorb a hunk of desert is if they thought there might be more here than just sand."

"The staff," I whispered, the pieces falling into place. "You said yourself that they've been looking for it so they can use it to tear down *all* the realm walls, but they can't feel it. Only I can, so what if their new tactic is to absorb places with natural phenomena to force me to look for it on *their* territory, just like I had to do with the slingshot?"

He parked the car and got out, taking the manna with him. When he came back, the bag was empty but when we started driving, the thump-thump-thump from the flat tire was gone.

"Then they'll be coming for this realm sooner than I expected," he finally answered, his tone hardening. "In fact, they might already be here."

Of all the things I least expected to see in the middle of a desert, a castle had to top that list. Yet there it was, sprawling across a couple acres, with a watchtower that loomed majestically over one corner. The fact that I could see it at all meant the castle had battery-powered emergency lights, and they showed off white walls, Spanish-style tile roofs and multiple curved archways. With its size and opulence, it would be the first place that demons picked to set up their headquarters. Say what you will about evil fallen angels; they weren't a pitchfork-and-brimstone crowd. Instead, they liked to live in style, and the fancier, the better.

Which begged the question, "Why are we here?" I asked.

Adrian killed his headlights, using the faint illumination from the castle to drive off-road. The sand was much softer here, with the peaks and valleys you'd expect from a normal desert. It was slow going, and I thought we'd get stuck a few times. It took almost twenty minutes to go a hundred yards, but Adrian finally parked the car beneath a Joshua tree jutting out from the hill. We'd be invisible here, unless you went trekking through the sand, which must be what we were about to do.

"The gateway's here," Adrian replied. "Makes sense. Whoever absorbed this realm would want it by the castle so they could keep pulling in tourists from the other side."

Anger burned through me. That's similar to what had happened with Jasmine. She and her boyfriend had stayed at a bed-and-breakfast that had a realm gateway in the innkeeper's office; a place no guest would feel wary about entering, and one they'd rigged so that select guests wouldn't be able to leave.

I chased the memory away as we got out of the car, closing our doors quietly. We'd seen other cars parked in front of the castle, but who knew if they all belonged to innocent tourists? One of them might be from the same demon that had dropped this realm onto this place. He or she had to be here somewhere. It took incredible power to make a realm, Adrian had told me, and that power couldn't be harnessed from long distance.

Adrian gestured for me to follow as he started up a steep hill. I did, looking around warily. I couldn't see much, but my eyes *were* starting to adjust to the dark. Months ago, after journeying to multiple demon realms, I'd been able to see almost as well as Adrian. Repeated use brought out the perks of my lineage. Too bad my hatred of the realms had stopped me from practicing my night vision since then.

My cell phone rang, the sound shattering the quiet and startling me so much, I almost dropped it. I'd had it in my hand in case Jasmine or Costa responded to my texts, but I hadn't really believed I'd hear from them on this side of the realm.

Adrian snatched it, hitting Answer before the next loud ring. "Are you out?" was his single hushed question.

"We got out," I heard Costa respond, and the rush of relief I felt was so intense, it weakened my knees. "You?"

"Still here," Adrian whispered. "We're—"

The light from the phone went dead. As anticipated, the best the signal could manage was a few seconds, but that was enough. We now knew that Jasmine and Costa were safe. Brutus, too, since he'd been hiding from the sun in the tour bus. I was so happy, I could have spun around in giddy circles.

Adrian gave it back to me after setting the call alert on vibrate. I put it in one of the zippered pouches in my pants. We

wouldn't need it again until we were out of this realm, and
hopefully, that would be soon.

Adrian paused when we reached the low wall that ran around
one side of the sprawling Mediterranean-style structure.

"The gateway's somewhere inside the house," he said, once
more feeling the air as if it had form. "From the sounds, all the
people are on the lower level, so let's start at the top."

I didn't get a chance to ask how he intended for us to do
that. Adrian ran to the corner of what looked like an exterior
courtyard, where grapevines twined up to the second floor. He
brushed the vines aside, revealing lattice and thin, hollowed-out
logs that must have been there for additional support. Adrian
grasped one of the thin logs, but instead of vaulting himself up,
he gestured to me.

"You first."

I went over to him, intending to fit my feet in the lattice
spaces and climb. Before I could do that, Adrian grasped me
low around the hips and pushed. Suddenly, I was scrambling to
grab the roof tiles so I didn't slide off the second floor. I knew
he was strong, but I was hardly a waif of a girl, and here he'd
almost shot-putted me onto the second floor with a single push.

Then I was scrambling back to get out of his way as he vaulted
himself upward next. Good thing the roof only had a mild
slope, because the barrel-shaped tiles were slick with the cold.
Adrian raised himself into a crouch and grasped my hand, leading me across the roof. I followed, mimicking his low profile,
only to stop abruptly when we reached the exterior flue of a
chimney. My right arm begun to burn with a sudden, startling
pain. Adrian stopped at the same time, touching the stones on
the chimney.

"There," he said with dark satisfaction. "The gateway is right
below this."

The pain in my arm grew more intense. I grabbed it with
a yelp, and when I pushed up my sleeve, I was shocked to see

the slingshot-turned-tattoo change from a dull brown color to a rich, shimmering gold. Pain radiated from each loop of the former rope where it curled around my arm, until the entire marking felt as if it were on fire.

"What's wrong?" Adrian said, not seeing the odd golden glow because my hand covered the parts that were visible.

At first, I could only shake my head in pained confusion. I had no idea why the slingshot tattoo was now burning as though it had been inked onto my flesh with acid. It had never done that before…wait. Yes, it had. Once.

I glanced at the chimney, then at the tiles beneath us. Somewhere below us was the gateway, according to Adrian. But maybe that wasn't the only dark object in the house.

"Adrian," I whispered, uncovering my right hand so he could see the new, golden sheen on my supernatural tattoo. "I think the demon who made this realm might be here."

CHAPTER TWELVE

Adrian glanced at my arm and his eyes widened. Without another word, he picked me up and ran across the roof, somehow
managing to make his rapid steps almost soundless. When he
reached the darkest corner where one of the emergency lights
had burned out, he jumped down.

I stifled my grunt as we landed from that two-story drop
with a thud that reverberated in my bones. Before I could tell
him to put me down, he began running again, glancing behind himself several times. I did, too, but I didn't see anything.
I couldn't hear anything, either, except the wind and the now
barely perceptible sounds of the people inside. All in all, I took
that as a good thing. If I was right and a demon *was* inside, at
least it didn't seem to have spotted us.

Adrian ran over to a looming clock tower that was surrounded
by an iron fence. He easily scaled it, even with me still clutched
to his chest. Once on the other side, he ignored my demand to
be let down. He also ignored the door at the base of the tower
and went around to the exterior stairs. He ran up those as though
being chased, but unless he saw something I didn't, no one was
coming after us.

About two stories up, we came to another door, and this time, Adrian broke through it with one kick. The softly lit interior showed what appeared to be the mechanical guts of the clock that crowned the top of the tower. Adrian finally let me down inside here, but I had barely formed all the questions in my mind when he found the single emergency light and killed it, plunging the room into near-total darkness.

"What's going on?" I whispered, blindly reaching out.

His hands covered mine moments later. "Shh."

I stayed quiet, letting him guide me around the objects I'd only gotten a second to glimpse. I don't know how he made his way without running into things, or how he found the staircase that took us at least another story higher in the tower. But he did, and a bracing, icy wind greeted us when we reached the top, which had large lookout points cut into the stone. At once, Adrian broke the small lights that lit up the exterior clock. If the castle hadn't been near enough to see the lights that still illuminated it, the night would've resembled a wall of pitch.

"We should be safe here for a while."

Adrian's voice was low, but it wasn't the whisper he'd used before. That, combined with his words, eased the knot that had formed in my stomach since my otherworldly tattoo had begun to glow and burn. Then he looked around, leading me to a corner where only a tiny window interrupted the stone.

"This spot should have the least amount of wind, and the stone walls will still retain a little heat from before."

He paused on the word *before*, and I took in a slow, choppy breath. Right, *before*, when this tower and everything around it was being warmed by a bright desert sun. Now, nothing in this place would ever see the sun again. Another gust of wind blew by, a plaintive noise that might have been a coyote's howl echoing on it, and I closed my eyes in silent grief.

No sunlight meant that every living thing here would die of starvation, if the cold didn't kill them first. I wanted to howl, too, at the horrible fate that had literally dropped onto this place and everything in it. *Find something else to fight for*, Costa had urged me just days ago, and as I looked around, I knew that I had. If I could stop even *one* more place from suffering the awful future that awaited this one, it would be well worth the fight, whatever it cost me.

In the meantime, though, I could do nothing. The realization was no less bitter for its roots in logic. The staff wasn't here, so all I could do was survive this realm in order to live to fight demons another day. I leaned back against the wall, a small, inadvertent sound leaving me when my back was warmed by the faint heat in the stones that would soon be gone.

"Why'd we come here?" I asked after a long moment. "Why didn't we go back to the car?"

Adrian slid down the wall until he was resting on his haunches next to me.

"When people are afraid, they tend to stay indoors," he replied, his tone matter-of-fact. "Add in the dark and the cold, and you almost never find them in exposed places outside. That's why the demons and minions who arrive here will first look for humans in houses when they do their initial round-up. Then they'll search all the cars, and eventually, they'll get around to other open-area places, like the top of this tower. That means we should have a day or two at least to sneak past them to get to the gateway."

Again, his almost casual way of describing this bothered me on many levels, but I had to focus on getting out of here.

"What if I'm wrong?" My voice was soft in case I wasn't, and supernatural ears might be close by. "What if there is no demon, and the only people in that castle are a bunch of terrified humans?"

Adrian took my right hand and slid the jacket farther up my arm. "Do you see anything?"

It was very dark, but with the residual glow from the nearby castle, I could make out enough to see that the slingshot had faded back to its normal brown color, not to mention that my arm no longer hurt. "No. Not anymore."

He let me go, and I thought I glimpsed a small, tight smile. "Exactly. The slingshot was glowing and now it's not. To me, that means the demon is no longer near enough to active it."

Activate it. I glanced at my arm again. That was one way to describe what had happened. Then I looked back at Adrian. If I concentrated, his features become clearer.

"I think it, ah, activated before, when you first came back and took out Snake Hands," I told him. "I didn't see the glow because of my long sleeves, but I felt the same pain. Maybe the slingshot embedded itself in my arm as a sort of…demonic early-detection system?"

Adrian looked at my arm, and this time, I was sure I caught a glimpse of a smile. "Maybe. Figures Zach wouldn't have given us a heads-up about that. He does love his surprises."

I let out a watery laugh. "Archons, right?"

Adrian laughed, too, and a thread of hope wormed its way through my depression over this area's future. I'd gladly take the pain that came with the tattoo's "activation" if it was warning us that a demon was near. We needed all the help we could get when it came to fighting demons, and if we won, no other place would have to suffer this same fate.

Adrian began to rummage through his jacket pockets. After a moment, he handed me a plastic bottle and something rectangular.

"Water and a power bar," he said, his tone turning wry. "Hardly the romantic dinner I'd planned to have with you, but the jackets only have room for necessities."

I gratefully uncapped the bottle and took a long swallow, then paused before my next one. "Where's yours?"

He waved a hand. "I don't want any right now."

I knew him well enough to recognize a deliberately vague

answer, and I gave him a look that he should've had no trouble deciphering. "That's not what I asked you."

With an unintelligible mutter, he pulled out an identical water bottle. "See? Happy now?"

I waited, drumming my nails for emphasis. "And?"

This time, I made out what he said under his breath, and it was a Demonish curse word. "And what?" he finished with.

"*And* you don't have any food, unlike what you tried to get me to believe," I pointed out.

"No, I said I didn't want any right now, with 'any' referring to my water. I can't help it that you assumed I meant food, too," he countered smoothly.

I gritted my teeth. Why couldn't men just admit it when they were busted? "Lies of omission are still lies, Adrian."

His look said that he disagreed, and I wanted to shake him. We were only talking about chocolate now, but if he still didn't believe that lies of omission counted, what would he do when the stakes were higher? The same thing he'd done months ago when he'd hidden the truth of my real destiny from me? "Your chocolate is getting cold," he added with infuriating glibness.

If we weren't in a subzero realm with a demon possibly in the nearby castle, I would've given him a piece of my mind about the entire subject. But now wasn't the time. So instead, I gave him an arch smile as I split the power bar in half. "No, *our* chocolate is getting cold."

"Ivy," he began.

"Oh, who's assuming now?" I mocked. "You thought I wanted the whole thing, but I never said that, did I?"

Maybe my eyes were adjusting even more to the dark, because now I could see him glowering at me. "Don't be stubborn."

I laughed at that. "You of all people should talk."

"There's more in the car, I'll get some later—"

"Then *we'll* get some later," I interrupted, quiet but firm. "If it comes to a demon fight, you'll need your strength because you're the only one who can take them down. My skills have improved, but minions are hard enough for me. I couldn't win if I faced off against a demon, and we both know it."

That sealed the deal. Adrian was trying to be chivalrous—an admittedly unfamiliar characteristic for him—but no one would know more than he about the importance of keeping himself at his lethal, fighting best.

"Fine," he said, accepting half of the power bar.

I clicked the tip of mine with his. "Cheers."

A smile hovered over his lips. "That's usually reserved for drinks, so save it for one of the bottles of Cristal I intend to crack open as soon as we're back on the bus."

My eyes widened. "You brought *champagne* on a relic-hunting trip where our best hope is to end up ass-deep in demon ash?"

His smile spread into a grin. "I'd break out every kind of liquor ever invented to celebrate being ass-deep in demon ash."

"Good point," I said, with a little laugh. "I really need to start looking at the bright side of things."

His expression changed, that grin fading. When he spoke, his tone had changed, too, becoming darker and more luxuriant. "I had other motives behind the champagne. One of those bottles is just for us, and we'll open it to celebrate what will happen after I fulfill my promise to you."

I glanced away. Once again, he'd skipped the "chance" part of my conditions and gone right for the panty-dropping expectation. Given my reaction to him this afternoon, I couldn't really blame him for being confident, but did I really want to risk my heart again? I'd agreed to give him another chance only because I thought it was impossible. Since then, he kept talking about it as if it were a sure thing. I'd brushed it off, but now, I had to deal with the possibility that he might pull it off. And if he did...

I looked back at him, asking the questions I'd been wondering about for the past several days. "Then what? Let's say you *do* prove that you won't betray me again, and I agree to celebrate with lots of sex and champagne. Is that all you want?"

It was as close to asking him if he still loved me as I dared, but the need to know burned as much as my tattoo had before. Adrian set down his half of the broken chocolate bar, then turned to face me fully.

"For longer than you can imagine, I thought I existed only to betray and to kill." Not even his controlled tone could mask the fierce resonance in his words. "And I loved being the weapon that would save Demetrius and the rest of the demons. They had raised me, rescued me and my mother from the Archons, or so I thought. Then I found out that my mother had been murdered by Demetrius and he'd used his shape-shifting abilities for decades to fool me into believing that she was still alive. Everything Demetrius and the other demons had told me was a lie... well, everything except for my fate as the last Judian."

He paused, a small, bitter smile curling his mouth. "After that, I couldn't stand to think of the future, and I couldn't stand to remember my past. The only thing that numbed my pain and rage was fighting the demons who'd once been my people, so I resigned myself to doing that for the rest of my life. Then, months ago, that same pain and rage compelled me to spend time with the one person I most wanted to avoid. The last Davidian."

He took my hands, twining his fingers through mine, and when he spoke again, the harsh bleakness had left his tone.

"I didn't want to know you, like you, need you, or most of all, love you, but I did. I still do. You *are* my destiny, Ivy, just not how everyone predicted. Now, when I think of the future, I think of spending it with you. The past still tears at me, but I can't change it, and if I help you find the staff, then I'll save more people than I've harmed. *That's* what I'm fighting for, and as you can see, it's a hell of a lot more than just champagne and sex."

I stared at him, feeling as though every word had struck me right in the heart. Emotions I'd fought came roaring to the surface, making the words *I love you, too,* tremble on the edge of my lips.

But if I said them, I wouldn't be able to hold anything back, and I had to. This was more than bad relationship timing: destiny said that we were supernaturally doomed as a couple. I might want to believe that Adrian could beat his fate, but how could I throw caution to the winds in the middle of a demon realm, let alone an apocalyptic war? If I couldn't even wait until Adrian made good on his promise to prove that he wouldn't betray me again, then I had no business resuming a relationship where the fallout could be far more serious than rebreaking my heart.

"I still care for you," I said, my voice cracking from everything I wouldn't allow myself to say. "And I want that chance to see if we'd work out. But right now... I can't."

His arms closed around me and he held me tight enough to almost force the air out of my lungs. I must've made a gasping sound because he released me, his hands gripping my shoulders instead. They kept flexing, as if he were having difficulty holding in his strength, and when he pressed his forehead against mine, his ragged breaths fell onto my cheeks.

"I know, but I'm not giving up, and you shouldn't, either. Besides, love and lust aside, I don't want to break my promise to you. I want you to *know* that you can trust me, both with your life, your sister's and everyone else's."

If it were only my life at risk. But it wasn't, and I was relieved that he understood that. Jasmine had been through too much for me to make that decision for her, and the same was true for everyone else. Still, I wanted him to know what his vow meant to me. I reached out, stroking his face. "Adrian, I—"

His hand clapped over my mouth with a suddenness that startled me. Then fear replaced my surprise when he rose and pulled me up with him, his heart hammering hard enough for me to feel the vibrations against my cheek.

"It can't be," he muttered in a barely audible whisper.

I pulled his hand away and turned around, looking at the only thing I could see in the darkness—the castle. Then I stared, my mind nearly going blank with disbelief.

How did Adrian know? was my first coherent thought. We'd been sitting well below the window, so he wouldn't have been able to see the demon that now strode out from the castle and into the parking lot.

My next thought was a silent scream. *How is he still alive?* He should be ashes along with every other demon I'd killed in the Bennington realm!

But he wasn't. I didn't need to see the demon's pale, pale skin or his long black hair to recognize him. The shadows emanating from him were horrifyingly familiar. They curled around the demon, haloing him with pure, impenetrable darkness that swallowed all the lights behind him.

Adrian yanked me down until we were both hidden beneath the window again. *Speak of the devil and he shall appear* ran through my mind. Adrian had just said how much he hated the demon who'd raised him, and now Demetrius was here. Alive. And looking as frightening and powerful as ever.

Both of us barely breathed as we waited to see if we'd been discovered. An agonizing few minutes later, the sounds of a car starting up and pulling away had Adrian peeking over the ledge.

"He's gone," he said with relief.

"How is he even alive?" I finally asked aloud, still reeling. "I should've killed Demetrius when I wiped out the Bennington realm!"

"I thought you did," Adrian replied grimly. "But either he was too strong to be taken out by the slingshot, or he found a way out."

Then he shook his head as if to clear it. When he looked back at me, his expression was harder than the stone walls that surrounded us. "We need to get through that gateway, Ivy. Now."

CHAPTER THIRTEEN

We didn't know how soon Demetrius would return, so Adrian gave up any attempts to be stealthy. After checking my tattoo to make sure that it wasn't glowing, he strode through the courtyard and up to the front of the house, flinging open the door as though he owned the place.

As expected, only the emergency lights were on, but compared to the tower, it was practically daylight inside. I followed Adrian, clutching the bag of grave dirt in my hand, as we entered the opulent castle.

A blazing fireplace lit up the large room, and under different circumstances, I would've loved to spend time there. As it was, I barely noticed the beauty around me. My quick, danger-evaluating glance registered that the walls were sand colored, the floor was Mexican tile and a huge chandelier hung between three balconies that overlooked the room. What held my full attention were the couches and chairs set up around the large fireplace, because none of them were empty.

"Who are you?" a wiry man wearing an early-nineteenth-century costume demanded.

"Don't worry, we're not staying," Adrian growled, catch-

ing my hand when I started to slow down. "Gateway, Ivy, remember?"

"There are at least a dozen people here," I hissed. "We can't
leave them behind!"

"They might not be the only ones here," he reminded me,
his voice very low. "You want them close by if we find out that
Demetrius didn't come here alone?"

No, I didn't. Costa had once been taken hostage by a demon.
I didn't want the same to happen to any of these people until
we made sure that the gateway was here and it was demon-free.

"We'll be back," I told the crowd huddled by the fireplace,
hurrying to keep up with Adrian's strides. "Don't anyone leave."

As soon as I said it, I realized the brutal irony of my directive.
They *couldn't* leave. Not unless we helped them.

"You can't go up there!" the costumed man called after us,
but I didn't stop. Neither did Adrian. He took the stairs two at
a time once we reached the staircase, drawn to the second floor
by a force I couldn't sense or see. I kept glancing at my hand
as I followed. No eerie golden glow, no pain. So far, so good.

The second-floor staircase landing opened into an even more
gorgeous room, with stained glass windows and a curved ceiling decorated with row upon row of engraved wood. It had another fireplace, with more artfully arranged furniture in front
of it. This time, no one was gathered around the fireplace, and
Adrian went right for it, shoving the fancy couches and chairs
out of his way. Then he held out his hand, and I was shocked
to see it disappear as if rubbed out by a magic eraser.

"The gateway's right here," he said, drawing his hand back,
which made it whole again. "But it's so new, it doesn't feel stable
yet. Come here, Ivy. It could close up any minute."

"I'm not going anywhere without those people," I protested.

Adrian made it to me in two long strides. "I'll come back for
them," he said through gritted teeth. "I can go through without
you, but you can't cross the gateway without me."

"I left you behind in a demon realm once," I snapped. "I'm never doing that again, so we can waste time arguing, or we can get those people and then *all* get out of here."

He muttered a particularly foul Demonish curse, but with a short nod, he gave up the fight. We were almost at the staircase when my arm suddenly flamed with pain, coinciding with a loud whooshing sound behind us.

I didn't need to turn around to know that we were no longer alone in the room.

"Fuck," Adrian hissed, shoving me toward the stairs. "Run!"

I did, for the first few steps. Then I spun around, remembering that I had the hallowed grave dirt. I burst back into the room to see Adrian smash a grand piano over someone's head. The wood from the piano immediately took on a pale, shiny glaze and then exploded outward, revealing an African-American man with white hair and eerie, albino-like eyes. Being brained by a baby grand didn't seem to faze the demon, either. He grinned, saying something very fast in Demonish. I didn't know what, but I recognized one word: Adrian's name.

"Oh shit," I whispered.

The demon knew who Adrian was. So much for Zach saying that Adrian wouldn't need to be disguised with Archon glamour. Then again, who else would be strong enough to treat a piano like a baseball bat?

The demon swung his gaze toward me next. Adrian took advantage of his distraction and hurled a fireplace poker at him. The poker sunk into the demon's chest, impaling him. Adrian immediately chucked a chair, the other couch and the coffee table at him next. My right arm was throbbing with pain, but I got into the mix and flung a handful of grave dirt at the demon.

To my surprise, nothing happened, and Adrian stopped his furniture assault to shove me back toward the staircase.

"I told you, run!" he warned me. "He's—!"

That's all Adrian got out before the furniture covering the

demon exploded away. In the next moment, he had grabbed Adrian. Almost at once, a blue tinge covered Adrian's skin, followed by a shiny white layer that resembled ice. *Frostbite*, I realized in horror, remembering the glazed sheen that had overtaken the wood from the piano. That's why Adrian had been fighting this demon with furniture instead of his fists. Somehow, the demon must be able to freeze everything that he touched.

And everything he'd touched had frozen so rapidly, it had ended up exploding.

"No!" I screamed, grabbing the remaining grave dirt and throwing it at the demon.

Not only did it fail to make the demon release Adrian, he grinned at me as if I'd amused him. His teeth were filed into icicle-like points, and those pale, white-on-white eyes seemed to burn into mine. A choking sound escaped Adrian and his arms began to flail in a jerky, uncoordinated way. Panic overwhelmed me, making the pain from my now golden tattoo feel almost blissful by comparison. The demon was killing Adrian right before my eyes, and the only weapon I had wasn't working!

It's not your only weapon.

The words whispered across my mind, so faint that I barely heard them. I don't know why I looked down at my right hand, but I did. Even with my jacket covering me to the wrist, the tattoo of the ancient slingshot was glowing so brightly that it lit up the space around me. In fact, the incredible light radiating from it made the image of the rope that wrapped around my fingers and hand look almost...real.

Without thought, I grasped a section and pulled. If I would've paused to consider what I was doing, I never would've done it, let alone kept pulling when I felt the unmistakable give of something tangible beneath my skin.

The demon's grin faded into a look of disbelief. I didn't pull anymore; I yanked, agony searing up my arm as if I'd sliced it open to the bone. But when I glanced at my right arm, my skin was unbroken. And I now held a long, golden rope that was very, very real—and thrummed with enough supernatural power to make my teeth rattle.

As if everything were happening in slow motion, I saw myself grab a fragment of wood and fit it into the sling's loop. Saw the demon drop Adrian and charge toward me. Watched me dodge him and spin the rope, then snap it at him. Then felt the icy, paralyzing power of his abilities as the demon's hands closed over my legs, but in moments, that grip loosened, then vanished.

I fell to the floor, my legs feeling like they'd been turned into popsicles. The demon's face was right next to mine as my head banged onto the tile, and I glimpsed a cut on his forehead. Before I could roll away from him in instinctive defense, his features began to splinter, crack and dissolve. By the time I'd hauled myself into a sitting position, he was nothing more than a pile of ashes on the ground next to me.

CHAPTER FOURTEEN

"What is happening?" a male voice demanded.

I didn't reply. I dragged myself over to Adrian, needing to use my upper body because my legs still wouldn't work. He was curled into a ball, and the blue tinge clinging to his skin scared me so much, I almost burst into tears. When I reached him, I wrapped myself around him, trying to use my body to warm his. He was barely breathing, and his skin was so cold, it took only seconds to realize that he needed a lot more warmth. Now.

I summoned all the strength I had to drag him over to the fireplace. The tiles in front of it were hot, and I laid him over them. Then I grabbed the poker from the demon's ashes. It was so icy after being embedded in the demon's body that it stuck to my hands, so I simultaneously froze and burned as I used it to stoke the fire higher. Once it was blazing, I threw myself on top of Adrian, hoping the trifecta of heat coming from all sides would reverse the awful effects of the demon's touch.

Nearby, demands for answers grew louder, but I kept ignoring them. All my attention was on Adrian, whose skin was slowly losing that terrifying bluish color. I barely noticed the agony shooting through me as the slingshot began to wind itself back into my right arm as if it were a snake returning to its home. I did notice Adrian wince when a section of the rope brushed across him, but I was so happy to see him coming back around that I didn't pause to wonder why.

"Adrian? Can you hear me?" I asked, lightly shaking him.

He made a noise. More moan than a word, but it was a response. Then he tried again, and this time, I understood him.

"That...hurt," he croaked.

Relief crashed into me with such force, I could no longer control my tears. They spilled from my eyes even as I laughed from the sheer, giddy joy of him being alive.

"So much," I agreed, climbing off him so he had room to maneuver. "I still can't feel my legs."

That was true, but the slingshot was back to being twined around my finger, wrist and forearm as if it were no more than the tattoo it now resembled. If I wasn't sitting next to a pile of demon ashes, I would've sworn that I'd imagined it reforming into the hallowed weapon, but the ash was there. So was the pain, and the last time I'd felt anything this excruciating was when I'd used the slingshot to wipe out Adrian's former realm.

Adrian looked at the ashes on the floor next to us, then at my right arm. His hand landed on my tattoo, which was still shimmering with that iridescent golden color. With a yelp, he let go and a red welt appeared on his palm.

"Son of a bitch," Adrian breathed. "It still works."

Tremors ran over me as the shock from the last several minutes faded enough for me to fully accept that.

"Not like it used to." My voice was shaky, yet even as I spoke, I began to pull myself together. "But enough."

More than enough. Having a weapon that could kill demons built into my arm was an incredible gift. So what if I was only able to kill them one at a time? That might not be as scary as how the slingshot had simultaneously wiped hundreds of them out the first time I had used it, but everyone had thought it was defunct after that, if you counted how it had resembled nothing more than a tattoo on my arm.

Adrian sat up very slowly. Every movement was clearly painful for him, and seeing it made tears well in my eyes for a different reason this time.

"I'm sorry," I whispered. "I distracted you, that's why he was able to grab you. I shouldn't have gotten in your way."

He pulled me into his arms. His embrace was chilly, but it was still the best thing I'd ever felt. "It's not your fault," he murmured. "I couldn't beat him. Oblivion was one of the oldest, deadliest demons in existence. Demetrius wasn't playing when he brought him here as backup."

Costume Man picked that moment to lose his cool. "I *demand* to know what's happening!" he snapped as he stomped over to us.

Adrian let me go, then pushed himself off the floor and rose. His movements were far slower than normal, but the stare he leveled at Costume Man was full of warning.

"You're not in Kansas anymore, Toto, and if you want to go home, you'll shut up and do what we say."

"I'm a park ranger as well as the tour guide for Scotty's Castle," Costume Man said, recovering. "If you don't want to get arrested, you'll do what *I* say."

To punctuate his point, Costume Man, aka the park ranger, pulled out a gun. Before I could react, Adrian had knocked it out of his hand. Even in his weakened condition, he was far faster than a normal person.

"Anyone else want to test me?" Adrian all but growled.

The costumed ranger paled, and the people who'd come upstairs with him looked equally intimidated. I didn't want them to be frightened of us, so I tried another way.

"Sir, something awful has happened to this place. We're going to help get everyone out of here, but we don't have a lot of time to explain, so you'll just need to—"

"What are you?" a white-haired woman hissed, interrupting me. "You killed that man and turned him into, into *nothing!*"

"He wasn't a man," I answered truthfully.

"Don't listen to her," the ranger whispered to the older woman. "We just have to wait until the other man comes back. He said that he was getting help."

"You mean the man with the long black hair?" Adrian's snort was derisive. "Oh, he's getting help, all right, but not for you. He's a demon, and he's bringing more demons with him."

I sucked in a breath at his bluntness. So much for easing people into the truth about the supernatural!

"I'm not going to listen to this," the white-headed woman said. Then she wagged her cell phone at me. "As soon as I get a signal, I'm calling the police!"

Either my legs had recovered from the demon's freezing touch, or sheer frustration got me back on my feet. "Even if you could, the police can't help you. I know it sounds incredible, but you're not in the same world you were in before. You're in a parallel realm, and yes, demons live on this side. That's why we need to get everyone back to where they came from."

Perhaps not surprisingly, they didn't listen. I'd seen glimpses of the realms all my life, and the first time I heard what they really were, I didn't believe it, either. With several mutters and glances back at the pile of ashes, the people left.

Adrian sighed. "No one believes the truth until it's too late. That's why Demetrius fed them that 'getting help' crap. He wants them docile until he's done rounding everyone up."

I took a few steps, trying to force the debilitating iciness out of my legs. The warmth from the nearby fireplace beckoned me closer for many reasons. The gateway was right in front of it, and all I needed to do was let Adrian take me through, and we'd be safe. He was right; Demetrius or another demon could show up any minute. But how could I live with myself if I didn't try harder to save the people downstairs, too?

"I'm not giving up," I told Adrian, and began heading for the staircase on my still-wobbly legs.

He came after me and spun me around. "You think they'll listen? You took out a demon in *front* of them, and they still don't believe what's going on. Speaking of that, you got lucky nailing the demon in the head without really aiming. You might not get that lucky again, which is why we need to go now."

I knew he was right, but Jasmine's face flashed in my mind, as did my parents'. Maybe no one had been able to help them when they'd been in situations just like this, or maybe someone had, yet had chosen not to. How could I look my sister in the eye if I walked away from these people now? How could I stand to remember my parents if I showed the same apathy that minions had when they'd contributed to my parents' deaths?

"I have to try one more time," I insisted, pulling away from Adrian.

His jaw clenched, but he didn't stop me as I hobbled past him. Maybe he couldn't stand the thought of leaving these people behind, either. He might not be up to his full strength, but I was pretty sure he could still throw me over his shoulder and force me through the gateway, if he really wanted to.

I made it down the stairs without tripping, which took a lot of effort. Then I carefully made my way into the grand entry room. The people who'd witnessed what had happened upstairs were huddled up with the rest of the group, and from the hostile glances my way, it wasn't hard to guess what they'd been talking about.

"Whatever you heard, all of you need to come with me if you want to get out of here." Then I took a deep breath. There was no way to tell them what had happened without sounding crazy, so I just plowed ahead. "This place has been pulled into another realm and demons are coming to enslave you, but there's a gateway upstairs that will send you back home."

The white-haired woman shook her finger at me. "Don't listen to her! She's crazy and she's *evil*. I told you, she killed a man and turned him into *dirt*!"

"He wasn't a man, he was a demon, and there's more where he came from," Adrian retorted, coming up behind me. "If you want to live, you'll let us get you out of here."

"This is ridiculous," a bespectacled, well-dressed man sputtered. "I don't know what sort of con you're trying to pull, but that other man said there had been an unexpected eclipse. That's all, and he left to get help—"

"Look around," I snapped, waving at the window. "Not only has it been pitch-black for hours, the desert is now *frozen*. No eclipse could do that, and no con artist could, either. I know it's a lot to take in, but you need to accept that you're in another realm so that you can get the hell on *out* of it!"

"Demons? Realms? You expect us to believe that?" he muttered, to murmurs of agreement from the rest of them.

I contemplated how long it would take to knock them all out, carry them upstairs and drag them one by one through the gateway. Too long, judging from how I could hardly walk, and Adrian looked better, but not by much.

"You have another explanation for how a dark, freezing version of this world suddenly fell on you?" I countered, trying to force them past their denial. "If you don't, you might want to start listening to the crazy one."

"You gave it your best shot, but they're not listening, and we have to go," Adrian muttered, tugging my arm.

I planted my feet, going for one last argument. "I wish I could prove the existence of demons and other realms to you, but I don't have time. You don't trust me? Fine, trust your own eyes. Eclipses last minutes, not hours. They don't shut off everything that isn't battery-operated, knock out cell signals and freeze deserts. You know this, so if it's not an eclipse, then it's something that shouldn't be possible, and yet it *is*. So *please*, come upstairs with us, and we'll take you through the gateway and prove that we can get you home."

I put all of my desperation into those last few words, trying also to say with my eyes what I couldn't seem to convey vocally. Glasses Guy turned away. So did the costumed ranger, the white-haired lady and most of the rest of them. But, with several hesitant glances, a family of four stepped forward.

"We'll come," the father said, picking up his little girl.

"Take them upstairs," I told Adrian, fighting back a surge of tears. "Please, the rest of you, come with us. Like I said, we'll prove to you that we can get you out of here."

They began to back away instead, egged on by the white-haired lady's continual, muttered accusations and their own disbelief. Adrian led the family to the staircase and, after a few, long moments where I futilely hoped that at least one other person would change their mind, I followed them upstairs. I was almost at the top when a scream made me run the last few steps. I tripped, but made it into the trashed music room in time to see the two parents beating at the stone around the fireplace.

"Wait!" the mother was crying, while the father stuck his hands in the flames as if trying to snatch something back.

"It's okay," I reassured them, doing an odd hop-run into the room. "He'll be right back, I promise!"

No sooner did I say that than Adrian appeared, almost knocking the parents over with his sudden entry. He didn't pause to explain, as I continued to do, but grabbed both of them in a bear hug and then lunged at the fireplace. They disappeared as if the flames had somehow swallowed them. I knew what was going on, but to be honest, it was still a little freaky looking.

The costumed ranger picked that moment to run into the room. He had a candlestick in his hands, of all things, and he brandished it at me. "Where are they? What did you do to them?"

"Nothing," I began, but Adrian's reappearance cut me off.

He grasped me around the shoulders, and I noticed that he was breathing heavy and his color didn't look good.

"Are you all right?" I asked, worried enough to ignore the ranger's sudden yell of "What the *hell*?"

"Oblivion did a number on me, and crossing the realms is making it worse." Adrian's words were choppy between his labored breaths. "I've only got one more trip left in me, Ivy."

I turned at once to the ranger. "Please," I started to say, but then Adrian went immobile so abruptly, I looked back at him in concern. He was staring over my shoulder, and when I glanced that way, the ranger was no longer alone in the doorway.

Demetrius stood behind him.

CHAPTER FIFTEEN

My tattoo roared to agonizing, glowing life, but with a surge of panic, I realized that I didn't have anything to put into the sling. I should've stuffed my pockets with projectiles as soon as I realized that the weapon could manifest itself, but I'd been focused on trying to save Adrian. Then I'd turned my attention to saving the rest of the people, thinking with my heart, not my survival instinct.

Adrian drew me tighter against him, and I expected him to launch us through the gateway even though Demetrius was sure to follow. Could I pull the sling out of my arm and find something to hurl at Demetrius before the demon caught us on the other side? From how fast Adrian had traversed between the realms, I doubted it. Fear caused my heartbeat to slam against my ribs, but Adrian didn't pull us through the gateway. Instead, he let out a low, almost satisfied-sounding laugh as he stared at his demonic foster father.

"Demetrius, I hoped you'd come back before we left. Zach's on the other side of this gateway." Adrian gave weight to the lie by flicking a taunting glance between the fireplace and the demon. "Come with us. I'd love to see him kick your ass again."

Instead of responding, Demetrius looked my way, and those coal-black eyes seemed to burn into mine. Whatever disguise Zach had glamoured me with didn't matter; he knew it was me, and the virulent hatred in his gaze raised gooseflesh over me despite my close proximity to the fire. Then he turned his attention back to Adrian, and that hatred melted away. In fact, something like exasperated affection crossed his features.

"My son, haven't you had enough of your rebellion yet?"

"I'm just getting started," Adrian replied, his tone luxuriant with hatred.

The ranger laid a heavy hand on Demetrius's shoulder, unable to see the ominous shadows that came from the demon. "This boy here is your son? He—"

One of those shadows sliced across the ranger's throat, turning his words into horrible choking sounds. He fell to his knees, blood spurting out from his neck. Then that lethal shadow rejoined the rest of the swirls behind Demetrius after bending toward me in what could only be called a wave.

"How did you make it out of my old realm, anyway?" Adrian asked, with none of the shock I felt over what had just happened. "Ivy decimated it. You should be ash right now."

"There are two kinds of demons," Demetrius said, his tone light. Almost bantering. "The kind that stand around to discover what the Davidian can do with a hallowed weapon, and the kind that hasten to the nearest exit to avoid finding out."

Adrian snorted. "So, you ran for your life like the coward that you are."

"Name-calling?" Demetrius scoffed with mild reproof. "Such a human trait. Didn't I teach you better?"

Adrian's laugh was low and ugly. "Oh, you taught me many things that I will spend the rest of my life unlearning. Love to stay and chat, but Zach's waiting."

Then he flung us backward, and the gut-churning, free-falling sensations of crossing from one realm into another began.

They culminated with me landing face first in a room that looked identical to the one we'd left, except that none of the furniture was broken and it was far warmer in here.

Adrian hauled me up before I could even say *ow* at my face-plant. "He'll be right behind us," he muttered, half carrying, half propelling me out of the room at a run.

I tried to keep up, cursing my wobbly, still-icy-feeling legs. "But you told him that Zach was here."

He grunted. "That might buy us a few minutes, but he'll call my bluff, guaranteed."

"Then let me get something for the sling!" I protested.

Adrian's arm tightened around me as he forced me to run down the stairs at a pace I could barely manage. "Don't bother. If you're close enough to hit him with the slingshot, then Demetrius is close enough to kill you with his shadows."

I still wanted to grab something that could be used as a projectile, but Adrian's ashen coloring combined with his labored breathing made me channel all my energy into running under my own power instead. He looked more awful than I'd ever seen, and it wasn't just from crossing the realms. He'd gotten a full-body assault hug from Oblivion, and here I was, having trouble recovering after only getting a brief grab on the legs.

We made it into the main room downstairs when Adrian suddenly slowed. The family of four he'd pulled through was by the front door. Next to them was a police officer, and the cop went for his gun as soon as he saw us.

Adrian pushed me aside so hard that I fell. "I told you, no police," he growled as he launched himself at the cop.

A gunshot went off and I screamed. Adrian's velocity caused him to land on the cop, and for a few, frenzied seconds, the two of them rolled on the ground, knocking over anything in their way. I ran over, but in the moments it took me to get to them, another shot went off, and the pile of limbs went still.

"Adrian!" I screamed.

His dark gold head lifted. Blood smeared his face and he was paler than I'd ever seen him, but he managed a grin.

"Minions. Easy to kill," he muttered. Then he slumped over the cop's body, which was starting to disintegrate into ashes.

I rolled Adrian over, sucking in an anguished breath as I saw the bloody hole in his stomach. He'd been shot, and we'd used up all the manna we'd carried with us!

"Help me carry him over to the couch," I told the father, who was staring in shock at the ashes that, moments ago, had been a police officer. "*Help* me," I repeated. "Grab his legs, I'll get his shoulders."

After another dazed look at the ashes, the father complied. We got Adrian onto the couch, and I pulled out my cell phone, letting out a relieved sound when I saw that it still worked.

"What happened to him? What's going on?" the mother pleaded as she clutched her two sobbing children.

"He wasn't human," I replied, dialing Costa's number. "Adrian knew a minion would probably respond to a hysterical call about people being transported from a dark, icy version of this world. That's why he told you not to call the police... Costa!" I said when he answered. "Where are you?"

"Where are *you*?" was Costa's instant reply. "Are you out?"

"Yes. We're at Scotty's Castle and Adrian's really hurt." My voice cracked on the last word, but I refused to break down. Adrian's life depended on me keeping it together. "We need manna and a way out of here. Right away."

"Got it. We're about forty minutes east of Scotty's on 276, so we'll be there soon."

"Forty minutes?" I glanced at a window, which showed that night had already fallen. "That's too long."

In the dark, Demetrius could walk around freely on this side on the realm. I started stuffing every sturdy, decorative knick-knack I came across into my jacket. They weren't as durable as rocks, but they were the best I could come up with at the moment. Adrian had said that they wouldn't do any good if Demetrius were that close, but I'd rather have a bad chance than no chance at all. Demetrius could show up any second. The minion cop had gotten here lightning fast despite how it had only been minutes since Adrian had pulled the family through the gateway...or had it been longer?

"How long have you been here?" I asked the father. At his confused look, I elaborated. "How long has it been since Adrian brought you through the fireplace? Ten minutes? Twenty?"

"About an hour," the father answered, and his wife gave a frightened nod of agreement.

I almost whooped with relief. That's right, time moved differently in the realms, sometimes faster, sometimes slower. Adrian had said that it might take Demetrius a few minutes to decide to call his bluff. With minutes there equating to about an hour on this side, we might have enough time to get away.

And the minion cop hadn't arrived here by gateway, so that meant there was a car here that I could steal.

"Get going," I told Costa, formulating my plan. "I'll meet you on the way."

CHAPTER SIXTEEN

All the tourists' cars had been pulled into the realm along with their owners, but as it turned out, the cop's car wasn't the only one in the parking lot. A gleaming black Ferrari was parked right outside the entrance to Scotty's Castle.

"Demetrius," I muttered. It had to be his. Only he and Oblivion had come through the gateway, and Oblivion turned everything he touched to ice, so he couldn't have driven this or any other vehicle.

Out of curiosity, I tried the door. It was unlocked, with the keys resting on the passenger seat, no less. My lips curled into a nasty smile. Demetrius's arrogance knew no bounds, but in this case, that was a good thing.

I smashed the side mirrors and the rearview mirror, then turned to the father, who waited at the doorway with Adrian stretched out on a sheet behind him.

"Change of plans," I announced. "You're not coming with me. You and your family are taking the cop's car instead. Head for the nearest city, and then ditch the car once you get there."

"B-but—" he stammered.

"You're safer alone. Demons are coming for us," I snapped.

"Plus, Adrian told you not to call the police, yet you did, and that nearly got him killed. You're going to make it up to him by doing exactly what I say. Now, help me get him in the car."

The two parents grabbed one end of the sheet and I took the other. Together, we used it like a stretcher to carry Adrian over to the car. It helped that Demetrius had been rude enough to park in a handicap spot right by the entrance. It also helped that he'd chosen to ride with the Ferrari's convertible top down. Because of that, we were able to get him in the passenger seat much easier than if we'd been maneuvering around a roof.

Still, I winced at every bump and jostle. I didn't need to be a doctor to know that moving someone with a bullet wound was very dangerous, but staying here was even more so. Once Adrian was situated, I turned to the family.

"Take your kids and leave now, and don't tell anyone what happened here, ever. They have cops in every city, and they don't like loose ends."

"We won't say anything," the wife said, with a nervous glance at her husband.

I gave a pointed look at her two small children. "For their sakes, I hope you mean it. Now, go."

After that, I followed my own advice and put the Ferrari in Reverse. Even with normal pressure on the gas pedal, the car shot backward with unbelievable speed, causing me to almost hit a light pole. I gave a worried glance at Adrian. I'd put a seat belt on him, which had probably saved him from hitting the dashboard from the car's momentum, but had the sudden jerk damaged things in him that I couldn't see?

If it had, then it was all the more reason to get to the manna as quickly as possible. With far less pressure on the gas pedal, I straightened the car out and got onto the road. 267 was a long, lonely stretch of highway, but in this case, that was a good thing. I had a fast car and no traffic to worry about, and I intended to make the most of both.

"Hang in there," I whispered to Adrian. "It won't be long."

His only reply was a soft moan. I held tight to the steering wheel and gave the car more gas. It responded at once, bulleting down the road. I went as fast as I dared over the hilly terrain, cursing the curves and the lack of flatness in this section of the desert. This car was so powerful, one little error on my part could cause a crash, and I couldn't risk that. Besides, if memory served, the topography would level out soon. Then I could open the throttle up and—

A yelp escaped me as pain shot through my right arm. I glanced at it with dread and saw that the tattoo was starting to shimmer with gold. Even though I knew what that meant, I couldn't stop myself from looking behind me. Through my wildly whipping hair, I saw a wall of darkness rushing toward me, and in the middle of that darkness was a pale, grinning face.

Demetrius hadn't waited minutes to call Adrian's bluff. With the time conversion from that realm to this one, he must have only waited seconds.

Despite a turn coming up, I gunned the gas. The back end of the car swung with a terrifying lurch, but then all four wheels returned to the ground. As soon as they did, I hit the gas again. This was hazardous, but anything less was suicide. Demetrius's shadows could rip the car apart around us. After all, he'd almost killed me in a car the first time he and I had met.

I risked another glance behind me. No more lethal shadows or leering face, but that didn't make me feel any better. It only meant that the demon must be changing his tactics since he would never give up unless forced. I gripped the steering wheel with my left hand and began digging through my pockets with my right. When I felt several hard objects, I put them on my lap. Then, with a quick prayer that this wouldn't be the last thing I ever did, I braced my knees against the steering wheel and took both my hands off it.

At this speed, even the slight change in pressure caused the

car to drift to the side. My left elbow joined my knees on the
steering wheel to level it out, then I yanked at the glowing,
throbbing tattoo with all the panic I had in me.

Either my agonized scream woke Adrian, or it was the sling
as it came out and a loop seared his skin. He jerked upright, his
head swiveling around to seek out the danger. When he saw me
knee-driving at ninety miles an hour, he grabbed the wheel even
though it meant more contact with the glowing, hallowed rope.

"Demetrius is here," I gasped out, fear superseding the awful
pain the ancient weapon caused. "He's right behind us!"

As soon as I said it, razors sliced over my head, so fast that I
was blinded by blood running into my eyes before I had a chance
to feel the pain. Adrian shouted, swerving the car, and another
slice took me in the shoulder instead of my head. That's when
I realized what was happening.

Demetrius was no longer behind us. He was on top of us.

Amid my fear, agony and panic, another emotion grew. Rage.
Demetrius had ordered my parents' murder, imprisoned my sister, branded me as a killer and fugitive in the human world and
tried to kill me more times than I could count. Starting now, I
wouldn't let him take anything else from me.

"Hold the wheel!" I shouted, wiping the blood from my eyes.

Then, with one foot still on the gas, I put a hard object in
the loop of the sling and twisted around, snapping the weapon
at the shadows poised above me for another strike. The projectile sailed right through them, but an unearthly screech let me
know that I'd scored a hit. The shadows recoiled, and for an
instant, I saw the demon within them. Demetrius's mouth was
open in a howl, and something like black blood poured from it.

With a blind grab, I notched another object in the sling and
let it fly. This time, the shadows pulled back before I could
hit them. They whipped around the car, aiming for the tires.
Adrian's swerve kept them from reaching their goal, but it

slammed me against the door and knocked my foot from the pedal.

The car slowed at once. I reached in my lap, but the projectiles were now gone, scattered somewhere on the floor. Adrian was half on top of me, keeping the car on the road but also keeping me from getting more projectiles from my pockets. Above us, Demetrius drew his shadows inward, winding up for a final, fatal strike, all the while smiling at me with his mouth still stained from his blood.

With nothing else to use, I ripped the necklace from my throat. As those deadly shadows descended, I balled the large diamond into the notch on the sling and hurled it at the demon.

Demetrius yanked his shadows around him like a shield. The diamond necklace disappeared inside that darkness, and for a heart-stopping second, nothing happened. Then the shadows exploded into wisps of smoke and an agonized roar reverberated through the night, so loud that it shook the ground beneath us.

Adrian shoved his leg past mine to hit the gas pedal. The car shot forward, flinging me against the seat. Once more, blood clouded my vision from my freely running head wounds, but I saw a body drop out of the sky behind us, and when it landed on the road, it didn't move.

I turned around, grinning at Adrian even though I was racked with pain and also pretty sure I was about to pass out.

"Best birthday present ever," I managed to croak.

Something large and winged rushed toward us from the opposite end of the road. Fear had me feeling around for something to hurl at it, until I saw its red, glowing eyes.

Brutus's victorious swoop around our car was the last thing I saw before I passed out from relief, or blood loss, or both.

CHAPTER SEVENTEEN

The smell of fresh-brewed coffee woke me. I inhaled, fantasizing about a cup with lots of sugar and cream, when I remembered what had happened right before I lost consciousness.

"Adrian," I gasped as I opened my eyes.

My sister's face came into focus. Jasmine's forehead was creased with worry, but at that, it cleared and she flashed me a strained, if rueful, smile.

"If he's the first thing you think of, then that means you're back to your old self."

I sat up, my hand going instinctively to my head. No bandages or slashes, so I'd been healed. Had he?

"Is he okay?" I asked, looking around, but Jasmine and I were the only ones in the bus's bedroom.

"He's fine now," she said, to my great relief. "Although he was half-dead when Brutus flew the two of you back to us. Took all the manna we had on the bus to heal both of you."

I sat up, and when the room seemed to tilt, that's when I realized that my wounds might be healed, but I wasn't all the way recovered. "That was smart, sending Brutus ahead of you.

I passed out right after he got there, and I don't know if Adrian could've managed to drive to you in his condition."

"Probably not," Jasmine said. Then she laughed, though it sounded more choked than amused. "Guess I can't hate Adrian anymore, considering that he took a bullet and what looked like a hell of a beating in order to get you out of that realm."

"I hope you do stop," I said, holding her stare. "You don't need to like him, but he hasn't done anything to earn your hatred."

She ran a hand through the white streak in her hair. "He has by being one of them."

"A Judian?" I sighed. "He can't help that any more than I can help being the last Davidian."

"Not that," she said. "A demon. I don't care if he is technically human, he's just like them. They're also totally ruthless except when it comes to whatever *they* care about, and if they want something, they'll stomp over anyone and everything to get it, too."

It was so close to the concern I'd felt when Adrian drove away from those stranded motorists without a backward glance that I simply stared at her for a moment. Could she be right? *No*, I decided, shoving those fears away. *She can't be.*

"Circumstances have forced Adrian to be single-minded and ruthless. They've forced me to be that way sometimes, too," I said, conviction growing as I thought about the people I'd had to leave behind in the realm. I hadn't *wanted* to; I'd had no choice. Neither had Adrian, most of the time. That didn't mean either of us were heartless to the point of resembling demons. Jasmine just didn't understand.

Jasmine let out a ragged breath. "Maybe I shouldn't be judging Adrian. I've done awful things, too."

"No you haven't," I said at once.

She looked away, and her shoulders started to tremble. "I—I didn't tell you this before, but they tortured Tommy to get me to answer questions about you. I didn't want to, but what they did to him…" Her voice cracked and tears spilled down her face. "It broke me. I told them everything. I sold you out, Ivy."

The pain in her voice was so raw, it tore at me. I couldn't imagine how awful it had been for her, seeing her boyfriend tortured by the most sadistic creatures in existence. I tried to speak, to tell her that I understood, but she held up her hand almost violently.

"Afterward, they killed Tommy anyway, and they laughed at me for believing that they'd let him live if I told them what they wanted to know. After that, I wanted to die, too, but the hate…it kept me going. It was the *only* thing that did, and now, if I let it go, I don't think I'll be able to make it," she finished in an agonized whisper before dissolving into tears.

"Yes, you will," I said, taking her hands and gripping them. "You're strong, Jasmine. So much stronger than they'll ever be, no matter how many powers they have. And you didn't sell me out. You didn't know where I was or what I was doing the whole time the demons had you, so don't feel guilty about that a moment longer." My voice rose as I tried to force her to look at me. "And even if you *had* known and you told them, I would still love you. You're my sister, and nothing will ever change that."

She finally looked up, and the mixture of hope and heartbreak in her gaze was painful to witness. "You mean that?"

"Of course I do," I said, putting all the conviction I had into my voice. "Forever."

Then, she did something she hadn't done since we were kids. She threw her arms around me and cried.

Half an hour later, Jasmine used a reflective surface in the bathroom to make sure that she'd cleaned away all the evidence of her tears. I hadn't been wearing mascara like her, so all I'd needed to do was splash some water on my face and blow my nose a few times before I was good as new.

"I'll try not to hate Adrian anymore," Jaz called out from the bathroom, "but it's a lot harder for me to believe the best about him like you do, especially when I've heard so much about his worst from the demons who held me captive."

I shuddered, glad I hadn't heard what she had. Adrian had told me the generalities about his past, but I never wanted to know the details. "I understand, and I don't expect miracles." Then I let out a brief, ironic laugh. "Okay, I guess I do, but I'm reserving that for finding the staff and being able to use it."

She cocked her head. "Why wouldn't you be able to use it?"

I looked away, blaming my recent blood loss for the slip. Jasmine hadn't seen me wield the slingshot, so she didn't know that using it had almost killed me, and the staff was supposed to be more powerful by *a lot*. On my optimistic days, I gave myself a fifty-fifty chance of surviving it. Still, what could I do? *Not* try to stop the walls between the realms from crumbling? Even if I could live with myself if I did nothing to prevent the mass slaughter that would follow—and I couldn't, not after what I'd seen—I wouldn't survive the aftermath, either. So, likely death or not, the staff was the best chance I had.

I just wasn't able to tell Jasmine that using it would probably be the last thing I ever did. Not yet. She was still too battered emotionally to deal with that.

Lies of omission are still lies, an inner voice seemed to taunt. Was it only last night that I'd said that to Adrian? So much had happened since then, it seemed like a long time ago. "Oh, you know," I said, forcing a fake laugh. "Performance anxiety. I used to freak out before my chorus solos, too."

I couldn't tell her the truth, even if it made me a total hypocrite. I'd rather suffer her justified anger later than hurt her more now while she was already bleeding on the inside from countless emotional wounds.

"I remember." Jasmine's smile told me that she bought the lie, which was a relief. "But you were great with those, and you'll be great with this, too. Mom and Dad—" her voice cracked "—they'd be so proud of you, Ivy."

I didn't expect the tears that spilled down my cheeks as if they'd been longing to escape. I tried so hard not to openly grieve for our parents, both to be strong for Jasmine and to avoid the pain that buried me every time I allowed myself to dwell on their deaths. They had adopted me after I'd been left by a highway like so much trash. Raised me with the same love and devotion they'd shown to their biological daughter, and tried in every way to help me overcome a psychological affliction that turned out to be a supernatural destiny.

There was no way to get over so great a loss. My only coping mechanism was to back-burner it. That's why I forced another fake smile as I tucked my sister's hair behind her ear.

"They'd be proud of you, too."

And they'd want her to be happy. I swiped at my eyes, resolve drying my tears. If I succeeded, she'd have a chance to be, and so would Costa, Adrian and countless other people. What was a little probable death compared to that?

"I'm going to take a shower," I told her, scratching a hand through my hair and feeling something grainy. "If I'm not mistaken, I've got dried blood all over me."

Our bus stopped and started during my shower, but I didn't think much of it until I came out into the bus's general living area, looked around and realized that someone was missing.

"Where's Adrian?"

Costa was driving, and he glanced back at me with a wave. "Out getting another car since he had to leave his Challenger behind. You know this beast is too slow and cumbersome. We'll need something with power when there's another emergency."

"When?" I repeated, with a hollow little laugh. "What a glass-half-empty thought."

Costa gave me a sardonic grin. "You're the only optimist on this road trip, Ivy."

Brutus was in his usual place behind the driver's seat, a blanket covering him from head to clawed toe. As I approached, he began to wiggle in anticipation. I put my arms around him, ending up in his lap when he grabbed me. Then, with happy-sounding grunts, he began licking my face through the blanket.

"You're a big softie trapped in a scary gargoyle's body," I told him, but I didn't mind. He must've snatched me and Adrian right out of the convertible, saving us from crashing in our badly injured conditions. That was well worth a few face licks.

"Who's the best, Brutus?" I continued, patting his huge head. He responded with a series of chuffs that were obvious translations of *I am, I am!* so I patted and praised him again.

Jasmine watched with a sort of morbid fascination. "Mom and Dad should've let you get another puppy when we were little," she finally muttered. "You've lost it, Ives."

"Friends come in all shapes and sizes," I replied pertly. "And that includes two-ton, demonically altered reptiles."

Jasmine shook her head, but as she turned away, I caught a glimpse of a smile. Brutus had gone from terrifying her to making her wary to now garnering a smile. In time, she'd come to realize that the fearsome guard she'd seen when she was trapped in a demon realm didn't truly represent all that Brutus was.

Come to think of it, the same could be said for her perception of Adrian, although she'd probably accept Brutus quicker.

After I was done praising Brutus for his rescue, I had that cup of coffee and fixed something for breakfast, or lunch since it was well past noon. Then I surprised myself by falling asleep on the couch. I hadn't realized I was still so tired, but I must have been, because it was dark out when I woke up. I suppressed my instant shudder at seeing blackness pressed against the windows as if it were a malevolent force trying to get in. It felt too soon since the last time the darkness I saw had been a real, living thing that had tried to kill me.

"Don't worry, we're on hallowed ground."

Adrian's voice came from the back of the bus, then he emerged from the bathroom still towel drying his hair. I didn't know how he'd known that I'd woken up, or how he'd known about the instant dread that had overtaken me at the darkness outside, but his words calmed me. So did seeing him without any bullet holes, blood or bluish-tinged skin. I got up and went to him, and he enfolded me in a hug that seemed to whisper promises to my soul that I gladly drank in.

"Um." My sister cleared her throat, and that's the first I realized that she was nearby, too. "I'd say get a room, but with one so close, I'm afraid that you might actually do it."

I turned, seeing her sitting in the passenger seat despite the bus being parked. "Was that a joke?" I asked in wonder.

She flashed me a small smile. "I hope so."

I laughed, letting go of Adrian rather reluctantly. "Even if I was tempted into letting him slide from his promise to prove that he won't betray me, he swears that he won't do it."

Adrian arched a brow at Jasmine as if to say, *Bet you didn't expect that.* From her expression, he was right.

"Did I miss anything?" Costa said, coming inside the bus.

"Nothing you want to know about," Jasmine muttered.

Now that everyone was here, I wanted to update them on the most significant thing that had happened during our escape from the realm. "I have something to tell you that should make you feel better." I cleared my throat. "I, um, think I killed Demetrius."

Saying the words made me both happy and fearful. I wanted to celebrate, and at the same time, I was half-afraid that the demon would magically show up to prove me wrong.

Jasmine's eyes widened. "Really?"

"Isn't he already dead?" was Costa's surprised question.

Adrian made a low, vicious sound. "He survived what happened in Bennington, and while I hope Ivy's right, I won't believe he's truly dead until I dance in his ashes."

"But how could you kill him?" Costa looked confused. "The sling's gone, and I thought that only Archons can kill demons."

I held up my arm. "Turns out, the slingshot isn't gone. It's just dormant until a demon gets close. Then it turns back into the real thing, except it only kills them one at a time."

Jasmine and Costa stared at the markings in disbelief. Adrian laid his hand over the tattoo, smiling a bit grimly.

"She's telling the truth, and I'd have the burn marks to prove it, if you hadn't stuffed me full of manna last night."

"It burns me, too," I said, with a hollow laugh. "I just don't get any visible welts. At least it doesn't hurt as much as it did the first time I used it."

Adrian glanced back and forth between me and the tattoo before meeting my eyes. "I don't think the weapon's potency has diminished. I think you've gotten stronger and better able to withstand the pain. In fact—" his expression took on a hard, assessing look "—with it, now we have something to use to build up your tolerance to the staff. A hallowed weapon is the best way to train you to withstand another hallowed weapon."

I didn't like the sound of this. "How? I have to be very close to a demon to activate the slingshot, and I don't want to risk my life hanging out with demons anytime soon."

The hardness in Adrian's expression didn't lessen even as a slight smile curled his lips.

"I might know a way around that."

CHAPTER EIGHTEEN

I felt a pang of nostalgia as I looked around the campus of Marquette University in Milwaukee, Wisconsin. If my life had turned out differently, I'd be close to finishing my junior year at the College of William and Mary. Jasmine would be wrapping up her freshman year there, and our parents would be looking forward to having both of us home for the summer.

Instead, we were orphaned dropouts who were sneaking onto campus with a gargoyle disguised as a seagull, a former demon-realm captive and the last descendant of Judas. No wonder there were moments when part of me thought that this was just one long, extremely strange dream. Yet here we were, and somewhere on this campus was the place that Adrian apparently called home. He didn't live here as a student, of course. In fact, according to him, no one knew that he lived here at all.

I had felt the thrum of hallowed ground as soon as we stepped onto the campus. Since this was a Catholic and Jesuit school, that explained why. There were more than a few churches on-site, but I noticed that the supernatural vibrations grew the closer we came to our destination. By the time we reached St. Joan's

Chapel, my nerves felt like they'd been transformed into guitar strings during a concert.

With its medieval architecture, the small stone chapel looked like it belonged next to the ruins of a castle on a lonely European hill. Not surrounded by multistoried lecture halls on the grounds of a modern American university. Evening mass had just ended, judging by the people spilling out of the chapel. I smiled at them as we walked up the stone steps, ignoring the many curious glances aimed at Brutus. If they thought that a seagull tottering behind us looked strange, they'd really freak out if they could see Brutus's true form.

"I still don't think this is a good idea," Costa muttered.

From her expression, Jasmine agreed, but she stayed silent. Adrian gave them a quick, measuring look before replying.

"Once again, anyone who wants to can stay back at the bus."

"As soon as I make sure that Ivy's really safe, I'm out of here," Jasmine said briskly. "Until then, I'm staying."

This time, Adrian's silvery-blue eyes lingered on me. "I'm not saying it'll be easy, but it should be as safe as regular target practice."

"Sure, if you ignore the part about the target being a living, bloodthirsty demon," Jasmine said under her breath.

I had to admit, that had given me pause the first time Adrian had told me his plan, but I knew as well as he did how important it was to train for the staff. Jasmine didn't, so she'd reacted as though Adrian were trying to fulfill his destiny by betraying me. By the time she'd calmed down enough to hear him explain the safeguards, we were halfway to Milwaukee.

Now that the moment had arrived, however, I felt more than a little nervous. Not because I thought that Adrian was about to pull a Judas, but because I was dreading the pain to come. As we walked into the chapel, my right arm began to tingle as if the sling was beginning to wake up. Made sense; according to Adrian, the demon was about thirty feet below where we were standing.

The interior of the chapel wasn't heavily decorated, but what was there was beautiful. Wooden chairs contrasted with the ancient stone walls and stained glass window mosaics. The ceiling was surprisingly low and flat until it neared the altar, and then it arced upward a full story and became shaped like an octagon that had been cut in half. The chapel was now empty of students, but a priest in full vestments stopped Adrian when he started to go behind the carved altar.

"My son, what are you—?"

"It's Adrian, Father Louis," he interrupted him, smiling wryly.

"Adrian!" the priest said with obvious happiness. "What an impressive new disguise. I'm so glad to see you. It's been so long, I was beginning to grow worried."

"This is no disguise. For once, you're seeing the real me, and as for being away," Adrian replied, reaching out to draw me forward, "you'll understand once you meet the reason why. Ivy, this is Father Louis. Zach brought me to him when I was fresh out of the realms, and he took me in and gave me a crash course on humanity. Father Louis, this is Ivy."

I said hello and shook hands with Father Louis, but when it came time to let go, the priest didn't. Instead, the white-haired father began to tremble as he stared at the tattoo snaking from my finger to my forearm.

"Adrian," he whispered. "Is it… Is—is she…?" He seemed too shocked to finish the sentence, so Adrian did.

"Yes, she is the last Davidian, and yes, that is David's slingshot embedded inside her skin," he said almost gently.

To my great consternation, the priest dropped to his knees, mumbling prayers in Latin. He kept hold of my hand, though, and for an old guy, he had a good grip. Then he pressed a kiss to the tattooed loop around my finger.

"Sanguine David, armorum Dei," he breathed, finally releasing me. "Blood of David, weapon of God."

I backed up as soon as I could, unnerved by the misplaced worship. If this priest knew me, he'd haul me over to the nearest confessional booth and then bolt it shut until I'd disclosed all my sins, which would take a while.

Adrian flashed me a grin. "Don't let this bother you. Father Louis is an emotional guy. You should've seen his reaction when Zach told him who *I* was. He dumped a vat of holy water over my head and began reciting the exorcist's prayer."

I couldn't help but snicker at the mental image, which lessened the awkwardness of the moment. After crossing himself, Father Louis rose, smiling at me with a sheepish expression.

"My apologies, miss. I was unprepared. Believing in something is not quite the same as seeing it in the flesh."

I reassured him that all was well while I mulled the truth of that statement. Months ago, I had believed the slingshot would work because everyone had told me it would, but still, I'd been blown away by actually *seeing* demons and minions fall by the hundreds from it. No wonder the good father had lost a little of his cool after Adrian told him who I was. Seeing and believing *were* two different things.

And sometimes, believing and trusting were two different things, too. I knew that God was real because of everything I'd been through, yet I still struggled to trust in Him. After all, it seemed reckless at best to hinge the fate of the world on a twenty-one-year-old who was far from the smartest or bravest that humanity had to offer. Any divine being that thought *that* was a good idea was deserving of a few doubts, if you asked me.

"You remember Costa, and this is Ivy's sister, Jasmine," Adrian continued the introductions. "We're here so Ivy can build up her tolerance to the staff. The sling comes out in the presence of demons, which is why we need to see Blinky."

"The demon's name is Blinky?" Jasmine asked in disbelief.

Adrian snorted. "He refused to tell us his real name and I don't recognize him, so we had to call him something. You'll understand why we picked that when you see him."

"Please, allow me to watch the sling's manifestation," Father Louis said, his voice almost trembling with excitement.

Adrian clapped him on the back. "Get me a bag of a hundred percent, hand-tossed grave dirt, and you've got a deal. The last priest I went through must've mixed regular soil in with the batch since it did nothing but piss off the demon it landed on."

Father Louis beamed. "Done."

I now knew why the grave dirt we'd used hadn't worked on Oblivion. Father Louis hurried to the front of the chapel. I thought he was leaving to get the agreed-upon hallowed dirt, but instead, he locked the chapel doors and came back.

"You never did explain how Blinky managed to be on hallowed ground without exploding or something," I said to Adrian.

He smiled, and for the briefest moment, he reminded me of Demetrius. The demon was the only other person I'd seen who could convey such dark expectancy with a mere curl of his lips.

"You're about to find out, but I'll give you a hint—if hallowed objects exist, then so do their counterparts."

With that, Adrian grabbed one of the four pillars that flanked the altar and turned it on its axis. With a grinding sound, the entire altar and part of the stone floor beneath lifted up on its side, causing the candlesticks and velvet cloth to crash onto the floor. The new position revealed a square, open space beneath the altar, with stairs that led down.

"You've heard of trap doors, well, this is a trap altar," Adrian said, his grin turning challenging. "Follow me."

CHAPTER NINETEEN

Father Louis took one of the altar's fallen candles, lit it and brought it down with us. Without that single flickering flame, we wouldn't be able to see anything. Well, most of us wouldn't. My eyes were already adjusting to the dark. As I'd told Costa, my abilities were like a muscle; the more I used them, the more they were there when I needed them.

"What kind of a church is this?" Jasmine whispered as we descended the stairs. The tunnel around us was so narrow, if I stretched out my arms, I'd hit the wall. That's why Brutus had to stay up in the chapel. Even though the staircase descended only about fifteen feet, there was no way Brutus would fit in this tiny space. I hoped no one in our group was claustrophobic. Even I was starting to feel twitchy from our cramped quarters.

"A very special one," Father Louis replied. He didn't sound unnerved by our surroundings. In fact, the old priest sounded almost giddy. "It originally came from the French village of Chasse-sur-Rhône. No one knows how old the chapel is. Some say five hundred years old, some say a thousand."

I was more surprised to hear of its original location than to hear of its age. "Someone moved an entire stone chapel all the way from France to here?"

"Oh, it didn't come here first," Father Louis said, further surprising me. "Its first destination was New York. It stayed there forty years and miraculously survived a fire that leveled the castle next to it. Then the chapel was inherited by another family, and they had it transported stone by stone to here."

"Why would anyone cart around an entire chapel once, let alone twice?" Jasmine asked, voicing my own thoughts. "You could build several new ones with much less time, money and hassle."

Father Louis reached out, touching the stone walls fondly. "There's something special about this place. If you stayed here any length of time, you'd feel it. Right, Adrian?"

Adrian was still at the front of our procession, and at that, he threw a glance over his shoulder at the priest.

"I don't know that I've felt something special, but it is the only place I've kept coming back to, so I suppose that counts for something."

All I felt was the thrum of hallowed ground across my senses, which, although stronger from the multiple churches on the campus, wasn't unusual. Maybe Father Louis was just romanticizing because the chapel had such an unusual history.

"How did you come to have a trapped demon down here, anyway?" I asked.

Adrian opened a small door at the end of the staircase—and something hit me with a full-body punch, knocking me back into Father Louis and Costa. With my momentum, I flattened them against the staircase.

"What is it, what is it?" Jasmine cried.

I looked around, dazed. "I don't know."

And I didn't. I couldn't find the cause of the force that had thrown me on my ass. All I saw was darkness behind the small door that Adrian had left open as he rushed to me.

Then I felt it; an indescribable pull toward something beyond that door. My heart began to pound and every hallowed sensor in my body began screaming out an alert. The reaction was so intense, I barely noticed the pain as the slingshot began to glow and uncurl itself from my arm.

"Oh my God, it's here," I whispered. Then I said it louder as excitement mingled with my certainty. "The staff is *here!*"

"What?" Jasmine said with disbelief.

Father Louis, still flattened on the staircase next to me, bowed his head in awed reverence. *"In nominee Patris, et Filli, et Spiritus Sancti,"* he began to intone.

"Ugh, anything but that," a disgusted voice said, with the same Demonish accent Adrian had.

My head whipped around. That hadn't come from Costa, who was farther up the staircase. It came from beyond the open door.

"Shut up, Blinky," Adrian snapped. He cradled my head, wincing as the now fully extended sling grazed his arm. "Are you okay, Ivy?"

Actually, between the slingshot and my overloaded hallowed sensors, I felt like I was being split in two and barbecued. Despite that, I managed to smile. We'd found the staff! No more fruitless searching, no more worrying about it falling into demons' hands, no more realms swallowing innocent people and places. I'd start dancing in glee, if I could move yet.

"I'm fine, but I need help up."

Very gently, Adrian lifted me to my feet. Costa helped Father Louis up even though the old priest had fallen on top of him, and Jasmine edged by them to get to me.

"Are you sure about that— Hey, look! It doesn't hurt when I touch it," Jasmine said in surprise, holding up a piece of the glowing, golden sling.

"Huh?" I said, stunned into a grunted response. "How?" I added a bit more eloquently.

"Supernaturally charged objects only react to people who can harness supernatural power, like you and me," Adrian replied, holding up his thickly gloved hands. He'd also worn gloves the first time I met him. At the time, I'd thought it was because he didn't want to leave fingerprints after kidnapping me. "But to a normal person like Jasmine, the sling is nothing more than ordinary rope," he finished.

"But you can't use the slingshot, Adrian. Only I or a descendant of Goliath can, so why does it burn you?" I wondered.

Adrian's expression became shadowed with more than our dark surroundings. "It's hallowed. My abilities are derived from opposing forces, so whenever something hallowed touches my skin, I have an adverse reaction, and the more powerful the object, the more intense the reaction. That's why I always wear gloves."

Jasmine looked away, but not before I saw a knowing look cross her features. I began to wind the sling around my hand. I didn't need it to brush against Adrian again and have the subsequent welt be another reminder to Jaz about his lineage. Besides, I must have a decent amount of darkness in me, too, because the slingshot burned me like fire whenever it activated.

"I'm sure that Moses's staff is here," I said, getting back to the point. "Every hallowed sensor I have is ringing off the hook, so it must be somewhere inside that room."

"Moses's staff?" that unfamiliar voice repeated, followed by low, disdainful laughter. "Who did you bring here, Adrian? A delusional treasure hunter or an extraordinary idiot?"

"I brought the last Davidian," Adrian shot back, "and you're about to watch her recover the second-most-hallowed weapon in existence."

CHAPTER TWENTY

That statement was greeted by silence. I tested my legs and found that I was able to stand again. Wow. This hadn't happened when I found the slingshot. Then, I'd just felt a full-body alert and a strange pulling sensation that had led me to its location. How powerful must the staff be if just being in its vicinity was enough to knock me off my feet?

Too powerful.

As soon as the depressing thought crossed my mind, I shoved it back. I had to do this, no matter the consequences. On the bright side, at least it would be over soon.

"Let's do this," I said, and walked into the small room that a glance showed to be a crypt.

A man stood next to a stone burial vault, which was the only furniture in the room. He looked to be my Dad's age, with thick brown hair, pale skin and a ramrod-straight posture that reminded me of a marine at full attention. That was where his human similarities ended. He was shirtless, which revealed odd extensions of flesh beneath his arms that looked like flaps, as if he were wearing a base-jumping suit made of skin. That wasn't what made me stop and stare in fascinated horror, though. It was his eyes. All several dozen of them.

Eyes covered his entire upper body, even on those skin flaps. Worse, they followed my every movement, as if just being there wasn't creeptastic enough. I was so, so glad that he had on a pair of baggy pants. If those eyes were all over him, I didn't want to know.

Then I met the gaze of the eyes in his normal-looking face, and really shuddered. No human could infuse such raw, unadulterated evil into their gaze. Not even minions could. Demons had a monopoly on that, and this one seemed to be the grand master of it. I felt chilled all the way to my soul as I stared at him. If I didn't have a demon-killing weapon wrapped around my hand, I might have walked out right then.

But I did, and more than that, I could feel an even more powerful weapon inside this room. So, I stared back and tried not to let him see how rattled he made me feel.

"Why does he have eyes all over him?" I asked Adrian in an admirably calm voice.

"Blinky used to be a seraph," Adrian said, giving me a slanting look. "Seraphim were one of the highest levels of angels, radiating light like firestorms, but Blinky lost all that, plus his feathers, when he rebelled during the Fall."

Demons were so evil; I often forgot that many of them used to be angels. I hadn't heard of a serpah before and had never guessed that an angel—fallen or otherwise—could look this freaky. Being covered with feathers and radiating light would have helped, but still. With those strange, wide flaps sprouting from his upper arms, back and legs, Blinky looked like a cross between a man and a manta ray. Add in the dozens of eyes covering him, and once again, my preconceived notions about angels had been proven wrong. One day, I had to pick up a Bible and research this stuff.

"She is the Davidian?" the seraph-turned-demon replied, with a disdainful snort. "You *must* be joking."

The insult chased away the last of my unease. "Blinky, is it?" I said, my tone cool. "I totally get why they named you that. You're an ophthalmologist's dream."

He smiled, and that simple stretch of his lips managed to ooze malevolence.

Jasmine walked in, took one look at the demon, and then walked out, visibly shaken. Adrian stopped me when I started to go after her.

"Costa'll make sure she's okay," he said. With a single glance at the demon, Costa left, looking relieved to do so.

"Don't touch the circles around him," Adrian warned me. "They'll hurt you because they mark the limits of the cursed earth."

"Cursed earth?" I repeated, and leaned down, but didn't touch the three separate lines that formed circles around the demon. The one closest to me appeared to be made of pale, loose sand, the second ring looked like it was ashes laminated into the stone floor, and the third was formed from a dark stain that resembled dried blood.

Adrian knelt next to me, his finger resting near the pale sand circle. "Yep. We poured and then glazed over these lines around Blinky after we let the hallowed ground knock him out. I told you that hallowed items have their counterparts. This first ring is made up of the ground bones of Moloch, a half demon who ordered child sacrifices for his worship. The next ring contains ashes from the Tower of Babel, and the third contains spilled blood from the first battle between Archons and demons. Put items like these together, and they turn whatever ground they rest on into condemned earth, making the space where Blinky stands as safe as home base."

I was openmouthed at the history behind these innocuous-looking circles. "Where did you even *get* those things?"

He arched an amused brow. "Former demon prince, remember?"

Right, I kept forgetting that. So, that's how Blinky could survive beneath a chapel. The cursed earth formed an invisible shield under him and around him. It also explained why there were no locks on the door to this crypt. If the demon took one step outside of his tiny, protected space, it would be his last.

And I now also knew that cursed objects would hurt me in the same way that hallowed ones hurt demons, but that didn't tell me everything.

"You never told me how you ended up trapping a demon in the first place," I reminded Adrian.

He shrugged. "I ran into Blinky a couple years ago while he was trolling for students to supply a nearby realm. I forced him onto hallowed ground, which almost killed him, and then I made this section for him in the crypt so I could interrogate him about the slingshot. I told you, at first, I was looking for it because I wanted to kill Demetrius. It wasn't until later that I discovered I couldn't use it even if I did find it."

No, Zach had hidden that from Adrian, much as the Archon had hidden a lot of important things from me. I continued to look around the room, seeing more strange circles drawn into the walls. They even went over the door, which was still open after Jasmine and Costa's hasty exit.

"What are those?"

"Muters," Adrian replied. "They cancel out the vibes left by supernatural objects. That way, other demons can't follow their trails back to the source and find Blinky."

"That's why I didn't feel the staff before." I let out a shaky laugh. "Those 'muters' must've dulled its vibe, too."

And when Adrian had opened the door, it broke the muting circle, allowing the staff's residual power to light up my hallowed sensors enough to knock me off my feet. Now for the really hard part.

"Miss, please, where is it?" Father Louis asked anxiously.

As if it had been marked with an X, I went over to a section of wall only about two feet outside of the demon's circle. Lucky for us, whoever had buried the staff hadn't hidden it a few steps over, or we'd have another big problem on our hands. I pressed my hand against the wall. Power reached out to zap my palm, and I smiled despite the fresh spurt of pain.

"It's right behind here."

Adrian turned to Father Louis. "We'll need a power drill, work gloves and lots of cloth." To me, he said, "You're not touching it, Ivy. Not yet. I'll pull it out, and then we'll lock it up somewhere safe while you build up your tolerance to it."

I wasn't ashamed of how relieved that made me. More time to train was a good idea. It gave me a better chance at surviving.

"Ooh, give Moses's staff to the Judian, splendid idea," Blinky mocked, breaking through my happiness.

Adrian shot him a dangerous look. "See that rope wrapped around her hand? It's David's slingshot, and while I haven't been able to kill you these past few years, it can."

Father Louis left after muttering something in Latin that made the demon's mouth curl down. "Superstitious old fool," he said contemptuously. Then the pale green eyes all over him narrowed as he stared at me. "You must know that the staff will kill you if you attempt to use it."

My worst fears spoken aloud. I couldn't let him know that he'd scored a hit, though. "The slingshot didn't," I said, holding out the glowing rope around my hand for emphasis.

"A mere toy," the demon scoffed. "Its claim to fame was killing one giant. Moses's staff brought an entire nation to its knees with plagues so fearsome, their like has never been seen before or since."

"One more word to her," Adrian said through gritted teeth, "and you won't live long enough to see the staff."

Blinky waved a hand, as though suddenly bored with us. We

spent a tense few minutes in that silent standoff until footsteps on the staircase had my head swiveling toward the door. Father Louis bustled into the room, slightly flushed, and he dropped several items by Adrian's feet.

"I already had most of what you needed here for when we do repairs," he said, his words breathier from his exertions. "The drill was at the hall next door, which is under construction."

Adrian snorted. "You stole it?"

"Borrowed," the priest replied promptly. "I'll return it as soon as we are done."

An hour later, Adrian had carved out one of the stone blocks that made up the wall. I almost held my breath as I saw the outline of something in the narrow space between these stones and the next layer of rock. Adrian glanced at me, his expression so inscrutable, his features could have been carved from the walls surrounding us. Then, very slowly, he pulled out an oblong object wrapped in dark, stained cloths.

I took in a long breath. Father Louis fell to his knees, and for the first time, the demon looked afraid.

Then Adrian drew the cloth away, revealing what was inside. I stared, cocking my head in confusion. That didn't look like a staff. I wasn't an expert on them, but wasn't a staff essentially a long wooden stick? This was stone, and unless the low lights were playing tricks on me, it looked like a tablet.

Then low, cruelly satisfied laughter broke through the shocked silence in the crypt.

"Looks like your illustrious hallowed sensors dialed a wrong number, Davidian," the demon drawled.

CHAPTER TWENTY-ONE

"That can't be," I muttered, going over to Adrian and grabbing the tablet. It felt supernaturally limp in my hands, but when I brushed the cloth around it, power overloaded my senses enough to almost knock me over again.

"What the hell?" I exclaimed in surprise.

The demon grunted. "Come closer and I'll show you."

I ignored that. Adrian didn't. He lasered another death stare at Blinky before returning his attention to me.

"What is it, Ivy?"

"It's the cloth."

He wouldn't know because he was wearing industrialized, superthick work gloves, protecting his bare skin from the supernatural forces emanating from the cloth. I grabbed a large handful to be sure, then screamed at the paralyzing pain shooting through me. It brought me to my knees, and through the sound of my own gasps, I heard the demon's taunting laughter.

"How delicious. It wasn't the staff that called you down here. It was merely the cloth that it used to be wrapped in."

I wanted to tell him to shut up, but I couldn't catch my breath. I dropped the cloth, backing away from it as though it were a poisonous snake. My body ached right down to the marrow in my bones, and I hadn't felt anything that excruciating since I'd used the slingshot for the first time.

"I—I think he's right," I got out, shuddering from the residual spikes of pain. "It's the cloth. Something hallowed was in it, and whatever it was, it imprinted the cloth with more power than the slingshot ever had."

I didn't want to dwell on what that meant. Not now. All I wanted to do was get away from the thing that had made me feel like razor wire was being shoved through my veins.

Father Louis rose and went over to where Adrian stood. He held the candlestick up to the tablet, or the decoy, as I now mentally referred to it. After a moment, he began to trace his fingers over the images on it, but right when it looked like he was about to speak, Blinky beat him to it.

"If the staff's mere covering sends you cringing to your knees, then the staff itself will *definitely* kill you." A short, contemptuous laugh. "What a joke you are, Davidian."

His words cut me to the core. That's what I was worried about, too.

Adrian stared at the demon, so incensed that a vein in his temple started to noticeably throb. Without warning, he threw the stained, ancient-looking cloth at him.

The demon howled so loud, I thought my eardrums would rupture. He flung the cloth away and vaulted into the air, those strange skin flaps flaring out and revealing themselves to be three distinct pairs of batlike wings. Large, swelling blisters began to form all over him, even on his many eyes. They grew, bubbling up until he looked even more monstrous. The cloth had hurt me because I couldn't handle its power, but this was a supernatural version of an extreme allergic reaction as a hallowed object touched pure evil.

I was sure the demon had it coming, and for more than taunting me with my probable impending failure and death.

Still, it was unsettling to see Adrian's obvious enjoyment as he snatched up the cloth and hurled it onto Blinky again, turning the demon's blisters into oozing burns. With more ear-piercing screams, the demon threw it off. His three sets of wings flapped madly, but he had nowhere to fly. Every time he approached the limits of the cursed earth, he screamed again, as if everything beyond the invisible cylinder of those supernatural rings was almost as painful to touch as the cloth. Finally, he gave up trying to fly and huddled behind the burial vault in an attempt to hide from another volley.

"Who's cringing on their knees now?" Adrian asked pitilessly.

"That's enough," I said, grossed out as every defensive movement the demon made caused his boils to burst open.

"Not until I say it is," Adrian retorted, throwing the cloth back onto Blinky and seeming to savor his new screams.

I didn't. It was one thing to teach Blinky to watch his mouth and another to reduce him to a festering, oozing pile of wounds. This side of Adrian was disturbing, to say the least. I'd told him to stop and he'd refused, so he wasn't doing this to defend me anymore. No, this was all about him wanting revenge for more than any insults lobbed at me.

"Then do it alone," I said, and walked out.

Father Louis followed me back upstairs. He either wanted to look at the tablet under stronger light, or he, too, didn't want to witness any more of Blinky's torment. Once I was back in the chapel, I spotted Jasmine and Costa, but I didn't see Brutus. Jasmine and Costa were as far away from the secret staircase as they could get while still being inside the chapel, and they each had a Starbucks cup in their hands. When I approached, Jasmine nodded at the extra one on the chair next to her.

"Brought some for you, Ivy."

"Thanks."

I sat down and took a long, grateful gulp. It was lukewarm,

not hot, but I didn't care. It was sweet, familiar and safe. I needed that combination so badly right now, if I could've, I might have bathed in it.

"Is Adrian still digging for the staff?" Jasmine asked.

I stared at her, only then remembering that she hadn't seen any of what had happened. "No. It, ah, wasn't there, after all."

"But you were so sure," she said in surprise.

"I was wrong," was my slightly shaky reply.

Costa gave me a sharp look. I pretended to be too absorbed in taking another gulp of coffee to respond to it.

"I've figured it out," Father Louis said, thankfully breaking the loaded moment. "The tablet is covered in runes."

"What're those?" Jasmine asked.

"An ancient form of alphabet," I replied. Take that, scoffers who said it was a waste of time to major in history.

"I don't know how to translate them, but one of the professors here might," Father Louis went on as if we hadn't spoken. He hadn't taken his eyes off the tablet, either. He seemed enthralled by it. "If this was left where the staff used to be, perhaps the writing on it will tell us where it is now."

"This must be the map," I said in wonder, remembering Zach's comment the day we started on this trip. He'd said that Adrian had to come because he would lead us to a map "of sorts." I'd thought he'd meant a drawing with a version of "X marks the spot" for the staff, but he must have meant the tablet instead!

"Oh, that's something," Jasmine said, her smile slipping as she stared at me. "You don't seem too happy by that, Ivy."

I *was* happy, but I was almost more afraid than ever that if we found the staff, I wouldn't be strong enough to use it to save the realm walls. Since I wouldn't worry my sister by telling her the truth about why I was having a hard time finding my inner cheerleader at the moment, I mumbled, "I, ah, I'm just—"

"Tired," Adrian filled in, coming up from the underground staircase. "Using her abilities takes a lot out of her."

"Yep, I'm tired," I agreed, giving him a grateful look.

Adrian's gaze lingered on me before he turned to Costa. "The tablet must be the map Zach mentioned. I can read a little runic, so I'll take a stab at translating it, but it'll take a while. Why don't you and Jasmine go grab some dinner? There's a few restaurants close by and most of the campus is on hallowed ground, so you should be safe."

From Costa's skeptical expression, he knew there was a lot more going on. Then his half shrug seemed to say, *I'll play along now, but I'll get the truth out of you later.*

Out loud, he said, "I could stand to eat something. What about you, Jasmine? Hungry?"

"Starving," my sister replied, rising. "Ivy? You coming?"

I wanted as far away as I could get from the boil-covered demon and his taunting reminders of my impending failure, but what I said was, "No, I'm not hungry. Besides, I should stay in case Adrian figures out what the tablet says."

"Oh." Jasmine looked disappointed, but she also looked clueless about anything else going on, so I was relieved even as guilt pricked me. *I'll tell her soon,* I promised myself. Just not tonight. "Well, I'll bring you back something, in case you change your mind."

"Thanks," I said, smiling even though it felt like my face might crack from the strain. "Maybe get something for Brutus, too. Where is he, anyway?"

Costa shrugged. "Getting his nightly exercise, and hopefully not eating any stray cats he comes across."

"Then definitely get him something," I said, shuddering.

With assurances that they would, Jasmine and Costa left. Adrian went over to the altar, turned the same pillar on its axis and then got out of the way as the stone slab slowly lowered until the altar covered the hidden staircase again.

"Father Louis," he said, "why don't you take some pictures

of the tablet, then find that professor and see if he can read the runes on it."

The old priest beamed. "It's late, but I am sure he will forgive me for troubling him." Then he pulled a cell phone from his robes and snapped a few pictures of the tablet.

"Aren't you going to try to read it first?" I asked Adrian.

He shrugged. "I can't read a word of runic."

I stared at him. "You lied."

A smile tugged his lips. "Not to you. I never promised not to lie to Costa or Jasmine."

"We *really* need to talk about your definition of the truth," I said, and at the same time, a part of me realized that I was just as bad when it came to Jasmine. But to protect her, I told that part, and tried to ignore how it whispered *bullshit* back at me.

"Now, children, no quarreling," Father Oliver chided.

Adrian snorted. "I'm over a hundred and forty years old, and you're calling me a child?"

The priest waved a hand. "Then act your age." With that, he left, almost skipping with glee over his errand.

Adrian locked the door behind him, leaning against it once he turned around.

"Now what?" I asked, feeling tired for real now.

Adrian glanced up at the ceiling. "Now I show you the place I briefly called home."

CHAPTER TWENTY-TWO

I'd wondered why the ceiling of the chapel was so low in comparison with its high, sloped roof. Now I knew. The upstairs had been converted into a large loft, and as a security measure, almost no one else could see it.

"Zach glamoured this so that it's only visible to Judians, Davidians and Archons," Adrian explained, leading me up the sharply winding staircase. "Everyone else who walks into the chapel sees a ceiling that goes all the way up to the rafters, and where you see the staircase, they see the sacristy."

"Nice," I said, meaning more than the glamour acting as a security system. The loft extended the length of the chapel, and it was furnished with butter-soft leather couches, a TV, several bookshelves, a claw-foot tub and bathroom fixtures, and a bed that looked to be covered in silk. The walls and ceiling were all dark, paneled wood, giving it a warm, cozy atmosphere. Up here, I could almost forget there was a secret crypt beneath the chapel that caged a very dangerous, very mouthy demon, and I wanted to forget that. In fact, I wanted to forget every terrible or destined thing that had been weighing on me for the past several months and just be a plain, normal *girl,* even if only for an hour or so.

"Not like what I'd picture you to live in, though," I added, thinking of the sapphire-colored castle in his luxurious, frightening former realm.

Adrian's smile had a self-deprecating slant. "Took a while to get used to, but it also reinforced my decision every time I looked around. The old Adrian would've never lived here. The person I chose to become was glad for the peace that this place brought, even if that peace came in small, plain packaging."

Then he drew me into his arms. "That's why I sent the rest of them away and brought you up here," he murmured. "You need to stop thinking about everything that demon said and find your own peace. So, for the rest of the evening, there's no destiny you need to fulfill, no brave mask you need to put on and no one you have to try to save. There's only a hot bath, a bottle of wine and a massage that'll make your body feel like it floated away."

It was exactly what I'd been thinking, and his knowing I needed that made it resonate all the more. All of it sounded so good, a soft moan escaped me. Adrian chuckled, tilting my head back.

"Save those for the massage. I expect to hear a lot more of them once my hands are all over you."

He laughed again at my sharp intake of breath, his light brush of lips more of a tease than a kiss. Then, with a final wink, he walked away.

I waited until he descended the staircase to start my bath, adding some shampoo to the running tap so there'd be bubbles. Then I took my clothes off and sank into the tub. It was obviously built for a person Adrian's size, which meant that I could fully stretch out without touching either end of it. Instead, I floated in the hot, bubbly water, closing my eyes and letting out a sigh as I slowly, slowly started to relax.

"Here."

His voice made my eyelids fly open again. A half-full wineglass suspended over me was the first thing I saw, but instead of taking it, my hands flew to cover certain parts of me. Adrian's low chuckle brought a flush to my cheeks.

"I've seen you naked before, Ivy. Don't you remember?"

"That was my top half only!"

"Besides, those bubbles are very concealing," he went on, as if I hadn't spoken. "Go on, drink your wine, and I'll get started on your massage."

"Now?" I burst out.

Another chuckle slid along my senses with its own caress. "Of course. Nothing is more soothing than a hot water massage, especially with a glass of wine."

"Adrian…" I couldn't begin to articulate all the reasons why this was a bad idea, so I settled on the most obvious. "There's no way I'll be able to relax with me being naked and you—you *not* being blind."

His brow arched. "Is that your only objection?"

With that, he set the wineglass down and went into the bedroom portion of the loft. After rummaging through a drawer for a moment, he came back with a long, black piece of fabric that I told myself was a man's tie because any other option sent my mind straight to places it shouldn't go.

Then, his mouth still curled in a grin that was part amused, part dangerously sensual, he tied the fabric over his eyes, covering them completely.

"There," he said, voice low and throaty. "Now I'm blind."

I should still tell him to leave. I really, really should. But, somehow, the words stuck in my throat. Maybe what I needed was some wine to get them out. I reached over the side of the tub, grabbed the glass with a soapy hand and drained most of it, all the while unable to tear my eyes away from him.

Adrian walked over to the tub, his steps never hesitating. Was that because of how well he knew the loft's layout, or because he could still see? My mouth felt like it went dry, so I finished the wine and pressed the glass into his hand. He took it from me and poured another, not spilling a drop. Were his senses that sharp? Or was the blindfold somehow see-through? This time, my hand shook a little as I accepted it. Another swallow later, and I put it down.

"Lay back, Ivy."

He seemed to be staring right at me as he said it, although that black swath of fabric was still covering his eyes. I repeated to myself that this was a bad idea even as I did what he said. Adrian went around to the back of the tub, kneeling so that he had better access. Then his hands settled on my shoulders and he began to rub in firm, duplicate patterns that found my tenseness and relentlessly coaxed it into lessening.

Oh, the feel of those strong, smooth strokes on my skin! They were blissful, soothing and enticing all at the same time. A soft sound escaped me, not a sigh, not a moan. Something else.

After several more minutes of that pleasurable attention, his thumbs slid up, kneading my neck while his fingers and palms continued to do truly wonderful things to my shoulders. Unbidden, I squirmed to give him better access, and that slight movement shifted the water around me, causing the hidden waves to stroke me in much more intimate places.

"Your skin is so soft," Adrian breathed, brushing my neck with his lips for the briefest moment before leaning back. "I can't get enough of touching you."

Then his hands went lower, massaging the length of my back with strong, supple movements. They skillfully manipulated my tendons and muscles, played along my rib cage like piano keys, and teased my spine with short, hard little pinches that had me arching in bliss. Water rippled over me with every shift of his hands, and sometimes, his mouth skipped across my flesh, vanishing before I could savor the feel of it, and replaced by more deep, soothing circles.

Whether it was the wine or the drug-like effects of his touch, my upper body began to feel as if had been replaced with melted caramel. Even my arms were limp after he'd rubbed them from fingers to shoulders. Each breath filled my lungs with warm, humid air and my eyelids felt heavy, but I kept them open. Water had spilled over him from his movements, highlighting his muscles more clearly than oil, and watching his hands move over me was as mesmerizing as it was arousing.

"Do you know how much I love touching you this way?"

His thick, growled voice made gooseflesh race over me even though I was submerged in hot water. In reply, I parted my lips and tilted my head up. He leaned forward until his mouth grazed mine, and a low laugh teased my lips.

"Did you want something else, Ivy?"

"Yes," I breathed. "You."

And I reached up, grabbing his hair and pulling his head down until his mouth slanted over mine.

For a few mind-shattering moments, there was nothing except the fierce sensuality of his kiss and the scald of excitement I felt when he hauled me out of the tub. Water sloshed everywhere, soaking him and the floor as he picked me up and carried me over to the bed. He didn't stop kissing me, and when he laid me against the silk-covered bedding, I was gasping for breath against his mouth. Then his body covered mine and his hands moved over me in ways that erased my prior relaxation, replacing it with tingling, pulse-pounding need.

That's why a noise of sheer protest left me when he suddenly sat up, holding me down when I moved to follow him.

"Shh. Something's wrong."

His words and the harsh urgency in his tone turned my desire to fear. I let go of him, looking all around but not seeing anything. What was it?

Then a loud, very familiar snarling sound came from outside, followed by a hard thump above us that shook the entire ceiling from its impact.

"Brutus," Adrian said darkly. "He feels it, too."

"What is it?" I said, pulling the sheet around me.

Adrian leaped off the bed, grabbing my clothes and throwing them at me. "Something big is coming."

I began pulling on my clothes without checking to see if they were inside out. "Another demon realm?"

Adrian looked at the wall as if he could see beyond it, and his body was so tense, it seemed as though one hard blow could shatter him where he stood.

"No, but if I'm right, it's just as bad."

CHAPTER TWENTY-THREE

The words were barely out of his mouth when the whole chapel began to shake. Brutus's snarl turned into a roar, and I was suddenly hit with the same invisible force I'd felt when I thought I'd located the staff. In the next moment, a crashing sound reverberated throughout the chapel.

"Brutus, *larastra*!" Adrian shouted, grabbing me and pulling me toward the opposite wall with his body covering mine.

Before I could ask anything, wood exploded from the ceiling. Then another tremendous bash showered the loft with shattered stone tiles. A third bash caved in a section of the ceiling and revealed Brutus, who was using his great bulk like a battering ram. The tub overturned, spilling water everywhere, when Brutus's fourth and final bash created a hole large enough for the gargoyle to fit through. Adrian shoved me at Brutus, yelling *"Tarate!"* at the gargoyle, before spinning around and running toward the entrance to the loft.

My right arm flamed with pain at the same moment that I saw something impossible: the eye-covered demon bursting up through the floor with all the power of his three sets of batlike wings. Brutus beat his own powerful wings and I was propelled backward through the chapel's ceiling, gripped in the gargoyle's mighty arms. Another rush of wings had me looking down at the chapel and campus from several stories up, and what I saw was equally awful and unbelievable.

Black funnel clouds were snaking their way horizontally through the buildings. The campus lights went out, plunging the area into darkness. Only soundless lightning flashing across the sky provided brief illumination, and it showed people spilling out from those thin, pitch-colored clouds. Wherever they went, screams followed, and ice and blood was left in their wake.

"Brutus, go back!" I ordered, realizing what was happening.

This area wasn't being swallowed by a demon realm. Instead, it was being flooded by one. I didn't know if the walls of the nearby realm had crumbled, allowing that malevolent, freezing world to spill out onto this one the same way water spilled out into nearby towns after a large dam had burst, or if a powerful demon had orchestrated the realm breach. Either way, Blinky had taken advantage and had used one of those leaked realm swaths like a series of supernatural stepping stones to walk right over the hallowed ground of his prison, and as I was well aware, Blinky was *not* in a good mood.

"Go back," I repeated to Brutus when he kept flying me farther away. *"Tarate, tarate!"*

He only flew faster. I struggled uselessly, all the while cursing myself for not learning more Demonish, and cursing Adrian for ordering the gargoyle to fly me away. Why would he do that when I was the only one who had a weapon that could kill demons? It's not like Adrian could've forgotten that!

Brutus didn't slow down until I saw the tour bus below us. We'd parked it well away from the campus because we'd taken the smaller, less conspicuous new Mustang to the chapel. That meant the bus wasn't near those dangerous realm swaths, and when I saw the Mustang parked next to it, I realized that neither were Jasmine and Costa.

Relief mixed with my seething impatience. They were safe, but Adrian wasn't. As soon as Brutus landed and let me go, I began shouting orders to the gargoyle.

"Brutus, *tarate*! Get Adrian, now!"

Brutus chuffed and beat his wings, soaring up into the night. Hopefully, Adrian's name and the Demonish word for *go* were enough for Brutus to understand what to do, but I wasn't about to leave that to chance. I ran into the bus, so frenzied that I barely noticed Jasmine and Costa's guilty expressions as they both leaped up from the couch.

"Give me the Mustang's keys," I demanded.

Costa pulled them out of his pockets far too slowly. "What's going on?"

"Realm wall's crumbling," I said as I strode over and snatched them from him. "I gotta get Adrian."

Jasmine grabbed my arm. "Wait, we'll come with you. You can't go alone, it's too dangerous!"

"That's why you can't come with me," I snapped. "Blinky is out, and with the realm bleeding all over the campus, there's more where that demon came from."

I shook Jaz off, ignoring her insistence to come with me and Costa's urgings for me to wait. Then I ran outside, slamming the door on the Mustang and locking it. I'd just thrown the car into gear and hit the gas when a dark figure appeared right in front of me.

I slammed on the brakes when his face was revealed in the headlights, but still, I banged into him. Zach didn't react in anger at nearly being run over. Instead, the Archon's mouth quirked, as if I'd amused him by hitting him.

"Get out of the car," he said in a pleasant voice.

I revved the engine instead. "Move away, Zach! You're not stopping me from going after Adrian."

"No, I'm not," he agreed mildly. "But if you get out, I can get you there much faster and safer."

I hesitated only a second before killing the engine and getting out of the car. Archons claimed that they never lied, and so far, that hadn't been disproven. If Zach really could get me to Adrian faster, I wouldn't waste any more time arguing.

And if he was about to prove that Archons *could* lie, then I'd find a way to make him pay.

"Let's go," I said. "Are we going to fly or something?"

I'd never seen him do that, but if a gargoyle could fly, an Archon should be able to. With another faint smile, Zach shook his head. Then he grasped my hand and pulled.

I fell forward into blinding light. For a moment, I felt like *I* was the one flying because my body was suddenly weightless, soaring and free. Then the light crystallized into colors and shapes. Warmth poured over me, soft grass teased my feet and, when I inhaled, the air was scented so heavily with flowers and flora that breathing it in felt like the world's most extravagant aromatherapy treatment. I looked at Zach, and for a split second, I saw something bright and formless shimmering inside him.

Then it faded into his normal appearance of a young, attractive African-American man with close-cropped hair and deep, walnut-colored eyes. Another glance showed that we were in the middle of a vast, flowering field, with lush trees offering shade from the warm, radiant sunshine. Blue-tinged mountains cradled the horizon, and sparkling creeks wound through the valleys below. Everything was so beautiful, it looked like Zach had pulled me inside a Monet painting, but instead of being charmed, I was panicked.

"What is this? You promised to take me to Adrian!"

"And I will," Zach replied, his faint eye roll adding, *O ye of little faith.* "He's right through that door."

I looked around, seeing nothing but the same exquisite landscape. "What door?"

"The invisible one," Zach replied, maddening me. "It can't be seen, Ivy. Only felt, so stretch out your hands and feel it."

I clenched my fists instead. "We don't have time for this. Adrian could be dying right now."

"He's not," Zach said, his tone turning sharp. "And it's past time you learned what you already should have figured out. Everything the demons have is a duplicate of something else."

"What the hell is that supposed to mean?" I snapped.

Zach shot me a warning look for my choice of words. "Adrian isn't hurt at the moment, but that could change, if you choose to keep arguing with me instead of doing what I say."

I wanted to slap him, but I didn't because he might smite me on the spot. Plus, he was right; the longer I argued, the longer it would take for me to get to Adrian.

So, I thrust out my arms and began to walk. I looked ridiculous, as if I was trying out for a spot in an old-style zombie movie, and worse, I didn't feel anything. Right as I was about to demand that Zach at least play hot or cold to give me a hint on which direction, something sizzled across my hands.

I stopped, reaching out again after I'd instinctively yanked them back. Another sizzle, this time up to my forearms, and right before my eyes, my hands disappeared.

I swung around, staring at Zach with awed comprehension. "Adrian just showed me that hallowed objects have evil counterparts, and if everything demons have is a duplicate of something else, then there aren't just demon realms and demon gateways. There are also Archon realms and gateways, so this—" my wave indicated the bright, stunningly beautiful landscape around us "—is an *Archon* realm."

Zach smiled; a pure, genuine smile without any of his usual irony, sarcasm or challenge. The difference was night and day, and for a moment, I again glimpsed that incredible, ethereal form that pulsed against the edges of his skin, reminding me that his body was only meant to cover up what he really was.

"Close," he replied. "Archons do come and go from places like this, but we dwell in the higher realms. This realm and others like it were originally made for humans. After the fall of man, all of them were sealed off, yet they still have gateways."

Stories I'd long ago dismissed as myths filled in what he didn't say, and I looked around with a fresh sense of awe.

"Eden," I breathed. "This realm is *Eden*, or at least, one of the Edens." And if it was a realm… "Time moves differently here, doesn't it? That's why you're not concerned about getting me to Adrian."

Another smile, though this one had his usual, ironic edge. "Haven't you noticed that if you merely stop worrying for a few minutes, you are able to think far more clearly?

"Have you seen my life?" I countered. "It's been a nonstop roller coaster of stress, danger and impossible expectations, so worry-free contemplation time? *Not* in large supply."

Zach sighed. "Your mind should rule your circumstances, not the other way around."

My fingers began to drum against my leg. "Easy for an all-powerful Archon to say."

His eyes blazed with light for a brief moment. "I am not all-powerful. I can be hurt and killed, as can those I love. Our differences are fewer than you allow yourself to believe."

Hardly. If I had his abilities, people wouldn't be dying on the streets of Marquette University right now. Zach knew what was going on, yet instead of helping them, he was lecturing me about worrying and willpower. He might not be in a hurry to save anyone, but I was.

"Is that so?" Zach said, raising a brow. "What if I told you that Adrian will survive tonight, but many people won't, unless you do something to help them? Would you still be in a hurry to return, if you knew that only strangers' lives were in danger instead of Adrian's?"

He really thought Adrian's was the only life I cared about? "Can I cross through the gateway without you?"

Zach's lips curled; *definitely* not a real smile this time. "Yes.

When you get to the other side, mark the spot where you came out. Then, return the same way. No one can follow unless you pull them through, so on this side, you're safe."

My irritation with him vanished with this news. "I can pull anyone over here with me?"

"Anyone," Zach repeated, challenge edging his tone. "Except demons, of course. Archons can't cross into their worlds and demons can't cross into ours. So, what will you do?"

I gave Zach a hard look as I stretched out my hands, feeling for the energy surge that marked the gateway. He might be content with letting people die when he could do something about it, but I wasn't.

"Just you watch."

CHAPTER TWENTY-FOUR

I landed on the other side with my usual grace, which meant face-first into the pavement. Oh well, so I'd never be a ballerina, big deal. I jumped up, shook my head to clear it and looked around, my eyes taking a second to adjust after the brightness of the Eden realms.

The campus looked like a war zone. Black, snakelike clouds were still strafed through several buildings, but either the view was different from the ground or there weren't as many as I'd first thought. Despite that, I couldn't count all the people that were running around in a panic, and more than a few fires had started. Surprisingly—or not surprisingly, considering how infiltrated minions tended to be in places near demon realms—I didn't see any police or firefighters.

My brave words to Zach now landed on me with the force of a thousand bricks. These people had no one to help them. I wasn't a superhero and I wasn't nearly up to the task of being a savior, but I was all they had, so I had to make this count.

First, I had to mark the gateway. A glance around showed that I'd spilled out onto West Wisconsin Avenue, in front of Zilber Hall. I didn't have anything to write with—hell, I didn't even have a bra, underwear or shoes!—so I used the only thing I had to mark the site. My blood.

I ran over to the no-parking sign and ripped it off. Then I used one of the sharp metal edges to gouge my arm, smearing the blood over the spot where the energy pulses were the strongest. I left the sign there, too, but it would probably get blown off. An unnatural windstorm swirled around the campus, no doubt caused by the demon realm spilling out onto this place.

As soon as I'd marked the gateway, I ran to the nearest median. The narrow strip between the streets was lined with trees and shrubs, but I wasn't there to admire the aesthetics. I was looking for rocks.

After digging madly through the dirt, I found some, and stuffed a couple handfuls of them into my pockets. My tattoo was starting to change from brown to gold, but it hadn't uncurled into a weapon yet. I must not be close enough to the demons that were riding through the realm spillage as if it were their own personal monorail. Time to change that.

I kept the biggest rock in my hand and ran toward where the screams were the loudest. The landscape of buildings, streets and churches looked completely different than when Adrian, Jasmine, Costa and I had strolled through here hours ago. Darkness had since claimed it, and that darkness was more than the absence of light. It was a living, writhing force that brought death and terror, literally, judging from the minions and demons that spilled out of those snakelike plumes.

"Make for the churches!" I began to shout at the people. "Everyone, get to hallowed ground as fast as you can!"

I repeated that chant over and over, only to be ignored by all who heard it. Up ahead, a minion dragged a screaming girl who resembled my former dorm mate toward one of those dark flumes. I ran toward them, but they disappeared into the realm tentacle before I could reach them, and I couldn't cross it to save her. I wanted to scream out of sheer frustration. Instead, I channeled my raging emotions into something else. If no one would listen to me and run for hallowed ground, then I would force the minions to pick on someone their own size.

I flung myself right into the midst of two more minions, who were forcibly corralling a group of students toward another realm flume. My adrenaline was so high, I smashed the rock over the first minion's head, then ducked under the punch the second one threw before head-butting him in the midsection. He hadn't been expecting my strength, so it knocked him flat, and then I slammed my foot down onto his neck.

The crunch I felt coincided with him going completely limp. A rush of wind warned me to whirl, and the minion whose head I'd bashed missed tackling me by only an inch. His momentum sent him sprawling, and I leaped onto his back before he could roll over and attack me again. With all of my strength, I smashed the rock into his head again. This time, I felt his skull give, and when I jumped off, he was as dead as his now disintegrating friend.

"Head for the nearest church!" I ordered the stunned group of students. "As long as one of those black flumes isn't on it, you'll be safe."

"Screw this," one of the guys muttered, running off. With a frightened bleat at the bodies turning to ash, the other girls followed him, and none of them were headed toward a church.

My teeth ground together. So many innocent people were getting hurt, killed and kidnapped right now, and as these crowds and the tourists at Scotty's Castle had taught, everyone was too panicked to do what I said. My best bet was to distract the demons and minions from continuing their evil roundup, and I happened to know the perfect bait. Me.

"I am Ivy Jenkins, the last Davidian!" I yelled, holding up my right arm with its now glowing, uncurling sling for emphasis. "Come and get me, demons!"

All the demons and minions within earshot stopped what they

were doing and began to run toward me. *Oh shit*, I thought, realizing that there were more of them than I had anticipated. A lot more. I didn't even have enough rocks on me to take out half their number, but I didn't have to fight them. All I had to do was outrun them. So, I spun around and ran.

My plan to distract them from hurting innocent people worked. Within a staggeringly short amount of time, it looked like I was leading a macabre version of a parade. Gleaming-eyed minions outnumbered their masters by about five to one, but quick looks behind me revealed that at least ten demons were hot on my heels. None of them had wings, though one had the head of an owl, another had long horns and another had Medusa-like snakes protruding from her head.

I began to notch rocks in my sling and hurl them at the horde without really aiming. I didn't have the time to. I was already running as fast I could while using a supernatural weapon that made my arm feel as though it had been set on fire. Add that to avoiding those winding realm tunnels that more demons could be hiding in, plus trying to run away from the most populated areas to give the people a chance to get away, and it shouldn't have surprised me that I felled very few of the monsters chasing me.

That was fine, I reminded myself, putting everything I had into increasing my speed. I knew where the Archon gateway was, and once I was through it, none of them could follow. In the Eden realm, I could gather all the rocks I needed and come back through the gateway with my slingshot blazing. They wouldn't even know what hit them.

A large man stepped out from behind one of the buildings, and relief swelled in me when I recognized him even though he was still about a hundred yards away.

"Ivy, this way!" Adrian shouted, motioning me toward him.

I changed course and headed toward him instead of taking the next right toward the Eden gateway. With more relief, I noted that Adrian didn't look hurt after his tangle with Blinky. In fact, he didn't even look wet from my bathwater anymore, and when had he found the time to change clothes? He hadn't been wearing that outfit the last time I saw him—

Realization hit me and I skidded to a stop a good twenty yards away from him. This might *look* like Adrian, yet it couldn't be. And I only knew one demon who could shape-shift into someone's exact likeness, but he was supposed to be dead. Again.

"Demetrius," I panted.

Adrian's form blurred. The unfamiliar clothes that had tipped me off turned into shadows that spread over the demon like a layer of oil. In the next instant, it parted, revealing pale skin, long black hair, a dark pink mouth and the blackest eyes I'd ever seen.

"So," Demetrius drawled. "You're not as stupid as I thought you'd be."

I had another moment to note that his shadows hugged his frame instead of towering behind him in their usual, formidable array. Then reality slammed home. I had succeeded in luring minions and demons away from the helpless, panicked people on campus, but Demetrius's shape-shifting trick had caused me to veer away from the gateway. Now I was trapped between a murderous crowd at my back and a far more deadly obstacle in front of me, and I was all out of rocks.

"The realm leak wasn't a result of crumbling walls, was it? *You* spilled the realm onto the campus," I accused, trying to stall so I could figure out my next move.

"Of course," Demetrius replied with naked satisfaction. Then his voice lowered to a hiss. "You destroyed my shadows." He took a step toward me, rage contorting his features. "You will suffer for that."

In response, I began to spin the sling. He didn't know the notch that was supposed to hold a rock was empty. Besides, the rope itself was hallowed. It might not kill him, but if it touched him, it would hurt, and I intended to lash him with it until he was distracted enough for me to run by him.

"One more step, and I'll finish the job I started with your shadows," I warned.

He smiled, so satisfied and chilling that I knew my bluff has failed. "If you could, you would have already done so."

I refused to be deterred by how easily he'd called my bluff. *He's only one demon*, I reminded myself, spinning the sling faster. And without his shadows, he was no bigger than an average man. I risked a quick glance behind me. Grins began to wreath the faces of the demons and minions who'd chased me. Shouts rang out, and I recognized enough Demonish to know that they were suggesting different ways to kill me.

Not today, I thought fiercely, about to turn back to Demetrius and lash him with my sling. Then something in the sky caught my eye. The crowd didn't see it. They were all facing me.

A large form swooped down behind them and began ripping a path through the center of the murderous horde. Glowing, red eyes appeared between the bloody row, and a fierce surge of pride coursed through me. It was Brutus, plowing through the crowd with incredible velocity, his granite-hard wings cutting down everything in his path as if it was grass and he was the lawn mower.

"No!" Demetrius roared.

I ran toward Brutus, not caring that I was also heading toward the remains of the bloodthirsty crowd. Nothing short of a surface-to-air missile could stop Brutus.

His head and shoulders were so large, I hadn't noticed Adrian crouched behind him until his arm shot out, hand extended for me to grab. I reached up—and a horned demon lunged at me, knocking my hand away. In the same instant, he grabbed Adrian's arm and yanked. With Brutus's continued velocity in the opposite direction, Adrian was ripped from the gargoyle's back.

Multiple shouts sounded as Adrian fell into the crowd. I

rushed toward him, but then was snatched up as Brutus's wild grab for me sank his claws into my shoulders. I screamed as those claws dug deep, hauling me above the crowd. Brutus tried to grab Adrian next, yet he had already been swarmed. Denied of their chance to watch me get murdered, the minions and demons tore at Adrian with all of their unspent vengeance. His arms flashed in a flurry of ferocity as he fought them, but in moments, he was overcome. There were simply too many of them.

"No!" Demetrius shouted again. "Stop!"

I thought that furious roar was directed at me. Brutus was beating his wings, but we were flying right at Demetrius, and even without his lethal shadows, we were low enough that Demetrius could reach me with one good jump. I braced myself to fight. To my complete disbelief, Demetrius ran right past us, throwing himself into the group that surrounded Adrian.

"Get your hands off my son!" he howled.

My own screams drowned out everything as Brutus shifted his grip, his claws tearing out of my flesh as he dropped me, only to grab me in a firmer grip a second later. In this new position, I was able to reach for the harness around his neck, and I hauled myself from his arms up to his back. My shoulders flamed from the multiple puncture wounds and the added agony from the hallowed sling being activated, but I gritted my teeth and wound the reins around my fingers.

Pulling up meant *fly higher*, pulling down meant *dive*, and pulling straight out meant *cruising*. Adrian hadn't taught me what position meant *murder all the bad guys*, but I intended to find out.

"Come on, Brutus," I yelled. "Let's do this!"

CHAPTER TWENTY-FIVE

I pulled up, and Brutus began to blast us into the sky. Even though I was in a frenzy to get back to Adrian, we needed the velocity. Once we were about a hundred stories up, I turned Brutus so he'd have plenty of space to circle back around to the remains of the crowd, and then I yanked the reins down.

Brutus dove so fast that it looked like the ground was rushing upward to meet us. At the last moment, he leveled out and headed toward the crowd without me even needing to steer.

"Good boy!" I shouted. "You know exactly what we're doing!"

Then, I tucked my head behind his bulky shoulders the way Adrian had. Otherwise, at this speed, I'd decapitate myself when Brutus collided with the crowd, and I wanted other peoples' heads to roll, not mine. Right before we hit, I gripped Brutus as tight as I could and braced for all I was worth.

Despite that, when Brutus plowed into the minions and demons, the impact almost knocked me off his back. Blood spattered me and countless thuds felt like they were rattling my bones as body parts were sheared off from the bladelike effect of his wings. If I didn't trust him so much, I'd worry that

Adrian would inadvertently be cut down, too. But I did trust Brutus, so I held on for dear life as the gargoyle hacked his way through the crowd.

When we came out on the other side, Brutus swung around so fast that my legs flew out behind me. Only my grip on the reins kept me from being launched off, and when I scrambled back on and saw what was left of the crowd, I was stunned.

Ashes littered the ground in piles that coated the body parts Brutus had just hacked off so ruthlessly. Only a few people were left standing. The rest were all dead, and that hadn't been Brutus's doing. Despite the gargoyle's best efforts, he could only kill minions, and there had been a lot more demons here. For a moment, I didn't understand. Then I heard a furious bellow followed by a voice I knew all too well.

"I told you not to touch him," Demetrius snarled, grabbing one of those few remaining figures. His shadows stabbed out from his hands, their reach minuscule compared to before, but the pale-haired demon in his grasp screamed. Then dark, smoking holes appeared in those small stab wounds. They grew, spreading all over the pale-haired demon's body, until they turned the screaming demon into ashes right before my eyes. It only took seconds, and the remaining demons exchanged a look of terror before running for the nearest realm plume.

Then, something moved in the heap of ashes and body parts, followed by the sound of Adrian groaning. Brutus heard it, too. He let out a warning snarl and flared his wings into chopping position. Then he began to lumber toward the demon.

"Stay back," Demetrius snapped, and I was so shocked at what I saw next, I actually pulled on Brutus's reins to stop him.

Unless I was hallucinating, I was watching the most evil demon I'd ever encountered gently lift Adrian's prone form from the ashes. He wiped them off Adrian's face, revealing bloodstains and more than a few slashes. Adrian groaned again, but he didn't open his eyes, and his limbs had the kind of looseness that spoke of a severe concussion or something worse.

"You killed your own kind to protect him," I said, still shocked beyond belief. "Why?"

Demetrius looked at me. His usual, venomous hatred quickly filled his dark gaze, but in the instant before it, I saw something I would've sworn was impossible from a demon.

Love.

Despite all the horrible things he'd done to Adrian, and despite the fact that Demetrius was as close to evil incarnate as anything could come, he truly loved Adrian. If I hadn't seen the proof for myself, I would never have believed it.

"He is my son." The words were spit at me, then his voice softened as he looked back at Adrian. "Minions can't kill him, but demons could, and they weren't obeying my orders to stop."

His words sank in, bringing with them a realization that rocked me. I didn't want to believe it, but in that moment, the truth was too obvious to be denied. Demetrius's revelation that only demons could kill Adrian just confirmed what I now knew all the way to my soul. Demetrius had been hiding the truth in plain sight every time he referred to Adrian as "my son."

"You're his father," I breathed. "His *real* father."

Demetrius set Adrian down and rose. Brutus reared up in a threatening manner, but the demon didn't move toward me. Instead, he smiled, and the wisps of his shadows sliced the air around him as if yearning to be cutting into my flesh.

"The only reason I'm letting you live is because Adrian needs manna and I don't have any." Demetrius's tone was light, yet his gaze held no less hatred. "So, take my son and heal him, Davidian. I'll save killing you for the next time we meet."

With that, Demetrius raised his arms, and the unnatural wind that had been swirling around the campus picked up speed, increasing until it felt like a hurricane had landed on us. More incredible was how the black tunnels began to pull back, leaving the buildings and returning to the realm they had spilled out from. Flashes of lightning revealed that realm. In it, as if looking through a dark, frozen mirror, I caught a glimpse of all the buildings, streets and cars that were here, but over there, they were desolate and ice-covered. Then, with a rush of wind strong enough to knock Brutus back a few feet, Demetrius, the realm and all of those encroaching tunnels simply disappeared.

As if on cue, police and fire truck sirens began to ring out. I looked back at Adrian. The ashes around him were gone, as were the body parts that had turned to ash during Demetrius's mind-blowing display of power. I wasn't sure if this was a trick or if Demetrius was really letting me go so I could heal him.

Didn't matter. I slid off Brutus's back and grabbed some of the rocks that the gale-force winds had scattered across the ground. If this was a trick, I'd be ready. With rocks in my pocket and one notched in my sling, I ran over to Adrian.

Brutus beat me there, and his wings formed a protective shield around us as I knelt beside Adrian. He was still unconscious, and he was covered in so much blood and soot that I had to feel him to judge which wound needed immediate attention.

A crashing sound made me jerk up with my sling at the ready. Relief filled me when I saw that it wasn't Demetrius or another demon, but a familiar bus driving over fallen tree limbs, rubble and other debris left after the realm tunnels' retreat.

"Get in," Jasmine urged, opening the door. Then she yelled, "Adrian's down!" at Costa, and jumped out of the bus.

"Is he dead?" she asked, hurrying over.

I continued to search Adrian with my hands. The worst of his wounds seemed to be his head and a very nasty gash on his stomach. "No, but he's hurt pretty bad."

"We don't have any more manna," Jasmine said, telling me something I already knew, not that I had been about to share that information with Demetrius.

I glanced at the bus, then back at the street sign that Demetrius's unearthly winds had blown over.

"Help me load Adrian into the bus, then follow me. I think I know where we can get some."

CHAPTER TWENTY-SIX

I wasn't about to put Demetrius's promise to kill me the next time we met to the test, so I didn't go into the Eden realm alone. I pulled Adrian, Jasmine, Costa and even Brutus into the stunningly gorgeous realm. Now, no one could be taken as a hostage while I got the manna that Adrian needed. Zach was our supplier, so either he had some, or he knew where to get it.

Once through, Brutus took one look at the endless sunlight and ran for the nearest set of bushes. Zach seemed to be in the exact same spot that he'd been before, so either he'd been waiting on me, or he was really comfortable in that position. I knew it wasn't the time difference. What had been about half an hour on the other side should have equated to a lot longer here.

"I need manna," I stated. The words were simple, but my thoughts conveyed everything I didn't want Jasmine and Costa to overhear. *How could you not have told Adrian who his real father was? I know that you knew! You always know things like that!*

"Jasmine, Costa, would you go down to the tree with the white flowers at the bottom of the hill?" Zach replied. "Bring me several of their blooms. They contain manna."

I gave Zach an incredulous look as Costa took Jasmine's arm and started down the hill. "Manna grows on trees?"

He shrugged. "Where else did you think it came from?"

I clenched my fists to keep from doing something rash. Then I knelt beside Adrian and began applying pressure to his head and stomach wounds, all the while cursing Zach with my thoughts. We hoarded manna like gold because Zach only gave us a little at a time, yet it literally grew on trees in realms that he had un-limited access to? Unbelievable!

"You now have unlimited access to them, so you no longer need me for your supply," he replied in an unruffled tone.

My fists clenched tighter on the wadded-up fabric I held to Adrian's stomach. "That's information we could have used sev-eral months ago," I managed to say very calmly.

His pointed glance settled on my clenched hand. "Until you passed the first challenge and the slingshot merged with your body, you wouldn't have been able to enter them."

"But I'm a Davidian," I protested. "Judians can cross into demon realms, so I should be able to cross into Archon ones."

He let out a snort that somehow managed to sound both el-egant and imperious. "The forces that guard these realms are much stronger than the ones that guard the demon worlds. No bloodline is enough to give a human the ability to cross into them. Only the hallowed weapon in your flesh is powerful enough." Then Zach shocked me by adding, "You can't tell Adrian about Demetrius," as casually as if he were remarking about the weather.

"No way," I said at once. "I know what it's like to have peo-ple conceal *really important information* about your lineage from you. Adrian might have done that to me when we first met, but it was wrong, and I won't do the same to him."

"Will you never take anything on faith?" Zach muttered, holding up a hand when I started to respond. "If you need a rea-son, here it is. Tell Adrian now, and you will both die."

I didn't take those words as a threat. If Zach wanted us dead, we would be, many times over, so he must be warning us based on foreknowledge. Times like this, he seemed to want us to succeed, although his habit of sitting on the sidelines during most of our battles was an infuriating way for him to show it.

"Fine," I said, shooting a guilty look at Adrian while thinking, *I'm sorry.* "I won't tell him. But Demetrius might, now that he knows I know."

Zach made a dismissive motion. "Don't worry about him."

"Oh, sure, a demon with enough power to spill realms onto us *or* sweep them back up is nothing to be concerned about. His being Adrian's biological father *and* my superevil archnemesis is just the icing on the relaxation cake."

Zach's mouth twitched at my acid tone. "As I told you before, your mind and your willpower needs to rule your circumstances, not the other way around."

"And as I told you, easy for you to say," I muttered, but Jasmine and Costa's return had us leaving it at that.

"Is this enough?" Jasmine asked, holding a bundle out.

Zach glanced at the blooms that were shaped like a trumpet's horn. Costa had taken his shirt off and used it as a basket, allowing them to collect dozens of the white flowers.

"This will do," he said. "Crush them together. The pollen will coat the petals and turn the entire mixture into manna."

"Can I keep your shirt?" I asked Costa. I had nothing else to use as a container while I crushed the flowers. This realm might be stunning, but it lacked some basic conveniences.

"Of course," he said. "Need help?"

I spread his shirt flat on the ground and began crushing up the flowers. "I've got it."

Jasmine looked around, her expression reminding me of when we were kids and our parents took us to Disneyland. "This place...it's so beautiful, it doesn't even seem real."

"Yes," Zach agreed, with none of her awe. "That is why we

took the survivors from the Bennington realm to these worlds. Their tranquility assists with the healing process."

Costa made such a bitter-sounding noise that I looked up from my task. "I don't remember getting any angelic rehab after *my* time in the demon realms," he said in a steely tone.

"Me, neither," Jasmine added, her expression hardening.

Zach's arm swept out in a wide arc. "If you feel cheated and you want to stay in this one, then stay."

I paused in crushing the flowers. "Are you serious?" Jasmine and I asked at the same time.

Zach's stare was level, and uncompromising. "Yes. In fact, any of you can stay here as long as you wish, but remember, by doing so, you lose your chance to be a participant in this war."

I began crushing the flowers with more force than necessary. "That's not a real offer for me. I'm the last Davidian, so if I sat this war out by staying here, the realm walls would crumble and countless places around the world would look like the campus we just left."

"Correct," Zach replied in that infuriatingly calm tone.

I glared at him. "That's no choice, and you know it."

Zach glared back, only his eyes had lights shimmering in them. "It is a choice, and it comes down to this. You living happily here, or leaving this place to save strangers who will never even know what you did, let alone thank you for it."

"Demetrius, is that you?" I replied mockingly. "Because Zach, Archon Who Only Follows Orders, would never try to talk me out of fulfilling my much-anticipated destiny."

"Do you remember my telling you that Adrian's fate was in his own hands?" Zach replied, his tone far more sharp. "So is yours. The Creator gave all humans free will, and that gift is so strong, not even destiny can overcome it."

Everyone's eyes were suddenly fixed on me. My heart began to race, but I tried not to show how affected I was as I crushed the last of the blooms into the sticky, crumb-like substance.

Then I spread some onto Adrian's head and stomach while my thoughts careened over this unexpected offer.

What if me, Adrian, Jasmine and Costa *did* ride out the fall of the realm walls in a beautiful world where demons could never harm us? As I well knew, even if I found the staff, I might not be able to wield it long enough to fix the walls. The more likely scenario was my touching it, falling over dead and having demons dance around my corpse as they used the staff to send all the realm walls crashing down.

In fact, might it be *better* for everyone if I stayed? Sure, some realm walls would crumble, but not all of them, and if only *some* fell, then the majority of people would live. After all, if I stayed here, then the staff stayed lost. Demons had already struck out for millennia trying to find it on their own and I doubted their luck would change anytime soon. If I stayed, then demons couldn't find the staff through me, and if Adrian, Costa and Jasmine happened to stay with me, well, what was wrong with that? Weren't they also entitled to a little happiness after everything they'd been through?

Zach stared at me, hearing every thought as if I were speaking them out loud. His expression didn't change, but his dark, steady gaze reflected the truth of my rationalizations, and I hated what I saw in their reflection.

I didn't want to die, and I *really* didn't want the people I loved to die, either. There was nothing wrong with that, unless I was willing to trade our safeties for the lives of untold millions. If I was willing to do that, then I was as evil as the creatures I despised with every fiber of my being.

I looked at Jasmine and Costa. My sister's gaze was filled with silent urgings for me to take this way out. Costa's was jaded, a little knowing, and I flashed back to our conversation several days ago, although with everything that had happened, it felt like several years ago. *You need to find something else to fight for,* he'd said. I hadn't believed him then, but faced with such a momentous choice now, I knew that he was right.

I couldn't just fight for the people I loved. I also had to fight for everyone who couldn't fight for themselves, for everyone who didn't know there was a war going on around them, and for all those who'd suffered and died at the hands of demons and minions, my parents included.

"I don't understand your boss," I finally said to Zach, "but I have to believe that my bloodline and my abilities have given me a real chance to win this war, and I hope—" My voice hitched before I finished strongly with, "I hope if those two things aren't enough, your boss will care enough to make up the difference, but either way, I have to do this. So thanks for the offer, Zach, but no thanks."

A moan jerked my attention back to Adrian. His eyes opened, and he sat up, that horrible gash on the back of his head healed, as was the deep slash in his stomach.

"What happened?" he muttered thickly. "What'd I miss?"

"Nothing," I said, shooting a quelling look at Jasmine when she opened her mouth to respond. "Nothing at all."

CHAPTER TWENTY-SEVEN

Adrian had a barrage of questions that I fielded while trying not to out-and-out lie. How did we get away from Demetrius? What did I mean Demetrius had pulled the realm back into itself? Why would he do that? I was endlessly grateful that Costa and Jasmine hadn't witnessed any of this, so my explanations, although not the full truth, went unchallenged.

"Demetrius still doesn't want you dead, so when the other demons kept trying to kill you, he pulled the realm back to stop them," I'd said, leaving out the crucial reason *why*. "Plus, his shadows are mostly gone, so I don't think he felt up to taking on me with my slingshot and Brutus with his guillotine wings."

Answering his question of "What is this place?" was much easier. After I was done explaining about light realms, he looked around, disbelief stamped on his features.

"I didn't know these even existed. None of the demons ever talked about them, and neither did any minions."

I let out a shaky laugh. "Until a little over an hour ago, I didn't know they existed, either."

"Thanks for keeping that a secret," Adrian said to Zach, followed at once by "And nice of you to *finally* show up."

"If you are not the Ancient of Days, I am not required to run to you when you call," Zach replied almost airily.

Adrian glowered at him before returning his attention to me. "I'm surprised you couldn't see glimpses of these realms, especially since you can catch glimpses of demon ones."

"Nope," I said, the irony of that hitting me. "Guess I have enough darkness in me for hallowed weapons to hurt me, too, and for me to see the demon realms, but not enough light in me to see the Archon realms. If I didn't have the slingshot melded into my arm, I couldn't even cross into them, either."

Adrian stopped pacing to grasp me by the shoulders. "Doesn't matter. I'll be your darkness when you need it," he promised in a low, throaty voice.

"And I'll be your light," I replied at once.

His mouth crushed mine in a kiss that ended far too soon. "You already are," he whispered when he lifted his head.

Then he let me go to pace again, and I could almost see him snapping back into battle mode. "We need to get back to the campus. I have to get that tablet from Father Louis, and we need to get Brutus."

"Brutus is here," I said, gesturing toward the tall bushes the gargoyle was hiding in. "But you're right, we need to go back, especially since we have plenty of manna to help people."

Adrian gave a cursory look at the residue still smeared on his stomach. "How much did Zach give us?"

"He didn't. It grows on trees here," Costa supplied.

Adrian stopped in midpace to nail Zach with a glare. "Really?" he asked with sarcastic accusation.

"My thoughts exactly," I muttered before yelling, "Brutus!"

The gargoyle came out from the bushes, cringing and using his wings like a huge umbrella to block against the sun.

"Don't worry, we're going back to the darkness," I told him as I began walking toward the gateway that led to the campus.

Adrian and Brutus followed me. Costa did, too, but when

Jasmine began to fall in line, I stopped, turning around to face her. "You don't have to go. Why don't you rest a little here?"

She let out an exasperated noise. "I know I can't fight like the rest of you, but if the realm tunnels are gone, then the demons are, too, so none of us should need to. Besides, I can help by treating any seriously injured people with manna."

I hadn't meant to insult her, so I said, "Great," in a hurried manner and thrust Costa's shirt at her. "Good thinking."

She gave me a look that said she knew when she was being patronized. "I'm not stupid, Ivy. I know my limits."

Costa sidled up and placed a casual arm around Jasmine's shoulders. "She's also tougher than she looks. You're not the only person I trained when you were living at my house, Ivy."

When had that happened? Jasmine and I had practically been joined at the hip for those two months, and I hadn't seen Costa train her once. The only way I would have missed that was if they'd been sneaking out to do her training while I was asleep, or perhaps during one of my many trips to the grocery store...

All at once, I remembered their guilty expressions when they'd jumped up from the couch after I stormed into the bus earlier. My eyes narrowed as I looked at them. Was this the only thing they'd been hiding from me? Or was there something more?

"Great" was all I said, but I made a mental note to corner Jasmine later and find out if anything was going on with her and Costa. Not that Costa was a bad guy, but Jasmine was only eighteen, and Costa was...well, a lot, *lot* older.

Yes, I was being a total hypocrite by letting their age difference concern me since Adrian was over a century older than I was, but I couldn't help it. She was my little sister. If I didn't look out for her, who would?

I was still wondering if something more than friendship had been brewing between Jasmine and Costa when I pulled Brutus through the gateway first. But when we tumbled onto the street in front of Zilber Hall, the horrible aftermath from the realm spilling onto the campus chased everything else from my mind.

Fire trucks were lined up on several streets, spraying water onto the still-smoldering buildings. So many cop cars had their red-and-blue lights flashing that it cast a weird strobe effect over the campus. New ambulances were arriving as fast as other ones were leaving, their sirens almost indiscernible over the equally loud wails from the fire trucks and police cars. Students were either huddled together in groups, or were running around screaming out names as they searched for missing friends.

It was so awful, no one had noticed me and Brutus suddenly stumbling onto the sidewalk. Judging from the few people I made eye contact with, they were too shell-shocked to care even if they had seen us appear out of nowhere. We'd been in the light realm for at least half an hour, but on this end, it looked like it had only been minutes since Demetrius had pulled the realm tunnels back, so chaos still reigned.

"Keep an eye out for demons," I told the gargoyle, patting him on his wings. "I'm going back for the rest of them."

Once I had everyone back on this side, we scattered; Jasmine and Costa to treat the injured that the paramedics hadn't gotten to yet, and me and Adrian to find Father Louis.

We went to St. Joan's Chapel first. The roof had a huge hole from where Brutus forced his way inside to get to me, but I was surprised to see that the chapel doors looked like they'd been blown off with dynamite.

"Blinky," Adrian said by way of explanation, flashing me a quick, wry grin. "That demon *really* wanted to kill me."

Considering that Adrian had kept him locked up for the past several years, I didn't doubt it. "You shouldn't have sent me away with Brutus," I muttered. "Seriously, Adrian, don't ever do that again."

"I needed to slow him down to make sure you got away," he replied without the slightest hint of remorse.

I stopped our brisk pace to grab him. "I'm not the same girl you rescued all those months ago. I can take care of myself now, especially with the hallowed weapon in my arm. Your staying behind could've gotten you killed, just like your diving into a crowd of demons with Brutus almost got you killed. All I had to do was run by Demetrius and get to the Archon gateway, and I would've been fine. Stop thinking that you need to save me, Adrian." My voice softened. "Saving people is my job, re-member?"

His expression flashed between fury and tenderness, until I wasn't sure if he was going to kiss me or shake me. "I can't help it," he finally replied. "I see you in danger, and my world nar-rows to only one thought. Keep you safe."

He sounded so frustrated that I took his hand, pulling it up to kiss his knuckles despite all the dirt and blood on them.

"I love that you feel that way," I said with all sincerity, "but we both need to expand our worlds beyond concern for each other if we're going to win this war."

He looked like he was going to say something else, and then his mouth closed with an audible click. Instead, he brushed my face with his hand and turned around.

"Father Louis's car is still in the parking lot, so he didn't leave the campus," he said, getting back to the task at hand. "I'll try his cell."

Adrian pulled his phone out of his jeans pocket, then let out a snort. "Guess I should've known."

It was smashed as well as soaked from my bathwater, his blood and the blood of who-knew-how-many minions and demons who had tried to kill him. Adrian attempted to use it anyway, and then threw it down when the screen didn't even power on.

"We'll borrow one," I said, looking around to see if any of the people near us had one.

"Don't bother," Adrian replied, striding toward the chapel. "There's a phone inside here."

CHAPTER TWENTY-EIGHT

Father Louis didn't answer his cell phone. A sobbing student did, and from the details Adrian managed to get out of the hysterical guy, we headed over to the Jesuit Residence. I already feared the worst, but seeing the doors blown off the multistoried building the same way the chapel doors had been destroyed confirmed it.

"Blinky came here," I said, shooting a grim look at Adrian. "Do you think—?"

"Yes," he replied in a stony voice. "He went after Father Louis to get the map."

I didn't know if the Jesuit Residence had been on hallowed ground, but when I saw the long, ice-slicked puddle that snaked up to the building and continued past those decimated doors, I realized it didn't matter. A realm tunnel had spilled out here, allowing Blinky and any other demon all the access they wanted.

There was also blood. A lot of blood, and I tried not to step in the crimson swaths as we walked inside the building. The first thing I saw was two guys who looked to be my age, hugging each other in the corner. Two cops were with them, one getting their statements while the other cordoned off an area around a large, sodden hump in the biggest puddle of blood.

The last several cops I'd seen had been minions, so I kept my hands near the knives strapped under my shirt as we approached. We hadn't just used the phone back at the chapel. We'd also re-supplied ourselves with weapons from Adrian's stash in his loft. My right arm hadn't begun to hurt or glow, so at least there didn't seem to be any demons nearby.

"Officer," Adrian said, striding up to the cop by the blood puddle. "I need to see that man. I know him."

The cop turned to face Adrian. His face was very pale, but I was relieved when his eyes didn't show any unearthly flash of light in them. He was human, then, and just pale from shock.

"There's not much left to see," the officer replied, shaking his head. "Someone butchered him."

I closed my eyes. I hadn't wanted to believe that the bloody hump on the floor was Father Louis, even though deep down, I'd known that it was. He'd been such a kindly old man, and now he was gone, and in a horrible manner. It wasn't right.

"Not someone, some*thing*," one of the young Jesuits suddenly shouted. "I told you, it wasn't human!"

I went over to the two men, giving Adrian a sideways glance that I hoped he could interpret. One of these guys had the good father's cell phone, and if Blinky had taken the tablet, it was now our only link to the runes written on it.

"I've seen things tonight that defied explanation, too," I told them, mustering up some tears, which wasn't hard to do con-sidering how bad I felt about Father Louis's gruesome demise. "It's just so...so awful!"

With that, I flung my arms around the two guys, letting out loud, fake sobs. They hugged me back, either out of sympathy or continued trauma over what they'd seen. As soon as their heads were close, I halted my sobs to whisper an urgent message.

"Give me the priest's cell phone. These cops will never be-lieve what you saw, but I do, and I need what's on the phone to stop those creatures from hurting anyone else."

They reared back, giving me a startled look, but I only clutched them tighter and sobbed even louder.

"If you want Father Louis avenged, give me the phone," I hissed between those fake sobs. "Quickly!"

Something hard was pressed to my stomach. I grabbed it, slipping the phone inside my pocket before hugging the two men for real this time. "Thank you," I whispered.

Then, I turned around to see Adrian kneeling next to the bloody remains of Father Louis, ignoring the other cop's demands to back away. Adrian lifted the father's sodden robes, feeling around for a moment, and rose, his expression grim.

"It's not here," he said, ignoring the cops who were now both pointing their guns at him.

I was dismayed, but not surprised. Zach might not have been the only celestial being who knew that there was a map to the staff's location. Blinky had been there when we discovered the tablet, so he knew that it had been with the staff. Even if he hadn't heard of the map, he would've known the tablet was a clue, and he must have overheard Father Louis saying he was taking it to get the runes translated. If not for Father Louis's excitement in taking all those pictures, Blinky would have made off with our only link to the staff's location.

"Don't worry," I replied, patting my pocket. "I've got the photos."

Adrian glanced at the cops, who were ordering him to get on the ground with his hands on top of his head. Then he threw a challenging smile my way. "Think you can keep up?"

I snorted, understanding his meaning. "Can you?"

And then we both ran out of the building so fast, the officers could do nothing to stop us.

I told myself that it only made sense to return to the light realm. So far, the campus appeared to be minion- and demon-free, but I would be putting everyone's lives in danger if Demetrius or anyone like him returned to make another attempt at killing me. After all, they might have extra motivation now that Blinky had the tablet. With it, they might not even need me to find the staff anymore. For all we knew, its exact location was carved into the ancient stone block.

If I were being honest, however, I'd admit that I brought everyone back here because I wanted to. The safety, the sun, the warmth, the flower-strewn meadows that were so beautiful, it wouldn't surprise me if a unicorn appeared and suddenly started frolicking in them... I didn't want to let any of this go. Not yet. Being here felt like giving my soul some much-needed Xanax. Besides, apparently we had plenty to eat, too.

"There's fruit trees!" Jasmine announced after returning from a short walk with Costa.

Adrian shot her a jaded look. "Let me guess—apple?"

From her unfettered smile, she missed the irony, although Costa gave him an appreciative grin. "Yep, all kinds," she said happily. "Plus, olive trees, avocado trees and almond trees."

I'd be delighted to browse through the trees snacking on fruits and nuts, for more reasons than the simple fact that I was hungry. But, much as I loved everything about this realm, I had to get back on the hunt for the staff. I hadn't been lying when I told those Jesuits that I intended to avenge Father Louis's death, and everyone else who'd been killed tonight.

"You and Costa help yourselves. Adrian and I need to find Zach," I said. We'd been here for over an hour, but the Archon hadn't shown up. Maybe he was in another corner of this realm.

Adrian stood so fast, I realized he'd only been sitting with me because he thought I needed the rest. "Let's go."

Costa arched a brow. "Impatient to get your favor, huh?" he drawled with a knowing look that almost caused me to blush.

"We don't need Zach for that," I hastily said, then as Adrian swung a surprised glance my way, I amended, "Okay, not only for that. Zach is who-knows-how-old, right? And he knows all kinds of things, so maybe he knows how to read runes, too."

"He might," Adrian said, his expression turning thoughtful. "It's definitely worth a shot. I have no idea who Father Louis was going to show the tablet to, so that's a dead end, and for obvious reasons, I don't want just anyone looking at it."

"I do in fact read runic," a voice stated from nearby.

I turned around. Zach hadn't been behind us seconds ago, of course, but now, he was lounging a little higher on the grassy knoll as serenely as if he'd just roused himself from a nap. His ability to suddenly appear—and disappear—was something that continued to unnerve me, but at this moment, I was so glad to see him that I didn't point that out.

"Look at these photos of the tablet," I said, tossing Father Louis's cell at him. "Can you read the runes?"

Zach scrolled through the pictures. A little line stitched between his brows, as if he were concentrating very hard or having trouble seeing through the sun's glare on the screen.

"It's drawn by someone who obviously wasn't an expert in runic," he finally said, "but roughly translated, it says 'It is back in its holy home.'"

"What is that supposed to mean?" I burst out. "That's not a map, it's the vaguest riddle ever!"

"Maybe not," Adrian said, starting to pace. "Remember the history of St. Joan's Chapel that Father Louis told us about? The chapel originally came from France, so what if its old site is the 'holy home' that the staff was taken back to?"

"But there'd be nothing there now, right?" Jasmine asked, beating me to the same question.

"There might be a leftover slab, or something else to mark where the church was," Costa said, giving Adrian an appraising look. "And if Zach can read runes, the demon that snatched the tablet might be able to, also. Or he's bringing it to somebody who can, so it'll be a race to see who gets there first."

Adrian's features hardened as he looked at me. "We'll need to use demon realms to get there. A plane would take too long."

He didn't say out loud what the rest of his expression confirmed. The demons would know that their realms would be the fastest way for us to travel, too, so they'd be expecting us.

I wanted to go back to those frozen, pitch-black realms and fight more demons about as much as I wanted to brush my teeth with razors, but I got up at once. "Just give me a minute. I want to make sure I've got enough rocks for whatever happens."

"There is another alternative," Zach pointed out.

Adrian's stare was like a laser. "Are you finally going to fight with us side by side?"

Zach's dismissive gesture wasn't quite a shrug. "You know that Archons cannot enter the dark worlds, and as I have often reminded you, I only intercede when I am ordered, which I have not been in this case."

Adrian turned away, muttering, "Figures."

I didn't say anything, but I couldn't stop the stab of hurt I felt. After everything that had happened, Zach still didn't regard us as anything aside from obligatory tasks to be dealt with if the appropriate instructions came down? Not that I'd been so naive as to think the powerful Archon regarded us as friends, but I'd hoped... I'd hoped that he *cared*.

Jasmine came up to me, taking my hand. When I saw my hurt mirrored on her features, I forced my expression into a smile.

"Don't worry, we've got this," I told her, glad that my voice sounded light and confident. I'd had to give so many false reassurances over the past few months; I was finally getting good at them. To Zach, I simply said, "What alternative?"

In the time it took me to look from my sister to him, his features became impassive, though his dark stare reminded me that he'd heard all my thoughts. Still, for a split second, I saw something in his expression. It was gone so fast, I couldn't tell if it had been pity or contempt, but whatever it was, he'd felt it strongly enough to crack his usual inscrutableness.

"These realms are not bound by the limitations of their dark counterparts," he replied, nothing in his tone giving a hint to what he was feeling. "Each one of them contains a vortex that connects them together, so those with the ability to enter them can then be transported anywhere in the world where light realms exist. You need only to think of the destination you wish to go when you use the gateway, and it will take you there."

"Wow," I said, so impressed that I stopped trying to decipher Zach's elusive emotion. "You're saying that I can just *think* my way to where we need to go? Talk about an upgrade from using the demon realms to travel!"

"Anywhere other light realms exist, huh?" Adrian looked from me to Zach, but instead of being awed like I was, an expression of deliberate calculation took over his features. "And where might those be? France, I hope?"

Zach arched a brow. "You should know. These realms are in the same places where demon realms are. Every time they strike into your world, we strike back."

Now I was really impressed, and in the midst of that, also a little ashamed. I'd just been thinking about how Zach didn't care about us, and I regularly bemoaned how the rest of his kind as well as his boss didn't do enough to help humanity. But hearing about this made me wonder if there was a lot more going on behind the scenes in this war. For all our sakes, I hoped so.

"I'll get lots of rocks just in case, but other than that—" this time, my smile was real "—let's take a trip to France."

"Just me, Ivy and Brutus are going," Adrian said when Jasmine left my side and started gathering up her things.

Costa looked as surprised as my sister did. "Why?" he asked. "Ivy didn't have any trouble pulling all of us through."

A muscle flexed in Adrian's jaw. "If you're my friend, Costa, don't press this. Just stay here."

"*I'm* asking," Jasmine said, striding over to Adrian. "Why?"

I'd assumed it was to keep them safe since demons might be waiting for us there, which was why Adrian's reply stunned me.

"Demetrius dropped a realm on us within a few hours of our arrival in Death Valley. Then he leaked one onto us only a few hours after we showed up at the campus." Adrian's voice, already sharp, became harder than diamonds. "Once is coincidence, but twice is a pattern, and both times, the two of you were conveniently out of harm's way. That's why neither of you is coming with us now because I don't know which of you has been going behind our backs with Demetrius."

CHAPTER TWENTY-NINE

After a moment of shocked silence, I found my voice. "That's impossible. Neither of them would ever do that." Then, louder, "Jasmine, Costa, tell him you'd never do that!"

"Of course I wouldn't!" was my sister's immediate response. "You know how horrible I felt about what I told the demons when they tortured Tommy. Do you think I'd ever do anything even resembling that again?"

The stare Costa leveled at Adrian was full of anger. "After all these years, I never thought I'd *have* to say that I wouldn't betray you," Costa bit out.

"See?" I said. "You're wrong, Adrian!"

Adrian turned to Zach, who I just realized had remained ominously silent. "Well?" Adrian asked. "You know almost everything, so tell me, am I wrong?"

Zach let his gaze rest on each of us before replying, and though it only took moments, the tension grew and stretched, until my nerves felt as if they were about to snap.

"You are correct. One of you *has* been alerting Demetrius," Zach replied.

An explosion seemed to go off in my mind, making Jasmine's

sputtered denials and Costa's angry protestations fade into white
noise. As if I'd never seen them before, I stared back and forth
between the sister I loved and the friend I trusted. I didn't want
to believe it was true, but Archons never lied, and if I didn't
focus on how this bombshell ripped me apart emotionally, I'd
recognize that each of them had motive.

Jasmine had made it no secret that she lumped Adrian together with demons, to the point where she partially blamed
Adrian for her boyfriend's death as well as her awful treatment
in his former realm. What if that hatred had driven her to do
something terrible, like trying to get him killed? It wouldn't
be hard for her to reach Demetrius. All she would've had to do
was say his name in an unbroken mirror, and he would appear.

Costa knew that, too, and as he'd told me recently, he still had
difficulty forgiving Adrian for what had happened to him while
he was enslaved in Adrian's realm. Hadn't Costa also said that
he'd do anything to avenge his friend Tomas? Tomas had died
trying to help Adrian and me, and while it was minions who'd
shot him, maybe Costa blamed Adrian, too. After all, Tomas
wouldn't have been in Mexico to get shot if not for Adrian asking for Tomas's help.

It had to be Costa, I decided, reining in my spiraling emotions. Jasmine might hate Adrian, but she'd never risk me getting killed, too, and she knew I was number one on the demons'
hit list. Costa might like me, but if he was that determined to
punish Adrian by turning him over to Demetrius, he wouldn't
call it off on my account. We'd been though a lot, but at the end
of the day, I didn't mean nearly as much to him as Tomas had.

"...this is bullshit!" my sister was saying, and her screech cut
through my inner wrestling match.

"You bet it is," Costa flared, his dark brown eyes almost flashing in his agitation. "I know it wasn't *me*, and I was with Jasmine
both times, so it couldn't have been her, either!"

"You sure about that?" Adrian asked, his tone softer, but no less harsh. "She never left your side to go into another room for a moment? Would you even remember if she had?"

My gaze swung to Adrian. "It's *not* her," I snapped.

From the pitying look he gave me, he'd also come to his own conclusions about who'd done it, only he'd landed on Jasmine.

"It's not her," I insisted. "Jasmine would never do that to me, and Costa admitted before that he's still pissed at you! Hell, he's also never believed I'd be able to wield the staff without getting killed, so it's not like he'd think my death would take the rest of the world down with me. He already thinks everyone is doomed."

Costa replied with a burst of Greek that sounded as furious as he looked, and with his handsome features mottled from rage, that was saying something. Whatever his tirade was, it pissed Adrian off to a fantastic degree, too, because Zach had to catch his fist before he slammed it into Costa's face.

"Was that a confession?" Jasmine cried, coming over to me.

The look Costa threw our way was more scalding than his response. "Quit acting, Jasmine! We both know it has to be you."

"Fuck you, no it isn't!" she screamed back at him.

Zach still had ahold of Adrian's wrist, and when Adrian attempted to pull free, the Archon tightened his grip.

"Not until you are in control," Zach said coldly.

"If you'd just confirm who it is, we can end all this," Adrian snarled.

"No," Zach replied. "Until you are able to figure it out for yourself, you are not ready to accept the truth."

His cryptic response only made things worse, but when Zach didn't want to reveal something, all the raging in the world wouldn't make him. Plus, while we were fighting, demons could be descending on that former church site in France. As serious as the prospect of Costa's betrayal was—and after Zach's comment, I was 100 percent convinced it was Costa because that's the only truth Adrian wasn't ready to accept—getting the staff before the demons found it had to come first.

"Stop it, everyone," I said, raising my voice to a shout. "We have a staff to get, so Jasmine, Costa, you two are waiting here. You'll be safe," I added with a hard glance at Zach, whose oblique nod confirmed that he was staying with them. Good, because now, I didn't trust Costa around Jasmine. "When we get back, we'll figure this out."

Zach released Adrian's wrist. He rubbed it while his gaze landed on the three of them, seeming to make silent promises that I couldn't decipher. Then at last, he looked at me.

"Ready when you are, Ivy."

It felt like I had twenty pounds of rocks in my pockets. Good thing I'd worn jeans to the campus last night. If I'd had on a skirt, I wouldn't have been able to store nearly as much. I still didn't have on a bra, not having found it during our brief, former visit to Adrian's loft. I did have knives, holstered and strapped beneath my thankfully baggy T-shirt. As for shoes, well, I hadn't found mine in the trashed loft. If I hadn't been so upset by the betrayal revelation, I might have remembered to ask Jasmine if I could borrow her shoes before we left.

I hadn't been thinking about my feet, though. My thoughts had been split between Costa's betrayal and the possible fight we were walking into. Those thoughts were briefly put on hold when we tumbled out of the light realm in Lyon, France, which was as close as we could get to the chapel's original location of Chasse-sur-Rhône. We landed in a wooded area, with a huge, towering white structure that looked like a cross between a castle and a church looming above us. Amber-pink rays of sunrise highlighted the gorgeous Gothic building, making it appear to be a vision from the medieval past. If Brutus weren't so afraid of the sun, the gargoyle would've looked perfect soaring around the high, pointed turrets.

From Brutus's cringing, he wouldn't be doing any soaring in the sunshine soon. The leafy trees kept most of those bright rays off us, but too much was getting through for his liking, and with the time jump, that would only get worse. I'd estimated it to be around midnight in Milwaukee when we left. Here, it was the beginning of the day.

"What's that?" I asked, pointing at the castle/church.

Adrian glanced up. "The Basilica of Notre Dame. I wasn't sure where the light realm would spit us out, but I've been here before. Like Zach said, there's a dark realm nearby, and the basilica is a tourist trap, so there should be lots of cars."

I don't know why I thought that meant we were going to rent one. Neither of us had our passports or other identification, and I certainly didn't have any money. But still, I was surprised when Adrian snuck around to a parking lot, picked out an older-looking van and smashed out the back window.

Brutus shared none of my hesitation. He practically flew over and dove into the back door Adrian held open. I hurried over, too, but far more cautiously, looking around to see if anyone had seen and was now calling the police.

So far, no one was. I got in the passenger seat and Adrian got in the front. As soon as he did, he ripped some wires down from the base of the steering wheel, and in moments, had the van revved up and moving.

"How long have you known how to hot-wire?" I asked.

He flashed a sly grin my way. "Since the invention of cars. The newer models are harder, though. That's why I picked this one. It's big enough for Brutus and old enough not to have an alarm, let alone better safety measures beneath the wheel."

I felt bad about stealing someone's car, but consoled myself with the thought that if the person knew why we needed it, he or she wouldn't mind. What was a little car theft compared to trying to stop a demon apocalypse?

"Here," Adrian said, handing me Costa's cell phone. "Pull

up directions to Chasse-sur-Rhône. I don't think it's far, but it's been a long time since I've been in this area, so I could be wrong."

I did, feeling encouraged when I saw that it was only twenty miles away. Then I googled information about the chapel. Back in the fifteen hundreds, it had been called the Chapelle de St. Martin de Sayssul, and while I couldn't find an exact location for the old site, it said that it had been along the Rhône River Valley. Since Chasse-sur-Rhône was only three square miles in total, my plan was to start by the river and keep walking until I felt something hallowed. With luck, we'd grab the staff and be back in the nearest light realm before the owner of this van even realized that it had been stolen.

If we weren't lucky, then the police coming after us for a carjacking would be the least of our concerns.

"I'm sorry," Adrian suddenly said, giving me a guarded look. "Are you okay?"

I took in a deep breath, knowing he wasn't talking about traversing through the realms. "No, I'm not okay that we were sold out by a close friend, and I'm even less okay knowing that you still think it was Jasmine. She wouldn't do that, Adrian. No matter how much she doesn't like you, she'd never risk my life that way. I know her."

He let out a short grunt. "I know Costa, too. If he wanted me dead, he'd come at me head-on, not sneak behind my back, and if it's not him, then it has to be her."

"It's not," I said, my tone sharper. "I'd bet my life and yours on that, and since you know how I feel about you, you should know I wouldn't say that unless I was sure."

The look he gave me was gentle, and when he spoke, his voice was soft. "I believe that's true of the Jasmine you're remembering. But this one spent several weeks being tormented by Demetrius. That would break anybody, so the person she is now isn't the same person you grew up with. This Jasmine is hard, or she wouldn't have survived. This Jasmine might even think she's protecting you by getting rid of me, and she might have rationalized the danger she put you in by betting that I'd sacrifice myself to save you, and in that, she'd be right."

Some of my anger drained away as I looked at him. Yes, Adrian had proved more than once that he'd sacrifice himself to make sure I was safe. It didn't mean I agreed with him about Jasmine, but it meant I'd forgive him for doubting her.

And, when he finally realized that it had been Costa, I'd be there for him. That kind of betrayal bit deep, especially given Adrian's absolute belief that it couldn't be his friend, but simple numbers meant that if it wasn't Jasmine, it had to be Costa. After all, I knew it hadn't been *me*, and of course it hadn't been Adrian...

A dark thought teased my mind. I rejected it at once, mentally slamming the door shut on it. Adrian would never do that, destiny be damned. I'd been willing to bet my life that it wasn't Jasmine, and I'd bet it again that it couldn't be Adrian.

Yet that nagging thought continued to worm its way through my subconscious, returning as fast as I kept rejecting it. *He's half-demon*, it whispered, *and he's betrayed you before*. With 50 percent of his nature contaminated by evil and 100 percent of his destiny predicting that he'd be the one who would deliver me to demons, could I really be sure that it wasn't him?

Yes, I thought fiercely. And in about twenty minutes when we got to the former chapel site, I'd prove it by hopefully finding the staff and letting Adrian remove it from the ground. That's how sure I was that he would never betray me again.

Just like your ancestors, that thought mocked. They'd been sure, too. So sure that they'd bet *their* lives, and lost them.

CHAPTER THIRTY

I had never been to France before, but if I didn't die and the world didn't get splattered with demon realms, I'd love to come back. The tiny commune might not be nearly as popular as France's other cities, but it reminded me of a secluded glen, and the river we walked along only made it more picturesque. Adrian had his arm around me, and the relative silence of the early morning cast a hushed, peaceful lull over the area. If not for our circumstances, it might have been romantic.

"I've been here once before," Adrian remarked.

I was surprised. Had he been everywhere? Probably, I reminded myself. Adrian had had at least two normal life spans to travel, plus with access to realm vortexes, I supposed I shouldn't be surprised that he'd gotten around. "When?"

He gave me a sardonic smile. "The first time I slipped Demetrius's watch and explored the human world. I couldn't do it near my realm because too many people would recognize me, so I went through a vortex and it spit me out by the basilica. The sunshine, the cars, all the people... I'd never seen anything like it before. It freaked me out, so I started running and didn't stop until I reached this town. It was quiet here, so I stayed for a day, just taking it all in with amazement." Then his smile vanished. "Demetrius had such a fit when I went home that it took me a year to risk exploring this world again."

Brutus snarled as he darted from tree to tree, and that shattered my fascination with Adrian's story. Adrian whirled, looking for danger, and I pulled out a knife while I checked my arm. My slingshot wasn't glowing and no one seemed to be around. When Brutus snarled again, I realized he was doing it in general grumpiness about being out in the sun. He'd wanted to stay in the van, but we didn't know if we'd need a quick aerial getaway, let alone the protection of his lethal wings. Now those snarls, combined with his baleful looks, were his way of letting us know what he thought of that plan.

"Feeling anything yet?" Adrian asked, relaxing when he saw that Brutus was just expressing his displeasure.

"Just my toes getting cold," I replied.

Adrian glanced down, as if just now remembering that I didn't have on any shoes. "Aw, crap. Here, you can wear mine."

I stopped him in the process of kicking his off. "Don't bother. Your feet are twice as big, so I'd only trip."

He began to walk faster, his gaze darting around. "If we're lucky, this won't take long."

As if on cue, my senses began to perk up. A low, dinging vibration felt like it hummed along my subconscious, picking up in intensity as we continued to walk. By the time we'd gone another hundred yards, those dings had turned into inner gongs.

"Something's here," I said, keeping my voice low.

Adrian's hand tightened around the knife he had holstered in his jeans pocket. "Minions or demons?" he asked softly.

"Neither," I said, with a quick look around to make sure that I wasn't speaking too soon. "Something hallowed."

I began to walk away from the river, letting the supernatural sensor inside me guide my steps. Adrian and Brutus followed me, the latter snarling even louder when I took us well outside of the shelter of trees that had hugged the riverbank. Up ahead, I saw a line of warehouses, but in the clearing before that, on the gentle rise of a small hill, there was a crumbling stone structure that looked to be several hundred years old. Next to that, on a flat section of earth, I felt the ground beneath me change from grass and dirt to something harder. And the hardened ground sent my hallowed radar into overdrive, although it didn't physically knock me over or hurt to be near it the way it had when I'd walked into the crypt under the chapel at the campus.

"Here," I said, my voice a little hoarse from the mystical energy pouring into me.

Adrian knelt beside me, pulling at the grass. It didn't take long before he revealed large, flat stones. Judging from their size and placement, these weren't natural formations. They were the base of a structure that was no longer here.

And the hallowed item contained somewhere beneath these stones felt like it was calling out to me.

"Okay, let's get started," Adrian said with obvious relish.

I looked around, realizing that in our haste to get here, we'd forgotten something very important. Namely, any tools that we could dig the staff out with.

"Um," I began, hoping that there was a French version of a Home Depot nearby, but Adrian just started talking to Brutus in Demonish. When he was finished, the gargoyle went over to the slab and pounded his broad, leathery heel onto it.

The impact shook the ground. Brutus beat his wings to increase his momentum, and his foot repeatedly slammed down to the accompanying sounds of stone breaking. He used so much force, I was worried that he'd hurt himself, but his apelike features actually looked like his version of happy. Maybe he was. He now had something to take out his frustration on, and he was making that stone slab pay for his being out in sunlight.

But when Brutus had stomped his way down about three feet, I caught a flash of purple among the pale gray stones. Then shards of the same color flew out, and when one of them hit me, the supernatural vibes coming from it made me realize that it was different from the other stones in more than color.

"Stop!" I said, and Brutus paused with his thickly muscled leg still in midstomp.

I went over to the slab, looking down at the small crater that Brutus had made. Most of the shattered rocks inside the hole were pale gray to match the slab. But a few shards of purple remained at the bottom, and I followed their trail to a hollow purple rectangle embedded inside the stone blocks. When I touched it, power sizzled through my veins.

"Is that it?" Adrian asked, crouching next to me.

I jumped into the hole for a better look. Then, even though it hurt, I stuck my hand inside the rectangular purple casing, sliding it in until I'd gloved my arm almost to my shoulder.

"No," I said, glad that the pain wasn't as bad as when I'd touched the cloth back at the campus chapel. "But I think that this used to be its casing."

Considering its location and the power coming from it, it had to have been in contact with an extremely hallowed item. So, why did the power coming from it feel far fainter than the power that the cloth had given off? If not for the long, rectangular shape of the casing and the inlaid gold etchings in the form of locusts, frogs and a large river or sea, I'd think that the casing had once contained another hallowed artifact instead of the staff. But the shape and etchings were too specific to be anything else, not to mention that this was where the former chapel that had housed the staff used to be.

Maybe time made the difference, I mused. It had been almost a hundred years since the chapel had resided here. If it had been that long since the staff had been in the purple casing, that could account for the lessening of the supernatural imprint it had left.

But the staff *had* been here. I knew that as surely as I'd known that I'd found David's slingshot when I touched it for the first time, but it wasn't in the box now. I withdrew my arm, and while the pain lessened at once, trepidation replaced it.

Only Adrian and I knew that the staff was no longer here. If Blinky or another demon had managed to translate the runes on the tablet, they could show up any second, and they wouldn't be in a talking mood. We'd beaten them here, but that didn't mean we were safe.

"Ivy," Adrian said, and the urgency in his voice told me that he'd come to the same conclusion. "We need to leave. Now."

Adrian drove like a proverbial bat out of hell back to the basilica. We had sirens blaring behind us for the last five minutes, but Adrian drove the van right into the wooded section that led to the gateway. When the van could go no farther, he had Brutus fly us the rest of the way. We'd marked the tree closest to the gateway, not that I needed the big *X* to know where it was. Being in contact with the staff's casing had put my hallowed senses into overdrive. I could've found the gateway blindfolded and with both hands tied behind my back.

"Come on," I said when we reached it, and held my arms out. Shouts in French plus the sound of crashing through the woods meant that the police were almost upon us.

Adrian ducked under my right arm and Brutus hunched to fit under my left, but when I was about to pull them through the gateway, Adrian stopped me.

"Don't go back to the realm where Jasmine and Costa are. Think of New York City instead."

I didn't ask why. There was no time. The last thing I saw before I pulled everyone through the gateway was a group of policemen bursting out from the trees, but by the time the officers reached us, me, Adrian and Brutus were long gone.

We tumbled out on the other side of the gateway to land with a splash into foul-tasting, chilly water. I coughed, trying to expel what I'd inadvertently swallowed, and Brutus let out a howl that blasted my eardrums. He shot out of the water as if fired from a cannon, flying around in mad dips and turns. It was night here, but Brutus was easy to see against the huge, lighted bridge above us, not to mention the wall of brightly illuminated buildings on either side of the waterway.

Adrian pounded on my back to help me cough out the water. Once I was breathing normally again, he withdrew his knife and carved an *X* onto the stone support beam next to us.

"This looks like the Brooklyn Bridge," he said, the knife disappearing under the water to presumably go back into his pants. "Remember that."

"Gateway's under the Brooklyn Bridge, got it," I said. Not only was the water cold, it also had a current. If Adrian hadn't hauled me against him and held on to a corner of the bridge's support beam, we would have floated down the waterway by now.

"Brutus!" Adrian called out, and the gargoyle swooped back toward us. When he got close, I saw that his expression was as incensed as a newly bathed cat's, and I wondered if this was the first time that Brutus had ever gotten wet.

"I know, boy, we're getting out of here," Adrian muttered.

He let me go and said something in Demonish. Brutus dipped down and grabbed Adrian with his clawed hands, then flung him high over his head. Before I had time to wonder if Brutus had lost his mind, he swooped down under Adrian, who landed on Brutus's back and grabbed the reins as if he were a cowboy stuntman. If I wasn't busy treading water while floating past the bridge, I would've given them a round of applause.

Then Brutus flew down and angled himself toward me, and I grabbed the arm that Adrian held out to me. He hauled me up with a lot less flair, not that I wanted to duplicate his aerial acrobatics. When he settled me in front of him, I gripped the base of Brutus's wings to steady myself, and hugged my legs to the gargoyle's sides to keep from sliding off.

"When did you learn to do that?" I asked, raising my voice to be heard against the wind.

Adrian's mouth touched my ear as he leaned down. "During one of the long, lonely nights when Zach kept me from you." Then he pulled the reins to the right, and Brutus turned, flying us back toward the large city across the bridge.

"Stay high," Adrian shouted to Brutus.

The rest of what he said was in Demonish, so I didn't understand it. Not that I was trying to translate based on the few words that I knew. I was too busy staring at the endless glittering cityscape beneath us. Some buildings were so tall that a quick swoop downward would've had Brutus brushing their roofs. Other, smaller buildings seemed to crouch next to the skyscrapers as if seeking shelter in their shadows. Brake lights and headlights colored the streets below with lines of red and white, and all the various noises were so loud that they drifted up to us as a dull hum even from our height.

Brutus flew us toward a large, darkened section within this brightly lit concrete maze. As he descended and I saw the tops of trees, I realized that this must be Central Park. Brutus landed next to a small bridge, and as soon as we slid off, he shook out his wings, expelling the last of the water from them.

By this time, I'd figured out why we were in New York. "You think the staff might be here," I said through teeth that were starting to chatter. Summer or not, being soaked in a cold river and then flown around at high altitudes was enough to make anyone chilly.

"Father Louis said that the chapel's first stop in America had been New York, although he didn't say where. Still—" he flashed me a quick grin "—five minutes on Google will fix that. We know that the staff used to be in the chapel's other, previous locations, and since the demons didn't beat us to it in France, it might be here."

"It's definitely worth checking out," I agreed.

Adrian's gaze swept over me, lingering in certain spots. "Plus, I know a safe place we can stay in the city, so after we check the chapel's old site, we'll go there. First, though, I need to call my friend to get you some dry clothes and shoes."

Dry clothes sounded so good. So did a shower. Not only was I wet and chilly, I could smell things that I didn't want to think about. That river hadn't been hygienic, to say the least.

"What about Brutus?"

Adrian patted the gargoyle. "He can fly around Central Park and then get some fish out of the bay. He's got to be hungry."

At the mention of food, my stomach let out a disturbingly loud noise, as if I needed reminding that it had been over a day since I'd eaten. Adrian heard it and he pulled me into his arms.

"Sorry this has been so rough on you," he breathed.

I let out a choked laugh. "Me? You're the one who's gotten slashed up, shot up and beaten to a pulp recently."

He waved a hand, as if those were only minor nuisances. "I've been through much worse, and for a lot longer."

That's right, Demetrius had spent decades training Adrian under extremely brutal circumstances, all so Adrian could become the most lethal Judian who'd ever lived. *Half-Judian*, a dark inner whisper reminded me. The other half was demon. His lineage literally consisted of "evil" and "more evil." What would Adrian do once he found that out? Would it change his determination to help me fight against demons and minions? *Could* he bring himself to stand with me against Demetrius, if he knew that Demetrius was his real father?

I pushed those thoughts back. Half, whole, whatever Adrian was, I trusted him. More than that, I loved him. That's why when he murmured, "Stay here, Ivy. Costa's cell is soaked, so I need to get to a phone to call my friend," and then left me alone in the park, I stayed.

Two hours later, I was worried enough about him to regret this decision. I started heading out of the park, determined to look for Adrian, when I saw a figure running toward me and realized that it was him.

"I've got a car waiting at the entrance," he said, grabbing my hand. Then he yelled out, "Brutus! You need to follow us."

The gargoyle, who'd waited with me while Adrian was away, chuffed in understanding. Then he flapped his great wings and soared above us as I followed Adrian out of the park.

CHAPTER THIRTY-ONE

By "car," Adrian meant limousine, I soon found out. All the mirrors on it had been removed, and in the plush interior, on one of the leather seats, a long coat, new clothes, shoes and, more important, food, were waiting for me. I'd mostly dried off by now, but I still changed into the new bra, underwear and ankle-length pink dress while holding the coat over me for modesty's sake. Adrian turned away as well while I changed, but that was probably to hide his smile. Yes, I knew I was being ridiculous, and yet still, I couldn't bring myself to strip naked in front of him. Plus, though the driver's privacy window was up, there was someone else in the car with us, too.

Adrian must have changed clothes on the way to getting me. He'd traded his denim pants and T-shirt for a pair of black slacks and a formal white shirt that looked like it could've been paired with a tuxedo. I would've asked where he got such nice clothes for the both of us, but the delicious smells emanating from the plastic covered container took priority.

After I wolfed down the food, which turned out to be an unexpectedly fancy meal of filet minion, mashed potatoes and mixed grilled vegetables, I finally put on my new shoes. Once

I did, I decided I might never take them off. My poor feet were bruised, cracked and split in so many places from running around barefoot, a pedicurist would scream in horror if she saw them.

Now fed, clothed and properly shod, I asked the obvious question. "Who is your friend in the city? Bill Gates?"

He snorted. "No. He's a hotel manager. This is the hotel limo, and he got our clothes and food from the hotel, too."

"Oh." Made sense. Then I added, "I hope he doesn't get in trouble for all this."

Adrian gave me a sideways smile. "He won't. He's on good terms with the hotel's owner."

"What's that for?" I asked, gesturing to a large cooler shoved against the limo's other section of seats.

Adrian glanced at it. "Hunks of raw meat for Brutus, in case he doesn't get lucky with fish in the bay later."

I leaned back against the leather seats. Even with Adrian's large frame filling up half this section, it was so spacious that I almost could've stretched out. I didn't, of course. I was so tired, I'd probably pass out, and we still had work to do.

"You found out where the old chapel site is?"

He nodded, looking thoughtful. "It's at an old estate in Jericho, Long Island. Actually, I, ah, know the place."

"You do?" I asked in surprise.

For some reason, he seemed uneasy about the topic. "Yes, but I didn't notice anything special about the chapel back then."

"What is this place? Why were you there?"

He shifted in his seat, as if suddenly having trouble getting comfortable. "It used to be a huge chateau, but it nearly burned to the ground back in the 1960s. There's not much left of it now. Just servants' quarters, stables, that sort of thing."

I didn't know if this really was a sore subject for him, or if my being overly tired was the reason why it seemed like he was avoiding my question. "And how did you know it?" I repeated.

His face became shuttered, confirming my suspicions. "Because Demetrius was the one who set it on fire."

"What?" I asked with a gasp.

His shoulders tightened. "The sixties were around the time that I started exploring the human world. Long Island wasn't far from the Bennington realm, and the couple who owned the chateau traveled a lot. So, when I was in the area and they weren't home, I used to stay there."

My mouth was still agape. "You squatted in their house?"

He gave me a glare that was half defensive, half arrogant. "I was used to ruling my own realm. It gave me expensive tastes, but I didn't want to leave a money trail that Demetrius could follow. Needless to say, he didn't encourage my explorations in the human world."

I could figure out the rest. "So, when Demetrius found out that you regularly crashed at this chateau, he burned it down out of spite?"

Adrian's smile held all the iciness of a demon realm. "And told me he'd do the same to any other human place I frequented."

That sounded like Demetrius, but I was struck by something else. "You realize that you happened to stay at two out of the three places where the staff has been," I pointed out.

He opened his mouth to speak, then paused. "If the staff's at the old Graenan estate, that's true," he finally said.

I grunted. "Proving once again that fate has a twisted sense of humor."

The staff might have been right under Demetrius's nose when he set that fire, and he hadn't known it. Thank God that demons didn't have the ability to sense hallowed objects, or Demetrius could've sent the realm walls crashing down decades ago.

Beyond the window, buildings and urban areas were starting to be replaced by trees and a much more rural-looking setting.

"Let's hope the staff is still there," I said, giving Adrian a tired, if impish, smile. "If you send Demetrius a selfie of you holding it next to that house's ruins, he might combust with rage and save us the trouble of killing him."

The former chateau was on over ten acres of land in an area where the other estates also had a lot of elbow room. Obviously, this area still catered to the wealthy. We had to park outside the estate's closed gates, and if we'd been in a regular car instead of a limo, I felt sure that someone would've called the police to report an attempted robbery.

Of course, our fancy ride wasn't the only thing that helped. The late hour did, too. At just after three in the morning, any normal resident would be in bed. If I didn't have a life-or-death task in front of me, that's where I'd be. Jet lag had nothing on realm lag. I'd been bouncing back and forth between so many time zones without sleep; if I started speaking in tongues out of sheer exhaustion, I wouldn't be surprised.

That's why I didn't object when, safely out of sight from our limo driver, Adrian had Brutus land and then we climbed on his back. I might not like traveling via Gargoyle Airlines, but I didn't think I had a ten-acre trek in me at the moment.

Brutus had barely taken off when my hallowed sensors started to perk up. They grew stronger over the time it took him to fly us to the ruins, and when he set us down next to the charred remains of an abandoned chateau, they were vibrating.

"Feel anything?" Adrian asked.

"Yep," I responded. "For starters, now I'm awake, and the readings I'm getting feel stronger than the ones in France."

"Are they stronger than the ones that were at the campus chapel?" he asked at once.

I sent my senses out as I followed that inner sensor to the far side of the rubble that marked the main house. "No," I said at last. Then I pointed to an overgrown section of weeds that looked out of place even for abandoned ruins. "From what I'm feeling, that's where the chapel used to be."

Adrian looked back and forth between the weeds and the crumbled wall next to it. From his expression, he was restructuring how the house used to look when it was whole, and part of me wished I could've seen what was in his mind's eye.

"I remember it now," he finally said. "It's unbelievable that it wasn't destroyed by the fire, too."

The chapel had been located right next to the main house, which hadn't survived the blaze, yet somehow, it had. "Something must have saved it," I said quietly.

That "something" had to be divine intervention, although I didn't say it out loud. I might have conflicted feelings about the Great Being, but I had no doubt that He wouldn't let a fire destroy one of His famed, destiny-fulfilling weapons.

I bent down and touched the section of ground where the pulses were the strongest. The supernatural version of red alert that seemed to follow the staff was there, and it was stronger than in France, but...it still felt like echoes compared to touching the wall in the crypt beneath the campus chapel.

"Unless its casing has been spelled to mute its effect, the staff isn't here," I said with a heavy sense of disappointment. "I think it used to be, though. I can feel traces of it."

And if I went by my time-lessens-the-effect theory, then the staff had followed the migration of the chapel, first being in France, then here, and then at Marquette University. Why had someone bothered to ship it along with the disassembled chapel to all of those places? They must have known how valuable the staff was to go to such trouble. Most important, if it wasn't in any of the previous three "holy homes" it had resided in before, where was it *now*?

"Maybe there's another tablet or clue underneath this slab," I said, choosing to be optimistic that we hadn't come all the way here for nothing. "Or maybe the staff is here and there's a reason why I don't feel it. I say we dig and make sure that the staff's supernatural vibes aren't being muted with symbols like they were back in the Marquette chapel."

CHAPTER THIRTY-TWO

My optimism proved, well, too optimistic. Brutus dug until he could have buried himself in the hole he'd made, but the site beneath the former chapel's location yielded nothing except dirt. Adrian gave him the contents of the cooler for his efforts, which turned out to be thirty pounds of raw meat. Brutus gobbled it up in much the same way I'd devoured my dinner earlier. Then Adrian gave him instructions to follow us until we reached the city. Once there, Brutus was free to fly around at will. Once more, I was grateful for the Archon glamour that made him look like a seagull to everyone except me, Adrian and Archons. Otherwise, a gargoyle flying around New York City would garner international headlines.

As we headed back to the hotel that Adrian told me we were staying at, I was torn between feeling tired, frustrated and out of ideas. My moodiness didn't make for much conversation. The tablet was our only clue to the staff's location, but we'd been to every "holy home" that it had referred to, and turned up nothing. Now what?

"Maybe we missed something at the Milwaukee campus," I announced after almost an hour of silence. "What if the tablet wasn't the only clue stuck inside the crypt's walls? Of course, now it'll be a nightmare to go back and give the crypt another look-see. The place must be crawling with every government agency possible after an obvious supernatural attack—"

"You think anyone who doesn't already know about demons is going to have any idea what happened there?" Adrian interrupted.

I stared at him. "Demons and minions were coming out of realm tunnels and dragging people right back into them. This was too big, too public, to be swept under a rug."

Adrian gave me a jaded look as he pressed a button and a TV screen came down from the roof of the limo. "Demons have minions placed in positions of power all around the world. They'll have come up with an explanation that has nothing to do with the truth, believe me."

When the TV powered on and Adrian picked a news channel, he was proved correct. "Chemical weapons attack on campus!" read the graphic behind the news anchor. "Mass casualties after domestic terrorism. Government vows retaliation."

"You've got to be kidding me," I said in disgust. "Where are all the cell phone videos that could prove what happened?"

"If they don't get confiscated, they'll be explained away, discredited or, most likely, never make the airwaves," Adrian replied. "It might end up online on one of those conspiracy sites, but who pays attention to that stuff when it's paired next to photos of Bigfoot, Nessie and Chupacabra?"

I was stopped from commenting about that when the limo pulled up to the Waldorf Astoria. I was surprised when the driver opened our door and we got out. Adrian seemed to know where he was going, and he led me inside a jaw-droppingly extravagant lobby decorated in gold and white, with marble floors that looked like they belonged at the Vatican in Rome.

He'd said that his friend in the city was a hotel manager. "Is this where your friend works?" I whispered, dazzled.

Adrian led me to the elevators, a little smirk hovering over his lips. "Yes, and he's also the only one who knows who the real owner of this hotel is."

"Who's that?" At Adrian's single arched brow, I stared at him in disbelief. "*You?* No way."

The elevator doors opened and we went inside. He swiped a card in the slot and then pressed the button for the Towers.

"You've heard of people selling their souls for money," he said in a conversational tone. "Sometimes, that really happens. Take the former owner of this hotel. He sold his soul to a demon decades ago, but then like they all do, came to regret it."

"You don't say?" I muttered, still trying to take this in.

"I told you that when I stopped believing all the lies demons had told me, I turned to drugs to ease my guilt over what I'd done. That's when I met Trent. He was also hitting the chemicals because his time was almost up. We got to talking, and when he told me who he owed his debt to, I told him I'd fix the problem." He paused to give me a sardonic smile. "Trent was my first stab at redemption."

"But you can't kill demons. Only Archons, other demons or one of the three hallowed weapons can. So how did you fix it?"

Adrian shrugged. "I made sure that the demon who was coming to collect his soul got killed. As you said, I couldn't kill him myself, but I made it worth another demon's while to take him out for me. Then I came back and told Trent that he was free. He was so grateful, he started the paperwork to sign his hotel over to me. Took a few years since we had to make it look like an overseas corporation bought it so Demetrius and other demons wouldn't find out and ruin it as a safe space for me."

I was still having a hard time believing this, not that it was the craziest thing I'd heard tonight, let alone ever. "And you actually let him give you this hotel?"

Adrian laughed outright, coinciding with the elevator doors opening. "Of course. For one, Trent said that he was done with

money because of what it had driven him to do. For another—"
the grin he flashed me was wicked "—I *really* liked this place."

He led me over to a set of doors marked Historic Suite with
a comment of "The Presidential Suite is already occupied."

"Then I insist on going home," I replied flippantly. Then I
didn't say anything at all as Adrian opened the doors and I got
my first glimpse of the room, or rooms to be more accurate.

The first room looked like a foyer on extravagant steroids,
and it opened into a full dining room with crystal stemware that
would've sent my mother running over in rapture, if she were
still alive to see it. After that was a living room with a wall-to-
wall Oriental rug, a fireplace and furniture that looked too expensive to actually sit on.

The next room was cozier, but no less opulent. The couch
to my left looked like it was upholstered in red velvet, and the
red-and-gold-striped love seat across from it appeared to be silk.
Thick drapes only let part of the cityscape peek in from the
floor-to-ceiling windows, and there was a second sitting area
by another fireplace.

Everything was so luxurious that it actually took Adrian's
abrupt question of "What are you doing here?" for me to notice
that the chair across from those couches wasn't empty.

Zach set down the travel magazine he'd been reading, putting it back with the others that were decoratively displayed on
the table in front of him.

"For all the many times I've been to this city, I have never
seen a Broadway play," he remarked, replying to a question that
neither one of us had asked.

"What are you doing here?" I repeated, coming toward him.
"Where's Jasmine?"

He gave me a look as if the answer were obvious. "The same
place you left her."

"With Costa?" I burst out. "He could hurt her!"

"He would never do that," Adrian said before Zach had a chance to reply.

That reignited my irritation with him over his incorrect assumption about Jasmine. "My sister *isn't* the one who told Demetrius where we were."

"That's the only explanation that makes sense," Adrian shot back. Then his tone softened. "Costa could've gotten me killed a thousand times over these past few years. He didn't. Our location only started being reported back to our enemies when your sister started traveling with us."

I turned away, and he caught me by the shoulders. "I know it's hard, Ivy, but look at the facts. Demetrius didn't find us here or in France, yet it only took him hours to drop realms on us before, when Jasmine wasn't locked up in a light realm where she can't communicate with him or any other demon. Do you really think that's a coincidence?"

My jaw tightened. "I don't think it's coincidence, but I also know it's not Jasmine who's been selling us out."

Zach let out a sigh as he stood up. "I did not come here to listen to the two of you fight. Ivy, your sister is safe—you have my word. Adrian, you wanted me to perform a service for you. If that is still the case, I can do so now."

Adrian dropped his hands from my shoulders and turned to give Zach an amazed look. "You know I still want you to, but with everything that's going on, maybe now isn't the time."

"Now is the only time I will do it," Zach replied in a mild tone. "As I have often reminded you, I am not yours to command, and soon, I will have far more urgent matters to attend to."

Adrian's muscled tensed, as if he were fighting an inner battle. "Then now works for me," he said in a tight voice.

"Very well," Zach replied, still in that unruffled way. "*If* Ivy agrees to it. If she does not, then I will do nothing, and I know that you haven't told her what this request entails."

I was still upset over Adrian believing that Jasmine was the traitor, but I was also wildly curious. Zach had assured me that Jasmine was safe, so I wasn't worried about her, and no one was trying to kill us, which made this as good of a time as any to find out what Adrian's mysterious request was. Not that it was necessary anymore, though.

I touched his hands, which remained clenched at his sides. "After everything that's happened, you have nothing to prove to me or to anyone else. I know you won't betray me again, so whatever you thought you needed Zach to do, you don't."

He unclenched his fists and his hands rose to caress my neck and then my face, making me shiver under his touch.

"What I should have told you before was that I *want* to do this. You are everything to me, and this way I can show you that as well as be closer to you."

I leaned into him, letting my hands drift over his shoulders. "I know another way that we can be closer, but it requires Zach *leaving*."

Adrian laughed, low, knowing and oh-so enticing. "We'll do that afterward, I promise."

In my peripheral vision, I saw Zach roll his eyes with barely contained irritation, and it was all I could do not to laugh. If double entendres irritated Zach, I'd make it a point to talk sexy to Adrian every time the Archon was near. Payback for all of Zach's infuriating evasiveness in the past.

"Okay," I said, smiling. "So, what do you want Zach to do?"

His gaze never wavered as he stared at me. "In simplest terms, a soul tethering. Zach ties mine to yours, and after that, I couldn't betray you even if I wanted to because doing so would subject me to the same consequences. We'd be linked in a way that nothing on earth, under it or over it could alter."

My mouth opened, but for a few moments, I couldn't form words. I don't know what I'd thought it would be. Whatever my musings, nothing had come close to this.

"You're serious?" I finally got out.

His fingers tightened around my face, yet his touch remained achingly gentle. "I've never been more serious about anything in my life."

"But that's so, so—"

"Permanent?" Zach supplied drily.

I barely glanced at him. "Yes, permanent," I breathed. "Eternally permanent."

A smile flittered over Adrian's lips. "That's my favorite part. I love you, Ivy, and that more than anything else is why I want this. But my destiny has also been hanging over me my entire life, and since I'm breaking that destiny, I want the proof of it to be written all over my soul."

"Adrian..." I was so overwhelmed, I didn't know what to say.

He dropped his hands and stepped back, concern washing over his features. "This is a one-way tethering, if that's what you're worried about. You wouldn't be linking your soul to mine. Everything about you would still stay the same—"

"Why would you think I'd want a one-way-only tethering?" I interrupted.

His expression cleared, becoming completely blank, and he took another step back. "If you don't want me to do it, that's fine," he said in a very controlled tone.

"Adrian!" I grabbed him, almost shaking him for how badly he'd misunderstood me. "I meant, why would you think that I *wouldn't* want to do the same thing with you?"

He started to smile, and seeing it caused something bright and beautiful to bubble up inside me, making my answering grin wide and almost witless with joy.

"You do?" he asked, the question coming out almost breathy.

I tangled my arms around his neck, feeling a tear start to slip from the corner of my eye. "Of course I do."

He kissed me, and I didn't care about the Archon watching us. All I cared about was how his arms molded me to him, the searing passion that built as his mouth moved over mine and the happiness I felt, which rivaled everything else.

A cough sounded, and then Adrian and I were wrenched apart by invisible arms. Zach approached us, a regally haughty expression on his face.

"I agreed to perform a soul-tethering ceremony, not to oversee its celebratory consummation, so if you're still interested in the former, you need to stop the latter. Now."

"Sorry," Adrian said, but his grin made it clear that he wasn't sorry in the least.

Neither was I. "I'm sure it's nothing you haven't seen a billion times before," I teased Zach.

His glare was priceless. "That assumes that I have never had anything better to do, which is patently untrue."

Adrian went over and clapped him on the back. "Whatever you say, secret voyeur. Now, you said you had to do this right away or not at all, but exactly how long do we have?"

Zach thought for a moment. "Two hours."

"All right," Adrian said, giving Zach another back slap and ignoring the scowl he got in response. "Ivy, you have to hurry and get ready. I know the perfect place to do the ritual in."

I cast a disbelieving look around at our lavish surroundings. "This isn't nice enough for you?"

His gaze glinted with determination. "We've had so few chances to make good memories with everything that's happened since we met. Since we can only do this once, I want to make sure it's something you'll never forget." Then his mouth curled as humor mixed in with his usual arrogance. "Besides, a hotel room? I do have my pride as a former prince, you know."

Part of me couldn't believe that this was really about to happen, yet the rest of me wasn't the least surprised. So many momentous events in my life had been thrown at me with nary a warning of *catch!* that this seemed par for the course. Yes, it was a destiny-altering tethering that would bind us together in ways I still didn't really understand. Yes, we still had to figure out a way to find the staff before more realms started clobbering this world, and yes, a permanent, soul-binding ritual kinda meant that I'd end up with a demon for a father-in-law, so...it was a lot to take in.

This was my life, however, and although we didn't have a lot of wiggle room on our to-do list, if I'd learned anything over the past several months, it was that we had to live every moment to the fullest because any one of them could be our last. Put in that light, it would be foolish *not* to make the most of our soul-tethering ritual. As Adrian had said, it was a once-in-a-lifetime experience.

"So tell me, where do you want to go to say goodbye to your days as a *single* former demon prince?" I asked with a grin.

Adrian kissed me with such passion that I almost forgot what we were talking about. "Get showered and dressed, and I'll show you," he murmured against my lips.

Then he spun around, saying to Zach, "Stay here with Ivy. I'll be right back."

CHAPTER THIRTY-THREE

In a high-end hotel like this, I expected the bathroom to be stocked with toiletries, and I was right. After I showered to get all of the nasty river water, dirt and blood off me, then blow-dried my hair, I left the black-and-white marble bathroom to find a gorgeous new dress laid out on the king-size bed.

The duvet on the bed was royal blue, which made the pearlescent dress stand out more vividly against the dark fabric. I touched the bottom of the dress, which flared out mermaid-style against the fitted body, and the material slipped like raindrops through my fingers. I'd say that it was silk, except that it was diaphanous, and the color was the most beautiful blend of white, pink and pale gray. If I had to name the blend of colors, I'd call it ashes of dawn, and the dress was so beautiful, I was almost afraid to put it on.

Of course I did, and then spun around just to see the fabric billow around my legs. It was strapless except for the single thin swath of fabric over my left shoulder, so I wouldn't be able to wear my bra. At least with the snug, square cut and the thicker, opaque material across the chest, I didn't need one.

I did need shoes, though, and I was glad to see a pair of heels by the bottom of the bed. They fit, although like the dress, they were a little too small. Still, I was amazed that Adrian had managed to find anything this nice, let alone close to my size. The clock showed a quarter to five in the morning, so no shops would be open. Guess the same hotel store that Adrian had gotten our other clothes at had fancier attire, as well. And as the hotel owner, Adrian must have unlimited access.

I ran a hand through my hair, wishing I could style it into something prettier, but my hair spray and curling iron were back in the bus. So was my makeup bag, not that I could have done a great job of primping without being able to look at myself. All the mirrors in this suite had either been broken or removed. Adrian's friend, the manager, must have had employees scurrying like mad to do that during our fruitless drive to Long Island.

"No need to be concerned," a voice said from behind me. "Your appearance is quite pleasant."

I swung around, stunned more by his words than by how Zach had snuck up on me. "Was that a *compliment*?"

His expression remained serious even as the faintest smile pulled at his mouth. "Compliments cater to vanity. This was merely my stating an observation."

"Bullshit," I said with an amused snort. "You just gave me a compliment. Be a big Archon and own it."

"Are you ready, Ivy?" Adrian asked from the other room.

I gave my hair a final swipe before letting the dark brown waves settle naturally around my shoulders. "Yes."

Adrian walked in, having showered in the bathroom adjoining the suite's other, smaller bedroom. It had been less than an hour since I'd seen him, and in that time, he'd not only managed to get me a beautiful new dress; he'd also found an elegant black suit for himself. His dark gold hair was slightly tousled, as if he'd been running around after his shower, which he must have been, considering all he'd done. His jaw was smooth from a fresh shave, and his silver-rimmed, deep blue eyes had never resembled sapphires more than they did now as he stared at me.

"You're stunning," he said in a hoarse voice.

Zach arched a brow at me. "See? *That* is a compliment."

Adrian crossed the short distance between us and pulled me into his arms, but when I tilted my face up, he didn't kiss me. Instead, he caught my hand, pressing something hard into it.

I opened my hand and gasped. A large, oval-shaped diamond winked up at me, but in addition to the fiery colors it reflected from the overhead light, it also glittered with…darkness. I didn't understand how until I held the ring by its platinum loop and saw black diamond baguettes beneath the center stone, their color reflecting outward.

Darkness and light, just like the two of us.

I swallowed several times, but my throat still burned from the emotion overloading me. Adrian couldn't have gotten this from a hotel store, and he'd had no time to go anywhere else.

"When? I mean, how?" I choked out.

"I bought it after you told me you didn't want to see me again." Each low, rasped word slammed right into my heart. "I've been carrying it around for months, promising myself that one day, if I didn't give up, I'd see you wear it."

With tears blurring my vision, I held my hand out, and Adrian slid the ring onto my finger.

"I only have one more hour," Zach said, breaking a moment I would've wanted to live in forever. "We will need all of it."

Adrian raised my hand to his mouth and kissed it right above the ring. Then, with a wide smile, he turned to Zach.

"Let's do this."

We all rode in the limo, but our destination turned out to be so close that we could have walked to it: St. Patrick's Cathedral. If the past hour hadn't been such a whirlwind of the impossible made real, I would've been impressed to see Brutus perched on one of the cathedral's soaring towers, beating his wings as if claiming it for himself. Then Zach walked up to the massive doors of the elaborately styled, multistory church and, with a burst of light from his hands, broke the locks open.

I followed Adrian inside. Brutus landed with a thump moments later, and then the gargoyle entered the church. If I'd thought the exterior was impressive, the interior put it to shame. Instead of pale gray-colored stone rising majestically into tall, pointed peaks, the inside walls were warm amber shades, and that effect was deepened by the countless candles that Zach somehow caused to blaze with light as we walked down the long aisle.

When we reached the altar, the curved archways and magnificent stained glass windows faded into insignificance as I turned to face Adrian. His gaze was almost feral in its intentness, but a smile curved his lips as he stared down at me.

"Do you like it?"

"It's more than memorable." Even my whisper sounded loud in the huge, empty building. "It's unforgettable."

"Adrian," Zach said, suddenly sounding even more formal than his usual stuffy style. "Take Ivy's hand."

He did, and the warm curl of his fingers around mine stilled my nervousness. I didn't know what this ritual involved, but my experience with the supernatural made me brace for a lot of pain. Still, I'd go through agony with a smile to prolong this moment. For longer than I could imagine, Adrian had been told that his choices had already been made for him. That no matter what he did or what he wanted, his life would culminate in an awful, unavoidable betrayal. Yet still, he'd fought with everything he had, and now, I was about to be an integral part of his victory.

And my victory, too. In my darkest days, I'd thought what I felt for Adrian was fate's cruel twist on top of an already impossible destiny. After all, I wasn't some great savior, prophecy or no prophecy. I was just a girl doing the best I could while knowing that it probably wouldn't be enough. But right now, I didn't have to be the last Davidian, with all of the expectations, pressures and supernatural challenges that came with that title. I could just be Ivy, and as I looked at Adrian, I didn't see the last Judian, either. I saw the man I loved and wanted to spend the rest of my life with, however long or short that turned out to be. I thought I'd known what happiness was, but those instances had been mere shadows and glimpses of what I felt now, with Adrian holding my hand and Zach about to tether our souls together.

"Ivy," Zach said. "Take Adrian's hand."

I did. With our hands clasped right to right and left to left, our arms formed a loose X between us. Zach closed his eyes, held his palms up and began to speak in a language I'd only heard once before.

Demonish sounded beautiful yet harsh, with each syllable a melody broken by roughness at the last moment. I didn't know the official name of the language it had originated from, but that was what Zach was speaking now. Angel-speak, I'd called it the other time I'd heard it, and I'd thought that memory had exaggerated its indescribable exquisiteness. Instead, it had dulled it. Listening to it was like having every stunning visual I'd ever seen transformed into acoustics and then poured into my mind. It was hypnotic, euphoric, and when I felt wetness on my cheeks, I realized that it had brought me to tears.

Then light began to halo Zach, until it consumed his trademark blue hoodie and jeans, leaving him clothed in brightness that rivaled the stars. That light overflowed Zach, spilling out to encompass the altar, Adrian and even myself.

I closed my eyes against the searing brightness, and still light filled my vision. Zach's voice changed, turning into what sounded like the roar of multitudes. The sound was piercing, painful and beauteous all at the same time. My mind and body ached from sensory overload, until I would've run out of an instinctive need to protect myself, but I couldn't move. I couldn't even pull my hands away from Adrian's though it suddenly felt as if I was falling from a great height.

I would've screamed, but then something ripped out of me with such force that I felt torn in two. Before I could begin to process that, a tidal wave crashed into me, flooding the parts that had been ripped away. For a few brief moments, I was no longer only Ivy. I was someone else, too.

I grew up in a darkly glittering world where strange and beautiful demons gave me and my mother everything we wanted, especially the shadow man, Demetrius. To save this world, I learned to fight, wanting nothing more than to erase the fear in my mother's eyes when she spoke of Archons and to see the pride in Demetrius's when I finally fulfilled my destiny to save her, him and the rest of our people.

Then I discover the ugliness I hadn't been shown before in our realms. I sneak out and visit the half light, half dark world and discover it's different from everything I've been told. It holds real beauty, and I've become a monster. I seek death by searching for the Archons I've long been warned about, yet when one finds me, he doesn't kill me. Instead, he shows me the truth. Demetrius and the person I thought was my mother were one and the same. He'd killed her, then used her likeness my whole life to trick me.

My rage consumes me. I will deny my people their victory by refusing to fulfill the fate I'd once longed for. I will never go near the last David-ian, let alone betray her.

And then she appears…

I fell back into myself, until all I could feel were my own aches and pains. Adrian's thoughts, emotions and memories were no longer slamming into my consciousness with feature-film-like clarity. When I dragged my eyelids open, we were both slumped on the floor in front of the altar, our bodies twisted away from each other, yet our hands still clasped together.

"It is done," Zach said from above us.

He was standing only a few feet away, and yet his voice sounded far-off. Maybe that was from the blood still roaring through my ears, or from my ragged breaths as I tried to get ahold of myself mentally and physically.

Adrian's eyes met mine. His face was ashen and his hair was tangled as if a windstorm had blown through here. For all I knew, it had. I certainly felt like more had happened than merely falling to the floor. If I had one, it hurt.

"You okay?" he rasped, sitting up.

I sat up, too, and leaned against the altar, trying to even out my gasping by taking in slow, deep breaths. "Mostly."

He didn't say anything. Then he pulled his hands free and looked up at Zach. In a voice that echoed like the rumbling of thunder, Adrian said, "*Why* didn't you tell me that Demetrius was my father?"

CHAPTER THIRTY-FOUR

I was so shocked that he knew, I found the strength to get to my feet. Adrian got up, too, and though a fine tremor ran through his body, he strode over to Zach.

"Why?" Adrian repeated.

"How did you find out?" I asked.

He shot a single, sharp glance at me. "The same way you probably know all my secrets now, too."

He'd experienced the same accelerated, virtual reality replay of *my* life, as well? I suppose it made sense, since the soul tethering had gone both ways.

"Adrian, I'm so sorry," I whispered.

This time, the look he gave me was pained. "I know why you didn't tell me. I saw that, too."

He saw it, but did he forgive me? I wished I knew, but the ability to know his thoughts and feelings seemed to have ended with my regaining consciousness.

Zach drew himself up to his full height, although he was still several inches shorter than Adrian's six-six height. "If I had told you, you would have refused to do the soul-binding ritual with Ivy."

"Of course I would have!" Adrian burst out. "I'm half-*demon*. I would never knowingly taint Ivy's soul with that!"

"Taint? Adrian, don't say that," I gasped.

His arm shot out with such violence that he snapped a brass candlestick pillar right in half. "Don't. I can't stand to think about what I've done, let alone hear you justify it."

He was shaking, and I didn't know if it was from rage, regret or an urge to rip Zach limb from limb. When I came closer and saw Adrian's face, I realized that it was all three.

"There is more," Zach said, ignoring how I started to wave my hands in the universal gesture for *Stop!* Whatever it was, didn't he see that Adrian couldn't take it right now?

"What?" Adrian asked, the single word almost spit out.

For a moment, light glowed behind Zach's deep brown eyes, and I felt real fear. If Zach struck out at Adrian, he would kill him, and there would be nothing I could do to stop him. The lethal, mystic weapon in my arm worked on demons, not Archons.

Then Zach folded his arms and assumed his usual detached, cool demeanor. For once, I was relieved that humans seemed to be too beneath him for him to get worked up about.

"I told you that one of you had been alerting Demetrius to your location," Zach said, not blinking under Adrian's furious stare. "You were correct in believing that it couldn't be Costa, as Ivy was correct believing that it could not be Jasmine."

"Then who?" I demanded before the truth slammed into me.

Adrian didn't move, but for the briefest second, his features crumbled. Then they hardened until I wasn't sure I recognized the person I'd just supernaturally bound myself to.

"Me." Adrian laughed, a sound that more resembled rocks being ground together than an indication of amusement. "That's why Demetrius always knew who I was no matter what disguise you glamoured me with, right? Somehow, he can *feel* me."

Zach lifted his shoulder in acknowledgment. "As deep calls to deep, blood calls to blood."

Adrian spun around, striding past me. When he was halfway down the aisle, I realized he wasn't just pacing like he normally did when he was upset. He was *leaving*.

"Wait!" I shouted, energy returning to my limbs as I ran after him.

"Your tie to Demetrius is now broken," Zach called out.

Adrian stopped so abruptly that I had to pivot to avoid smashing into him. "What did you say?"

Zach didn't move from his spot in front of the altar. At the other end of the church, Brutus chuffed, then rose from his position behind the last pew. That's when I realized that at some time during our binding ritual, the gargoyle had run to the back of the church to hide from the light.

"Your tie to Demetrius is now broken," Zach repeated, speaking slowly so there could be no misunderstanding. "It broke the moment I tied your soul to Ivy's."

"How?" Adrian asked, holding his arm out when I came nearer. "Don't," he said without looking at me.

"Screw that." I flared, grabbing the arm he was using to ward me off. "I knew who your real father was when I agreed to tether my soul to yours, and I did it because I didn't care. *You* are who I want, and you are not him."

"Ivy." He said my name as if it were painful. "I'm part of him, and because of that, I led him to you all those times. Because of me, he nearly killed you. He might be in New York right now, looking for you through me. You can't expect me to forgive myself for that."

"Yes, I can," I said, touching his face and refusing to back down when he flinched. "You didn't know, and each time Demetrius found us, you did everything you could to protect me, even when we first met and you couldn't stand being near me."

I couldn't feel his emotions, but I didn't need to as I saw his features twist with pain. "I always wanted to be near you," he said in a ragged voice. "The only person I ever wanted to get away from was myself."

I threw my arms around him, tightening my grip when his whole body tensed. "I don't ever want to be without you, either, and I wouldn't care if that meant Demetrius was always hot on our heels. We'd find a way around him, just like we found a way around our fates. If we can beat destiny, beating Demetrius should be easy."

He laughed, although it sounded choked. "You always make me want to believe in the impossible, even when I know better."

"In this case, you don't know better, but I do," I said, pulling his head down and kissing him until his mouth lost its stiffness. "You're mine," I whispered against his lips. "And I'm yours, from now until hell freezes over, or until we beat it back to where it came from."

He stared at me, and in his eyes I saw tinges of hope. Behind that was ruthlessness and an almost animalistic determination to destroy those who'd caused us so much harm.

That was fine. Hate was useful sometimes, and Adrian would need all of his before we were done. But he needed something else more, and I wasn't afraid because he had that, too.

Love. I saw that in his gaze, as well. Felt it in his hands as they touched me, in his arms as they wrapped tightly around me, then felt it seethe from his mouth as he claimed mine with a desperation that put passion to shame.

When he finally lifted his head, my lips felt swollen and my breath came in pants. Despite that, I would have kissed him again at once if not for the very loud, very deliberate *harrumph* from the front of the church.

"As I was saying," Zach stated, his tone daring us to ignore him again, "your bond to Demetrius has now been fractured. Tethering your soul to Ivy's introduced enough of a supernatural disruption that Demetrius will no longer be able to track you through your blood tie."

"Maybe we should head back to the light realm, anyway," I murmured. "We've been here for hours. As you said, Demetrius could already be in the city looking for us."

"You can't go back," Zach replied, stunning me. "You also chose to tether your soul to his, so as Adrian's bond with you fractured his tie to Demetrius, so your bond to him fractured your access to the light realms."

Shock and disbelief made me ask, "I can't enter the light realms anymore? At all?"

"Not unless I or another Archon pulls you through their gateways," Zach replied.

Adrian's hand slid down my arm in a comforting way even as he sent a truly furious look at Zach. "Why did you wait until it was too late to warn her of that?"

"Ivy, would you rather have access to the light realms or have Adrian by your side?" Zach responded, answering a question with a question.

I closed my eyes. The light realms were more than the only demon-free places in existence plus an endless source of manna; they were also portals that could take us anywhere in the world. Having access to them had been a priceless advantage…unless that price would have cost me Adrian.

"You already know the answer," I said, opening my eyes.

The stare Zach leveled at Adrian was pointed. "And that is why I did not bother to tell her beforehand. Now, my time is finished here. Return to your hotel. You will be safe there. Even if Demetrius was using your link to follow you, now that it is severed, this city is too populated for him to find you before I return. I will see you at dusk."

With that, Zach disappeared. "Wait!" I said, but of course, the altar remained empty. How Zach loved his disappearing acts.

Adrian shook his head. "Typical." Then he took my arm. "Sun's almost up. Even if Demetrius did follow me here, he can't stay long enough to find us. This city has millions of people, so even if he sent every minion he made to look for us, they wouldn't find us, either. I say we go back to the hotel like Zach suggested and then leave with him tonight."

"All right," I said, thinking that if Zach hadn't promised to return, I'd have no way to get Jasmine and Costa out of the light realms. I gave the braided tattoo around my arm a wry glance. As far as it was concerned, the locks on the realm gateways had been changed.

Voices suddenly filled the cathedral as three priests entered from a side door near the front of the church. Then they stopped short when they saw us.

"How did you get in here?" one of them asked, almost sputtering in his indignation.

Adrian snorted as he held open the door for Brutus and me to leave. "Believe me, Father, that's a long story."

CHAPTER THIRTY-FIVE

The limo was still parked near the Cathedral, but Brutus was too big to fit inside, so Adrian sent the driver away and we walked back to the hotel. Brutus cringed at each new beam of light as the sun rose. At least the tall buildings kept most of the bright rays from reaching him, and being with us seemed to calm him a little, too. When we entered the Waldorf through the private entrance on 50th Street, the sun was fully up. Brutus hurried into the hotel, and the doorman didn't even blink at the Archon glamour that made it appear as if we'd gone for a dawn stroll with our pet seagull.

It made me wonder what other strange sights the doorman had seen, but I didn't pause to ask. I was so exhausted, I was running on fumes, and yet a nervous energy filled me as we entered the elevator, which was thankfully large enough to fit two adults and a hulking gargoyle.

Adrian had fulfilled his promise to prove that he wouldn't betray me again. And since we were now alone—sort of—with almost a day between now and when we'd see Zach again, with a nice, big bed waiting for us…well. Granted, Adrian had to be as worn-out as I was, so if he stumbled into the bedroom and fell right asleep, I'd completely understand. I might even pass out as soon as my head hit a pillow, too. But—more tingles of anticipation went through me—what if he didn't want to sleep?

The doors opened onto the Towers floor and we went into the Historic Suite. Adrian threw his coat onto the nearest chair in the foyer and then led Brutus into the side bedroom. I heard drapes being drawn and Adrian speaking in Demonish, followed by chuffs from Brutus, then the sound of water running.

I went into the master bedroom, struck anew by its loveliness. Royal blue drapes hung from the ceiling to frame the entire bed while white pillows and sheets provided a snowy contrast against the deep blue blankets. Crystal lamps adorned the nightstands as well as the end tables around the nearby love seat. A dark wood entertainment center with a flat-screen TV faced the bed, not that I wanted to watch anything right now. I also didn't want to look at the view from the windows, even though from this high up, it was really something.

I'd kicked off my heels and finished drawing the drapes when Adrian walked in. He didn't say anything. He didn't need to. One look into his eyes, and I knew I'd been wrong about his wanting to sleep in the other room. Or sleep at all.

In two long strides, he had me in his arms. My heartbeat sped up as his mouth closed over mine. His kiss was hard, yet when his tongue twined with mine and his hands began moving over me, I pressed myself closer. My weariness vanished, replaced by a long-denied desire. I wrapped my arms around his neck, moaning when he brought our bodies together so I could feel how much he wanted me. Then I gripped him tighter as his hands began to stroke and squeeze my ass. Those knowing, firm touches sent pleasure right through to the other side of me, making it feel as if he were touching something else. Without conscious thought, I rubbed against him, feeling his throbbing flesh through the thin layers of our clothes.

The sound he made was more growl than moan. He picked

me up, and when my legs wrapped around his waist, he rubbed that jutting hardness right against my clitoris. I cried out at the instant, exquisite tightening that made my whole body clench with pleasure.

Then he carried me over to the bed, and when his body covered mine, he kissed me again. After a long, mind-numbing moment, he drew away, lifting me up with him. My heart pounded as I felt the zipper on my dress being dragged down. He stared at me as he pulled my dress off, catching the side of my panties when he reached my hips. He bunched them and the rest of my dress in his hand until all of it cleared my feet, then he tossed everything onto the floor. The fierce, unbridled hunger in his gaze made my heart pound with need that felt very close to desperation.

"You're beautiful," he breathed. "So fucking beautiful."

His voice was harsh with lust. I pulled at his shirt, wanting to feel his bare skin next to mine.

"Take off your clothes," I said in a voice so husky, I barely recognized it.

He pulled his shirt over his head and tossed it aside. Golden-colored skin covered broad shoulders, a thickly muscled chest and arms that could've been carved from steel. My breath caught as I ran my hands over him, feeling the erotic juxtaposition of silky skin over rock-hard muscles. His eyes closed, as if savoring the feel of me touching him, then his hand went to his pants. When he pulled his zipper down, revealing his cock straining out of the top of his briefs, I almost gasped.

We're going to need Magnums, was my first thought, followed instantly by, *Do we even have any condoms?*

"Adrian," I said hoarsely, "do you have protection?" I hoped he'd gotten that when he was out getting our other stuff!

Instead of answering, he pulled his pants and briefs off. If I'd thought he looked magnificent the other time I'd seen him naked, that was nothing compared to the sight of him naked and fully erect. Anticipation mingled with my lust. I didn't know if I'd be able to take all of him, but oh, I intended to find out.

He held my gaze as he got into bed and settled himself on top of me. When I felt his body—skin to skin and hardness to softness—an inner throb deep inside increased until it almost matched the same thundering pace of my heartbeat.

"We don't need protection," he murmured, kissing the corner of my mouth while his hands started to roam over me again.

I disagreed, but I was having a hard time formulating words at the moment. His dark gold hair brushed my face in teasing wisps, his hard chest rubbed my nipples, making them even stiffer, and his knee rested against my inner thigh, only inches from where I was wet with need. He felt so large, so warm, so *good*, and that wasn't even counting his hands, which slid over me with sensual dominance, claiming every part he touched.

"I had a vasectomy," he breathed, and I was so overwhelmed by the sensations coursing through me, it took me a second to process that.

"Oh." That was all I was capable of saying as his palm climbed up my thigh.

"I've also been tested, and I'm clean," he whispered before his mouth covered mine.

The last of my concerns vanished. I opened my lips, meeting his tongue with my own. I loved the way he kissed me, as if he'd never get another chance to show me how much he wanted me. I moaned as his mouth continued to move over mine. Each stroke of his tongue aroused me more, and when his hand reached my center and his thumb circled my clitoris, my cry was muffled by his kiss. Then his fingers probed my depths, and I arched, my nails digging into his shoulders.

"You feel so good."

He growled the words as his mouth left mine to slide down my body. He stopped at my breasts, laving my nipple for a few spine-tingling moments, then sucked strongly at the same moment that his finger penetrated deeply inside me.

My back left the bed as pleasure bowed my spine. Cries spilled out of my mouth when he started to rub in a rhythmic way. My nerve endings tightened and twisted with each stroke, and my heart beat so fast that I felt dizzy. I knew my nails were digging into his shoulders hard enough to leave marks, but I couldn't make myself stop. I didn't feel in control of my body. Adrian was in control, and he sucked on my nipples while his fingers made me mindless with need.

That's why I wasn't embarrassed when he spread my legs and his mouth descended between them. I didn't care about the cry that tore out of me at the first branding stroke of his tongue, or the way I arched against him to feel more. When he delved deeper, his tongue swirling faster and faster, it was too much. Rapture broke within me, flashing out from my center faster than I could sob out his name. I gripped his head as the climax shattered me, then fell back against the pillows, panting, as that sharp ecstasy faded into lingering, blissful tingles.

He rubbed his face against the blankets before rising up on his knees. I gasped for a different reason when he slid my thighs around his hips and his hard flesh touched my wet, soft folds. Then he bent down, closing his mouth over mine in a kiss that stole the rest of my breath from me.

"I love you."

He said the words against my lips as he thrust forward. His mouth muffled the cry I made at the sudden, sharp burn within. He stopped even as his muscles tensed as though they were about to snap. Then he smoothed the hair away from my face, kissing my bottom lip where I was biting it in unwitting reaction to that wounding fullness.

"Are you all right?" he whispered.

His gaze almost burned from lust, but concern etched his features and he didn't move. That didn't stop those deep, unfamiliar throbs from pulsating inside me. Seemingly of its own will, my flesh tightened around him, and he closed his eyes as a harsh, choked sound came out of him.

"Can you go slow?" I asked, my voice low and breathy. His eyes seemed to darken even though I knew that was impossible.

"Yes," he said, drawing the word out to match the measured, sinuous arch of his hips.

I gasped as he slid deeper, increasing that incredible feeling of fullness. Then another languorous twist of his hips had him pulling out, and though the stinging sensation lessened, it left a feeling of aching emptiness that was somehow worse. Tentatively, I raised my hips, closing my eyes as he slid slowly, deeply, back into me. Those unbelievable inner throbs intensified as hidden walls stretched to fit him, and the sensations made the lingering pain pale by comparison.

My hands slid down his back, feeling the bunch and flex of his muscles with every new movement. His tongue echoed the slow rhythm of his body as the pain faded and pleasure began to build. I moved against him, reveling in how tightly he gripped me. Our breaths were short, sharp moans that mingled between kisses, and his hands were sensual weapons that sought out my most sensitive spots and then conquered them with pleasure.

The intensity built, until I was writhing with the same mindless ecstasy I'd felt when he was going down on me, only this time, he prolonged it. My moans turned into cries that turned into shouts as he held an orgasm just outside of my reach. He kept bringing me to the brink only to slow down before that crucial moment. Then he repeated the exquisite torture, until I was raking my nails down his back and shouting things I never thought I'd hear from my own lips.

And I didn't care. My loins burned in the most glorious way, my heart pounded so fast that it was probably dangerous and I slammed my hips against Adrian's as if I were urging him to hurt me. He wasn't, even if we'd left "slow" in the dust a while ago. No, each hard, rapid thrust felt ruthlessly rapturous, and I twisted against him in urgent need for more.

Then he picked me up, holding my hips against his while he leaned back until I was half straddling him. The change in position caused him to penetrate so deep, I could barely stand it, yet I cried out with pleasure so intense that it brought me over the edge. As I came, he moved even faster, his thrusts rougher, until I felt his climax in the fierce way his grip tightened and the deep, wet spasms within me.

He fell back against the bed, taking me with him, which was good since I'd suddenly lost the ability to move. I was vibrating with pleasure and so worn-out that I was dizzy; a unique experience for me. When Adrian brushed his lips across mine, I was too tired to kiss him back, but I did smile. Right before I gave into that anesthetic mixture of afterglow and exhaustion, I whispered the words I hadn't told him since that night all those months ago when I'd pulled him out from under a pile of demon ashes.

"I love you, too, Adrian."

Then, at last, I fell asleep.

CHAPTER THIRTY-SIX

I woke up to the unfamiliar weight of a heavy arm draped across my body. It made me smile as I rolled over into Adrian's embrace. Yeah, I could definitely get used to this.

"Hey," I murmured, opening my eyes.

Adrian's eyes were open, too. In fact, he looked like he'd been awake for a while. "Hey, yourself," he said, and kissed me.

I kissed him back, but pushed him away when he began to deepen the kiss in a more serious way.

"Wait," I said, rolling away. I might be in a romantic mood, but my bladder wasn't. His shirt was on the floor, and I pulled it on before I hurried into the bathroom.

When I came out, Adrian was still stretched out on the bed, his muscled arms over his head and the sheets tangled around his hips. I enjoyed the sight of that so much, it took me several seconds to register the numbers on the clock behind him.

"I slept for ten hours?" I asked in disbelief.

His smile held a hint of wickedness. "You were tired. I can't take all the credit for that, but I'll take some."

Being up over thirty hours while bouncing back and forth between realms and time zones might have resulted in a lot of my tiredness, but Adrian definitely was responsible for some of it. And he was responsible for all my aches in very intimate places.

"Zach'll be here in about two hours," I said, mentally calculating when dusk was.

Adrian's smile grew. "That gives you only an hour to eat, shower and get dressed."

"An hour?" I teased, coming closer.

He lunged, using his incredible speed to grab me and throw me onto the bed before my next breath.

"Probably less," he murmured, giving me a scorching kiss.

In the end, I had just over thirty minutes to get ready. At some point while I'd been sleeping, Adrian had ordered room service, so I scarfed the sandwich, fries and iced tea he'd gotten for me as soon as I came out of the shower. Then I got dressed in the new clothes Adrian had managed to get, too.

I'd just finished putting on my jeans and lavender top when Zach appeared in the bedroom doorway. To his credit, he didn't so much as wink at the messy bed or clothes strewn on the floor.

"Time to go," he stated.

I looked at Adrian. "Do we need to check out?"

He let out an amused snort. "No, Ivy, it's fine."

I sighed as I fingered my new shirt, remembering that the nearest gateway was under the Brooklyn Bridge. "Guess all this is about to get wet."

"Don't worry," Adrian replied, going to the closet and pulling out a sealed plastic bag. "We've got more clothes."

"How long were you awake?" I asked in wonder.

He shrugged. "A while. I'm used to all that."

"Oh, I could tell," I replied, arching a meaningful brow.

His grin promised things I now knew he could deliver on. "I meant realm-hopping without sleep, but I love your dirty mind."

The sound Zach made must've been Archon for "enough already." "If you wish to go back to the realm, come with me now."

"We're coming," I said, and Adrian called out, "Brutus!"

The gargoyle came out of his room, giving a wary look at the windows, which still showed the soft light of dusk. Poor boy. Wait until he saw where we were going. But we wouldn't be staying long. Not when we couldn't leave unless Zach was there to pull us through the gateway. The Archon tended to disappear a lot, and we still had to search for the staff.

"After you," I said, sketching a theatric bow at Zach.

His mouth twitched in his usual version of a not-smile. "Marriage seems to agree with you."

Marriage. The word still felt foreign, as if it couldn't possibly apply to me, but I didn't argue. Adrian and I weren't just bound together by mere human legalities. We'd been soul-tethered. It didn't get more permanent than that.

When Adrian put his arm around me, his fingers trailing over that stunning, darkly glittering ring, I decided that I loved the word *marriage*. It meant that we were going to face whatever life or destiny threw at us together.

"Maybe I'll change my name," I mused as we left the suite for the elevator. "What's your last name again, Adrian?"

Something flashed across his face, as if I'd poked at an old wound. "I don't know," he replied lightly.

I could have kicked myself. I thought I'd simply forgotten it, but Adrian had been so young when Demetrius had taken him, he hadn't even known his full name. It's not as if his mother had been alive to tell him, either. Demetrius had seen to that.

"Well, you can always pick one, although I don't recommend Iscariot," I said, attempting to walk back the new, tense mood with my quip about Judas's last name.

Adrian's wry smile said he appreciated my stab at humor. "That wouldn't be my first choice, either."

"Or, maybe Zach knows what your mother's last name was?" I said, remembering that he had an encyclopedic knowledge of lineage, not to mention children. But when Zach's dark gaze landed on me, I knew I'd made a mistake.

"You inquire about Adrian's real mother, yet you've never asked me about yours."

I used walking through the busy lobby as an excuse not to respond. All my life, I thought I had known the basic story of my biological parents. Due to my mixed coloring, pediatricians had guessed that my father had been Caucasian, and my adoptive parents had believed that my mother had been an undocumented Hispanic immigrant who'd left me on the side of a highway when the tractor trailer she'd been hiding in jackknifed.

I hadn't hated my bio-mom for abandoning me. The Jenkinses had raised me better than that. Instead, the few times I'd thought about her, I'd pitied her for being desperate enough to give up her month-old newborn so she'd have a better chance at disappearing into this country. Her life in Mexico must have been truly awful. As for my bio-dad, well, I knew nothing about him. No Caucasians had been spotted escaping the tractor trailer the day of the accident, so he'd been gone by the time I was abandoned. Maybe he hadn't even known that he had a daughter.

That's what I'd believed, and the Jenkinses had showered me with so much love, I'd been fine with it. Then I'd met Zach and he'd ripped my world apart, first by telling me about my supernatural lineage and unwanted destiny, then by his comment about my birth mother. *Your real mother didn't leave you because she was running from the police. She did it to save you, just as your dreams revealed.*

He'd tried to tell me more, and I hadn't let him. I'd been too overwhelmed after finding out that my adoptive parents had been killed, Archons and demons were real and demons had my sister in one of their realms. Add in the part where my best chance at saving Jasmine involved a lost supernatural slingshot and an arrogant, secretive man who wanted nothing to do with me, and I'd been full up on what I could handle.

But Zach was right, I reflected as I got into the limo while Adrian gave Brutus instructions to follow us by air. I'd had chances since then to ask about my biological parents, and I hadn't. Why didn't I want to know? Was I afraid that the reality was worse than the fallacy I'd grown up believing?

I'd ask Zach after we found the staff, I decided, telling myself I wasn't taking the coward's way out. I was only being practical. Whatever the truth was, it could wait until then.

We tumbled into the light realm soaking wet from the East River. Well, all of us except Zach. He somehow emerged without a drop on him, then had the nerve to give me a condescending back pat as I coughed out the water I'd inadvertently swallowed.

Archons. They really rubbed in their superiority at times.

"Ivy!" Jasmine exclaimed, running over and hugging me despite getting dirty river water on her. "Are you okay? What happened? You were gone so long!"

"Just two days," I began, then stopped. Right, time moved differently here. "How long has it been on this side?"

Jasmine let me go, flipping back her odd streak of white hair. "Weeks," she said, a catch in her voice. "Zach came by an hour ago to say he was bringing you back soon, but before that, I hadn't seen him in weeks, either."

I turned to give the Archon a scathing look. "You promised me that you'd look out for my sister."

"And I did," he replied in that infuriatingly calm tone. "I left Jophiel to watch over them."

"You'd like him," Costa said to Adrian, giving him a hand slap instead of a hug. "He quotes Scripture *all* the time."

"And I missed that?" Adrian replied with heavy irony.

"Yeah, but—" Costa eyed the ring on my finger that Jasmine hadn't noticed yet "—guess you were busy with something else."

Adrian's hand covered mine, hiding the ring. "We were, but before we get to that, I owe both of you an apology."

Costa's brows rose, as if he'd never heard those words from Adrian before. My sister looked at our clasped hands and her mouth curled down, but all she said was, "For which thing?"

I shook my head at her choice of words. Good to know she still had her spiteful side even after being trapped with a Scripture-touting Archon for this timeline's version of weeks.

"For accusing you of betrayal."

The words fell flatly from Adrian, but his hand flexed around mine almost convulsively, indicating his true emotions.

"It wasn't you, Jasmine, although I was sure you'd done it," he went on. "And it wasn't you, Costa, although I thought you were the only other option. It was me."

My sister's features darkened until all the blood must have been rushing to her face. "You," she almost hissed. "Again."

"Not by choice," I said quickly, squeezing Adrian's hand hard. "This wasn't like before. Demetrius was, um, able to track Adrian through his blood, but none of us knew that."

Now Costa's brows really rose, although I wasn't going to tell them how. That was Adrian's secret to keep or to reveal.

"I'm sorry, too," I said, meaning it, but also trying to fill the new, ominous silence. "I thought it was you who'd snuck behind our backs to Demetrius, Costa. Please forgive me."

A muscle ticked in his jaw as he glanced at Adrian, then he gave us a lopsided smile. "I guess I'm sorry, too, because I thought it had to be Jasmine since I knew it wasn't me."

"And I thought it was you for the same reason," Jasmine said, with a pleading look at Costa. "I'm really sorry."

"Looks like we all are," Costa said, but I noticed that he took Jasmine's hand and no one else's. Then he turned to Adrian. "That must be powerful magic Demetrius is using." His tone was casual, but the look he gave Adrian made me wonder if he suspected the truth. "Do you have a way around it?"

"Yep, Zach fixed it, we're all good," I rushed to reply.

Adrian sighed. "I'm not hiding this from my best friend, Ivy, even if he's no longer my friend once I tell him."

"Tell me what?" Costa asked with open challenge.

Adrian dropped my hand and squared his shoulders. "I'm Demetrius's son," he said in an unwavering tone. "His real son."

CHAPTER THIRTY-SEVEN

We didn't have a chance to tell Jasmine and Costa about the binding ceremony. Not with how they took the news about Demetrius. Costa was the opposite of congratulatory, of course, but my sister just lost it. She railed at Adrian, at me and even at Zach, who pulled his usual disappearing act after her first shout at him. Finally, Costa suggested they take a walk.

"It'll give us time to think," Costa said, tugging her a step down the hill. "Let's sit by the river. You love that."

She snatched her hand away. "No. I'll go alone."

I stared at my sister as she stomped down the hill. I would've gone after her if I didn't believe my presence would do more harm than good. Right now, Jasmine might believe that this proved all her worst suspicions about Adrian, but after she calmed down, she'd realize it was no more Adrian's fault that Demetrius had fathered him than it was my fault for being the last Davidian. Sometimes, the only choice life gave you was how you handled the things you *didn't* choose.

"She's confused, angry and worried, but she's strong," I said once she was far enough away that she couldn't hear me. "She'll come around. She's handled everything else that's been thrown at her since demons kidnapped her six months ago."

Adrian's gaze held hints of sadness as he looked from Costa to me. "Maybe she can't handle this. It's about more than who my father is. It's also about who I am, and that's half-demon."

"You were half-demon when you worked with an Archon for years to rescue innocent people from becoming realm slaves," I said, my tone sharpening. "You were half-demon all the times you faced a horde of murderous minions and demons to protect me, and you were half-demon when you bound your soul to mine so you'd prove to me and everyone else that you weren't fulfilling your fate."

"You did what?" Costa said in disbelief.

Adrian glanced at him. "Living with demons taught me that trick, only this time, I used it against them instead of for them." To me, he said, "Demons tie humans' souls to theirs to create minions. It's how regular humans suddenly get superhuman strength, and also how demons ensure that minions won't betray them because, as you know, then the minions would suffer the same consequences. That's how I knew that Zach could tie my soul to yours. Any power that demons have first originated from Archons."

I gripped his hand. "See? Once more, you prove that your bloodline is just that—a bloodline. Not a template for who you are now or who you will be later."

He touched my face, his large, strong hands managing to be feather soft against my skin. "You believe that, and I love you for it. But I don't think most people share your opinion."

"Most don't," Costa agreed, ignoring the quelling look I sent him. "But some do, and I'm one of them."

Adrian stroked my face a final time before going over to Costa. "Thank you," he said, grasping Costa by the shoulders.

Costa rested his hands on Adrian's arms, leaning in until their foreheads touched. "For decades, I saw who you used to be, and

I hated that man. Then you rescued me and Tomas, and I spent the next several years seeing you fight to become someone else." Costa's voice thickened. "You did, and I love that man like a brother, no matter who his father might be."

Adrian pulled Costa into a hug that made tears prick my eyes, especially when Costa hugged him back just as hard. Then they separated, doing those awkward back slaps that men did when they were trying to downplay the fact that they'd experienced an emotional moment.

"Hey, I noticed something in those photos," Costa said, changing the subject, which Adrian seemed glad to do, too.

"The tablet ones?"

Costa patted his pants pocket, where I presumed Father Louis's phone was located. "Yep. There's no service here, so it was either look at those or listen to Jophiel recite entire books from the Old Testament."

Adrian grunted knowingly. "So, you chose the pics?"

"Memorized them until the battery died," Costa replied in a fervent voice.

I stifled a snort. Good thing Zach had walked away during Jasmine's tirade or he'd probably take issue with that comment.

"Anything would help," I told Costa. "We went to the places the tablet implied the staff would be, and while it *had* been there, it's not now, and there were no other maps or clues."

Costa scratched his chin. "I'm not sure this means anything, but in tiny letters on the back of the tablet, it said 'Made in Po-land.'"

"What?" I said in disbelief. The stone map with ancient runic writing that was our only clue to the second-most-hallowed weapon in the world had been mass-produced in *Poland*?

"Did whoever took the staff leave that as a fucking joke?" Adrian growled, echoing my next thoughts.

"Maybe it was a decoy?" Costa offered, giving a helpless shrug. "You know, to throw demons off, if they found it?"

"Then why bury it in a chapel?" Adrian burst out. "No demon could enter one. If I hadn't used dark objects to curse the ground, Blinky would've been fried on contact with the chapel."

"Maybe whoever left it assumed that minions could've found it and brought it to their master," I said, taking a wild stab.

Adrian's expression reflected all of the frustration I felt at this looking like yet another dead end. "Doubtful. What would a minion be doing in a church in the first place?"

Nothing I could think of. There wasn't anything remarkable enough about the chapel to draw that sort of attention to it. It was a small, hardly well-known one, and looked so unimpressive from the outside that no minion would feel compelled to search it for lost relics. In fact, if not for the chapel's unusual history of being moved from place to place, there would be nothing notable about it at all. It certainly hadn't been located in the center of a divinely parted sea or a locust storm, either.

Wait a minute. There hadn't been *anything* unusual about the area around the chapel. In fact, if Adrian hadn't trapped a demon there that he wanted me to practice my skills on, we would've never swung by Milwaukee, Wisconsin, and found the stone map in the first place. We certainly wouldn't have found the staff's prior locations, giving us a rough timeline of where it had been over the past hundred years...

All places that Adrian had also been very familiar with, and it wasn't the first time. He'd also been the former ruler of the same realm that David's slingshot had been hidden in. An idea slammed into my mind as if hurled by the slingshot supernaturally coiled inside my arm. *What if there wasn't just one map, but two?*

"With the realm bleeding onto the campus and demons slaughtering and kidnapping at will, we didn't have time to wonder why there was no weather or other natural phenomenon around the chapel," I said, interrupting Adrian and Costa's dispute over whether the stone tablet was a deliberate red herring or just what the staff's guardians had available to write their clue on. "We know the staff had been at St. Joan's for a few years at least, so that area should have been known for freaky weather or strange geographical incidents, right?"

"Yes," Adrian replied, drawing the word out as he realized the implications, too. "So should its old locations in France and Long Island, but I don't remember hearing about anomalies there, either. But we know the staff *does* affect its surroundings in powerful ways. That's why the sailing stones in Death Valley were our first stop. After that, I figured we'd check out Honduras, where fish rain from the sky every year, then the Taos Hum in New Mexico, then Venezuela for the Catatumbo lighting—"

"All places with freaky anomalies," I interrupted. "Especially the fish thing, but if we don't think the tablet is a joke or a decoy, then it's an authentic clue from whoever took the staff. In that case, nothing on it was accidental. So, maybe the 'Made in Poland' decal was left on there for a reason."

Adrian stared at me, my meaning sinking in. "You think the staff is in a church in Poland," he stated.

"I think it might be," I replied, and that wasn't even the craziest part of the theory that had taken over my mind.

Costa let out a disbelieving snort. "Talk about hiding a clue in plain sight! The decal was so small, anyone could have missed it."

"You didn't," I told him, with a grateful smile. "I probably never would have noticed it in those pictures."

He grunted. "You didn't have those pictures as your only escape from endless sermons."

No, but Costa had. Coincidence? I was starting to doubt it.

"So, let's assume we're right about the significance of 'Made in Poland,'" I said, continuing with my theory. "Was Poland on your list of places with freaky weather occurrences?"

"No," Adrian said, his arched brow questioning where I was going with this.

"When we get back to the real world, we can google Poland to see what parts have freaky natural occurrences," Costa said.

"We could do that," I agreed, taking a deep breath. What I was about to suggest sounded insane, but after all I'd been through, I was starting to believe that more than a series of random coincidences and flukes had led us to where we were now. Add in some cryptic Archon speech about a map "of sorts" and a staff that might be controlling a lot more than nature, and maybe we'd been looking at this puzzle from the wrong angle.

If not, well, then, this wouldn't be the first time that someone called me crazy. "The staff is what Moses used during his infamous standoff with Pharaoh, but what was the point?" I asked, plowing ahead with my theory.

Adrian lifted a brow. "To call down crushing plagues?"

"Yes, but what was the *point*?" I insisted. "Everyone knows the 'let my people go' line that Moses kept repeating to Pharaoh, and after the plagues, Pharaoh did. So, what if the staff's influence isn't limited to nature? What if, just like with Pharaoh, the staff's greatest accomplishment is influencing *man*?"

I began to pace, so consumed by my theory that I couldn't stand still any longer. "And if so, what if thousands of years later, the staff's influence caused two sets of people to do the exact same crazy thing? After all, it cost huge sums of money to have an obscure little chapel disassembled and moved brick by brick over thousands of miles just to be reassembled again, and for what? There's nothing special about the chapel! But we know that's what happened, and we know the staff moved with it from France to New York to Milwaukee. So what if the *staff* made both those chapel owners do something senseless and costly, just like Pharaoh did something that he would have considered senseless and costly by letting his entire enslaved work force leave? And if so, then instead of looking for the staff in places with freaky nature anomalies, should we be looking for it in places with freaky *human* anomalies?"

I was almost panting by the time I finished, having rushed through those last sentences without taking a single breath of air. When I was done, Adrian said nothing. Neither did Costa. They just stared at me, until the silence passed awkward and headed right into uncomfortable.

Okay, so they didn't seem to share my views on the staff. Wait until they heard the rest of my theory, and it was either tell them now or keep it to myself forever.

"There's more," I said. No way could I keep this to myself. "I found the slingshot in your former realm when I was looking for Jasmine. We found the tablet by going to your former home at the campus, the chapel's location in New York just *happened* to be at a chateau that you used to stay at, and its original location of Chasse-sur-Rhône in France just *happened* to be the first place you went to when you were exploring the human world. Yes, you've been all around in your very long life, but that's too many coincidences. I think the tablet isn't our only clue to the staff's location, Adrian. I think the *real* map is you, so let me ask you—have you ever been to Poland?"

If I thought they'd looked skeptical before, this time both Adrian and Costa's faces registered sheer disbelief. Then, after a silence that slashed across my nerves, Adrian's expression changed, becoming so hard and calculating that, for a split second, he reminded me of Demetrius.

"Yes, I've been to Poland," he said in a stiff voice.

I let out the breath I hadn't realized I'd been holding. Now, for the million-dollar question. "Any particular place?" If he'd been all over that country, it would blow a huge hole in my theory, but the look he gave me sent chills up my spine.

"There was one that I kept going back to."

"Was it a church?" Costa asked, his tone almost urgent.

Adrian answered while keeping his gaze locked with mine, and what I saw in its depths convinced me that I was right. "Calling it a church is an understatement."

Zach appeared, walking over as casually as if he hadn't left in an angelic huff. "Are you ready?"

"For what?" I asked, wary.

He smiled, a rare real one. "To go to the Salt Cathedral."

CHAPTER THIRTY-EIGHT

Zach led us through the gateway to Wieliczka, Poland. All of us, even though I had wanted Jasmine to stay behind. Zach refused, saying that he had important tasks to carry out and couldn't continue to act as our supernatural doorman. That analogy would have amused me if he didn't follow it up by disappearing as soon as he'd pulled the last of us through.

"This is just great." I could still feel the gateway, but true to Zach's warning, I could no longer cross through it. "Get your Archon ass back here, Zach! You can't strand us in a tiny foreign town with no passports, money, transportation or weapons!"

No response. I resisted the urge to give the gateway the middle finger only because I didn't think Zach could see it. The only person more upset than me was Brutus. He snarled at the bright light around us, hitching his wings up to cover himself. Then he glared at me as if to say, *More sunshine? How could you?*

"Don't worry," Adrian said, rubbing my back. "I can call someone and get what we need. We just need a phone."

Costa pulled out Father Luis's cell phone, tried to turn it on and then put it back. "Yep, battery's definitely dead."

I forced myself to relax. Okay, so we might have a long walk ahead of us, but there were worse things. At least it wasn't dark, making this area demon-free for a few more hours until the sun went down. After that, well, where there was a light realm, there was a demon one. I could only hope that it wouldn't drop on us or leak out onto us, either.

Adrian looked around. "I know this place. It's the town's version of an urban market."

The quaint buildings arranged in a square around us didn't strike me as that, but whatever, it meant that phones were close. And hey, one of the shop's names was even in English. Granted, it was called Fuck Luck Tattoos, but all I focused on was that if the title was in English, then someone in the shop probably spoke it.

Adrian must've felt the same way. He took my arm, murmuring, "Let's try here."

"I'll stay with Jasmine," Costa said. Brutus had already run toward the shop because it had a sun-blocking awning.

I glanced at my sister. She met my gaze, then deliberately looked at the diamond ring on my hand before looking back at me. After her blowup following Adrian's parentage reveal, I expected accusation in her stare, or anger, but instead, the only emotion I read was sadness that bordered on grief.

Don't let him hurt you, she mouthed at me. *Please.*

Adrian's back was turned, so he didn't see it. I closed my eyes for a moment, wishing I could reassure her that her fears were groundless. Adrian wouldn't betray me. He'd only hidden the true purpose of my destiny from me before because he'd been trying to help me, and while that had been a betrayal of my trust, he'd had good intentions. Just like I'd had good intentions when I'd hidden my knowledge of Demetrius from him.

Adrian tugged on my arm again, turning around. "Ivy?"

"Coming," I said, adding, "I'll be fine," to my sister. Then I went into the tattoo shop with Adrian.

The proprietor did speak English, and he agreed to let Adrian make an international call after he dropped a hundred-dollar bill onto the counter. I didn't think he'd had any money, so I was more than surprised to see several more Benjamins in his wallet. At my questioning look, Adrian shrugged.

"I brought some emergency cash along with our dry clothes."

"You didn't get *any* sleep earlier, did you?" I muttered.

Adrian only smiled as he accepted the phone from the proprietor and dialed. After a moment, he began to speak in French, judging from the few words I recognized. The conversation lasted about five minutes, and when Adrian hung up, he looked satisfied.

"We now have a hotel reservation and a car on the way. The rest of what we need will arrive tomorrow."

He knew someone who could get four fake passports within twenty-four hours? I was impressed. "Wow."

"The salt mine's just a few blocks up from here, isn't it?" Adrian asked, as if only casually inquiring.

"Yes," the black-haired, heavily tattooed man replied in accented English.

"Thanks." To me, Adrian said, "Want to walk by and see if it interests you?"

I translated the subtext and let out a short laugh. If I felt nothing at the mine, then I had been wrong about Adrian being the map and possibly everything else.

"We came all the way to Poland," I replied. "I sure as hell hope that it interests me."

Costa, Jasmine and Brutus came with us, even though the three of them hung well back. That was fine. I was focused on my hallowed sensor. So far, I didn't feel anything, and the closer we got to the mine, the more that worried me. I'd been so sure that I had figured out the real clues to finding the staff. Zach knowing without us telling him that we wanted to go to Poland only seemed to confirm that, but in retrospect, he'd never said that I'd gotten it right. He'd never said anything, in fact, except that he wasn't our doorman. Would Zach really drop us here if he knew that it was nothing more than a wild-goose chase based on a very incorrect assumption?

Yes, I thought grimly. He would. And probably be smug about it afterward, too.

When Adrian said, "This is it," I was still registering a zero on my hallowed meter. The small, rather plain-looking building in front of us didn't match with my mental picture of the home to a salt cathedral, either, although it *was* a mine so everything interesting was below.

"How deep is the mine?" I asked Adrian. Maybe that was the problem. I could be standing directly above the staff, and yet perhaps still be far enough away not to sense it.

"Very deep," Adrian replied. "Over a thousand feet. And the mine is also well over a hundred miles long."

I gaped at him. "Are you serious?" If it was that massive, it could take a full week of underground explorations before I picked up a hint of the staff, even if it was here!

"You don't feel anything?" Adrian asked, his tone light.

I knew him well enough by now to know that the more deliberately unconcerned Adrian sounded, the more he usually cared. "Not yet, but if it's under a thousand feet of solid rock because it's at the bottom of this thing, I wouldn't expect to."

So saying, I walked toward the entrance of the mine. At some point, this place had been turned into a tourist attraction, and signs in four different languages, English being one of them, told me where to go. Adrian caught up to me in a few strides. So did Brutus, who was eager to be inside anywhere.

"Stay here, Brutus," Adrian told the gargoyle when we entered the building. Then he spoke to him in Demonish, and the tourists ahead in the ticket line cocked their heads at us.

"You talking to bird?" the woman asked in stilted English.

"He's our pet," I told her, patting Brutus and stifling my smile as she goggled at that. "We just love seagulls."

Then, it was our turn to get tickets, and Adrian selected four for the Tourist route. He paid cash and then handed two tickets to Costa and Jasmine.

"You are in luck," the female teller remarked. "The English-speaking tour group needed four more to be complete."

"Let's hope our luck continues," I said under my breath, then gave the teller a parting smile as we joined the group.

Edgar, our tour's group leader, went over a brief history of how the mine was thousands of years old and used to be a major producer of salt for the area. I stopped listening after the first few minutes, tuning into my hallowed sensor instead. So far, it was still flatlined. After several more minutes of droning on, we were herded into the mine's version of an elevator and our descent began.

I was glad I was wearing jeans, but I soon realized that my blouse wasn't suited for this. With each story that we went down, the temperature seemed to plummet, until I was fighting a shiver when we stopped and got out at the first leg of the tour.

"Everything you see is made of salt," Edgar was saying, and I paused in my hallowed-finder mode to give an appreciative look around. Statues and what looked like 3-D paintings were carved into the walls, as detailed and impressive as anything I'd seen in a museum. I could understand why Edgar had to specify that all of this was salt, too. With its bluish-gray color, it more resembled granite than the stuff I sprinkled on my food.

An hour later, I was torn between being thoroughly impressed and very disappointed. We'd traveled down hundreds of carved steps, seen the magnificence of the Chapel of St. Kinga, which rivaled the basilica for beauty, in my opinion, as well as other caverns that were decorated with life-size statues acting out religious scenes. There was even an underground lake, with a light show playing across its glassy surface set to the music of

Chopin. Yet while I'd been awed by all the works of art around me, especially considering how they had been chiseled out by hand from solid rock salt, my hallowed sensor had been silent.

I didn't understand it. If there was ever an example of sense-less human behavior being influenced by a supercharged, hal-lowed object, this mine should be it. And still, I felt nothing hallowed at play here.

After we had lunch at the underground restaurant—yes, there was an underground restaurant—and the group was starting to reform, I pulled Adrian aside.

"We need to try going deeper," I told him. From our guide, I now knew that the Tourist tour only descended a quarter of the way down into the parts of the mine open to the public.

"Edgar," Adrian said, sidling up to our brown-haired, slightly portly guide. "This has been wonderful, but my wife wants to get more adventurous. We'll need to go back up to get tickets for the Miners or Mystery tours."

"I'm sorry, my friend, those require purchasing two weeks in advance," Edgar replied.

Adrian smiled at him and pulled out his wallet, fingering through the still-impressive stack of bills in it. "Are you sure there isn't *anything* you can do? I'd hate to disappoint her."

Edgar's features tightened in obvious offense. Great, we'd been assigned an honest, unbribable man as our guide. Now we were probably about to get kicked out entirely.

I rushed to place my hand over Adrian's wallet, giving Edgar my best guileless smile. "*So* sorry! I'm afraid we're a little too used to how things work in America. Plus, this is our honey-moon, so he's tripping all over himself trying to make me happy. I hope you excuse his exuberance. He meant no insult—"

I stopped my apologetic gushing when Edgar suddenly grabbed my hand. His grip tightened when I tried to pull away, and then Adrian's arm shot out, landing against Edgar's throat.

"Take your hands off her," Adrian said in a dangerous tone.

Costa sidled over, giving a concerned glance at the standoff. "Everything okay?" he asked quietly.

Edgar still hadn't relinquished my hand. He couldn't stop staring at it, even as Adrian increased the pressure to push his forearm deeper into Edgar's throat.

"Let. Go," Adrian said, each word heavy with threat.

"Wait," I breathed, realizing what Edgar was starting at. I pulled up my sleeve, revealing more of the braided-rope tattoo, and Edgar's eyes bugged. "You recognize this, don't you?"

"Yes," Edgar managed to say.

Adrian stared hard at Edgar. I hadn't seen any telltale shine over Edgar's eyes or other minion characteristics, and when Adrian dropped his arm, I knew he hadn't, either.

A small crowd had started to gather as members of our group stopped what they were doing to watch this. I ignored them and tapped Edgar's hand, which was still clasped over the lower part of my tattoo. "How do you know this mark?"

Edgar finally let go of me to rub his throat where Adrian had half throttled him. Then he shocked us all.

"Because I am one of the Guardians of the staff, and we have been waiting a long, long time for you, Davidian."

CHAPTER THIRTY-NINE

Edgar followed up his stunning announcement by pulling the fire alarm. We stayed below, but the remaining members of our group plus all the other tourists and most of the mine's employees were rushed up to the surface. Only Edgar and an old, spindly man he introduced as Piotr remained with the four of us, and as we waited for the mine to completely empty, Edgar told us its real history.

"Piotr and I are both Guardians. The roots of our order can be traced back to 660 BC, when the first of us smuggled priceless relics out of Jerusalem before the Babylonians invaded. Later, some of us became Templars, but our primary responsibility was always the same—guard the staff until the day of the last Davidian."

It was beyond unbelievable that a group of people had been expecting my arrival for over twenty-six hundred years. Then again, it was also unbelievable that I had a hallowed weapon even older than that supernaturally embedded into my arm, so who was I to judge?

"Is it here?" I asked, everything tensing in me.

Both Edgar and Piotr appeared surprised by the question. "Of course," Edgar said. "Can't you feel it?"

My breath exploded out of me as relief nearly weakened my knees. We'd finally found it!

"Ivy's only recently begun to embrace her abilities, so she's still learning how to hone them," Adrian replied.

Piotr still looked doubtful, but Edgar seemed satisfied by that. "It is also much deeper than where we stand."

"You were the Guardian entrusted with its location?" Piotr asked, sounding very surprised.

Edgar bowed his head. "Now that the awaited day has come, I can at last admit that I was the one chosen among our order."

"And where is the staff, exactly?" I prompted.

"Beneath the Russegger Chambers," Edgar replied.

Piotr looked at Edgar as if he'd lost his mind. "You alone out of dozens were entrusted with its location, and you were foresworn never to reveal it to anyone!"

"Except her," Edgar replied, gesturing to my right hand for emphasis. "As foretold, she bears the mark of the Davidian."

All this "foretold" stuff was starting to creep me out. Wait until these guys found out that I was here to retrieve the staff but wasn't going to use it yet. They might believe my lineage made me all that, whereas I knew I wasn't nearly strong enough to attempt to wield the staff yet. It would be safer for me to play Russian roulette with a half-full cylinder of bullets.

Piotr gave me another skeptical look, then turned back to Edgar. "I will ensure that all the chambers are empty and send the rest of the employees away. Only Guardians should be present for this."

Adrian began to strip the nearby restaurant tables of their tablecloths, clattering dishes and glasses to the floor. "We need lots of these to wrap it in," he muttered, and Costa hurried over to help.

Jasmine stayed with me, and I was startled when she came

closer and her hand slid into mine. Then I squeezed back, infinitely glad by the wordless gesture of support. She might be mad, worried and highly disapproving of recent events, but she was letting me know that, no matter what, she was there for me.

"So, you're the one who took the staff from the Milwaukee chapel and left the tablet behind as a clue?" Jasmine asked.

Edgar smiled. "Yes. And my predecessor was the one who journeyed with it from France to its two homes in America."

"Why move it so much?" I asked, glancing around at the mine. "At the bottom of this place seems pretty safe to me."

"We do as we're told," Edgar replied. "And the Messenger is never wrong. Shortly after it was moved from here to France, the mine flooded, so it would have been damaged had it remained. Then the Messenger told us to move it with the chapel from France to America. Less than twenty years later, Nazis overran France, and among their many cruelties, they were obsessed with stealing religious relics. Then the New York chateau burned in the 1960s and the Messenger told us to take the staff along with the chapel to Wisconsin. Ten years ago, when its responsibility fell to me, I obeyed the Messenger's instructions to bring it back home and leave the tablet as a clue for you."

"Who's this Messenger that tells you what to do?" I asked, suspicion growing along with my anger.

Once again, Edgar looked surprised that I didn't know. "Zacchaeus," he said, calling Zach by his full name.

Adrian responded with a slew of curses that mirrored my thoughts exactly. Just wait until I saw that Archon again! He'd known all along where the staff was because he's the one who'd been directing its movements for over two thousand years!

"Do not say such things," Edgar gasped, staring at Adrian in horror. "Zacchaeus is an officer of the Most High!"

"You don't know him like we do," I said grimly. "He let us run around like chickens with our heads off for weeks when he knew where the staff was the whole time. Worse, people got kidnapped and killed from the demons following us. Had Zach just told us where it was, he could have prevented all that."

"Damn right," Jasmine muttered. Costa grunted in agreement.

Edgar looked distressed as he glanced back and forth between us. "*You* cannot mean that," he finally said.

I let out a short laugh. "Sorry to disappoint you sooner rather than later, but I do." Then, because he looked on the verge of either giving me a lecture or bursting into tears, I added, "Why don't you take us down to the Russegger Chamber?"

Edgar pursed his lips as if holding back a reply, making me think he'd been leaning toward lecture instead of tears, but at last, he gave me a short nod.

"This way."

The elevator in the Danilowitcz Shaft was the only direct way in or out of the lowest portion of the mine, and it took us over four hundred feet straight down into the darkness. By the time we stopped, my ears had popped several times. I moved my jaw around in an attempt to relieve the pressure, but the worst part was that the pressure was the only new thing I felt.

"How far away from it are we now?" I asked Edgar.

"It is about seventy meters ahead, in the old mining tunnel past the chambers," he replied.

Since America was the only nation not on the metric system, I had no idea what that meant. "Two hundred feet," Adrian translated, catching my questioning look.

I tried not to remind myself that I'd felt the staff's former casings much sooner. Tried, and failed. Why wasn't I feeling it yet? It had to be at least ten times more powerful than the stuff it had been wrapped in, and yet I felt nothing!

"Are you sure it's still here?" I muttered under my breath.

Edgar heard that, and gave me a very offended look. "I have guarded it faithfully for the past twenty-five years."

Half his life, judging from how old he looked. And since he'd come from a long, long, long line of Guardians, he obviously took his job very seriously. That meant slacking on his part wasn't the problem. It must be me.

I took a deep breath, blowing it out slowly as we entered the chambers. Some of what we passed looked like science exhibits, with different types of salt, their ages and their chemical compositions behind glass walls. Others contained old machines and tools used in mining, and farther in were religious exhibits, like a wooden re-creation of the crucifixion. Through it all, I felt *nothing*...until we stepped into the mine tunnel.

"Ivy!" Jasmine cried when I suddenly lunged forward with no coordination and fell. Adrian reached me in the next instant, but though I could hear him speaking in a concerned tone, the words blurred into white noise.

Boom, boom, boom! went my hallowed sensor. Or maybe it was my heart. I couldn't tell the difference anymore. All I knew was that I was being yanked farther into the tunnel by a force I couldn't see, but though invisible, that force had a stronger hold over me than anything tangible ever could.

"Let me go," I heard myself snarl at Adrian, but he didn't. After several hard shakes, I could finally make out his words.

"Ivy, listen to me! Costa checked the door to the mine. It was warded to mute the staff's effects. That's why you couldn't feel it before, and why it hit you so hard all at once."

"I had no idea," I vaguely heard Edgar add. "Those markings have been there for centuries, but no one knew what they meant."

Some of the fog left my mind, so I processed what they were saying, yet it did nothing to stop my need to go forward. I had to reach the staff. Not doing so made every muscle ache as though I were being beaten from the inside.

"Let go." It was all I was capable of saying. If I could've caused the slingshot to come out, I might have started whipping Adrian with it. That's how deep the need ran to reach it.

Adrian's grip tightened on me instead. "I don't think she can help herself from touching it," he told Costa. "I'll have to get her past the muters again, then go in for the staff alone."

I was so appalled by this, my right hand connected with his jaw in a punch that rocked him backward. Still, he didn't let go, and when I went for another punch, he grabbed my fist, knocking my legs out from under me at the same time.

"Nice one, dear," he said through gritted teeth, "but we're getting you out of here before you go full Ronda Rousey on me."

"I cannot show the staff's location to anyone except the Davidian," Edgar insisted. "I've made vows."

Adrian gave him a glare I only half saw because I was still trying to wrest free. "I made vows, too, and one of them tethered my soul to this woman's, so you're going to show *me*."

"But you—" Edgar began. Then he stopped.

A horrible, metallic screeching sound filled the air, followed by an explosion that rocked the ground beneath us and sent ominous clouds of dust raining from the roof.

"No!" Edgar shouted, running back toward the chambers.

Adrian picked me up and ran after him. I fought as if I were deranged until the moment we crossed the entryway to the mine shaft. Then my need to reach the staff evaporated as quickly as those phantom pains that had overtaken my body.

"I'm okay, put me down," I urged, but Adrian ignored that, using his superior speed to race past Edgar and reach the first section of the chambers. A thick cloud of dust billowed out to meet us, and beyond that, more sounds of metal breaking followed by frightening tremors in the earth.

Pain shot up my arm and my tattoo suddenly glowed bright gold, lighting up the thick, chalky air around us. Adrian saw it and pivoted, reversing course so fast that it felt like my head might snap off from extreme whiplash. But in the next instant, two large snakes snapped their fangs at empty air instead of me, and as the dust cloud cleared, I saw the same snake-armed demon who'd tried to kill me weeks ago. Piotr was behind him, the old man looking all too smug, and when I saw dozens of eyes flashing through the dark, I knew that the snake-armed demon had brought friends. Lots of them.

"Adrian, Davidian," Vritra said, satisfaction practically oozing from his tone. "We meet again."

CHAPTER FORTY

"What did you do?" Edgar yelled at Piotr.

The old man stared at him defiantly. "Ensured my future, something being a Guardian has never done. Now that I've proved my worth, I will be transformed, as I deserve."

A minion wannabe. Now I'd seen everything. Adrian slowly let me down, and as soon as my feet touched the floor, I bent, picking up the loose rocks that the explosion had shaken free.

"There's no way out, Davidian," Vritra said in a pleasant tone. "Those explosions you felt were Piotr blowing a hidden charge to disable the elevator, and the second blast took out the staircase above the Dlugosz Chamber."

Edgar's stricken expression confirmed that we had no way out of here. "How could you?" he breathed to Piotr.

"Easily," Piotr bit back. "All it took was a few sticks of the dynamite, plus a mirror to summon Vritra. I have been serving him for the past three months." He turned smug eyes on Adrian. "Did you really believe that throwing him into an ocean could wound him indefinitely?" He chuckled before zeroing in on Edgar again. "You and the rest of our order might consider

it an honor to spend your life underground and in poverty, but
I don't."

I was actually wondering why Vritra and his minions hadn't
charged us yet. They had us trapped. What was he waiting for?

"We can proceed one of two ways," Vritra said, answering
my unspoken question. "I slaughter all of you, which is my personal preference. Or, whoever leads me to the staff gets to live,
and whoever doesn't dies."

So *that's* why! Piotr might have told Vritra before that the staff
was in the mine, but the mine was over a hundred miles long
and over a thousand feet deep, which was too vague to be useful
if you couldn't sense it. And before today, Piotr hadn't known
who among the dozens of Guardians had been entrusted with
its exact location. Now, Vritra needed me or Edgar to point him
to the staff, or even with it narrowed down to one mine shaft,
he'd spend countless days or weeks trying to find it.

"Don't do it, Edgar," I murmured.

He glanced at me, his gray gaze hard. "I was chosen because
I would rather die than betray my cause, so let this demon scum
do their worst."

The slingshot was now fully uncurled from my arm, and I
notched one of the salt rocks into it. "You heard the man," I
said, starting to spin the rope. "Take your offer and shove it."

Adrian pulled out two guns from holsters beneath his shirt.
So he'd gotten a lot of things while I was sleeping earlier. "I
kicked your ass before, Vritra. Love to do it again."

The snake-armed demon smiled as he glanced at Piotr. "Seems
they need more persuading. Blow the last charge."

What charge? I thought. Piotr's uneasy expression only increased my sense of foreboding. If Vritra didn't have over a dozen
minions in front of him, I'd start slinging rocks, but with his
minion shields, the projectiles wouldn't reach him.

"But, master, I may not survive, either—" Piotr began.

"Do it!" Vritra roared, his coiling serpents striking out at Piotr, their fangs missing him by mere inches.

Piotr lunged away from the deadly snakes, leaving the shelter of the minion crowd. That was all Adrian needed. A shot rang out and Piotr fell, clutching his bleeding chest. Adrian fired again, this time hitting the minion who threw himself in front of Piotr. From the tangle of legs surrounding him, I saw the spindly old man glaring at us, and even as blood bubbled from his lips, he pulled something out of his jacket and pressed it.

The explosion didn't sound as massive or as close as the previous ones, and though the ground shook, the walls stayed up and nothing caved in. For a few relieved moments, I thought that something had gone wrong with the blast. Then I heard a strange rushing sound that grew louder.

Edgar grabbed my arm. "Run! He's flooded the mine!"

Adrian began firing into the crowd at will as he backed up. Edgar was pulling at me for all he was worth, but this might be our only chance to kill Vritra. I aimed for his head and snapped the rope, sending a rock right at the demon. He ducked, and it hit the minion behind him. Furious, I notched another rock, but that rushing sound grew, and then water blasted into the chamber with enough force to knock the minions and Vritra over.

Adrian grabbed my hand and we ran back through the first chamber. When we reached the second, I heard water smash into the glass displays of the first room, breaking everything it its path. We ran faster, until we reached Jasmine and Costa, who'd gotten a big head start. I grabbed her and Adrian got Costa. Together, we propelled them forward faster than they could go on their own, but it wasn't enough. Water splashed around our ankles when we reached the fifth chamber, and by the time we got to the seventh one, it was up to our waists.

Worse, it wasn't only filled with glass, rocks and other dangerous debris. It had also carried along the minions and Vritra with it. Three snakes popped their heads out of the water next to me, and I lunged away just in time. Adrian released Costa and grabbed the snakes, tearing their heads off with a brutal yank. I screamed when three more appeared in the water behind him. He whirled, grabbing them and tearing, but too late. One of them latched on to his arm and those deadly fangs sank in.

"No!" I shouted.

Adrian grimaced as he pulled the snake head off his arm and threw it aside. I tried to run to him, but the water was now up to my chest, and I tripped over objects it hid from my view. Then Vritra emerged from the frothing waves. Decapitated snake heads swirled around him as he grabbed Adrian, his features a mask of rage. Adrian fought, but his movements were terrifyingly uncoordinated and his eyes looked unfocused.

The poison, I realized in horror. Adrian was half-demon, so most things couldn't kill him, but other demons could and, maybe, so could demon poison.

Arms grabbed me around the waist and pulled. Hard. I kicked to get free, but with everything shifting from the rising water, I lost my balance. Those arms pulled me under, and for a few frantic seconds, I fought to break the surface. My assailant kept dragging me back down, and amid my panic over lack of oxygen, I realized my error.

Instead of fighting to break the surface, I grabbed my assailant. Water blunted the effect of my punches and made my slingshot useless. My only advantage was that it also blunted the punches and kicks from the minion I was grappling with. I had to do something else. Fast.

With my lungs burning for oxygen, I felt around until I reached his face. It was easy to find, since he bit me viciously as soon as I grazed it. Instead of trying to pull free, I used my trapped hand as a map, and then shoved my thumb into his eye as hard as I could.

Frenzied kicking and fighting ensued. I absorbed every painful blow and held on, shoving my thumb deeper and twisting.

Those movements abruptly stopped and I twisted free, taking in huge gulps of air as soon as I cleared the surface.

"Ivy!" my sister screamed. I sloshed around, seeing her and Costa much farther ahead. The force of the water had swept them and several minions into the mine, but Adrian and Vritra were still in this chamber, and I was horrified by what I saw.

Vritra's hands were wrapped around Adrian's neck. Adrian was trying to pry the demon's hands free, but his eyelids were fluttering and he looked to be fading.

"You tore my throat out once," the demon hissed. "It's time I repaid you for that."

I lunged toward them, desperation allowing me to cut through the water with more power than I should have had. Then, because I had nothing else to use and Adrian's eyes were closing with a terrifying finality, I looped the sling around Vritra's head, planted my feet in his back and pulled with all of my might.

I fell backward into the water so suddenly that I was sure I'd failed. Then something bobbed against my chest, and I stared down at Vritra's decapitated head. His mouth was still moving in curses as his skin blackened and caved inward, then his head disappeared and ashes filled the water around me.

I swam over to Adrian. Ashes blackened his throat from Vritra's hands, but that was quickly washed away in the swirling water. It had risen until I could no longer feel the ground, and the ceiling was only a few feet away.

"Adrian!" I said, shaking him. His eyes fluttered and he smiled, but his veins were starting to turn black as the poison worked its way through his body.

I pulled him with me as I swam, keeping his head above the water. The only place left to go was the mine shaft where the staff was located. From the little I remembered of it, it went back a long way, so it might buy us time before the water reached the ceiling and drowned us all. Plus, once I crossed through the doorway, I wouldn't be thinking about anything except finding the staff.

Maybe that was a good thing, I grimly decided as I swam toward the mine shaft. The only way any of us would survive was if these waters suddenly, miraculously receded, and there was only one item in the world that could cause them to do that. It might kill me to use it, but if I didn't, we were all dead anyway, and if I was going down, I'd rather go down fighting.

I tightened my grip on Adrian and pushed us toward the doorway to the mine. Right before we crossed it, the entire cavern filled with light.

Zach appeared in the center of the water. Light radiated from the sword in his hand, growing in brightness, until the blade shone like a lightning bolt. He used it with ruthless accuracy, hacking into every minion that the rushing river swept his way. Ashes blackened the water and screams echoed in the mine as the minions tried to fight the current to swim away. They couldn't. Faster than my eye could follow, Zach hacked them to pieces, somehow not hindered at all by the chest-deep water.

"Ivy, hurry," Zach ordered me. "They're right behind you."

Who? I turned, and then gasped. At least a dozen more demons were crashing through the water in the chamber just beyond this one. From the shouts that echoed behind them, more were on the way. Piotr had blown the elevator to bits, ensuring we couldn't escape, but a four-hundred-foot drop was probably a fun free-fall for demons that had been waiting centuries or more to claim this staff for themselves. Or kill me, depending on their preference.

"Go!" Zach urged me. "I will hold them off." Then his teeth flashed in a smile that was nearly dazzling. "It seems I *don't* have more important things to do than act as your doorman."

I would have been stunned by the joke, let alone the smile, but there wasn't time. I pushed Adrian past Zach through the mine entryway, watching the Archon snatch him up with one hand while slicing a minion in two with that great, shining sword. He didn't seem hindered at all by holding Adrian above the water while fighting, so, taking a deep breath, I plunged through the mine entryway myself.

CHAPTER FORTY-ONE

As soon as I passed the warding symbols that had muted my link to the staff, my fear vanished. So did my aches from the multiple items I'd bashed into in the water, let alone the beating I'd taken from the minion who'd tried to drown me. All I could focus on was the staff, and it pulled me forward as if I'd been caught in a tractor beam.

I swam past Jasmine and Costa, not listening to what they said as I went farther into the mine. Something slashed into my leg, an old piece of equipment, perhaps, but not even the pain registered. All I could feel was the staff, and its power sizzled along my nerves from being in its proximity. *Closer,* it seemed to whisper, urging me forward. *Almost there.*

A hundred yards ahead, I stopped, facing the wall on my left. It was the same granite-gray color of the rest of the mine, its uneven surface no different than the rest of the rocks around it. Yet when I touched the stone, the power behind it seared my hand, and I would've snatched it away at once if I could feel the pain. For the strangest reason, I couldn't. I was too consumed with freeing the staff from its rocky confines.

I dug around the surface of the rock, knowing that the slab

acted as a natural door and my prize was right behind it. My hands and fingers tore and bled from the jagged edges of stone, but that didn't stop me, either. Neither did the water rising up to my chest as I continued to feel for a good handhold in order to pull the rock away. When I finally reached a spot where my fingers could curl around the stone at both ends, I pulled. The stone gave, but not enough. I increased my efforts, feeling my muscles strain as I heaved and pulled with all of my strength.

The rock slid toward me, and water rushed into the alcove it revealed. I barely noticed the carved stone figure of the old bearded man behind it. My eyes were fixed on the wooden staff in his raised hands. The statue held it in front of itself as if in supplication, and the staff was so long, it extended from the floor to well past the reach of those stone hands.

And the power that vibrated from it made the very air around me crackle with energy.

The slingshot in my arm throbbed, as if recognizing the power that ran through the staff. Without a single concern as to the repercussions, I grabbed it, removing it from the stone hands that were half-curled around it. Using the staff would save everyone. I knew that to my core, unlike the time I found the slingshot and had to keep trying until I mustered up enough faith to wield it.

But as soon as my hands closed around the staff, my mind felt like it emptied of everything that made me Ivy Jenkins. I wasn't concerned about the water that now swirled to my chin, the screams and howls that echoed down the tunnel from the supernatural death match, my sister, Costa or even Adrian. I didn't have purpose here. Something else did, and it was so overwhelming, so focused, that nothing else could sway it.

It made me hold the staff vertically, then raise my arms over my head. As soon as I did, power smashed into me with the force of a meteor landing. I would have crumbled beneath it, but that force held my legs as straight as the arms I kept extended over my head. That power grew, building, until it took over everything, even my breath. I was held completely immobile, with no more free will than a power line has over the electricity coursing through it, and as that power reached a crescendo that felt as if it would rip me asunder, I had a moment of complete, out-of-body clarity.

I could see the ruined elevator, the broken exhibit and all the smashed rocks now being pulled back into their original positions. Could feel the water reversing course and returning to the underground lake it had poured out from, then feel the walls of rock beneath it realign into the impenetrable barrier they had been before dynamite had blasted them away.

Then, with another bone-shaking surge of power, I felt that unstoppable, unbelievable energy flare out far beyond the confines of the mine. It expanded and grew, becoming too great for my mind to measure, and through it, I felt the gaps, tears and breaks in the realm walls. Another blast of power shattered my mind, and I felt them all being repaired. But it didn't stop. It continued to grow, surpassing comparison, until more, then all, the realm wall weaknesses were rebuilt. The gateways slammed shut and were sealed with impenetrable bonds, and though I couldn't hear them, I felt the screams of countless demons as they realized that they were now trapped within their dark, icy worlds.

Finally, the power began to dissipate, and with its absence, that invisible grip around me loosened. My knees gave way. I would have fallen, except I still had a death grip on the staff. Then it, too, seemed to disappear and I slumped to the stone floor. The water was now gone, but the floor of the mine was wet, and that cold surface seemed to increase the chilliness that had taken residence inside me.

I'd gotten it all wrong, I thought, bemused by the irony. I hadn't been the one wielding the staff, after all. Instead, the staff had wielded me.

"Ivy!" I heard someone shout, yet the voice sounded so far-off, I didn't recognize it. Then it said, "Oh God, she isn't breath-ing!" and I thought it might have been Jasmine, but I wasn't sure.

"Do something, she's dying!" I heard next, and almost smiled. Definitely Jasmine. I'd know that screech anywhere.

"I cannot." For some reason, Zach's voice sounded much closer, as if he were speaking right into my ear. "I have been ordered not to heal her or to raise her if she dies."

Figures, I thought, and would've shaken my head if I could move anything. I couldn't, though, and that revelation was im-mediately followed by another. I couldn't feel anything, either. No pain, which was a relief, but the nothingness, the discon-nect… Jasmine must be right. I was dying.

I was less depressed by that thought than I would've imag-ined. I mean, I'd spent the past several months worrying that using the staff would kill me, and now that it apparently had, I was oddly okay with it. I'd miss Jasmine, of course. Costa, too, and while my biggest regret was not having more time with Adrian, I felt so lucky, so glad, to have had one perfect, soul-sharing day with him. *I love you, Adrian*, I thought, slipping fur-ther away. *Always…*

"Bring him here," Zach said, his voice barely audible now. I thought I heard him say, "Join their hands," but I couldn't be sure. I was floating away, and it wasn't frightening at all. In fact, it felt kind of freeing…

A jolt slipped into me, tiny and yet potent, like a mild elec-tric shock. For the briefest second, it brought the pain and the noise back, and then it was gone. I was relieved by the silence and nothingness again. It was so peaceful here. If Adrian were somehow with me, it would be perfect—

Jolt. Jolt, jolt, jolt, jolt.

Noise crashed into me, along with more pain than I could stand. I tried to run from it but I couldn't move, even if now, I could feel in full, agonizing acuteness.

Ivy, I felt rather than heard Adrian whisper. *Use my strength to heal yourself. Come back to me.*

The pain was so intense, I was screaming, and at the same time, I knew I wasn't making any sound. I was trapped in a nightmare I couldn't wake up from, and each slow, fluttering beat of my heart sent more merciless, cascading pain through me.

Ivy, Adrian said more urgently. *Stop fighting and use my strength!*

I didn't know what he meant, but when he spoke, those jolts sizzled through me with more power. Could that be him, some-how? I wondered. Was I being shocked with a defibrillator? If so, then I was technically dead, but other people had come back from that. Could I?

When the next shock went through me, I stopped trying to run from it. Instead, I braced myself and absorbed it. It brought an avalanche of pain, but beyond that, I could hear Jasmine's voice again. And Adrian's, though his still seemed to be whispered into my mind instead of filtered through my ears.

That's it, Ivy. Take more.

Another shock, and I rode it without bracing this time. Light flashed before my eyes. Not the I-see-a-tunnel kind, but with flashes of faces bent over me and a babble of voices. Then another shock, and another, and I was riding a wave of pain that swept me right into full sound, color and sensation.

"Ivy!" my sister screamed. Then louder, "Costa, she opened her eyes!"

"Stop shouting," I tried to say, but couldn't. That's when I realized I had a large tube shoved down my throat. I couldn't seem to move anything except my eyes, and when they slid to my right, I saw Adrian in a hospital bed next to me. He also had a breathing tube and multiple machines around him, but his arm was stretched out as if reaching toward me.

That's when I looked down and saw that his hand was clasped around mine. Tears filled my eyes, overflowing onto my cheeks when I saw him blink once, slowly, and then his dark sapphire gaze met mine.

He couldn't talk, either, but he smiled, and when he did, I knew that both of us were going to be okay.

CHAPTER FORTY-TWO

It took three doses of manna over three days before I could walk again. Funny; I thought I'd mastered walking around age two, but over a week in a coma will mess your body up, it seemed. Adrian was either taking just as long to recover or he was holding himself back to match my pace out of solidarity.

My mobility problem wasn't the only new thing I woke up with. I also had another tattoo that ran from my neck all the way down the right side of my body, finally ending at my toes. The incredible detail of the gnarled wood staff looked as if it had taken an artist weeks to ink onto me, but I knew that it had only taken seconds as yet another hallowed weapon merged with my skin. I had no idea what this meant, but if my second tattoo was anything like the first one, it might come in handy one day.

Costa had arranged for us to recover in an abandoned church that he'd turned into a makeshift intensive care unit. How did he do all that? It turned out that months ago, Adrian had given him access to his accounts and contacts in case of an emergency. Since this had definitely qualified, Costa had made the most of both. We had an excellent doctor, two nurses and two physical therapists at our beck and call. They were wonderful people who never questioned the odd surroundings, lack of mirrors or complete confidentiality requirements. I was so grateful for all they'd done, but when it was time for them to leave, I was glad to see them go. That meant we were really recovered, and re-covered meant that we could finally start our lives again.

I couldn't wait to do that with Adrian.

That's why, when a familiar blue hoodie appeared in the corner of my eye as I was packing so we could catch our plane back to the States, my first reaction was to tense.

"Zach," I said without turning around. "What are you doing here?"

"You're still angry with me," he noted in his usual mild tone.

I shoved a shirt into my suitcase with more force than necessary. "Yep, although I owe you a thank-you for stopping the demons in the mine shaft, but then again, they wouldn't have been there if you'd told us where the staff was in the first place."

He came closer, forcing me to look at him unless I chose to walk away. "After everything you've been through, you still don't see it?"

"See what?" I asked. "Adrian trying to kick your ass as soon as he realizes you're here? Or see Jasmine get in line to do the same after him? You didn't make a lot of friends when you said you wouldn't heal me or raise me, even though you could have easily done one or the other."

"I have orders," Zach said, his dark gaze unwavering.

"Then maybe tell me why *He's* got it in for me?" I snapped, a soul-deep hurt bubbling to the surface. "I have done my best with all this, yet He specifically ordered you to let me stay dead if my best still ended up getting me killed?"

Zach sighed deeply. "You have the supernatural proof that billions of people long for, yet you have so little faith. When will you realize that nothing in your life has been left to chance? Take my not telling you about the staff."

"Yes, let's hear it," I muttered. He ignored that.

"If I had told you where it was the night you first decided to go after it, you would have been killed because you weren't ready. If I'd told you weeks ago when you left with Adrian seeking it, you both would have been killed—Adrian by the demons in the ambush, you as soon as you touched the staff because again, you weren't ready. If I'd told you right after the campus attack, same scenario. In fact, if you'd learned *at any time* before you did, you, Adrian, your sister and Costa would have died as a result. So tell me, Ivy, how have I wronged you with this?"

Frustration bubbled up in me. If he was telling the truth, then he hadn't. In fact, then I owed him another thank-you, and a big one, but it still felt wrong.

"All those people at the campus and back at the desert house," I whispered. "You're saying they died and got trapped in demon realms all so I could get tough enough to wield the staff? And that's supposed to, what, be an acceptable trade? Why didn't you help them? If you knew everything that was going to happen, you knew that, too, yet you did nothing. Why is that? Because you didn't care, or because your boss didn't?"

Zach's dark gaze glowed with specks of light. "You believe you would do better if the power of life and death was yours?"

I let out a harsh laugh, thinking of my parents, who'd been killed by demons because they were stirring up trouble over Jasmine's disappearance. Adrian's mother, slaughtered by Demetrius while she was trying to protect him. Father Louis, a good man, killed by Blinky. Edgar, a loyal Guardian, either drowned or killed outright in the mine ambush. Tomas, Costa and Adrian's friend, killed by minions in the desert. All the people demons and minions had pulled into the realm during the campus attack, and all the hopeless, abused ones I'd seen when I was searching the realms looking for the slingshot.

"I don't know if I'd do better, but some days, it looks hard to do worse," I said, meeting Zach's gaze.

"Prove it," Zach said, startling me. "All the dark realms are now sealed off. This keeps most demons off the earth, but also dooms the humans trapped in them. You, Ivy, and you alone have the ability to do something about that."

"How?" I asked, but deep down, I already knew.

"The final weapon," he replied, confirming it. "The spearhead of Longinus."

I was the last Davidian, so I should know this, but it didn't ring any bells. "Who was Longinus and why is his spearhead so important?"

"Longinus was the Roman solider who thrust his spear through the side of Jesus of Nazareth as he hung on the cross," Zach replied. Oh, right. *That.* "The spearhead is all that remains of the weapon," Zach continued, "but one thrust of it through the appointed gateway can create a door in all the realms that only humans can cross through. If you find it and use it, you will save all who manage to come out, but the spearhead is the strongest, most hallowed weapon of them all."

I'd just relearned how to walk after spending over a week in a coma because of the staff, so I don't know why I said what I did next. Maybe, I just had to hear it out loud.

"I have less than a million-to-one chance of surviving if I use it, right?"

"Yes," Zach said, and the single word was cruelly spoken. "And as you know, I will not raise you up if, or when, it kills you. So, Ivy, you who believe that you can do better by people, I say again—prove it. Be willing to almost assuredly sacrifice your life for theirs. Or—" his dark gaze became even more intense "—do not. No one can make you do this. Your fate, and theirs, is in your hands alone. By your will, hundreds of thousands of humans will either perish or get the chance to live. As you wished, the choice is yours."

A sob tore from my throat. This *wasn't* what I'd wished for! How could it be? I didn't want to die, especially now, when I had so much to live for. Why should all of this be dumped on me? I hadn't asked for this destiny, and I sure as hell wasn't the one who'd stood by while those people were enslaved by demons in the first place. So why were my options only limited to live, and doom many, or die, and save some?

"What about Adrian?" I asked, struck by an even more awful thought. "We're soul-tethered now. If I die, does that mean he dies, too?"

Zach's expression became shuttered. "Adrian is half-demon as well as the most powerful Judian ever. Your death would mortally wound him if he were only human, but his humanity is the smallest part of him. His Judian lineage plus his father's blood will ensure that he survives."

So I was the only one who had to die, if those people were to get a chance to live. I let out a short, despairing laugh. For months, I'd complained that I wanted my destiny in my own hands, and now it was. Worse, just minutes ago, I'd sworn that I could do a better job at playing God than the real God could. Now, as Zach had so bluntly pointed out, it was time to put my money where my mouth was—or my life where my convictions were. Talk about being careful what you wished for.

"Don't listen to him, Ivy," Adrian said, appearing in the room. He ran over to me and then gripped me by the arms. "Archons might not lie, but whatever he told you, it's an exaggeration and a trap. Don't you see? He *wants* you to die because that's what destiny says you're supposed to do. Screw destiny, you deserve to live! You've done enough."

Oh, I wanted to believe that! I wanted so, so badly to think that I'd given all I could, and to spend the next fifty or so years living happily with Adrian. But even as I considered that, those same reels of faces seared across my mind.

My parents. Father Louis, Edgar, Tomas, the people I'd pleaded with in the desert house, the ones I hadn't been able to save during the campus attack and every single, suffering person I'd seen in the demon realms. If I turned away now, I'd be saying their lives weren't worth saving, and all of them had wanted to live just as much as I did. How could I consider my life worth more than hundreds of thousands of lives just like theirs? And what kind of life would I even have, if that's the person I chose to become?

Zach said he'd given me a choice. No. No, he really hadn't. "Adrian…" I began.

He dropped his hands and spun away, lunging violently toward Zach. As soon as his hands closed over the Archon's throat, Zach simply disappeared.

He reappeared behind me. I turned around, and a flash of near-blinding light made me throw up my arm in front of my eyes. That light also stopped Adrian from charging at Zach again, and he, too, used his arm as a shield against the beams of light shooting out of Zach with the brightness of several nuclear detonations.

Even with my eyes closed and my arm shielding my face, it still felt as if the light was burning its way into the back of my skull. Then the painful light dimmed enough for me to risk opening my eyes. When I did, I gasped again, and lowered my arm.

Zach's trademark blue hoodie and jeans were in a heap on the floor. So was his human body, which looked like a crumpled-up flesh suit that someone had tried on and discarded at an elaborate costume shop. The being in front of me had no skin. No distinct form, either. Instead, amid that halo of incredible light, I saw what looked like wings made of lightning surrounding a shape that I guessed was humanoid only because I thought I saw arms and legs.

Then, just as abruptly as it had appeared, all the dazzling light was gone and a young man stared back at me with ordinary brown eyes and a mocha-colored face that was partially shielded by a low-hung hoodie.

"Why did you do that?" I managed to gasp out, blinking to get the hot spots out of my vision.

"Now that you have chosen to see your destiny through to its conclusion, I wanted you to see my true form," Zach said, his deep voice sounding slightly husky. "You have often wondered what I felt for humanity. I used to love it, but after many millennia watching your kind tear each other apart, I began to long for humanity to reap its well-earned judgment. Once it does, the last war between Archons and demons will be fought, and I will finally be able to avenge the blood of my fallen brothers and sisters."

I'd often wished that Zach would drop his cryptic way of speaking and just tell me what he was thinking, but now that he finally had, it hurt me to the core. "So, you've always wanted me to fail?" I said, fighting against the burn in my throat that threatened tears at this confirmation of one of my darkest fears.

"At first, yes," he admitted, a hard smile ghosting across his lips. "Yet my 'boss' forced me to watch over you. Witnessing your struggles, your pain and even your recklessness reminded me why I loved humanity to begin with. It wasn't because your race was ever good, or even better than it is now. Your race has always been fatally flawed, yet they are also ever hopeful. They might be cruel, yet they are also capable of great love, and while each of you is inherently selfish, you are also able to sacrifice, when the time comes." He shook his head slowly. "I am very powerful, yet I have never had to struggle against myself the way that your race does every day of your lives. Now that I am reminded of that, I no longer wish for humanity's end to hasten. My fallen brothers and sisters can wait a little longer for their vengeance."

Then Zach reached out, brushing my cheek in a gesture that I would've called affectionate, if he were anyone else. I was as stunned by that as I was by his many revelations. He hadn't painted a pretty picture of humanity, but we weren't pretty.

Still, most of us tried. I didn't have much to say for myself aside from that, and according to him, it was enough.

"But you still want Ivy to sacrifice her life," Adrian said, and the bitterness in his voice broke my heart. "Even now, Zach, you still don't care enough to help Ivy save her life. Instead, you want to help her to end it."

"Adrian, please," I said, reaching out to him.

"No," he said sharply, and the look he gave me chilled me to the bone. Those weren't his eyes. They were his father's eyes.

Just as suddenly, Adrian's gaze softened, making me mentally lash myself for ever thinking such an awful thing. Then he held out his arms, and I gratefully ran into them.

"You're right, I'm blaming him and it's not his fault," he said, kissing my face with light brushes of his lips. "We'll figure something out with the last weapon. We always do. You'll be okay, Ivy. I promise."

"I love you," I replied in a choked voice. "No matter what, I love you."

"I love you, too," he said, his voice deepening with single-minded intent. "More than you'll ever know. We'll get through this, I promise you. Both of us."

I held him tighter, glad for what had to be soothing lies despite his promises that he'd only tell me the truth. We both knew how this would end, but at the moment, I needed reassurance more than I needed honesty. Maybe Adrian did, too. He sounded like he really believed what he was saying, even though we both knew that he was most likely wrong.

Still, right now, we had each other. Life was only lived in the present, and so I'd put everything I had into whatever present we had left. From the tightening of his arms around me, I knew that Adrian would, too. Besides, it could take months or years to find the spearhead. I could grow stronger by that time, perhaps even strong enough to withstand the final weapon's devastating effects. Maybe, just maybe, I *would* beat those million-to-one odds. After all, destinies were sometimes made to be broken.

EPILOGUE

Adrian stood in front of a large mirror. He touched its smooth, unbroken surface, thinking that it had been years since he'd seen his reflection this well. Other reflective surfaces, like water or windows at night, never revealed things in such clear detail. In those, he wouldn't be able to see the hard set to his jaw or the flintlike look in his eyes as he spoke the name of the demon he'd never hated as much as he did now.

"Demetrius."

His reflection blurred and the mirror rippled as if it had become water. Then, in the center, a dark form appeared, growing larger until a very familiar man filled the frame. When Adrian saw the bright lights of a modern cityscape behind Demetrius, he let out a harsh laugh.

"You managed to avoid getting trapped in the realms along with the rest of them. Why am I not surprised?"

"Because you know me, my son," Demetrius said, a small, sly smile curving his mouth. "And if you didn't think I had a contingency plan in the event that the little Davidian succeeded, then you don't know me as well as you should."

"Let me guess. Cursed earth?" Adrian asked, with an ironic glance at the ground Demetrius stood on.

The demon's dark eyes gleamed. "Remember, I'm the person who taught you all your best tricks." Then he looked beyond Adrian. "You summon me from a church so that I cannot leave this mirror to come to you. Do you still fear me, even now that you know the truth of who I am?"

"No, I don't fear you," Adrian replied. That was the truth, even as he fought to make his tone light. He'd never let the demon in front of him see how tortured he was by doing this. Demetrius would only use it to his advantage, and Adrian had almost nothing left as it was. "But I sure as hell don't trust you."

Demetrius's shoulder lifted in a concurring shrug. "I suppose I do tend to misbehave."

Adrian stifled his snort. Demetrius *would* characterize untold millennia of horrible deeds that way. "I didn't come to banter or to catch up on what you've been doing. Real father or no, I still hate you, and I'd kill you if I could."

Instead of being angered, Demetrius grinned. "If not for your regrettable honesty, I'd be proud of you, my fierce, vengeful son. However, let me impart a word of fatherly advice. Next time, don't warn someone that you want to kill them. Tell them all is forgiven, then rip their heart out as soon as they turn their back."

Adrian gave him a pointed look. "My honesty comes from my mother, and I'm keeping it because it's all I have left of her."

Demetrius let out a sigh. "You say that as if I enjoyed killing her. I didn't, even though she deserved it by hiding her pregnancy and your birth from me. When I finally found out about you, I tried to reason with her, but she summoned Archons to fight against me. What choice did I have?"

The one where you didn't kill her, Adrian thought, but he didn't bother saying it. Demetrius's mind simply didn't work that way. Adrian would have a better chance explaining poetry to a cockroach, and he didn't have long until Ivy expected him back.

Ivy. Adrian steeled himself for what he had to do next. It felt
vile, as if he'd dunked his soul inside a vat of filth, but if he didn't
do this, she would die. He didn't care that he'd probably die with
her, despite overhearing Zach's assurances that his Judian and
demon natures would be strong enough to withstand her loss.
What Zach hadn't said, and yet the cunning Archon undoubt-
edly knew, was that without Ivy, he wouldn't want to go on.
But most of all, after everything that Ivy had been through, he
couldn't *let* her sacrifice herself this way. She deserved a chance
at happiness, and he hadn't been able to give her much, but he'd
damn well make sure that he could give her that.

"I'm soul-tied to Ivy now," Adrian stated, although he suspected that Demetrius knew that.

His father winced as if the words had injured him. "Yes, I can
sense the stink of her soul around yours from here."

"That means whatever happens to her happens to me, too,"
Adrian went on. Demetrius should know that, but he was taking no chances by guessing. "You might be a twisted, evil bas-
tard, but I'm probably the closest you've ever come to truly
loving someone. When Ivy was dying after wielding the staff,
I almost died, too. Ivy recovered because she siphoned enough
of my strength through our tie to survive."

"And you only had that strength because you are my son,"
Demetrius said, emphasizing those last two words, as if the truth
wasn't enough on its own.

Adrian met his father's gaze without flinching. "Yes, and you
want me to live. I won't, not with every demon and minion still
topside gunning for Ivy. I know you aren't the only one who
got out before the gateways closed, but remember this—if Ivy
dies, then I die, too, whether by the power of the spear or by
my own hand. I won't live without her. I refuse to."

"Ivy." For a moment, hatred blazed in Demetrius's gaze as he
said her name. Then, it vanished and he shrugged as if he didn't

care. "The other thing you get from your mother? Deplorable taste in lovers."

Adrian didn't crack a smile at Demetrius's backhanded insult to himself, although that was the closest he'd ever heard his father come to being self-deprecating.

"I can misdirect the other demons on this side from hunting Ivy down. As for the minions, I'm sure you can handle them on your own," Demetrius said. At Adrian's doubtful look, the demon waved a hand. "I'm not lying. Unlike the prior two weapons, I don't care if the little Davidian uses this one. Let her save some of the wretched meat bags trapped in the realms. She can't hurt my people with it, and they will eventually find a way to punch a hole though the walls and return on their own."

"But if Ivy uses the spearhead, it will kill her," Adrian said, hating himself but loving her enough to do this. "I've tried to convince her not to go after it, but I can't change her mind or stop her. As her abilities have grown, so has her need to save people. It's almost a compulsion now."

"Of course it is, it's her destiny," Demetrius said dismissively. Then he cocked his head, understanding dawning on his pale features. "But you don't want her to find the spearhead, let alone use it." A statement, not a question.

Adrian forced the single, damning word out between his gritted teeth. "Yes."

A slow smile spread across Demetrius's face, and it was filled with so much triumph that Adrian almost smashed the mirror right then. *You're wrong*, he thought savagely. *I'm not doing this to betray her. I'm doing this to save her!*

"Well, then, my son," Demetrius drawled. "It seems that we have a lot to talk about."

★ ★ ★ ★ ★

Turn the page for a sneak peek at
THE BRIGHTEST EMBERS,
the earth-shattering conclusion to
New York Times *bestselling author*
Jeaniene Frost's BROKEN DESTINY *series,*
in which fate goes head-to-head against true love...

I walked into the museum with a half demon holding my hand and a gargoyle waiting for me back at our car. As a History major, I'd often dreamed about going museum-hopping in Europe, but not once had I pictured doing it like *this*.

"We're here for the 4:00 p.m. tour," Adrian, my new husband and the aforementioned half demon, told the museum attendant.

"The 4:00 p.m. tour group is over there," she said, pointing toward a small cluster of people about a dozen feet away.

As we walked off, Adrian traced the braided rope tattoo on my right hand. My sleeve hid the rest of it, just like my high-necked blouse and long pants hid the remains of the second hallowed weapon that had supernaturally merged with my flesh. If the final hallowed weapon we were looking for was here, I'd no doubt end up with a third supernatural tattoo, too.

Of course, that tattoo would probably decorate my cold dead corpse, but I was trying not to think about that.

"Feel anything, Ivy?" Adrian asked in low voice.

I sent my senses outward and felt the distinct vibes that denoted being on hallowed ground, plus additional brushes of power from the various religious relics this museum housed. But

I didn't feel anything potent enough to punch a hole through every demon realm in existence, and that's the specific ancient relic we were after.

"No," I said, frustration coloring my tone.

I also hadn't felt that kind of power at St. Peter's Basilica in Rome last week, or the Hofburg Palace in Vienna earlier this week. Now we were at the Mother See of Holy Etchmiadzin complex in Vagharshapat, Armenia; the third place in the world to claim possession of the spearhead of Longinus, aka the Holy Lance, aka the final hallowed weapon that I was supposedly fated to wield.

Yet according to my lineage-derived radar that could sense hallowed objects, the famed spearhead wasn't here. The only reason I didn't walk out was in case wards were messing with my ability to feel it.

That didn't mean I was optimistic about our chances. "I suppose if the real spearhead was at one of the places it was supposed to be at, demons would've stolen it to use the power for themselves centuries ago," I muttered.

Someone close enough to overhear that gave me a startled look. I just waved at her. I wasn't worried about shocking her with the truth about demons, Archons—better known as angels—minions, or any of the other supernatural creatures I now knew were real. Hell, I could spend the next twenty minutes telling everyone here that all these things existed, and no one would believe me even if a bunch of demons were breathing down their necks while I spoke. Trust me, I knew that from experience.

"We had to check out this museum to be sure the spearhead wasn't hiding in plain sight," Adrian reminded me. Then he drew me closer, brushing back my dark brown hair.

"Besides," he murmured, leaning down until his mouth nearly touched mine. "This might not be a successful hallowed relic hunt, but it's turning into a great honeymoon."

My cheeks weren't the only parts of me to grow warm at his statement, yet instead of leaning into his lips, I pushed him back. The look in his eyes said he was about to kiss me in way more suited to our bedroom than a museum located in the headquarters of the Armenian Apostolic Church.

Still, Adrian was right. We might have struck out at finding the third hallowed weapon, but other than that, this had been the best month of my life. The second hallowed weapon had closed the gateways between the demon realms and our world, effectively locking the demons out. That made it a thousand times safer for me, Adrian, my sister, our friend Costa, and every other person in the world. Only minions were left on this side of the realms, and with their demon masters locked up, they seemed to be running scared instead of terrorizing anyone.

"Kiss me later, let's do the tour now," I told Adrian. "I might not feel anything, but the last weapon's power was blocked by wards. The spearhead will probably be warded, too, so maybe it's here and I just can't feel it yet."

"Maybe," Adrian said, his light tone belying the sudden darkening of his sapphire-colored gaze.

Then he straightened, and just like that, the teasing, passionate man I loved was replaced by a hardened fighter who'd been raised by demons to be the world's most effective killer. I took in a deep breath, reminding myself that the demons' efforts to make him their best weapon had backfired. Now, Adrian used his amazing abilities to fight demons instead of using them to help them.

Besides, he was only gearing up for a fight in case the spearhead really *was* here. If so, its incredible power would compel me into attempting to use it on the spot, and I wasn't ready to. Not yet. That's why Adrian would fight to the last ounce of his demonically-fueled, destiny-enhanced strength to stop me from touching the spearhead if it was here.

Because if I did, we both knew that it would kill me.

★ ★ ★

As it turned out, neither one of us had anything to worry about. One glance at the relic should've been enough to prove that it wasn't the real deal. Touching the glass around it to make sure it hadn't been protected by wards had almost been redundant. A first century Roman spearhead wasn't a short, flat, ornamental object that looked better suited to be a necklace than an ancient tool of war. It was a nasty, two-foot iron shank crowned with a sharp, pyramid-shaped point designed to impale someone even through protective armor.

No, this was another fake, and now, we had no idea where to look for the real spearhead. Adrian wasn't nearly as upset about that as I was, and he wasn't even trying to pretend otherwise.

"You could at least fake some disappointment," I said as we walked toward where our rental van was parked.

He gave me a sideways glance. "Then I'd be lying, and I thought we agreed there would be no more lies between us."

We had, but he didn't need to rub in how he'd much rather that I never found, let alone wielded, the spearhead. I could understand his reasons why, but if I gave this up, then countless thousands of innocent people would die.

"And I thought *you* agreed to support me," I said, the weight of all those lives making my tone sharper.

Adrian stopped and turned to face me. The sun was starting to set, casting artificial shades of red across his golden hair. His towering height, impressive physique, and gorgeous features had turned lots of heads as we walked, but he stared at me as if we were the only two people in this massive complex.

"I do support you." The smoothness in his tone didn't fool me. Unbreakable ties could also be made of the finest silk. "My every action is driven by my undying love for you, in fact. What more do you want than that?"

Put that way, what more could I want? Yet something still

felt…off, as if what Adrian *wasn't* saying was more important than his actual words.

Underneath my joy this past month, I'd also had a nagging feeling that I was missing an important detail. Of course, it could be that I just didn't know how to be truly happy. I'd never had a real relationship before, plus until six months ago, I and everyone else who knew me had believed that I was crazy.

"I know you're not chomping at the bit to find the spearhead because using it is dangerous for me," I said, exploring that nagging feeling. "But we agreed that we couldn't let the thousands of humans trapped in the demon realms die just because using it poses a risk. I've survived lots of risks before, remember?"

Adrian opened his mouth as if to argue, then closed it. "I know you have," he said, still in that easygoing tone. "You're just not ready to wield it yet. That's why I'm glad that none of these relics have been real. Later, when you've had more time to train, you'll be better prepared to handle it."

"Yeah, well, later better end up being sooner," I muttered. Those trapped people couldn't wait years for me to bulk up on my supernatural fortitude. They might not even have months. The demon realms had been brutal enough with the gateways open. With them closed, it would be far, far worse.

"Don't worry," Adrian said, intensity deepening his voice this time. "I'll keep you safe, Ivy. I promise."

I gave him a lopsided smile. Yes, between Adrian and our good friend Costa training me, my stamina, strength and skills had grown by leaps and bounds, which made me a lot safer for a lot of reasons. Who knew? It might be enough to keep me alive after wielding the weapon—assuming we ever found it.

I shook off that nagging feeling. It had to be me projecting paranoia plus my own inner turmoil onto Adrian. After all, aside from that first huge fight when I'd decided to go after the spearhead, Adrian hadn't argued with me once about it. He'd arranged these trips, helped me train, and been nothing but supportive about the whole thing. So, even though I felt like I'd grown an inner "trouble brewing" sensor in addition to my hallowed one, it had to be in my head.

"Fine," I said, my tone brightening. "Since the spearhead is a bust, do you know any good restaurants around here?"

I stopped speaking when Adrian flung me forward so hard, I would have hit the pavement face first if not for all the training I'd undergone. Instead, I immediately rolled, muscle memory taking over. Several loud pops sounded in quick succession above me, as rapid as fireworks, yet when they were followed by screams, I knew what they actually were. Gunfire.

"Ivy, run!" Adrian shouted.

I darted to the nearest car for coverage. Thank God we'd been on our way to the parking lot when whoever this was opened fire. Otherwise, I would've had nothing to use for cover. I was even more grateful that bullets weren't lethal to Adrian. He hadn't joined me behind the car, but ran in the direction of the shots. That would be suicidal for anyone except him. His half-demon bloodline meant that only another demon could kill Adrian.

"I'm good!" I shouted so Adrian wouldn't worry about me.

The car window above me shattered and a hole appeared an inch from my nose. Guess I wasn't good! Worse, the angle from that shot had been completely different than the first rounds. Shit. We were being attacked by at least two shooters.

I hit the ground and began to crawl toward another car, shredding my knees on the concrete, but not caring about the pain. Another shot winged the car nearest to me, and I lurched to the right, seeking shelter in the opposite direction.

"*Larastra!*" I shouted to Brutus, using the Demonish command Adrian had taught me. I hoped the gargoyle could hear me. Our rental van was all the way on the other side of the parking lot.

A familiar roar responded to my shouted command, followed by a much louder crashing sound. I fervently hoped it was my pet who'd caused that instead of a third attacker joining the mix, but I didn't dare pick my head up to look. Instead, I stayed as low as I could while I darted between the cars.

Glass kept exploding next to me, causing me to immediately pick new cars to hide behind. Soon, I felt like I was stuck in a deadly game of pinball. From the angle of the bullets, the shooter had to be on a roof, giving him a great view of the parking lot and my every move. I might not be able to hide, but I could run. I risked rising into a crouch to get better traction, and darted for a nearby truck. It was high enough off the ground that I should be able to crawl under it, and its bulky steel frame should provide more protection—

Pain erupted in my calf, followed immediately by a burn in my upper arm. I bit back my scream and didn't pause to see how badly I'd been hit. Instead, I lunged for the truck while trying to zigzag so I wasn't as easy of a target.

Before I reached it, a massive, winged beast landed on the car in front of me. The hood crumpled like a tin can under his weight, and I only had a second to hear the car alarm go off before the gargoyle's roar deafened me to everything else.

"Good boy!" I told him. "Who's getting steak tonight?"

Brutus spread out his leathery wings as if he knew I needed the cover to hide behind. I ran to him and immediately scrambled onto his back, using the harness he always wore now.

More cracks of gunfire sounded. From the way Brutus jerked, they'd hit him. His scaly hide was too thick for the bullets to penetrate and really injure him, but they must've stung. Brutus let out another roar, his talons shredding the car's hood in outrage. Then a beat of his mighty wings had us airborne. I didn't want him to merely fly us away, though. I wanted to stop this shooter before he hurt anyone else.

I pulled on the reins, directing Brutus to fly nearly straight up. Then, I angled him downward toward the roof of the museum Adrian and I had recently left. There was a small structure on that roof, like a short turret, and I glimpsed the barrel from a long sniper rifle protruding from the open window.

"Let's get him, boy!" I shouted, aiming Brutus right at that window. Then I hid behind the gargoyle's wide back.

Brutus knew what I wanted him to do. He drew in his massive wings at the last moment, leaving his body streamlined for maximum velocity. I braced when we burst through the window, his wide body taking out a lot of the wall, too. We landed with a thump that made all my bones rattle.

Screams caused me to hold on to Brutus with my thighs so I could shield my eyes from the flying shards of glass and stone. Brutus had landed on someone hard enough to make the guy's guts burst out of his sides. That concerned me until I saw the rifle in the dead guy's hands. When the shooter began to turn to ash, my suspicious proved correct.

This wasn't just any shooter. Only minions and demons turned to ash after they died. Since demons were locked away in their realms, not to mention we were on hallowed ground that they couldn't cross, the dead guy had to be a minion.

Brutus spun in a half circle, his long, leathery wings shooting out. Until then, I hadn't noticed the other guy crouched on the far side of the room. He sprawled forward under the blow, looking stunned as well as terrified. Light rolled over his eyes, as if he were an animal caught in a car's headlights. That inhuman trait outed him as a minion, too.

"N-n-nice birdie," he stuttered at Brutus.

Thanks to Archon glamour, he didn't see a massive, nine-foot-tall gargoyle with dragon-like wings and grayish-blue, reptilian skin. Instead, he and everyone else only saw a fluffy seagull. Granted, one that had somehow flown through a window and stomped his buddy to death, all while carrying a passenger on his back. No wonder the minion looked as if he didn't know whether to scream or to faint.

"Davidian," the minion said next, proving that he knew who I was, at least. "Have mercy on me."

"Mercy?" I repeated in disbelief. "You mean like the mercy minions show humans when you enslave them for your demon masters? Or the mercy demons showed my adoptive parents when they murdered them and pinned their deaths on me? Or maybe you mean the mercy demons showed my sister when they used her as bait in one of their countless attempts to kill me?"

He glared at me almost sullenly. "Who are you to judge? You've murdered hundreds of people."

"No, I've killed hundreds of *demons*," I corrected him, waving my tattooed right hand at him. "King David's ancient slingshot turned out to pack quite a punch, but I'll tell you what. I'll show you the same mercy you just showed me when you watched your friend use me as target practice."

His look became hopeful. "You'll let me run for it?"

"Make it to the door and you're a free man," I told him, loosening Brutus's reins. "Promise I won't stop you."

He whirled around—and Brutus lunged forward, biting him in half with one vicious snap of his huge jaws.

"Details matter," I said under my breath. "You should've made me promise not to let *him* stop you, either."

Once, I would have been horrified by seeing a man bit in half, but that person was long gone now. She'd been replaced by the new me, and the new me had been hardened from grief, betrayal, survival, and a whole lot of destiny and death.

Plus, if I'd let the minion go, he would have destroyed more peoples' lives. Now, the only thing he was destroying was the carpet as his ashes stained it black.

"Good boy," I said again to Brutus, holding on tighter when

his instant, happy wiggles were enough to almost unseat me. Brutus loved praise more than he loved life itself. "Now you'll get *two* steaks for dinner tonight."

ACKNOWLEDGMENTS

A book starts out as one person's idea, but with help, that idea turns into a written adventure that can be shared with thousands. That's why I'm so grateful to pen another acknowledgments page, because it means this particular adventure is now ready to be shared. As always, my first thanks go to God. Among many other things, He blessed me with a sufficiently strange mind, and let's face it: if I were normal, I probably wouldn't be able to think up this stuff *wink*. Endless gratitude also goes to my husband, who is my daily reminder that love is real and worth fighting for. Thanks also to my editor, Allison Carroll, for her careful attention to detail and her many helpful comments. Deepest thanks once again to my agent, Nancy Yost, for her fabulous business savvy as well as her support these past several years.

Since this is getting long, I'll try to be briefer, but I couldn't possibly wrap this up without thanking Melissa and Ilona for their encouragement and insight; to my family for their unconditional love; to the wonderful folks at Harlequin for their enthusiasm and support; to Blackstone Audio for making this story also available in audio format; to bloggers, reviewers and librarians for talking about my books and thus spreading the word; and last but certainly not least, to readers for taking the leap and trying them. Thank you forever for that. As I've said before— without readers, I'd still be telling these stories to myself.